FEEL the HEAT

ALSO BY KATE MEADER

All Fired Up

To Lynda, (with a "y")

FEEL the HEAT

Kate Meader

Love, laugh, eat!

Kate Meader.

FOREVER

NEW YORK   BOSTON

Forever
Hachette Book Group
237 Park Avenue, New York, NY 10017
www.hachettebookgroup.com
www.twitter.com/foreverromance

Printed in the United States of America

OPM

Originally published as an ebook
First mass market edition: January 2014

10 9 8 7 6 5 4 3 2 1

Forever is an imprint of Grand Central Publishing.
The Forever name and logo are trademarks of Hachette Book Group, Inc.

The Hachette Speakers Bureau provides a wide range of authors for speaking events. To find out more, go to www.hachettespeakersbureau.com or call (866) 376-6591.

The publisher is not responsible for websites (or their content) that are not owned by the publisher.

ATTENTION CORPORATIONS AND ORGANIZATIONS:

Most Hachette Book Group books are available at quantity discounts with bulk purchase for educational, business, or sales promotional use. For information, please call or write:

Special Markets Department, Hachette Book Group
237 Park Avenue, New York, NY 10017
Telephone: 1-800-222-6747 Fax: 1-800-477-5925

For Jimmie, who makes me laugh like no one else

Acknowledgments

No writer is an island, though it certainly feels lonely at times. It's such a comfort knowing there are amazing people in my life cheering me to the finish—and then shoving me over the start line for the next book.

Thanks to Nicole Resciniti at the Seymour Agency whose faith in me and all her authors knows no bounds. She saw potential (and a sexy chef hero) and pushed me to be better.

To Lauren Plude, my wonderful editor, and the team at Grand Central Publishing, thanks for carving out something great from the word lump I sent you. I will also be forever in debt to the lovely folks in the art department for my ab-tastic cover.

My promiscuity on the chapter contest circuit earned fantastic feedback and enough wins to encourage me to stay the course. Thanks to all the judges: I learned something from each and every one of you.

So many people helped with critiques and beta reads,

and I extend a warm, fuzzy blanket of gratitude to envelop you all: Gina Blechman, Jessica Briones, Michelle Frisque, Anna Geletka, Rebecca Lynn, Erin McCarthy, Angela Quarles, and Shannyn Schroeder. A special thank you goes to Amber Lin, whose keen insight and dirty mind has made me a better writer.

And finally to my writer girls in Chicago 4D, your dishing, drinking, and divaesque behavior has kept me informed, tipsy, and laughing throughout this past year. Cheers, ladies!

FEEL the HEAT

CHAPTER ONE

She should have been safely ensconced in the apartment above her family's restaurant, scarfing down leftover pasta and catching up on the reality show glut bursting her DVR. Instead, Lili DeLuca was considering a 3:00 a.m. stealth mission down a dark alley, wearing shiny blue Lycra hot pants and a star-spangled bustier. As ideas went, this one was as smart as bait.

Peeling off her Vespa helmet, she sent a longing look up to her bedroom window, then peered once more into the alley leading to the kitchen entrance of DeLuca's Ristorante. The door was still propped open. Light streamed out into the night. Brightness had never looked so wrong.

A busy Damen Avenue could usually be relied upon to assure an unaccompanied woman that she was not alone. Wicker Park, formerly a low-income haven for underfed artists and actors-slash-baristas, had grown into a dense jungle of expensive lofts, chic eateries, and shi-shi wine bars. Between those, O'Casey's Tap on the corner, and the regular influx of suburbanite good-timers, the streets were always full and safe.

But not tonight.

The bars had dribbled out their last drunks an hour ago, and by now, the 708ers were snoring soundly on their Sleep Number beds back in the burbs. Despite the stifling ninety-degree June heat, her neighborhood had never appeared so stark and cold. Living so close to work might have its perks, such as a thirty-second commute and the best Italian food in Chicago, but it was hard to see the upside in the face of that damn kitchen door, open like a gaping maw.

Maybe it was Marco. Her ex liked to use her family's business as his playpen, adamant that his investment accorded him certain privileges. A bottle of expensive Brunello here. A venue for an after-hours poker game there. Even a chance to impress, with his miserable culinary skills, the latest lithe blonde he was wearing. He'd cooked for Lili once. His linguine had been as limp as his...

Sloughing off those memories, she refocused on her current problem. Six hours ago, the Annual Superhero Extravaganza had seemed like a harmless way to rehabilitate her social life and get out there (oh, how she hated *there*). Guilting her into living was a favorite pastime of Gina's, and her cousin had persuaded her to attend with honeyed words.

Time to get back in the game, Lili. No, your thighs don't look like sides of beef in those shorts. The Batman with the wandering digits? He's not fat—he's just husky.

A husky Batman might come in handy right about now.

Leaving behind the safe hum of traffic, she crept toward the door. The garbage stench stung her nostrils. Something furry scurried behind one of the Dumpsters. A raucous riff from the Rolling Stones' "Brown Sugar" swelled and filled the space around her. Insanity had its own soundtrack.

You might be dressed like Wonder Woman, but that doesn't mean you should play the hero. Just take a look, then call someone.

She sneaked a peek around the door. Expensive kitchen equipment—*her* equipment—lay strewn with serving dishes, pots, and pans on the countertops. Renewed alarm streaked through her. This didn't look like the handiwork of Marco, who thought a *bain-marie* was the name of a girl he'd like to date.

So much for the plausible explanation. Some shithead was burglarizing her restaurant to the strains of Jagger and Richards.

The next move should have been obvious, but her cinder-block feet and racing brain warred all the same. Call someone. *Anyone.* Her father. Her cousin. That cute chocolate-eyed cop who stopped in for takeout on Fridays and insisted she give him a buzz at the first scent of trouble. She swallowed hard, desperate to stop her heart from escaping through her throat. It settled for careening around her chest like a pinball.

A cautious sniff caught an astringent blast of bleach that competed with the lingering basil aroma of Friday night's dinner service. Trembling, she nestled her camera, an eight-hundred-dollar Leica, inside her Vespa helmet, then squeezed her phone out of the tight pouch at the side of her shorts. She started to dial. *Nine. One...*

Her twitchy finger paused on hearing something more eerie than heart-stopping. From inside the walk-in fridge, a voice bounced off the stainless-steel interior. High-pitched. Indeterminate gender. Singing at the top of its lungs. It was also completely out of tune.

She repocketed her phone, pulled open the screen door, and quietly stepped inside. Damn feet had never known what was good for them.

Frantically, she searched for a weapon, and her gaze fell gratefully on the cast-iron frying pan resting on the butcher's block. She swapped it out for her helmet, appreciating how the new heft almost worked to stop her hand from shaking. Almost. Her blurred and frankly ridiculous reflection in the fridge's stainless steel should have given her pause; instead it emboldened her. She was dressed for action. She could do this.

Rounding the walk-in's door, she took stock of the enemy in a millisecond. Built like a tank, he had his back turned to her as he reached up to the top shelf for a container of her father's *ragù*. For the briefest of seconds, the incongruity gnawed at her gut. A tone-deaf, *ragù*-stealing brigand? So it didn't exactly gel, but he was in her restaurant.

In the middle of the night.

Any hesitancy to act was wiped away by his stutter-step backward and the corresponding spike in her adrenaline. She hurled the pan and allowed herself a gratifying instant to confirm his head got the full brunt. Wolfish howl, check. Then she slammed the door shut on his thieving ass.

It had been quite a nice ass, too.

Good grief, where had that come from? It must be relief because a drooling appreciation of criminal hot stuff was so not appropriate. She loosed a nervous giggle, then covered her mouth, trying to smother that wicked thought along with her chuckle. Naughty, naughty.

Now what, Shiny Shorts? Time to call in the cavalry, but as she pulled out her phone again, another thought pierced her veil of giddy triumph. By now, Fridge Bandit should have been making a fuss or bargaining for his freedom, yet a full minute had passed with not a peep.

Confident that the broken safety release on the walk-in's interior would keep him at bay, she laid her head and hands flush to the cool fridge door. Somewhere behind her, the music's *boom-boom* bass meshed with the walk-in's mechanical hum. Both now vibrated through her body while the *thump-thump* of her heart tripped out a ragged beat.

Still nothing from within that cold prison. New horror descended over her.

She had killed him.

Fortunately—or perhaps unfortunately—the panic of that dread conclusion was dislodged by the fridge door's sudden jerk outward, sending Lili into a rather graceless meet-cute with the kitchen floor. Butt first, of course.

So someone had fixed that safety lock, then.

Her former comrade, the frying pan, emerged like a mutant hand puppet, soon followed by a wrist and a hairy arm before the whole package materialized. Vaguely, something big, bad, and dangerous registered in her mind. He held the pan aloft to ward off an imminent attack, but he needn't have worried. Still grounded, superpowers severely diminished, she blinked and focused. Then she wished she hadn't bothered, as the tight knot of fear un-raveled to a cold flood of embarrassment.

"Jesus Christ, you could have bloody killed—" Fridge Bandit said. His mouth dropped open. Scantily clad superheroes flat on their butts often have that effect.

Thick black hair, green eyes flecked with gold, and a face straight out of a Renaissance painting were his most obvious assets. Lili postponed the full-body browse because she knew she was in trouble. Big trouble.

It was *him*.

He touched the back of his head, a not-so-subtle reminder of her transgression, and placed the pan down with all the care of someone disposing of a loaded weapon. His casual wave at the countertop behind her cut the music abruptly. Probably a skill he had acquired during an apprenticeship with the dark side of the Force.

"You all right, sweetheart?" he asked in the casual tone of one who doesn't really care about the answer. He pocketed an iPod remote and made a halfhearted move toward her. She held up the okay-hand. *Too late, buster.*

Lowering her eyes to check the girls, she exhaled in relief. No nip slips. She jumped to her feet, surreptitiously rubbed her sore rump, then cast a glance down to her red knee-high Sandro boots for inspiration. Nothing doing.

You're wearing a Wonder Woman costume and you just went all-out ninja on one of the most famous guys in the Western Hemisphere.

At last, she raised her eyes to his face, now creased in a frown.

"I'm Jack."

"I know who you are."

Lili figured anyone sporting a painted-on outfit like she

was probably had, oh, a ten-second ogle coming her way. Her ego might have taken a shot along with her behind, but she knew she had started the evening looking pretty darn good. Hell, four out of the five flabby-muscled Supermen at the party had thought so. With her overweight teens firmly in the past, she'd since embraced her size 14 figure, and on the days she felt less than attractive—for every woman suffered days like those—she had enough friends telling her to own it, girl, revel in those curves.

So here she stood, owning and reveling, while simultaneously forging a somewhat unorthodox path for feminism with her own leering appraisal.

Jack Kilroy's extraordinarily handsome mug was already branded into her brain. Not because she was a fan, heaven forbid, but because her sister, Cara, was constantly babbling about its perfection, usually while nagging everyone she knew to watch the cooking show she produced for him, *Kilroy's Kitchen. (Monday nights at seven on the Cooking Channel—don't forget, Lili!)* A hot-as-a-griddle Brit, he had risen to stardom in the last year, first with his TV show, then with his bestseller, *French Cooking for the Rest of Us.* And when not assailing the public with his chiseled good looks on food and lifestyle magazines, he could invariably be found plying his particular brand of brash foodie charm on the daytime talk-show circuit. He wasn't just smokin' in the kitchen, either. Recently, a contentious breakup with a soap star and a paparazzi punch-up had provided delicious fodder for the tabloids and cable news outlets alike.

The camera might add ten pounds, but in the flesh, Jack Kilroy was packing the sexy into a lean six-and-change frame. The matching set of broad shoulders didn't surprise her, but apparently the tribal tattoo on his right bicep did, judging by the shiver dancing a jig down her spine. It seemed so not British and just a little bit dangerous. Her gaze was drawn to his Black Sabbath T-shirt, which strained to contain what looked like extremely hard, and eminently touchable, chest muscles. Sculpted by years of lugging heavy-duty stockpots, no doubt. Long legs, wrapped in a pair of blue jeans that looked like an old friend, completed the very pleasant image.

Jack Kilroy was proof there was a God—and she was a woman.

"Is that your usual MO? Frying pan first, questions later?" he asked after giving her the anticipated once-over. He had used up his ten seconds while she had stretched her assessment to fifteen. Small victories. "Should I hold still and let you use your lasso to extract the truth from me?" He gestured to the coil of gold-colored rope hanging through a loop on her hip. If he expected her to act impressed by his knowledge of the Wonder Woman mythology, he'd be a long time waiting.

Maybe she was a little impressed.

"I thought you were stealing. I was about to call the police."

"You're telling me there's something worth stealing around here?"

Her body heated in outrage at his dismissive tone, though it could just as easily be because of the way his dark emerald eyes held hers. Bold and unwavering.

"Are you kidding? Some of this equipment has been in my family for generations." Right now, most of it had been pulled out from under the counters and was scattered willy-nilly on every available surface. "Like my *nonna's* pasta maker." She pointed to it, sitting all by its dusty lonesome on a countertop behind a rack of spices.

"That rusty old thing in the corner?"

"That's not rusty. It's vintage. I thought you Brits appreciated antiques."

"Sure, but my appreciation doesn't extend to food-poisoning hazards."

A protest died on her lips. Her father hadn't used that pasta maker in over ten years, so a zealous defense was probably unnecessary.

"So either I'm being punked or you're Cara's sister. Lilah, right?"

"Yes, Cara's sister," she confirmed, "and it's Lil—"

"I thought you were the hostess," he cut in. "Are frying pans the new meet-'n'-greet in Italian restaurants?"

It's three in the morning! she almost screamed. Clearly, the blow to his skull had impacted his short-term memory. On cue, he rubbed his head, then gripped the side of the countertop with such knuckle-whitening intensity that she worried he might pass out.

"I'm the restaurant's manager, actually, and I wasn't expecting you. If I'd known *Le Kilroy* would be gracing us with his exalted presence, I would have rolled out the red carpet we keep on hand for foreign dignitaries."

She sashayed over to the ice cabinet and glanced back in time to catch his gaze fixed to her butt like he was in some sort of trance. Oh, brother, not even a whack to the head could throw this guy off his game. With a couple of twists, she crafted an ice pack with a napkin and handed it to him. "How's your head?"

"Fine. How's your—" He motioned in the direction of

her rear with one hand while gingerly applying the ice pack with the other.

"Fine," she snapped back.

"I'll say," he said, adding a smirk for good measure.

Oh, for crying out loud. "Is that *your* usual MO? I can't believe you have so much success with the ladies." The gossip mags devoted pages to his revolving-door dating style. Only Hollywood fembots and half-starved models need apply. They clearly weren't in it for the food.

For her insolence, she got a blade of a look, one of those condescending ones they teach in English private schools, which for some ridiculous reason they called public schools.

"I've had no complaints."

She folded her arms in an effort to project a modicum of gravitas, which was mighty difficult considering what she was wearing. It didn't help that every breath took effort in her sweat-bonded costume. "So, care to explain?"

"What? Why I've had no complaints?"

"I mean, what you're doing in my family's restaurant at this ungodly hour."

"Oh, up to no good. Underhanded misdoings. Waiting for a superhero to take me down."

Okay, ten points for cute. She battled a smile. Lost the fight. Palms up, she indicated he should continue and it had better be good.

"I'm doing prep and inventory for the show. Didn't Cara tell you?"

Of course she hadn't told her. That's why she was asking, dunderhead. "I haven't checked my messages," she lied, trying to cover that she had and her sister hadn't deigned to fill her in. "I was busy all evening."

"Saving cats from trees and leaping tall buildings in a single bound, I suppose."

"Wrong superhero, dummy," she said, still ticked off that Cara had left her out of the loop. "You haven't explained why you're doing this prep and inventory *here*." It seemed pointless to remind him of the lateness of the hour.

"Because this is where we'll be taping the show, sweetheart. Jack Kilroy is going to put your little restaurant on the map."

* * *

Good thing Laurent had stepped out, because if he'd caught Jack referring to himself in the third person, he'd laugh his derrière off. That shit needed to stop. It was worth it, though, just to get this reaction. Wonder Woman's mouth fell open, giving her the appearance of an oxygen-deprived goldfish.

"Here? Why would you want to tape your stupid show here?"

Jack let the comment slide, though the snarky dig about his success with women had been irksome enough. Rather hypocritical, too, considering all that hip swaying and lady leering in his general direction.

"Believe me, it's not by choice. This place is far too small and some of the equipment is much too...*vintage* for what I need."

Contrary to his comment about the size and age of the kitchen, Jack felt a fondness bordering on nostalgia. The nearest stainless-steel counter was scuffed and cloudy with wear, the brushed patina a testament to the restaurant's many successful years. He loved these old places.

There was something innately comforting about using countertops that had seen so much action.

Returning his gaze to Cara's sister, he speculated on how enjoyable it might be to hoist her up on the counter and start a little action right here and now. That costume she was poured into had cinched her waist and boosted her breasts like some comic-book feat of structural engineering, creating an hourglass figure the likes of which one usually didn't see outside of a sixties-style burlesque show. A well-packaged, fine-figured woman with an arse so sweet he was already setting aside fantasy time for later. His head throbbed, but the lovely sight before him was the perfect salve.

As intended, his "too small" and "vintage" comments set her off on another round of fervent indignation. The wild hand gestures, the hastily-sought-for jibes, the churning eyes. Beautiful eyes, too, in a shade of blue not unlike curaçao liqueur, and with a humorous glint that had him trying not to smile at her even though he was incredibly pissed off at what she'd done. A woman—a very attractive woman—in an agitated state got him every time.

"This kitchen is not too small. It's perfect." She jabbed her finger at the burners and ovens lining the back wall. "We get through one hundred fifty covers every Saturday night using this *tiny* kitchen, and we don't need the Kilroy stamp of approval. We're already on the map."

"I never said tiny, but I'm full of admiration for how you've utilized the limited space."

That earned him a response somewhere between a grunt and a snort followed by a surprise move toward a heavy stand mixer. Surely she wasn't going to start cleaning up? He put a placating hand on her arm.

"Hey, don't worry. I'll put everything back the way I found it."

She glanced down at his hand resting on her golden skin. By the time her eyes had made the return trip, she was shooting sparks. *Back off.* Hooking a stray lock behind her ear, she returned to her task—cleaning up his mess and making him look like an arse. A cloud of unruly, cocoa brown hair pitched forward, obscuring her heart-shaped face and giving her a distinct lunatic vibe.

It would take more than a death stare and a shock of crazy curls to put him off. Teasing her was too much fun. "I'm pretty fast, love, and if you can move with superhero speed, we'd get it done in a jiffy."

Another push back of her hair revealed a pitying smile. "Don't ever claim to be fast, Kilroy. No woman wants to hear that."

Ouch.

Before he could muster a clever retort, the kitchen doors flew open, revealing Cara DeLuca, his producer, in full-on strut. Neither the crazy hour nor the mind-melting heat had stopped her from getting dressed to the hilt in a cream-colored suit and heels. Laurent, his sous-chef and trusty sidekick, ambled in behind her with his usual indolence and a tray of takeout coffee.

Cara's sister grumbled something that sounded like, "Kill me now."

Sibling drama alert. Unfortunately, with a younger sister determined to drive him around the bend, he was in a position to recognize the signs.

"Lili, what on earth are you wearing?" Cara gave a languid wave. "Oh, never mind."

Lili. He had called her *Lilah*. Lili was much better.

Lilah sounded like someone's maiden aunt. This woman didn't look like anyone's maiden aunt.

Cara's eyes darted around, analyzing the situation. His producer was nothing if not quick, which made her both good at her job and prone to snap judgments. The crew called her Lemon Tart, and not because she was sweet.

"Why are you holding your head like that?"

Jack cast a sideways glance at the sister. He wasn't planning to rat her out, but to her credit, she confessed immediately. In a manner of speaking.

"I thought it was that gang of classic-rock-loving, yet remarkably tuneless, thieves that have been pillaging Italian kitchens all over Chicago, and as I was already dressed for crime-fighting, instinct just took over, and I tried to lock your star in the fridge."

Laughter erupted from deep inside him, although he was fairly positive she had just insulted his beautiful singing voice. A muscle twitched near the corner of her mouth. Not quite a smile, but he still felt the warm buzz of victory.

"Lili, you can't go locking the talent up in a fridge," Cara chided.

"Or hitting it on the head with a frying pan," Jack added.

Cara's head swiveled *Exorcist*-style back to her sister. "You did what?"

Jack rubbed the back of his head, heightening the drama. "I don't think she broke the skin, but there'll be a bump there later."

Cara caressed his noggin and yelped like a pocketbook pup. "Oh my God, Lili, do you realize what could have happened if Jack got a concussion and had to go to the emergency room?"

"It might have improved his personality. He could do with a humility transplant," Lili offered, again with that cute muscle twitch that he suddenly wanted to lick.

Laurent had been suspiciously quiet, but now he stepped forward, and Jack braced himself for the Gallic charm offensive. As usual, his wingman looked bed-head disheveled, sandy hair sticking out every which way. His bright blue eyes twinkled in his friendly face as he launched into one of his patented gambits.

"Bonjour, I am Laurent Benoit. I work with Jack." It tripped off his tongue as *Zhaque*, sounding lazy and sexy and French. "You must be Cara's beautiful sister, Lili." He proffered his hand, and Lili hesitantly took it while the corners of Laurent's mouth hitched into a seductive grin. "*Enchanté*," he said, raising her hand to kiss it. This netted a husky laugh, which was a damn sight more than Jack had managed in the five minutes he had been alone with her. Man, that Frenchman was good.

"Now that's an accent I can get down with," Lili murmured.

Jack sighed. While his own British voice accounted for much of his success with American women, over the years he had lost more skirt to that French accent than he'd eaten bowls of bouillabaisse. Laurent—brilliant sous-chef, occasional best friend, and his most rigorous competition for the fairer sex—was the embodiment of the French lover. As good as he was in the kitchen, his talents would be just as well suited to tourism commercials. All he needed was a beret, a baguette, and a box of condoms.

Jack's head still hurt and weariness had set in bone-deep. He was sure he had lost consciousness for a few seconds in the fridge, and now he battled the dizziness that threatened to engulf him. Coffee. That's what he needed. Coffee and something to focus on. Something that wasn't curvy and soft-looking and radiating man-killer vibes.

"Any chance we can get on with what we were doing?" he sniped at Cara, more brusquely than he'd intended.

"Of course, Jack, babe. We'll let you continue." Dragging her sister by the arm, Cara marched her out of the kitchen with a portentous, "Liliana Sophia DeLuca, a word in the office, if you please."

Laurent stood with arms crossed, staring at the scene of departing female beauty. Jack eyed his friend. *Here it comes.*

"I think I'm in love," Laurent groaned. "Is she not the cutest *chérie* you have ever seen?"

A laugh rumbled in Jack's chest. "That's the fourth time you've fallen in love this year and it's only June."

"But did you not see her cute little nose wrinkle up when I offered her my hand? And that lovely derrière. What I wouldn't do for a piece of that."

"She might have 'zee lovely derrière,' but she's got a dangerous bowling arm." His fingers returned to the spot where the frying pan had connected. A bump was definitely forming.

Jack followed Laurent's gaze to the swing doors through which Cara and her sister had just exited. A sudden image of brushing his lips against Lili's and watching the pupils of those lovely eyes magnify in passion flitted pleasantly through his mind. It wasn't long before his imagination had wandered to stroking her inner thigh and inching below the hem of those tight, blue, shiny shorts.

Things were just getting interesting when the crash of a dropped serving pan knocked him back to the present. While Laurent muttered his apologies, Jack blinked to quell his overactive brain, the pain in his head briefly forgotten. Maybe he should apply that ice pack to his crotch.

Evie, his dragon-lady agent, had been clear. *Think of the contract, Jack. Keep your head down and your nose clean. And whatever happens, do not engage the local talent.* Right now, that imminent network deal was the rocket that would propel his brand into the stratosphere. No more rinky-dink cable shit. Instead he would spread his message of affordable haute cuisine to as wide an audience as possible and garner fame for all the right reasons.

Which meant grasping women were an unnecessary distraction, even a tasty piece like Cara's sister. He needed to forget about smart-tart birds with eyes and curves that would lead a good man, or one who was trying to be good, off the straight and narrow. After his last disastrous relationship, he wasn't looking to screw around with the help, even if she did have the best derrière in the Midwest.

* * *

Lili trudged after Cara into the restaurant's back office, her focus on the platinum-blond cascade that swished from her sister's ponytail. After three careful swipes of the swivel chair with a tissue from her purse, Cara sat, smoothing her cream silk skirt as she went.

"Nice costume," she said with a knowing smile. "Jack seemed to like it."

The absurdity of that statement canceled out the deceitful thrill Lili had felt while pinned by Jack Kilroy's assessing gaze. She'd been right not to trust it. A man like that—too good-looking, too charming, too *everything*—needed constant female attention to keep his ego afloat. Memories of her ex were still fresh: she'd been there, done that, bought the T-shirt.

Her long sweater hung on a hook inside the door, and she threw it on. "Have you seen Mom yet?"

Cara examined her nails, an avoidance tactic Lili immediately recognized because she was rather fond of using it herself. "I spoke to her on the phone. She sounds in good spirits. I was planning to drop off a gift later."

Lili bit back a catty response. Cara's ability to ignore the unpleasant was legendary and lately had become a source of ever-increasing resentment between them. Why bother to visit when nothing says *Congratulations on beating cancer, Mom* better than a fancy gift basket, delivered weekly like clockwork? It was too late, or maybe too early, for a sister-on-sister confrontation. Besides, there was something about all that fragile beauty of hers that made it impossible to hate her properly. Lili needed to change the subject, though it would probably take some sort of power tool to chisel off the sour look she knew was cemented on her face.

"Cara, you could have warned me about the British Invasion."

Her sister crossed her shapely legs and picked some imaginary fluff from her tulip-shaped skirt. Size 0 or 2, Lili was willing to bet, though she looked a little plumper than she had on visits past. Cara's thinness was both an object of envy and awe, and Lili wondered how her sister retained such a rigid grip on her self-control. Occasionally, Lili speculated that Cara's distinctly non-Italian attitude to food could mean just one thing: her sister must have been adopted. If only.

She shrugged in that don't-hate-me-'cause-I'm-beautiful way of hers. "I talked to Il Duce last night and he's on board."

Il Duce was the nickname for their father, coined to reflect his startling similarity to a certain Italian wartime dictator. Lili might be the de facto manager while her mother recovered, but her father was supreme ruler. She shouldn't have been surprised that he'd make an end run on this. Standard operating procedure.

By the way Cara quickly adopted a softer tone, Lili knew she hadn't hidden her hurt reaction in time. "It's a once-in-a-lifetime opportunity for the restaurant. Remember I told you we had Serafina's on Randolph lined up for the taping next week? Well, yesterday we find out they've had to close for health code violations. Rats!" She waved her hands in the air as if she'd seen the vermin with her own innocent eyes. "We were scrambling to find an alternative and I suggested our place to Jack. To be honest, Jack's really grateful Dad can help out."

In the five minutes Lili had spent with Jack Kilroy, gratitude was nowhere in evidence. In fact, he had acted like he was doing *them* the favor, though in reality, that wasn't too far from the truth. Her earlier braggadocio about DeLuca's healthy numbers couldn't disguise the trouble they were in, a perfect storm of external pressures and internal entrenchment. They were lucky to boast eighty covers on a Saturday, never mind the buck and a half she'd tossed out back in the kitchen. Weeknights were practically a ghost town. Classical Italian dining wasn't quite in vogue anymore, and as amazing as her father's food was, it was getting harder to compete with the hipper, trendier eateries that had popped up all over Wicker Park. Lili had ideas for taking their game to the next level. Lots of ideas. But her autocratic father refused to play ball.

"What do you think of him?" Cara asked, dragging Lili's thoughts reluctantly back to Jack Kilroy. "He gives good handsome, right?"

Lili gave a noncommittal shrug that did little to divest her of worry. Her sister had been drinking Jack Kilroy's Kool-Aid ever since her New York company, Foodie Productions, began handling his show back in January. It had been a real coup for Cara to get the gig, and to hear her sister speak, the future of mankind was riding on it. Though, how someone who despised food made her living producing food television was one of life's great mysteries.

In the interests of sisterly peace, Lili decided to feign some interest. "So why is he cooking in someone else's restaurant and not in a studio like the other hack chefs you see on TV? I'm surprised Lord Studly would be caught dead in a place like this."

"On occasion, Lord Studly is happy to lower himself to the level of the great unwashed." That accented voice swept over her like cut crystal. It really should come with a government health warning.

She turned and got the full blast. Wow, if he wasn't the incarnation of sin on a stick. *Focus on the face,* she told herself as her photographer eye drank in more details. A smattering of freckles dotted across his nose. A scar on his chin that was probably airbrushed out of magazine covers. And beautiful eyelashes, like silken, inky strands fringing his green eyes. Live-and-up-close Jack was much more impressive than small-screen Jack. She wondered how he might fare under her camera's gaze. Very well, she suspected.

Too late, she realized she was gawking, but funnily enough, he was gawking right back. Braining someone with cast-iron cookware was starting to look like a viable pickup strategy. She drew the edges of her sweater closer together. The scratchy brush of the wool heightened the new sensitivity of her skin, which felt like sunburn under Jack's ferocious gaze.

He blinked and held out her Vespa helmet. "Yours, I presume?"

She took it with a shaky hand, relieved to see her camera and phone were still safe inside. "Thanks," she muttered, wishing he didn't turn her into such a gloopy mess.

"You rode a motor bike in that getup?"

"A scooter, actually. What of it?"

"Just building a picture in my head."

Oh, for... never mind. She swiped all expression from her face. "The show?"

"Well," Cara said. "Here's the premise." She leaned forward as if she were making a pitch to a Hollywood producer. "It's a cooking contest pitting Jack against a host chef in a cuisine he's not so familiar with. Jack's specialty, of course, is French, so he's going up against other cuisines, preparing a brand-new menu and serving it to real restaurant customers. He'll be competing against Dad, and whoever gets the most votes wins. Simple, right? The show's brand-new. It's called *Jack of All Trades* and DeLuca's is going to be on the premiere episode!"

Lili settled in against the desk and switched her attention to Jack, who lounged against the door frame with an easy, devil-be-damned grace that said he was above it all.

Her father had won awards—*Chicago* magazine's Best Italian, two years running, albeit over ten years ago—and chefs came from far and wide to learn the secrets of his gnocchi. He was the true kitchen genius, not this walking ego who coasted on charm and cheekbones. Time to get her game face on. Never too early to start the trash talking.

"So, not so hot at *la cucina Italiana*, then?"

He appeared to be thinking hard about that, so Cara jumped into the pause. "There's also a twist. Jack gets to pick his own appetizers and dessert, but Dad chooses the pastas and the entrées for both chefs. And doesn't tell Jack until the day of the contest."

Better and better. Lili could think of several dishes that could pose last-minute problems. This might be fun. Her gaze traveled the long, lean body of British Beefcake. This might be a whole lot of fun.

"Oh, you're going down," Lili said, then winced as she realized that could be interpreted as flirty. So not her intention, especially as she sucked soccer balls at flirty.

Evidently he hadn't gotten the memo because his face lit up with a traffic-stopping smile. He probably had a million risqué comebacks on tap but he let that killer smile do all the work. Seeing it in person made a girl feel incredibly lucky.

He moved into the cramped office, inching closer like a jungle cat stalking something small and defenseless. While she was in no way defenseless, and no one would ever have characterized her as small, there was still something rather daunting about how he filled a space. Especially a confined space. A flushing tingle spread through her body and her nipples tightened. Although he couldn't possibly have seen *that*, he cocked his head and considered her as if he had. As if her body's reaction to him was the only possible response to a smile that dangerous.

"You think I have something to worry about?" he said in a tone that made it clear he had this one covered, honey.

Irritation over her hormonal meltdown turned her surly. "Oh, yeah. My father's going to take you to the woodshed, Brit Boy."

A slight twitch appeared like an errant comma at the corner of his no-longer-smiling mouth. "Don't worry, sweetheart. I think Brit Boy can cook a bowl of linguine and melt some mozzarella over a slab of veal. Italian's not the most challenging of cuisines, no offense to your father, and any restaurant would kill to be featured on my show. It's a guaranteed seat-filler for the next six months."

Apparently she didn't suck soccer balls at flirty; she sucked spectacularly. The great Jack Kilroy had just dismissed Italian cooking as barely worthy of his inestimable attention and, boy, did that stick in her craw.

"If you think it's that easy, perhaps you should stop by for dinner tonight. I think you'll find my father can melt cheese to rival any idiot box chef. Oh, a hotshot like you probably won't learn anything about food, but you might learn some manners."

He opened his mouth to speak, then seemed to think better of it. Good call.

Stepping around her, he thrust a piece of paper at Cara. "Here's what I need. I'll start testing dishes tomorrow." Pronouncement made, he stalked out of the office with all the flourish of a Shakespearean actor marching offstage.

Lili shook her head in disbelief. "I know he's your boss, Cara, but that guy's got some nerve walking in here and proclaiming Italian cuisine is easy. And you should have heard him dissing the kitchen and our equipment. Just who does he think he is?"

Cara picked a speck of invisible dust off her low-cut blouse and tousled her perfect, platinum-blond hair. "That, baby sister, is your birthday and Christmas presents all rolled up into one sexy, hunk-shaped package."

CHAPTER TWO

Lili grasped her sweater so tight it was starting to resemble the Baby Jesus' swaddling. Quietly, she pressed the office door shut, the hushed snick a marked contrast to her thunderous pulse.

"Hunk-shaped package? Please tell me that doesn't mean what I think it does."

"All that snarky back-and-forth, the sexual tension dripping in the air..." Cara fanned herself. "I've got goose bumps over here. I just knew you two would hit it off."

Hit it off? Well, she certainly had the "hit" part right. Jack Kilroy was the most arrogant, superior, arrogant—wait, she'd already said that—guy Lili had ever met, and she worked in the restaurant business where that personality type was as common as tiramisu on an Italian dessert menu. He also happened to be the hottest streak of male she had ever clapped eyes on, and unfortunately her nipples and her other body parts agreed wholeheartedly.

Bad body.

Take away the glittering green eyes, the scimitar-curved cheekbones, and the accent that made her knock-kneed, and he'd be nothing. Nada. Just a slab of beefy charisma with a few well-appointed muscles and a so-so smile. Okay, a gorgeous smile that hinted at good humor behind the amateur dramatics. Oh, hell, there was something about Jack Kilroy that turned her crank. If her life wasn't so complicated, if her family's business wasn't a breath away from collapse—if she wasn't such a coward—she'd be tearing open the wrapping on that hunk-shaped package before you could say "Happy Birthday, Lili."

Cara stood to lean against the desk, drawing Lili's envious gaze. Her sister had great thighs, directly attributable to her diet of coffee, PowerBars, and a borderline manic devotion to the treadmill.

"The show tapes Monday night. Jack has to do a spot-check on the new place he's opening in Chicago, and then he flies out to London on Tuesday for business. Now, I know you're out of practice, but I reckon that should give you enough time to get the job done." She added a conspiratorial wink.

Lili suppressed a compulsion to pop her one in the ovaries. "Cara, are you ill? On drugs?" She pressed her palm to her sister's forehead. No obvious signs of fever, but her eyes were wide as saucers. Oh yeah, she was high on smugness.

Cara lowered her voice to a whisper. "Lili, in case you haven't heard, Jack Kilroy is a complete man whore. He's so freaking needy he'll jump at any opportunity. Even *you* could manage to hit that."

Even *her*? So she wasn't the most adventurous sort when it came to men, but that one hit lower than she expected. "I'm not some charity case, you know. I have options."

Cara gave a dramatic eye roll, which made her look much younger than her twenty-nine years. "*Riiight*, options. How long has it been since things finished with Marco?"

Lili shifted uneasily. Since Marco had called time on their fling several months ago, her sex life had been on life support. The battery-operated kind. A night with a hot guy might be just the ticket, but Jack Kilroy? No amount of advanced yoga could get her in shape for a guy like that.

"It's been months, and Jack is more than up to the task," Cara continued blithely.

"Cara, I've seen the type he hooks up with." Ashley van Patten, soap diva, was enough to strike fear into the nether regions of any woman. Lili might have a voluptuous body type that a lot of guys went for, or claimed they did if she was to believe *Cosmopolitan*, but sex royalty like Jack Kilroy did not usually deign to slum among the little people.

"Lili, you're real and gorgeous and ten times hotter than the likes of Ashley. Best thing he ever did was dump her, though she got him back good in those interviews." Her sister chuckled. "'Naughty Nights with Kilroy.' He went into DEFCON Divo for that one."

Other tawdry tabloid headlines popped into Lili's head. *Duracell Jack. Kinky Kilroy*, and her favorite, *Red Hot Kilroy Peppers*. Headlines that summoned up wicked thoughts of Jack's hard body wrapped around her like a luscious lick of fire. Quickly, she doused that illicit blaze with a sobering wet blanket from her memory bank. The one where he had taken a paparazzo to task with his fists for daring to record Jack with his model-of-the-week.

"I'm sure beating the living daylights out of that poor photographer got him back on track. And the Victoria's Secret angel he hooked up with the week after would have kissed it all better," she said, feeling a mite ridiculous that she knew so much about a perfect stranger.

"Listen, who cares about the details? All you need to worry about is crooking your finger and watching how fast he comes running. And you heard what Ashley said. Wizard in the sack," Cara added, laying it on like a thick layer of cream cheese frosting.

Lili was sure he was the Voldemort of all things down and dirty, but he'd need several more blows to the head before he would take an interest in her. However, just before he dismissed her with that coal-dark look and cool put-down about Italian cuisine, there had been a moment when...

"Wait a second." Bone-chilling panic sloshed over her. "Does he already know about this brand of crazy you're selling?"

"Of course not. What do you think I am, some sort of pimp?"

"I think in your case, it would be a madam."

Cara curled her cupid-bow lips into that *saputa* smile Lili knew so well, the one that said that she was privy to some great wisdom that a pleb like her younger sister could never hope to attain. "Lili, you're only twenty-four. You should be out clubbing, hooking up with guys, and deleting their filthy text messages the next day."

Tears stinging her eyelids, Lili twisted away and focused on the great cathedrals of Italy calendar on the bulletin board, pinned next to the clipboard detailing last night's miserable numbers. Sometimes her sister displayed all the sensitivity of a grizzly on crack. Lili fought for neutral. *Take deep breaths. Think of a calm place. Better yet, think of Mom's shrimp linguine with lemon caper sauce followed by a slice—no, two slices—of ricotta cheesecake.* Self-pity did not coordinate in any way with the amazing boots she was rocking.

"Maybe I'd spend more time clubbing if I didn't have to look after Mom every day and then come here to work every night."

Cara rested her chin on Lili's shoulder and rubbed her arms, surprising Lili out of her ill humor. The DeLuca sisters weren't touchy-feely Italians, no cheek-pinching or bosom-clasping for them. Six months of air-kissing with D-listers had turned Cara soft.

"I'm sorry. I know you've been a trouper, looking after Mom this last year and a half. But she's been in remission for almost three months."

True, but fear, Lili's overriding emotion these days, still clenched her heart like a fist. If it wasn't dread that her mother's illness might return, it was needling anxiety at how rudderless Lili felt with her life stuck in a buffering pause. Neither did it help that her father disapproved of everything his youngest daughter did, from how she managed the restaurant to her impractical dream to make photography her life.

Cara carried on, oblivious. "I just think Jack might be good for you. A sexy rut to get you out of your sorry rut."

Lili faced her sister, every fiber pissy because she might be right. Traces of pity were etched on Cara's beautiful, fine-boned face.

"Now that Mom's better, you can get your life on track. Come to New York, go to graduate school, quit being Il Duce's lackey." She brightened. "I can get you a job at my company. We always need talented photographers for our publicity materials."

Lili managed a watery smile. Graduate school seemed as fuzzy as a Monet landscape now that all her savings had gone to her mother's medical care, or that was what she had taken to telling herself lately. Of course, if she really wanted it to happen... *Leave that rock alone.* Turning it over would only reveal those creepy-crawlies of self-doubt she went to considerable lengths not to acknowledge.

Cara was making the effort, so Lili tried to front it out. "I don't think I'm a good match for that kind of work. Shooting plates of coq au vin and crème brûlée..." She shuddered.

Her sister laughed, a naughty, girly giggle that sounded so good on her. "Well, maybe not. But I think you're a good match for someone I know. Nothing serious, just a hot and sweaty one-night stand." One eyelid dipped in a lascivious wink. "And I'm sure Jack would love if you snapped a photo of his coq—"

"Cara!" Lili had missed her sister's filthy-minded take on everything. Truth be told, she had missed her sister.

The idea of a hot and sweaty one-night stand with Jack Kilroy made her... well, hot and sweaty. What would Wonder Woman do? She'd take charge and kick some ass, that's what.

And given half a chance, she'd rip off Batman's cape and ride him senseless.

* * *

It didn't escape Jack's notice that at 9:00 p.m., DeLuca's Ristorante, in the usually hipster-sodden Wicker Park, wasn't exactly packed to the gills. More like a third full, if even. So far, the clientele had consisted of an older Italian crowd, most of whom looked like they'd caught a group ride in from central casting. Special-occasion diners or once-a-monthers, judging by how they were all dressed up in their Sunday best on a Saturday, complete with heirloom bling. That customer base might be good enough to keep things ticking over in a smaller place, but it couldn't possibly sustain an establishment this size in an area where overhead was high and competition was higher. Hard to fathom the night ending with seventy-five covers, never mind the one hundred fifty Cara's sister had boasted.

Still, the nostalgia he felt earlier about the well-worn countertops and equipment had stayed with him now that he was front of house. A snob to the toes of her designer shoes, Cara had implied her family's business was some sort of down-market, red-sauce emporium with plastic checkered tablecloths, but nothing could be further from the truth. It was a fairly stereotypical design as far as neighborhood eateries went—two dining rooms separated by a large arch, cherrywood tables covered with pristine white linens, chocolate leather banquettes, a fifty-foot bar, and the ubiquitous frescoed ceiling. A touch stodgy, reminiscent of a bygone era. Or maybe it was Dean Martin crooning in the background that left Jack feeling like he was stuck in a Rat Pack movie. Music for Italian Americans to conceive by.

The artsy photos dotting the walls might have kicked the old-world ambiance into modern if the subject matter had been a tad less run-of-the-mill. There was something arresting about the picture compositions, though. Off-kilter with strange angles of Italian types doing Italian things. Overhead shots of old men playing something like *boules*. Children having fun with wooden hoops and roller skates, showing snatched glimpses of legs and arms. Jack didn't know much about art except what he liked, and while the portraits whispered of comfort and familiarity, he recognized a quantum of quirky yearning to break free of the frames. Cara had told him her sister was an amateur photographer, but this work didn't really fit the image he had formed. Following that fiery display this morning, he would have expected something with more edge.

Speaking of edge, he looked up at the fidgeting server with the big eyes and even bigger hair who appeared to be perched on it. Either she was pleased to see him or she needed to pee.

"All right, sweetheart?"

Jack's drawl sent Italian Smurfette into a frenzy of hair twirling. A quick scan of the room confirmed half of the other servers went to the same salon. And they all looked alike. It was as if he'd been drop-shipped into the nickel slots aisle at Caesar's in Atlantic City.

"I just wanted to say how excited we are you're here, doing the show and everything," she gushed. "We're all big fans. Everyone's dying to meet you."

Jack found it hard to believe there was anyone left he

hadn't already met. For the last twenty minutes, his table had been inundated with DeLuca cousins who were dying to meet him. Looking into the lively face of the girl before him, he doled out one of his dazzling smiles, the ones he'd been told made his female fans horny. "I'm thrilled to be here. Really, I am."

Laurent shook his head and mouthed, *Score*.

Jack grinned and turned back to his fan girl. "What was your name again?"

"Gina. Gina DeLuca. I'm Cara's cousin." She motioned to Cara, who stood at the bar talking to her sister. The lovely Lili had covered up her shapely legs and stellar behind in black trousers, but the trade-off was a fitted shirt hugging that figure he'd been fantasizing about all afternoon. Jack would never have considered himself a hair man—was that even a thing?—but there was something about those riotous waves that heated his body like a furnace. She'd made an attempt to tame its nuttiness. While it was still on the big side, it appeared to have gone through some sort of anger management regimen since this morning.

Before the night was out, he would apologize to her for diminishing her father's cooking and all Italian cuisine. Yes, she had goaded him, but his response had been rude. And off-base. Eighteen months in Umbria had taught him plenty about the beautiful complexities of *la cucina Italiana*. Nevertheless, there was something both touching and exhilarating about her loyalty to her family. A hundred fifty covers, his arse. That little braggart.

"Did you want to hear about the specials?" the cousin asked, vying for his wandering attention. Without waiting for a response, she launched into a recitation of the additions to that night's menu. "We have two special appetizers tonight—*funghi arrosto*, which are wood-roasted mushrooms with pancetta, and *polpettine arrabbiate*. That's veal meatballs in a spicy sauce." She leaned in and pushed her hair back behind her ear, a gesture that reminded him of Lili. Christ, now he was being reminded of her? "The meatballs are spectacular."

"I'm sure they are," Jack murmured, indulging in a dutiful gander at her cleavage before diverting his gaze around her to eye Lili.

"Next up for *primi* are two special pastas. First we have ricotta gnocchi with sage and butter sauce." She pulled a card from her apron and consulted it while Jack tried to silence his inner critic. It was only a neighborhood joint; the staff couldn't be expected to memorize the specials in their entirety. "We also have *penne strascicate*—that means 'mixed up.' That's fresh penne pasta with sausage, tomatoes, onion, and thyme. It's a very old recipe from Tuscany. Uncle Tony says his mother used to make it for the family every Friday night back in Fiesole."

Jack itched to meet Uncle Tony—he especially wanted to see the man's kitchen at full tilt—but Cara had said her father preferred to wait until they'd been served their entrées. Sounded like some power thing. He was used to games like that when he dined in restaurants at the topmost echelon. It was unexpected in a midscale establishment, miles from Chicago's Restaurant Row.

The munchkin was gearing up for the homestretch. "Now for the *secondi. Bistecca fiorentina*, made with Chianina beef. That's for two people. And *branzino al forno*—whole sea bass, wood roasted." She edged closer to the table, bending over to give them another flash. At this rate, he was confident he'd be able to pick her breasts out of a lineup.

She lowered her voice to bedroom level. "Between you and me, I hate fish. And calling it by its Italian name doesn't make it taste any better." She chuckled and Laurent joined in, probably thinking he was onto a good thing. Clearly he hadn't noticed the Jupiter-sized rock weighing down her left hand. Jack kept his testiness in check. It irked him to no end when servers inserted their unsolicited opinions into the proceedings.

Although, given the size of the menu—the pages upon pages of every Italian specialty prepared since the fall of Rome that just screamed "waste" and "where the hell do I start?"—he supposed an opinion or two wasn't such a bad thing. Rather than wade through the tome before him, he made an executive decision. "Just bring us one each of the specials and a bottle of Brunello di Montalcino. And make the steak medium rare."

Once the server had bounced off, Laurent cleared his throat. "I thought after Ashley you had sworn off women."

Sworn off? Nah, he'd just encased his dick in concrete, that's all. Ashley had left Jack feeling contaminated and in need of a full-scale mind and body bleach. He had thought they had a connection, but in reality, he was just another tool in her quest for celebrity dominance. And once Jack became better known for his sex life than his kitchen expertise, he realized he had a problem. Casual hookups were no longer on the menu.

"You mean the busty munchkin? No chance." His traitorous eyes sought out Lili, who was busy showing a statuesque redhead and her plainly undeserving oaf of a date to a table. Finally, some diners under the age of forty.

"I'm talking about *ma chérie*, Lili."

Jack snapped his head back so sharply he winced. "Oh, she's your *chérie* now? She's far too young. She must be the same age as my sister."

"But she's not your sister," Laurent countered quickly, because no one wanted to dwell on a friend's sister when the potential of a mind-blowing lay was on the table. Jack silently agreed, not wanting to think about his sister either. Where Jules, ten years his junior, was scatter-brained and likely to lose her job at the drop of a hat, Lili projected a calm responsibility beyond her years. He had been watching her closely ever since he arrived, enjoying the ease with which she managed everyone, customers and staff alike.

Laurent coughed again. It was really annoying. "So if you are truly not interested, you won't mind if I take a shot?"

"You're asking permission? You never ask permission." A muscle clenched in Jack's midsection, but he chose to ignore it. Not trusting his instincts seemed to be the safest option these days.

Laurent smiled and, not for the first time in their fifteen-year friendship, Jack wanted to pummel him. "You saw her first."

Jack laughed off his discomfort, forcing his fists to cooperate. "That's awfully gallant of you. Have at it. Maybe you can bag the chatty cousin, too."

A few minutes later, Cara was back and Gina was struggling with the bottle of Brunello as if it were an enemy combatant. Following a quick sniff, Jack put the glass down on the table. The smell was akin to wet dog, indicating that the cork, and by extension, the wine, had been contaminated by a chemical compound.

"It's corked."

Her eyes grew wide in clear confusion.

"Bad. Appalling. Wretched." He tried not to sound too irritated, but come on.

Gina stole a peek at the bar before turning back to face them. "Are you sure you don't want to taste it first?"

Now it was Jack's turn for the wide eyes. If a guest— an expert—said the wine was undrinkable, then his word should be accepted without question. Laurent smirked, probably anticipating the reaming that inevitably followed when some sassy piece challenged the boss's authority, but before Jack could reply, Cara chimed in.

"Gina, you know that saying 'the customer is always right'? Well, it's a load of crap. But you know who is right? The chef with several fine dining establishments in three countries and six Michelin stars."

"Seven," Jack corrected instinctively. It should have been eight; that two-star rating for New York still rankled. And no matter how many times he told Cara that the restaurants received the ratings, not the chef, she always got it wrong.

Cara continued her defense of his superior nose. "And if Jack says the wine is corked, then it's corked. So toddle off and bring us another one." With a mutinous glare, Gina stormed to the bar.

Jack's fingers instinctively went to the throbbing bump on his head. It was going to be a long night.

"You need to do something," Lili's cousin Tad murmured from behind the bar. He nodded at the estrogen flock near the water station.

Yeah, yeah, didn't she know it. She hauled in a fortifying breath and strode over to the ringleader. Her second cousin, Angela, was fronting the charge, licking her lips and bombarding Jack's table with lustful gazes.

"If I have to tell you one more time to get back to work, tonight's tips will be dropped in St. Jude's collection plate at eight o'clock Mass tomorrow." Not that she'd be stepping across the church threshold herself—she might turn to ash—but her pious aunt Sylvia would be happy to make a donation on behalf of the servers at DeLuca's. Angela scowled while the rest of the girls separated in a flurry of giggles, throwing longing glances in Jack's direction.

Lili seated Mr. and Mrs. Castillo, here for their thirty-fifth wedding anniversary, and returned to gossip with Tad.

"So, Wonder Woman, huh?" her cousin asked, giving the bar a quick swipe with a damp cloth while he shot a glittering smile at a bouncy redhead on her way to the restroom. Ever the multitasker, her cousin. The poor girl's perk faltered as she wobbled on her heels, helpless in the face of Tad's blue-eyed, square-jawed, hint-of-scruff charm.

"Hey, I didn't look half bad in that costume," Lili protested.

"Yeah, I heard Kilroy thought so, too," Tad said. "And judging by the heat he's packing tonight, I'd lay good odds he spent his day thinking about peeling you *out* of that costume."

"Oh, hush."

But Tad was right. The air was thick with sex pheromones, and while ninety-five percent of it was one-way traffic from every female in the room to Jack's table, the remaining five percent was swimming upstream from the man himself to her spot at the hostess podium. With the scorching looks he was sending her way, she half expected the smoke alarms to go off any minute.

"What are you going to do about it?" Tad asked.

"What? Kilroy?"

Tad threw her a well-duh look. "Cara seems to think you've got an in. I thought she was talking out of her bony ass as usual, but now that I've witnessed the man in action, I'm inclined to agree."

"I'm not his type. You've seen the women he dates."

"Yeah, I wouldn't throw that Ashley out of bed for eating breadsticks. And then there was that lingerie model and one of those bikini babes from *Survivor*." Her cousin had clearly found a kindred penis in Jack Kilroy. "Yeah, you're probably right. How could you possibly stack up against those chicks?"

She knew he was being his usual sarcastic self, but it didn't stop a sigh escaping her lips.

"Babe, I jest," he added, his expression resolving to sympathy. "Trust me. *All* men like 'em curvy. It's like, programmed into our DNA."

Maybe, but Lili's DNA still screamed, *Danger!* An afternoon of Google-Fu had thrown up all she needed to know about the lives and lusts of Cara's star. Last summer, he'd been a minor-league TV chef on a fledgling network with fewer viewers than DeLuca's Tuesday night covers. Then along came Ashley van Patten, star of struggling soap opera *Tomorrow's Hope*. His people must have lunched with her people, angling to manufacture the next celebrity couple juggernaut. Jashley. Or Ashlack. Not as catchy as Brangelina, but it did the trick to reverse the slide of their respective ratings. Hers doubled. His tripled.

While their relationship ups-and-downs were entertaining, their train wreck breakup had been even more so: a public fight at one of those Hollywood mogul's shindigs that ended with Jack wearing a martini and Ashley coughing up a gallon of chlorinated water after she fell into the kidney-shaped pool. Not long after, he had punched a photographer who got all up in his grill on a London street. Lili obviously didn't have the dramatic flair to go toe-to-toe with Jack Kilroy.

"Ah, but still he stares." Tad grinned, interpreting her apprehensive expression correctly. "Worried your lady bits might go into shock, babe? I know it's been a looong while."

"Maybe he's not *my* type," she said, shooting for haughty.

"Liar," he said, then more casually, "We could make it interesting."

"How interesting?"

"Fifty bucks says you can't close the deal before he leaves town."

She shot him an impatient look. "How about twenty minutes on your hog?"

Tad answered with the family stare-down, a skill learned by all DeLucas while still in the cradle. "I've told you before, Lili. I don't think you can handle that much power." Her cousin had a Harley but refused to let her ride it. It was much more fun to take potshots at what he called her "tin cup runabout."

"Forget it," she said, turning away.

"Okay, ten minutes. But it doesn't matter because you're such a chicken. You won't go for it even if it's offered up on a platter." He sloped off to attend to a couple of cougars who had just stalked up and dug their claws into the bar.

Chicken. More like Little Miss Do Nothing, and though she knew Tad was only teasing, it still stung. Now that her mom was better, Lili should have been back on the life train, next stop grad school. Two years ago, she had plans to blow this Popsicle stand and finally transform into the person she had dreamed of as a tortured fat girl. Future Lili would be poised, self-assured, successful. Achieving an acceptable comfort level with her body should have instilled a similar confidence in her mind, but there were always those lingering doubts—about her artistic talent, her self-worth, her place in the world.

Until she got her restaurant back in the black, her place was at DeLuca's, doing everything in her power to ensure the family's future. Even if that meant enduring her father's viselike grip on the business and her dreams. She sighed. Rome wasn't built in a day, and neither was a new life.

Minutes later, Lili spotted a teed-off Gina approaching the bar with a bottle of wine in one hand, a corkscrew in the other, and a face that even her extremely patient fiancé might have reservations about. While her cousin shook and gesticulated her way through an explanation to her brother, Tad, Lili ambled over to see how her meddling services might be best employed.

She placed a protective arm around Gina's shoulders as the girl spluttered, "They...they shouldn't talk like that to people. I know he's a freaking genius chef, but that wine costs a lot of money. Telling me to toddle off. There's no need to be rude, you know?"

Lili's hackles rose as she contemplated tearing Jack Kilroy a new one. If that big shot big mouth with his behemoth restaurants and über-sensitive wine palate thought he could waltz in here and look down his British nose at everyone, he had chosen the wrong night to do it—and the wrong family to mess with. She pivoted quickly, only to bump chest-first into the object of her next tongue-lashing, who was doing a wonderful impersonation of a Stonehenge monolith.

He stepped back just as she placed a hand on his chest to...well, to stop him, she supposed. Mercy, if he wasn't incredibly solid and warm and undeniably male. He was definitely going to hear it. Once her brain unwarped and she could think straight.

She raised her eyes using his shirt buttons as her road map and blinked when she reached his face. He really was the most handsome man she had ever seen in person—movie-star gorgeous—and briefly her resolve wavered. But that shit-eating grin was enough to straighten her spine and snap her back to mountain pose. Yay, yoga.

"The next time you want to act like a card-carrying jackass with one of my staff, you should ask to see the manager." Her cheeks burned. He opened his mouth—*that crooked, sexy mouth*—and she put up a hand to stop him.

"You had better be a good tipper, Kilroy, because money's the only way you're getting out of this intact."

"Lili—" Gina tried to cut in.

Lili waved a hand. She had this.

His feet didn't move, but his upper body leaned in so close she caught the scent of his skin, woodsy and citrus, reminiscent of a Sorrentine lemon grove. New man smell, nothing like it. He combed his fingers through his thick—and more lustrous than it had a right to be—hair.

"I actually came to apologize to Gina. Cara was bang out of order and shouldn't have said what she did."

Gulp.

So maybe she didn't have it after all.

She shot a death glare at her cousin, who offered a wobbly smile in return.

"I'm sorry. I misunderstood the situation," Lili muttered before snapping in Italian, "Gina, take another bottle of Brunello to Mr. Kilroy's table. Then it's your turn to check the restrooms." Her cousin slunk off.

Lili turned back to the Duke of Hunk, who had crossed his arms over that barrel chest and appeared to be waiting for a more groveling apology than the one she'd just given.

"You're still here," she said.

"I am." He smiled.

She scowled because it was the opposite of smiling, and if she gave him the slightest opening, he would take it as some sort of encouragement.

"You seem tense," he said, his brazen grin widening.

"I have a lot to do and you're very distracting."

"You find me distracting, Lili?"

It was the first time he had said her name—correctly—and it sounded like a devil's whisper. Her heart pounded like a trip-hammer. She choked out a laugh because it was ridiculous to be affected by something so silly as a man saying her name, even when the way he said it was calculated to make pulse rates soar and panties plummet.

"Oh, I don't, but your siren call seems to have cast a spell on my girls. Maybe you should try to rein in your"—she flapped a hand and accidentally brushed against his chest, still solid, and warm, and male— "tendencies, so the rest of us can do our jobs."

"If you can't control your staff, that's not my problem. I feel like a tourist attraction over there with all the visits from your girls. Perhaps you should train them better."

Irritation simmered in her chest. She took great pride in how she ran DeLuca's and in how her employees behaved, but she reluctantly admitted that the excitement of Jack's visit might have led to a drop in everyone's game, including her own. She was such a girl.

"There is nothing wrong with how my staff is trained."

"So, trashing the fish special, arguing about the wine, and practically sitting in customers' laps is all part of the training program? I've suffered through enough cleavage *Italiana* to last a lifetime." His eyes gave an indolent dip. "Well, almost enough."

He was doing it again, that thing where he spoke and he looked and her body ignited, setting the women's movement back fifty years. His voice took a shivery road trip down her spine and back again. She tried to think of something to say, but her usual sass was out on a smoke break in the alley.

He tilted his head. "I understand this is a family business, but you may want to consider casting a wider net. Nepotism usually results in an inferior product."

At last, her voice returned from its sabbatical. "We

don't hire people because they're family." Well, except for Angela. And, um, maybe Gina. Both were unemployable. Dammit. "We hire people because they're good at their job. If you'd stop flirting with them and let them do that job, things might go a lot smoother."

He moved in, taking up a stance a hairsbreadth from her body. "Don't worry, I'm not interested in any of your waitresses," he said, his voice a silky caress. "I'm more than willing to aim higher. Maybe even as high as the hostess."

I'm the manager, you clod. Heart still slamming, she plastered on a bored smile. "Oh, please don't raise your standards for me, Kilroy. Just like I won't be lowering my standards to a fame-hungry megawhore like you."

Bingo. A flash of something flared in his eyes. Nothing so mundane as disappointment, more likely the annoyance that accompanies a bruised ego. Men like Jack Kilroy weren't used to being told they weren't good enough, especially by a member of the hoi polloi.

"So you believe everything you read online? Pity, you might have enjoyed a visit to the lower depths." With a theatrical turn, he strode to the end of the bar and took a seat.

Well, she sure showed him, but why didn't she feel better about it? Instead of the rush of empowerment she expected, she was left feeling like a nitwit. A turned-on nitwit. Who needed contraception when they had a mouth as big as hers?

Tad held up the keys to his Harley and jiggled them. "Poor Lili. Looks like you won't be feeling anything hot and hard between your legs anytime soon."

CHAPTER THREE

Jack leaned his elbows on the bar and steepled his fingers. He had reached a point where it was easier to take the hits than disabuse people of their precious preconceptions. *Hack. Sellout. Whore.* Since Ashley's post-breakup media blitzkrieg, he refused to read anything written about him, but tuning out an in-your-face insult like that required a different level of fortitude.

The less time he spent in his restaurants, the more he found himself on the receiving end of the snide, the smug, and the outright scornful. There was nothing he'd prefer than to be working the line at his New York kitchen, Thyme on Forty-seventh Street, instead of traipsing all over the country like a glorified carnival barker. Damn, he was tired. An unsettlingly soul-deep tired that had little to do with his road-warrior status. Keeping Jack Kilroy front and center had turned into the biggest challenge of his life, and not for the first time in the last six months, he questioned whether he was up for it any longer.

But the new show would be different. Less travel, studio-based, and a chance to take his brand to the next level. He didn't want to recommend a particular skillet; he wanted his name on the box. He didn't want one cookbook; he wanted twenty with translations in thirty languages. Mostly he wanted to show people how to make a restaurant-quality meal for a quarter of the price.

Preferably with Jack Kilroy–branded cookware.

Like any enterprise that required a public face and hard work, there were pitfalls. Lack of privacy for one. Bloodsuckers who made a living off gleefully reporting his mistakes and grabbing compromising pictures of him. Or the people he loved. His sister's face, scared and hunted, flashed before him. It was bad enough he continued to fail her every damn day; he couldn't even treat her to an unmolested dinner in public. What a cliché he had become. The brilliantly successful professional who couldn't negotiate the thorny path of his personal life. The notorious celebrity afraid to trust any woman who piqued his interest.

And we're back. That Cara's sister held him in such low esteem should have been enough to dismiss her as just another member of his know-it-all public, fond of regurgitating the crap spewed by every lurid tabloid outlet. Why, then, was his body zinging and every nerve on fire?

He had forgotten that feeling, that excitement when something new was starting. A new recipe. A new restaurant. A new woman. It galvanized him, helping him overcome the fatigue. Then he remembered his agent's admonishments and his bones ached, weary again.

Do not engage the local talent.

He risked a glance in Lili's direction. If only the local talent weren't so damn engaging.

The bartender tossed a coaster down and asked him what he needed. Some peace and quiet and a six-month holiday to sort out his life. Not that there was a chance in hell of getting it. He had five episodes to complete and a contract for his new show to negotiate. He had his Chicago restaurant to open and seven others to oversee so the quality wouldn't slip. At the ripe old age of thirty-three, everything he touched was golden, a far cry from that fourteen-year-old Brixton street thug who had been headed for the gutter, prison, or worse. Cooking had saved him and set him on the right path. Now he felt...He wasn't sure what he felt.

Oh yeah, tired.

He looked into the deep blue eyes of the bartender, an older Italian guy who could probably intuitively tell a troubled soul when he saw one. At least Jack hoped so.

In a heavy accent, the bartender offered, "How about some grappa?"

Jack gestured his surrender. "Lay it on me. Show me what I've been missing."

Twenty minutes later, he'd tried three different varieties of the pungent grape brandy and was feeling that comforting burn in the pit of his stomach. The bartender had explained how grappa was made and how the varieties differed from each other. It was quite the education. With that warm Italian-inflected English washing over him, Jack watched, entranced, as he expertly poured cocktails and manned the bar. He should poach this guy away when he opened his new restaurant.

Lili's scent, hot woman and floral, but more specifically vanilla with shades of hibiscus, reached him before she did and he felt that pleasurable prickle again. Grappa, like all alcohol, was a great leveler and summoned his magnanimous streak. He opened his mouth to apologize, but he couldn't actually remember what he was supposed to apologize for. There had to be something. With a woman like this, there was always something.

"Your appetizers have arrived and there's no way on earth we're serving them over here." She turned to leave.

"Hey, wait," he said, his hand brushing her arm.

She stood, fists at her waist, her stiff posture drawing his gaze to the flare of her hips, the slope of her breasts. Christ, she was a lot of woman.

"What?" she asked, still pissy.

"I'm surprised you'd take the time to give me a personal update on my first course." Though close to twenty-five minutes for appetizers was a bit much.

"I just want you to eat them how the chef intended. Hot instead of cold."

He blew out a breath. "Look, I'm sorry about insulting Italian cuisine this morning. I'm sure your father's a great cook and the meatballs are fantastic." It came out sarcastic, so not his intention. As well as being a great leveler, grappa turned guys into morons.

"He *is* a great cook. You won't eat better in Chicago."

"I don't doubt it." He flashed a conciliatory grin.

"Okay, then," she said, clearly thrown. Hey, it worked on housewives. She hovered for a moment, then turned heel and split.

"I am sorry about that," the grappa-pusher said, his brow lined with concern. "She is not normally so rude."

Jack waved the apology away. "No worries, mate. That's how she usually talks to me—or that's how she's only ever talked to me."

Another shot appeared before him. The man knew how to work it.

"She is right, though. The food here is quite good," Ol' Blue Eyes said, pouring a shot for himself. He clinked Jack's glass. *"Salute."*

Jack slammed it and peered at the man before him. It was time for this guy to step up and do what bartenders do—listen inattentively to some drunken digressions while dispensing old-world wisdom.

"Have you ever met a woman who annoys the hell out of you?" He paused to judge his next words carefully, his muddled brain already ascribing high-level importance to them. His head both pounded and spun like wet sneakers in a dryer. Drinking was not the cleverest of ideas.

"I mean, you just want to touch her, and if she's mouthy, kiss her to shut her up." He turned the shot glass over. When the idiotic rambling started, the night was pretty much kaput. Time to halt the crazy train at this station.

The bartender's face darkened and he spouted something in Italian that reeked of wisdom and portentousness. *Now we're cooking.* Jack lifted an eyebrow and waited to be wowed.

"It means 'Wine, women, and tobacco reduce one to ashes.' So my Liliana has made an impression?"

My Liliana? Jack's body wrenched in sobering alert; then his self-preservation instincts kicked in and he thrust out his hand. "I'm Jack Kilroy. Pleased to meet you."

The bartender laid down his towel and considered the outstretched hand for a heartbeat before taking it in his firm grasp.

"Tony DeLuca. Cara's and Liliana's father."

For fuck's sake, that's just sneaky. Tony's grip crushed him. Jack let his hand go slack; he might be tipsy, but he wasn't stupid. He studied the cherrywood bar for five seconds. Ten. When he looked up, he found Tony regarding him closely, his expression unreadable.

"Any chance I can see your kitchen in action?" Jack asked, throwing in a hopeful grin that the code of courtesy among professional chefs might drag this into the draw column. Not only that, but also the craving for action that might break his skin into hives at any moment needed to be assuaged. And if he couldn't get his fix with a woman, or one particular woman, then he'd take the next best thing—a visit to the kitchen of the man who would be his cooking rival for the next two days.

Tony's lips curled up into a not-quite-smile. *"Si, naturalmente."*

* * *

It seemed everyone and his brother had decided to stop in at O'Casey's, the after-work hangout for the DeLuca crew. As the smallest Irish bar in Chicago, its cozy dimensions did an admirable job of accelerating intimacy in case the beer wasn't flowing. Not that it wasn't flowing tonight. Jack was running a tab for the gang, who were knocking it back like they had to report to Cook County Correctional Center the next day.

Lili glanced over her shoulder to where her ex, Marco, was engrossed in conversation with the man himself, who had the glassy-eyed look of the condemned. She tried not to notice that Jack was a few inches taller than Marco or that he was broader and generally more...space-filling. She also tried not to notice the way a light dusting of chest hair poked above the V of Jack's shirt or how the rolled-up sleeves of his white button-down contrasted scrumptiously with his tanned forearms.

Jack Kilroy had it going on.

Sighing, she returned to the other man of the moment. Laurent had waylaid her the second she stepped through the bar door and was now on his third White Russian. Addled as he was, Lili still felt flattered to have such a quality charmer touching her bare arm and looking down her shirt at every opportunity. Her curiosity about Jack got the better of her, though, so she steered the conversation around to his friend.

"You and Jack have worked together a long time, then?"

"*Oui*. We met in Paris many years ago during our apprenticeship, but we didn't work together again until a few years later when he needed a sous-chef for his first restaurant in London. I have been with him for all his restaurant openings, but I am now based at Thyme on Forty-seventh in New York."

"You don't want to run your own restaurant?" It seemed strange he would be satisfied to remain in Jack's shadow, but then, that's what she'd been doing for years with Cara. Some people were just born to play sous-chef.

He hesitated, and while she would usually put it down to the alcohol, there was something faraway in his expression. "I would like to be in charge at Thyme but Jack is not one to give up the reins so easily. He likes to be in control."

Bet he does. The mere mention of that word in relation to Jack sent a long, shivering pulse through her body.

"But I like working with him," Laurent continued. "He's the smartest and most creative guy in the business." He inclined his head to hers, and the fumes knocked her sideways. His eyebrows arched up like accent marks. "Why are you so interested in Jack? You should be interested in me, *chérie*. The Italians and the French have always been close, *oui*?"

She pointed with her beer bottle. "Except when the Romans conquered France. And that whole Napoleon thing. And World War Two. But other than that, we've always got along exceptionally well." She grinned. "Not like the French and the British. Aren't you supposed to be terrible foes?"

"There is a lot of the rivalry, *oui*. But not between Jack and me. He is my best friend."

Aw, Lili couldn't help but be touched by his loyalty. After another few minutes of good-natured ogling, he excused himself to hit the restroom.

Gazing around the room, she spotted Tad at the other end of the bar chatting with Shannon, the buxom bartender who reminded Lili of a female Bond villain. The kind who could crush walnuts with her thighs. Her cousin sent an impudent smile her way and bowed in the direction of Jack, who now had his hands full trying to fend off the attentions of a gaggle of DeLuca women.

Do it, Tad's grin said.

Not on your life, her frown replied. After her mouthy put-down earlier, there was no way Jack would still be interested, and even if he threw his hat into her ring again, she was so rusty she wouldn't know what to do with it.

This night was a wash on the man front, but all was not lost. There were cookies. Double-chocolate chip cookies.

And they were waiting for her less than a block away in her apartment. She had just put a foot to the floor when a heady, expensive man scent, straight from the perfume counter at Macy's, stopped her cold.

"Hey, Lil." Marco was a sidler, one of his many talents. If his cologne weren't so potent, he might have had a promising career in Special Forces.

"*Ciao*, Marco."

"Exciting about the show, isn't it? It's going to be great for business." Her ex's favorite topic of conversation, after his Lamborghini, his Italian shirt maker, and his net worth, was how to make his twenty-five percent investment in DeLuca's worth the time he didn't want to put into it.

"Sure is," she said, all too aware of Marco's undertone. He was thinking about the personal loan he'd made to her father covering her mother's medical bills and how soon it might be repaid.

While he yammered on about getting a local news crew involved, she observed him closely, drinking in his golden looks, that deep baritone that used to make the hair on the nape of her neck stand on end, and his habit of talking too loudly when he got excited. This past winter, she had needed a warm body to get her by, and he had been kind enough to step up. Not exactly fireworks between the sheets, but he had given her what she needed—arms to hold her for a couple of hours when she felt overwhelmed by her mother, the restaurant, and her life half written. In true Lili fashion, she had listened to all his problems and kept quiet about her own. Then the inevitable happened: she fell for him hard just as he realized he could do much better.

He rolled his lips in, his usual signal that he didn't approve of something. He did that a lot. "I heard you're going to make a play for Kilroy."

Lili almost fell off her barstool. "Where'd you hear that?"

Marco delivered a condescending smile. He did that a lot, too. "Someone's running a book on it."

Madre di Dio, she was going to drown Tad in wet noodles. At Marco's sympathetic expression, Lili could feel the knuckles whitening on her clenched fist. It would be so easy to hit him on that square jaw. He wouldn't even see it coming because his gaze had already wandered to a boobs-on-a-stick blonde draped over the jukebox. She flexed her hand; Marco's hazy focus returned.

"I don't think Kilroy's your speed, Lil. Maybe you should stick with the frog. Aim a little lower."

Aim a little lower. Marco's words went down like Pepto—they tasted awful but they were probably good for her. She could fake it up to a point, but no way, no how could she pull a league jump of this magnitude.

A glass of clear liquid appeared in front of her with uncanny timing and a wink from Shannon. Tad saluted a bottoms-up cheer with his beer bottle. Marco raised a disapproving eyebrow. She knocked back the shot—ugh, mint schnapps—and her Benedict-Arnold hormones did the rest.

Pinned against the dartboard, Jack had been stunned into submission by a crescent-shaped line of brunette admirers with a blonde thrown in for variety. Lili watched as he engaged in a rally of repelling tactics, from slow nodding to diversionary swigs of his beer. The blonde loitered at his shoulder with intent, her hand glossing over his bicep. Angela was two baby steps short of clambering on top of him. Gina, despite her affianced status, was trying to outflank her cousin with a couple of undone shirt buttons and frenzied eyelash batting.

Jack's gaze locked onto Lili's, and she felt a sudden and startling jolt of attraction right down to her toes.

"Kilroy's working it, I see. You've got no chance there, Lil," Marco said, his tone jovial but laced with something else. She looked at her ex with interest. If it was possible for eyes to sneer, Marco's were doing it right now. Her own eyes were drawn back to the evening's entertainment and found Jack still staring above Angela's frizzy curls, his gaze direct and true. His sexy mouth hadn't moved a muscle but his eyes, in that rare green hue…they promised everything.

That look enveloped her like a curl of flame, immolating all her hesitation in a fiery burst. Just one night was all she asked. One night to see stars, to experience scorching passion, to get a little lost. A combination of the corrosive burn from the liquor and Marco's smug grin decided it. She was tired of aiming lower.

"Later, Marco."

Sidestepping him, she skirted around the fan club and addressed Jack. "Hey."

His eyes widened and shifted to a smoky darkness. "Hey, yourself."

"We should talk."

"We should?" he asked in a graveled voice that guaranteed talking would be low on the list for the rest of the evening.

"Logistics," she said, playing along. "Getting into the kitchen tomorrow to test your dishes. That kind of thing."

"Right, we should talk about that." He bowed to his rapt audience. "Ladies, business calls."

The ladies shot her unladylike glares aimed at sending her six feet under, twice. Jack tucked his hand under her elbow and with a gentle, but very deliberate, pressure propelled her toward the bar.

"How can I ever thank you?" he murmured close to her ear.

Lord, that accent. Combined with his touch and that delicious male spice, it set off a high-frequency vibration throughout her body.

"Oh, I'm sure I'll think of something."

CHAPTER FOUR

The crush at the bar was tight, the sliver of space between them shrinking fast, and Jack's world was all the better for it.

"I'm sorry about the girls," Lili said, not sounding sorry at all. "They're just excited."

He stole a look back at the kettle of vultures. *Excited* wasn't the word—more like *ravenous*.

"We don't get a lot of famous visitors," she added. "You've caused quite the stir."

"I'm not even that famous," he said, the familiar irritation creeping into his voice.

"They're easily impressed."

Evidently she wasn't, and that turned him on to an unreasonable degree. She pushed one of her dark curls behind her ears while he shoved a twitching hand into his pocket, wishing he could have got there first.

"So, did you enjoy the food?" she asked with a sly smile.

"It was amazing. Your father's a great chef." Lip service wasn't Jack's style. The pastas were out of this world, especially the fluffy, melt-in-your-mouth pillows of gnocchi. The steak was cooked flawlessly, the fish flaking off the bone. All the same, Jack wasn't too worried about the contest. He'd been cooking on the right side of perfection for years.

What did worry him was how he'd made an arse of himself in front of her father, and he cursed Cara for neglecting to give him a heads-up. Luckily, Tony had been a gracious host and gave him a tour of the kitchen, in spite of Jack's half-drunken drooling over his youngest daughter. A little acrimony might make for good TV, but he didn't want to be on Tony's shit list. He wasn't sure why.

"Ready to throw in the towel yet?" Lili asked.

"I never back down from a challenge."

She laughed, a low throaty chuckle that blossomed into something full and husky and left him scrounging for air. Her mouth was lush and he had to take breaks to stop himself from staring at her. From staring at her mouth and imagining what he'd like to do to it.

On one of his air-grasping sorties away from her mouth, he spied Laurent with a dangerously stacked blonde near the jukebox. So much for love Italian style. Not far off stood that Maximo-Mario guy, glaring in Jack's direction. Earlier, while he and Laurent waited for the staff to arrive, this loser had tried to lease him a building for Jack's new restaurant, the one he already had half built in Chicago's West Loop.

"What's the deal with him?" he asked, nodding in the loser's direction.

Lili's eyes sparkled, and Jack speculated that she might be buzzed.

"Marco? He's my father's business partner."

"My condolences," Jack muttered.

"And I used to date him."

A mouthful of beer went down the wrong way. "Jesus, my sincerest condolences."

Marco was speaking animatedly on his cell, though it had all the hallmarks of a one-sided conversation. He probably had the opening bars of Beethoven's Fifth as his ringtone and answered his phone with *Yello*. Tosspot.

Lili smiled thinly. "He's not so bad. He's actually quite sweet."

Oh no, he wasn't. Jack knew Marco's type. With his pinkie ring, his manicure, and his shark eyes, he was the embodiment of a flash geezer. As if that wasn't enough for Jack to hate him on sight, he sported the one thing no man over the age of twenty-one should ever leave the house with—a ponytail. That Lili had found him date-worthy, and maybe more, unsettled him.

"He can be…" Her voice hummed so low he had to lean in to hear her. Standard bar trick. "He just needs a little support."

"And that was your job? The great woman behind the little man?" What would it be like to have a woman like this at his back? Pretty damn nice, he was willing to bet. To come home and talk to her, to listen to that beautiful laugh, then bury his tension in her softness.

To come home and talk to her? That whack to the head must have knocked a few screws loose. How else to explain the leap from unbridled animal attraction to choosing china patterns and cozying up on the couch to *Law and Order* reruns?

For a while now, he'd been hovering on the edge of ready, but every potential relationship was fraught with suspicion about the other party's motives. After Ashley's tell-all to the tabloids—and it didn't matter that most of it was a bald-face lie—he was more careful now. More circumspect. He needed to keep that train of thought on the track and not get derailed with fantasies of waking up with Lili's soft body curled into his...Jesus.

Her mouth quirked like she could read his thoughts. "Doesn't every man need a great woman, or a great man, behind him?"

"What about the great woman? Doesn't she have her own needs?"

"All of us great women have needs." She wrapped her lips around the opening of her longneck beer and he stifled that groan he'd been fighting all fucking night. His dick twitched in commiseration.

Just to complete the circle of torture, he grabbed his beer from the bar and snuck a stealthy glance into the shadowy valley of her cleavage. White cotton bra, none too exciting, but those breasts...yes. They plumped up over the edges like succulent, golden peaches. His lips skimmed close to her ear, and he paused to breathe in her hair's scent as if he could store it for another day. Rosemary and mint.

"What kind of needs do you have, Lili?" he whispered.

"Oh, a guy with all his own teeth who's good at foot rubs and can give earth-shattering orgasms. Nothing special."

Ask a stupid question... Drawing back, he responded

to her salvo with his most penetrating gaze. She held it for a moment, but then a shiver of doubt crossed her face. Ducking her head, she took a long draught of her beer.

That little exchange told him two things.

It had been far too long since he'd had sex.

And he was officially in trouble.

The silence drew between them like a piñata poised to be hacked down, and he hesitated, knowing he was sending her mixed signals. When you devour a woman with every look, it's understandable she might have certain expectations. He wanted her, but he also wanted something he couldn't put a label on. Not yet.

Several thudding heartbeats later, she slid off the stool and pressed her body against his, her soft breasts teasing his ribs and prompting every nerve to revolt. With her hand flat on his chest, she tilted her face up and gave him the full benefit of those baby blues.

"Okay, I'm out," she said.

"You're what?"

"I'm out." Drawing back, she crossed her arms, which plumped up her cleavage to hazmat levels. "Jack, I'm not one for playing games."

"Neither am I."

She cocked a generous hip, projecting the don't-fuck-with-me thing perfectly. "Have you or have you not been staring the bejesus out of me since I brained you with that frying pan?"

"Well, yes—"

"And wouldn't any girl in my position interpret that as an indication of your interest?"

"I suppose so, but—"

"So you're all hat, no cattle. Or maybe we got our signals crossed."

"I thought we were having a nice chat," he said, sounding like a little old biddy in a tea shop. *A nice chat?*

She'd already checked out of their nice chat and was now surveying the crowd.

"Is Laurent still here?" she asked, her gaze taking inventory of the bar.

"Yes, he is but—" His heart stuttered. "Are you taking the piss?"

She fanned her waist with both hands. "Take a good look, Kilroy."

He took.

"I owe it all to spaghetti."

"Good line."

"Sophia Loren," she said, then added, "She's an Italian actress," in case he'd been living under a rock for the last thirty years, he supposed. She gave a wobbly, likely tipsy, pirouette, delivering a taste of all the angles. It was a very, very pleasant view.

"You had your chance, but you blew it. I think your sexy French minion will be more than willing to tap this." She turned and it took every iota of his strength not to reach out and stroke her very tappable arse. Cup it and squeeze it. Slap it so she cried out in surprise.

"Au revoir," she said with a racy smile over her shoulder, taking another step away from him and his raging hard-on. Then two more steps and she was out of his immediate orbit on her way toward the jukebox and...shit. Laurent.

That had *not* just happened.

A knot of negativity unraveled within him but he

wasn't ready to call it jealousy. Laurent would be too drunk to know what to do with her, anyway. He followed that bobbing cloud of hair, plowing his way through the wall of bodies that opened and closed behind her like quicksand.

Her little exclamation of disbelief when he grabbed her hand sent warmth spreading through his gut. Without looking at her, he dragged her toward the dim corridor near the restrooms and caged her against the wall, his hand still locked in hers. Not as private as he would have liked but he'd worked with worse. Much worse.

"Now, listen up, caveman," she panted. "Who the hell do you think you are?"

"I'm the bloke you do not want to mess with, sweetheart."

In his head, he had a whole raft of things to tell her, starting with how her cleavage was a menace and how she had better think twice the next time she pulled a stunt like that, but the sight—damn, the experience—of her glowing in the hallway's shadowy light checked his speech hard.

Breasts heaving, warm, womanly scent filling his mouth and nostrils so he could hardly breathe. Those already moist lips of hers parted and quivered, a microcosm of the shake now pulsing through her entire body.

"Don't do that again," he growled, ostensibly a continuation of his mission to reassert control. Sure it was. Somewhere along the way, their joined hands had interlaced and were now pinned to the wall by her cheek. Her hand seemed so small in his and when she squeezed, it felt like the most intimate of pleas. A plea answered when he squeezed back, drawing a spark of relief in her big eyes. And relief was catching because just the knowledge that she wanted him, not Laurent, not some random dick, did it for him right there.

Something caught in his throat as he claimed her mouth. Her name perhaps, more likely a swear. Lips explored, tongues tangled, creating a chemical explosion of sweet that startled his body to glittering life, as if it had been waiting for this moment to wake up. She let out a rough sound that spurred him on, and he redoubled his efforts and kissed her harder.

He coasted his free hand along her hip before, finally, he cupped her magnificent arse, enjoying the flawless fit in his palm. Her body unfurled for him and he hiked her up, then slipped between her legs, filling in the concave space of her sex with his own hardness. He reveled in the sensuous friction of her breasts against his chest. Another guttural sound escaped her, a sound of pure pleasure.

She hooked her leg behind his thigh for leverage and stroked that highly sensitive part of his body with the side of her foot. He moaned against her mouth. Loudly. Dazed, he broke away but didn't get far because she had a death grip on his hair.

"God, you taste good," he said, wishing she'd release his hair because his head still hurt from this morning.

She blinked rapidly. "I know—I mean, you too. You taste good, too."

He ran his tongue along his lips, confirming his findings. It had been so long since a woman had tasted this amazing. Hell, no woman had ever tasted this amazing.

"More," he grunted.

"God, yes—" But he had already gone in before she could get the words out, because he wasn't really asking permission. He would never have thought it possible, but the kiss became even more intense as it flowed through his body, buzzing his skin. She must have felt it, too, because she jerked her foot against the back of his leg, dragging another loud moan from him. The slanting pressure of her lips ratcheted up the tightness in his jeans.

He felt the heated trail of her hand between their bodies, down his chest, his abs, to places onward. The kiss expanded to harder, deeper, hotter. Her hand inched below his waistband, tickling his zipper, and Christ on the cross, if that wasn't amazing. She hovered there, so close to heaven, and his brain and dick cheered her on. *Lower, sweetheart. Touch me, baby, please.* His erection turned excruciating, and he swallowed a budding groan.

This had to stop.

At last they came up for air and hopefully a splash of cold-faced common sense. Unfortunately, sense had left the building towing any remaining oxygen in its wake. They both stared, hauling air like marathon runners.

"Let's go back to my place," she said, low and druggy. "I live over the restaurant."

Yes.

But.

That's when the niggle kicked in, not in his jeans where there was no niggle room whatsoever, but in the limbic centers of his brain. The parts that were in charge of lust, sadness, joy, and fear. He wanted her—every inch of him was in agreement on that score—but he had made some promises to himself these last few months, and a fuck-and-forget wasn't part of the plan. He needed more information.

"Maybe we should slow down. Talk a little first." She

looked befuddled. He tried again. "What happened to getting to know someone?"

She cracked a sexy smile with a side of condescension. "Jack, I'm not looking to know you."

No, she wasn't, unless you counted biblically. She was looking for the guy who indiscriminately dated and bedded famous women. A guy whose life could be reduced to adjectives, most of them unflattering. *That* guy.

Really he should be applauding the novelty of meeting a woman unimpressed by his fame, only to find she just wanted him for sex. It sure made for a nice twist on the usual "what can you do for me?" refrain. His gut churned in disappointment. There was some anger folded in there, though he couldn't be sure if it was directed at her or his own sorry self.

"Lili, this isn't a good idea."

She released his hand and it felt all wrong. "It's not?"

He shook his head and that felt all wrong, too.

"Are you . . . are you turning me down?"

"I'm afraid I am."

Her lips formed a soundless O that sent a shiver of dread through him. She raised her hand to her forehead. He agreed wholeheartedly. It was a real face-palm moment, for sure.

"But I thought—" She looked like she'd just found out Santa Claus didn't exist. Her fingertips stroked feverishly across her collarbone, as though the action might work to spirit her away from here. "Am I not good enough? Am I not . . . hot enough?"

At the tremor in her voice, he felt an answering lurch in his chest. "Sweetheart, that's not it. Maybe we could—"

"Don't sweetheart me." All the earlier promise of the

evening lay closed and shuttered in her tightly held stance. She palmed a light pressure to his shoulder to push him aside. He went easy.

"Lili, you're a very beautiful woman. This is just moving a little fast."

"Forget it." She rubbed a hint of moisture from her kiss-swollen bottom lip, wiping the taste of him from her. It was going to take much more than that to get the sweet memory of her out of his mouth.

Angling around him, she strode back into the bar, and not even her harried gait could disguise that sexy tilt to her hips or the pride with which she carried herself. He could go after her, tell her she'd had a lucky escape and wouldn't become part of the three-ring circus that was his life. He could tell her the truth, that he was tired of using and being used and he would like to get to know her better. Not that she'd believe him.

He didn't quite believe it himself.

CHAPTER FIVE

Lili was still shaking.

Fifteen minutes ago, she'd experienced both the hottest and most humiliating moments of her life. One right after the other. She jammed the toothbrush into her mouth with such vehemence that she grunted at the abrasive pain.

What in the name of all things good and holy had just happened with Jack Kilroy?

So she wasn't the brightest spark when it came to men. Consider Exhibit A, Marco Rossi, the man she had mooned over for six pathetic months. She had known it was a lost cause, but at one time the slightest glance from him had been enough to send her into a tizzy of anticipation, which usually fizzled quicker than a damp squib. Thankfully, she was cured of Marco.

Next up, Exhibit B, Jack Kilroy, with his epic chest and his hot mouth. No vaccine available against that. He had walked out of that fridge and into her flat-lining life, dazzling her with that easy smile and stupid accent. Cara and Tad had egged her on, and like an idiot, she had played into their rom-com script.

How could she have mistaken the nuclear heat rolling off the man in waves? The looks that promised he was picturing her naked. The appraisal of her body, first with his eyes, then with his hands. That mouth...that mouth that could do anything and have her begging for more. Begging for him to feast on her neck, her breasts, her belly, her—

The harsh blast of the intercom slashed through her pathetic fantasy. She rinsed the mouth that had just been kissed stupid. No, she could still taste him. *Essence de Kilroy.*

She had played a little, teased a lot, added in the empty threat of Laurent, and it had worked. He had followed the sure thing and then proceeded to blindside her. Even if he had been affected by their clinch—and she had definitely felt the affection when he ground his body into her like she was the mortar to his pestle—he clearly had a different agenda.

She hated guys with agendas.

The buzzer sounded again. Living in a neighborhood filled with bars usually guaranteed a few late-night visitors. No one she knew, just idiots who liked to press buzzers on a drunken dare and stumble on to the next target.

A few seconds ticked by. Another buzz. She knew who it was before she'd even pushed the Talk button.

"Yeah?"

"Lili, I need to see you." Jack's voice filled the room, crisp, British, and not in the least bit apologetic. Following a moment of silence on her end, he buzzed again. She pressed the button and listened to the ominous crackle.

"Lili, let me in so I can explain."

She bit down on her lip, praying that might work to stop her from screaming at him. Her finger depressed the Talk button again and caught him midsentence.

"—down and shut up," he said, followed by incomprehensible muttering.

"Did you just tell me to shut up?" she asked, incensed.

"No, not you." He sounded distant, like he was underwater; then his voice came in again so clearly that it startled her.

"Sweetheart, I can hear you breathing." She stopped. Breathing was overrated anyway. "Why don't you let me come up and we can talk about this like adults?"

Adults? She had wanted to do some very adult things with him and now he wanted to talk. Like adults. That suppressed scream yearned to break free of her throat. She caught muddled snatches of what he said next. Something about Laurent, then a torrent of French gibberish.

"I don't want to talk to you," Lili shouted, because a raised voice always got the job done.

"I need to explain."

"It's really not necessary. Please go away." And leave her alone with her humiliation.

The sound of a scuffle bounced through the intercom followed by more foreign babbling. A full minute passed.

"All right, you're going to be sorry," he said, inducing a flap of panic in her chest. Would he try to break in? Bang on her door until one of the neighbors called the cops? If only. It was worse. Much worse.

Jack Kilroy started to sing.

The caterwauling made by the most deluded of wannabe contestants on *American Idol* had nothing on this. Hearing such a sound blasting from her TV was one thing; listening to it through her intercom was quite another. His voice had not improved any since the last time she'd heard him mangling a tune, right before she clocked him with a frying pan.

"Lili, I just met a girl, she's called Lili…" This, to the tune of "Maria" from *West Side Story*.

Someone on the street cheered. Encouraged, Jack raised his voice a couple of inadvisable octaves. Another voice punctuated the lyrics with shouts of "Lili" a half-beat late. There was a pause as Jack told his accompanist in no uncertain terms to shut the fuck up.

The crazy galoot. All that charm in six feet two of hot, spicy male, and for a brief, brilliant moment, it was directed at her. This must be what being in love felt like—the swoopy sensation in her stomach, the lightness of her galloping heart, the notion that anything was possible because one guy chose to serenade one girl with an atonal rendition of a show tune.

It was silly to feel like this, a frivolous fakery, but she held on to it as she took the stairs, two at a time, and threw open the door to the street. Poking her head out, she found Jack arranged against a wall looking like some good ol' boy at a barn dance waiting for Ladies' Choice. All he was missing was a toothpick and a Stetson.

"What took you so long?" he said, gifting her with that so-help-her-God smile.

Along with all the other sensations, her legs now turned to water.

Laurent was sitting on the ground with his head between his knees. A couple of guys, helping each other along with the affection of the drunk, turned and shouted, "Lili!" Jack saluted them like they were old pals.

"You are an awful singer," she said, biting back a budding laugh. It wouldn't do to make it too easy on him.

His eyes crinkled with good humor. "What I lack in skill, I make up for in enthusiasm."

"Add that to the list of things no woman wants to hear."

He scrubbed a hand through his hair and his expression took a turn for the serious. "I want to explain."

Lili waved him off magnanimously. "Forget about it."

"I behaved terribly," he said.

"Right, just not terribly enough."

He pushed off from the wall, closing the gap between them, and his eyes did the full-body sweep. If that wasn't enough to haul her back to earth, the whispering night breeze reminded her she had changed into her version of jammies: gray sweat shorts and a thin-as-wax-paper tank top with SAVE THE TATAS emblazoned across her chest. And she wasn't wearing a bra. She crossed her arms to cover her nipples, which she suspected would start betraying her at any moment.

"You lost your leering privileges when you told me to take a hike."

Jack's sensual lips curved into a knowing grin. He opened his mouth to say what she assumed was something flippant. She cut him off at the pass.

"Jack Kilroy, your energy might be better employed explaining why you flirted your buns off, kissed me with all the technique of a marine mammal, and then dropped me when things got interesting." By *interesting*, she meant when her hand encountered that intriguing bulge between his legs. The tipping point, she would have thought, with any other guy.

"You're right, I did all that, although I think my kissing technique is slightly better than a marine mammal's." He managed to look both sexy and affronted.

"That's a matter of opinion."

"Well, you have to admit you provoked me."

"*I* provoked *you*?"

"Is Laurent still here?" he mimicked, sounding nothing like her in the slightest. "There's only so much a man can take."

Not for the first time in his presence, words failed her. He handily filled in the silence.

"I didn't stop because I'm not attracted to you or to teach you a lesson, though you probably deserved it for trying to use me."

Use him? This from the guy who blew through women like Gina blew through hairspray. In what crazy-ass universe did men worry about being used when a woman offered herself up on a platter?

"I wasn't trying to use you," she said, less sure now. "Well, no more than anyone who wants…"

His raised eyebrow challenged her to finish that sentence. No more than anyone who wants what? A night of wild, abandoned, no-strings sex with a guy you just met? That's what she had meant, but it rang sordid even in her head. Damn him.

He huffed a breath that rippled through the strands of dark hair brushing his forehead. "A lot of women I meet are only interested in screwing me because I'm on TV. And after a while, casual sex becomes really old."

This was said with all the blithe confidence of someone who has no problems getting casual sex on a regular basis. It was like a rich person saying money didn't matter. When you didn't have any or weren't getting any, it most definitely mattered.

"I wasn't interested in you because you're famous," she said, squelching her discomfort.

That earned her more of the judgmental eyebrow. "Right, you just want my body."

Well, yeah. She couldn't deny it, though she could do her best to ignore it and flip this table around. "Are you saying you're giving up your hound dog ways and retiring to a monastery?"

"I'm saying that now when I want to sleep with someone, I'd like to know more about her than just her cup size."

She folded her arms beneath her D-cups.

"Lili, any guy would be lucky to be with you, but one-night stands no longer interest me. In fact, I haven't slept with anyone in quite a while. These days, I'd rather get to know a girl first."

She barked out a laugh at the notion Jack had suspended his membership in Man Whores United. His eyes registered surprise. He was serious.

"You mean dating?" she squealed, as if the word were foreign to her.

His eyes locked on hers in a way that completely unnerved her. "Yes, dating. Do you have rules against dating fame-hungry megawhores?"

She should have known that would come back to bite her, but her unease about it was nothing compared to the emotion roiling through every cell of her body. Jack Kilroy—*the* Jack Kilroy—had asked her out on a date.

When a few awkward seconds passed and an obsequious game show host still hadn't jumped out to tell her it was all a hilarious prank, she regrouped.

"I don't have time for dating," she blurted. Not exactly true, but not exactly a lie either. What she didn't have time for were men who needed a woman to keep their inflated egos pumped up to supersize levels. She'd already traveled this road with Marco. For their few months together, she had felt warm and safe and . . . grateful. Grateful that the cute guy who wouldn't have looked at her twice in her fat days had come down from the mountain and shown poor ol' Lili what she'd been missing. Marco had turned on that winning smile, and after she got through the metaphorical throat clutch followed by a "who, me?" she had grasped at the opportunity a little too desperately.

Never again.

Eventually, she would meet someone sweetly average, a guy at her level, who didn't think he was doing her a favor by breathing the same air as her. Real life, not the stuff of romantic fantasy.

Some people might think a guy singing tunelessly through your intercom to snag your attention was romantic. Hopelessly romantic people. She kicked that thought to the curb. Now wasn't the time to get mushy.

"You live in New York. I live here. It would never work." But even before the words were on the warm night air, she felt the cool chill of regret.

"Right, it could never work." His eyes glinted as if he was thinking about how to make it work, which had the curious effect of making *her* think about how to make it work. This guy was good.

"How's your friend?" she asked, eager to pilot them to more neutral ground. Laurent had since fallen over and was now curled up on the sidewalk, probably imagining he had made it to the safety of his comfortable hotel bed.

"Not great. Frenchmen should be able to hold their liquor, what with them being weaned straight from breast milk to wine, but Laurent has always been a bit of a light-weight, bless his heart."

They looked down at the Frenchman-shaped puddle on the ground.

"I just need to get him into a cab." He didn't seem to be in a hurry. "Unless you want to offer us a bed for the night."

"That's a really bad idea." Lili gave Laurent a gentle shove with her foot and was rewarded with a reedy moan. "I don't think I'd trust a Frenchman, even an adorably inebriated one, in my apartment. He could probably make zee love while in zee coma."

"I'd protect you. And you're definitely not his type." Jack shrugged. "Despite all the Gallic swagger, he much prefers the company of sheep."

Laughter bubbled up from her gut. Jack Kilroy was charm personified, all shiny surfaces and glittering bon mots. She couldn't remember the last time she'd enjoyed talking to a guy this much. It had been even longer since her body had reacted with such...sizzle. When Jack touched her—when Jack plain looked at her—her body sizzled.

Laurent interrupted her musings, inching his way up Jack's leg like he was climbing a jungle gym. "'Allo, Lili." He draped his arm over Jack's shoulder and ex-pelled a juicy belch. "*Merde*, Jack, it is drunk out."

Jack murmured something in French that Lili didn't understand but could tell wasn't very nice. Propping his friend against the wall of her building, he held his palms up, willing Laurent to stay upright. Then he turned back to her and stepped in close. Too close.

"Before we go, I'll need you to take it back."

"Take what back?"

"What you said about my kissing technique."

Aw, poor little big shot needed massaging for his sore ego. "It's all so subjective. That suction thing might work for some girls, I suppose."

Another dangerous step and he had gripped her hips with both hands. Mercy, he was fast. "Give me another chance."

"Oh," she managed to eke out just as that smooth-talking mouth met hers. Her initial thought was gratitude that he was holding on to her, because her spine had dissolved. Her next was...she didn't have a next. The kiss hit her like a fifth of bourbon and with each luxurious swipe of his tongue, she fell deeper and deeper into oblivion.

Displaying his range, he cut a path of honeyed devastation along her jaw. "Am I doing better?"

"Hmm. Full letter grade improvement. B minus," she teased. "But I'm still not going to date you."

He laughed, a warm chocolaty sound against her neck that goose-bumped her heated flesh. "And I'm still not going to sleep with you. No matter how much you beg."

"Oh, I think I'll survive. We great women are used to enduring." Her hands caressed his strong back, shaping its tightly woven muscles. "You, on the other hand...How long has it been since you last had sex?"

"Four months"—he nipped her earlobe—"one

week"—his lips tickled the sensitive spot where her neck met her shoulder—"five days."

"Sounds terrible," she murmured as she rubbed her breasts against his chest. So much for keeping her nipples in check. They happily pebbled their pleasure at this latest turn of events.

"It hasn't been so bad," he said, his voice as thick as the humid night. "I just can't help flirting with gorgeous women."

Her mind heard the compliment, but before it could register fully, he moved in flush, making her gasp as his hardness rasped against her belly. A Darth Vader–like rumble reverberated in her head. *I have you now.* They just needed to get Laurent settled on her sofa, then let the good times roll.

Jack drew back to face her, his lust-blown eyes illuminated by the overhead streetlamp. "Lili, all joking aside, I'm serious about going on a date..." One hand dropped from her waist and traveled shakily to his forehead.

"Jack, are you okay?" She squeezed his beautifully muscled shoulder. She couldn't wait to kiss every inch of—

"I'm fine," he muttered just as his body crumpled and slid from her grasp. He made a surprisingly soft thud considering all that rock-hard muscle. As if in sympathy, Laurent slid down the wall with a well-oiled giggle.

Merde.

CHAPTER SIX

Who's the president of the United States?"

A muffled grunt was his response.

Lili drew the curtains apart, allowing watery early morning light to flood the hotel room. The sun's rays bathed the cathedral façade of the Wrigley building, and the soft glow glinting off the water almost convinced her the toxic Chicago River was appealing enough for a dip. Tourists trickled down Michigan Avenue on their way to breakfast, or just as likely biding their time waiting for Niketown to throw open its doors. God, she loved this city. Its beauty never failed to move her.

She stepped around to the other side of the humungous bed where beauty of a different variety hid beneath swathes of luxurious Egyptian cotton.

"Is that your final answer, then?" she asked cheerfully.

Jack poked his dark head above the sheet, shading his eyes. "Why is it so bright in here?"

"Oh, sorry." She hastily grasped at the curtains until

just a chink of sun infiltrated. The doctor had said he might be sensitive to light and sound for a while. She sat at the end of the bed. "So, who's the president of the United States?"

One eye, shadowed by eyelashes most women would give their firstborn for, peered at her. "These questions are stupid."

"I know, I know," she said soothingly.

"And that sounds patronizing."

"If only you'd do as you're told, it'd be a lot less painful." She cocked an eyebrow. "The president?"

"Woodrow bloody Wilson." He propped himself up and swiped the sleep from his eyes. After two hours in the ER, a battery of tests, and a boatload of painkillers, they had finally made it back to Jack's hotel. Per the doctor's instructions, she had woken him every couple of hours to pose interrogatory gems like *What's your name?* and *What city are you in?*

Now he looked crumpled and grumpy and panties-melting hot.

"Where did you sleep, Mrs. Kilroy?" he asked around a yawn. He even yawned sexily.

"On the sofa in the other room," she murmured, his casual reference to their faux marital status making her light-headed. Last night, the doctor had mistaken her for Jack's wife, a conclusion Jack found incredibly amusing. Lili hadn't had time to be amused—she was too busy having a mini-series of heart attacks, deathly worried she had caused him brain damage and deprived the culinary world of its leading light. After his dramatic collapse outside her door, he came to in less than a minute. It had only been the worst minute of her life.

"You should have slept in here with me, my blushing bride. This bed is huge. We could have gone days without finding each other."

"I hear people with brain injuries often have problems with impulse control," she said. Along with women who haven't had any in months. "Though I suppose I would have been safe with you, now that you're a born-again virgin and all."

"It would have been hard—I mean, difficult," he said, grinning. "But I think I would have managed."

He stretched and the sheet fell down to his waist, revealing a rather monumental chest with a pleasant ratio of hair to skin. Her mouth watered at his defined pecs and ridged abs, so tight she could bounce a British pound coin off them. *Absolutely ab-ulous*, she could hear Gina leering like a little devil on her shoulder. He was tan—not overly so, but enough to debunk the stereotype of the pasty Englishman. How she wished she had her camera.

"Do you...do you work out?" she asked, her voice as taut as the muscles on show.

"I have to. I'm a French chef. Mostly running, swimming, and—" He chuckled. "Hey, my face is up here."

Grabbing a pillow that had strayed to the end of the bed during his restless sleep, she lobbed it at his perfect face. "Maybe I'm just sick of looking at it."

He threw the pillow back at her. "You could always look at something else. That usually leads to my other form of exercise." His fingers fidgeted with the hem of the sheet.

"Keep that to yourself. I might swoon and then you'd have to take me to the emergency room."

Laughing, he stretched again, knowing full well the effect it had. Cocky bastard. "I'm absolutely starving. Please say you ordered room service."

"Of course I did. It's already here." As someone else was paying, she had taken the liberty of ordering one of everything. This was too much of an opportunity for a breakfast lover to resist.

"All right, be a good wife, then. Feed me."

Wife. Her stupid heart cranked out a few more beats than was safe, and she swallowed to calm it the hell down.

"No chance, Kilroy. I've already filed for an annulment." She walked toward the door, tugging down the Black Sabbath tee she had borrowed and spent the night inhaling. When she turned back, he was regarding her with glassy eyes. *Still got it, girl.*

"If you have problems standing up, I can always call Laurent in to help." If the dipso Frenchman wasn't having problems standing up himself. She had put in a quick phone call to his room ten minutes ago and confirmed that while not upright, Pepé Le Pew was at least conscious.

Five minutes later, she had redressed in her tank top and cargo pants, and they were enjoying breakfast in friendly silence. To Lili's regret, Jack had covered up with jeans and a Who T-shirt, the red, white, and blue target on his chest drawing her sharp focus.

I've got you in my crosshairs, Jack Kilroy. "How are you feeling?"

"All right. My head's still a bit fuzzy, but it doesn't hurt anymore. Painkillers are doing the trick." He sipped his coffee and slumped back onto the sofa. "Thanks for staying. It went above and beyond the duties of even a fake wife."

"I suppose I bear some responsibility with my frying pan—"

"Suppose? Oh, I'd say you bear the brunt, but don't feel you have to apologize or anything."

"I'm so sorry. When you hit the pavement, my heart just about stopped."

"Ah, you *do* care."

He shot her a smile so infectious it should be quarantined, and her stomach flipped, reminding her of the first time she had been favored with that slice of sun. Since then, she had thrown herself at the hottest chef in the country—the hottest guy in the country—and she should feel like an idiot, but she didn't. An incongruent mix of giddy and comfortable settled over her. What would Cara say if she saw her now?

"Oh, Cara," she said. "I need to call her and let her know you're still alive." Unsurprisingly, her sister had returned none of her messages. Cara was a big proponent of pill-assisted sleep, otherwise Lili was sure she'd be knocking Jack's door off its hinges demanding to know how her star was faring.

He groaned. "Please don't bring Cara into this. I've already got the DeLuca sister who knows what she's doing. I certainly don't need the one who's going to go into a tailspin at the mention of the word *concussion*." Rolling his tongue around his mouth, his gaze drifted over the smorgasbord before them. "I take it you like breakfast?"

"I like food," she said around bites of her second waffle. "Marco's fond of telling me the restaurant will never make any money because I eat all the profits."

"That's not a very nice thing to say."

No, it wasn't, but she was used to laughing off digs

about her weight. Spending most of her teenage years as the butt of fat jokes in high school had built up her defenses to the point that she'd come full circle to making excuses for how others felt about her abundant curves. Or maybe she was just used to making excuses for Marco. "He doesn't mean anything by it. I'm not exactly svelte."

Jack was studying her in a way that made her self-conscious. She tried to chew slower.

"You shouldn't listen to that tosser. You have a beautiful figure."

There he went again. *You taste good. You're a gorgeous woman. You have a beautiful figure.* And with the way his gaze branded her on every pass, she allowed herself a moment to enjoy the heady newness of feeling sinfully sexy. The nicest thing Marco had ever said was that her body felt "comfortable." Like she was a floor pillow.

Her skin had heated at his compliment, but acknowledging it with aplomb wasn't in her makeup. "Is a tosser the same as a wanker?"

"It is, but I find it has more of a ring to it." He was still staring. "You're very different from Cara."

She gave a rather unladylike snort. "You've got that right. No one ever believes we're sisters."

He looked thoughtful. "You seem like a very tight family."

"We're Italian," she said like that explained everything. It occurred to her that, courtesy of the rag mags, she knew everything and nothing about Jack Kilroy. "Do you have family across the pond?"

"Yeah, I have a sister. She's about your age and, like you, drives me batty."

She rather enjoyed the thrill of how comfortable it felt to be teased after such a short acquaintance. "Prerogative of the younger sibling. We must annoy our elders. What does she do?"

"She works in pubs for the most part," he said, his expression turning dark and disapproving in an instant. "Picking up glasses. I've tried to get her better jobs but she's not interested."

The steel underlying his words reminded her of her father when he sported his disappointed hat. On Il Duce's head, it was well worn and comfortable.

"Not everyone aspires to greatness. Maybe she's happy with what she's doing."

He stared at her like she had spoken Sanskrit. "How could she be?"

"You mean, how could she be related to you and not have the Kilroy imperative to vanquish everything in her path?"

"You know what I mean. She's smart but she doesn't try. She floats."

"And you hate floaters?"

"I love my sister." The slight break in his voice punched her in the gut. He took a sip of coffee and waited a moment. "I wasn't around much when she was growing up, and I don't think she got what she needed." He shook his head like he had given it some thought but the conclusion refused to tally with his expectations. "We don't really talk about the important stuff. I just worry about her."

Her heart squeezed. "She might not show it but I'm sure she appreciates it. Not everyone is good at the touchy-feely stuff."

He remained silent, his gaze on the plate-strewn coffee table, the air now heavy with his thoughts. With hers, too. She longed to comfort him, to reach out and brush the hair from his forehead like she had last night when she tended to his medical needs. It was a role she fell into easily—Lili the caregiver, the comforter, the unstinting support.

Her fingers twitched; his phone chirped.

"That's probably Cara now," Jack said. He gave a couple of taps, then scrutinized the screen for a long moment. Finally he jumped up, shaking his head like a dog coming out of water.

"Shit, shit, shit. This is not happening."

"What's going on?" she asked, worry spiking her pulse.

He paced the room, glowering at his phone. "I'll tell you what's bloody well going on. Somebody filmed us in that bar and now last night's snog is today's big news."

Hell to the no. Someone had posted that kiss? A skitter did the rounds in her stomach and she braced for full-scale panic. One, one thousand. Two, one thousand. Still relatively calm. Three, one thousand, four. By now, dread that her parents and everyone she knew would see that kiss should have set in, but oddly the flutter wasn't mutating into the flapping she expected. Unfortunately, she couldn't say the same for the other party to the proceedings.

Jack Kilroy was wigging out.

"Do I have one of your Muppet-haired cousins to thank for this?"

"What? No…" She considered it a moment before affirming her previous denial. "No one I know would do something like that. That's just…no."

"This is a complete disaster." He punctuated his conclusion with a violent hair rake and another scowl. It looked good on him, of course.

"I can see how it might be," she said, not seeing it at all. Though she was starting to appreciate what Cara meant when she called her boss a divo.

His jaw bunched so tight a simple touch might break it. "I'm supposed to be keeping it clean, playing it safe until I sign this contract."

"What contract?"

He waved his hand as if she should know what the hell he was talking about. "This new show I have in the works. It gets me off cable and onto network. It's huge and I'm not supposed to do anything to jeopardize it."

"And kissing a woman in a bar jeopardizes it? This isn't the 1950s."

"No one cares what you do when you're on cable, but network is another ball of wax entirely. All that drama with Ashley was fine back then, but this show is family friendly and I'm not supposed to be drawing any negative attention."

"But it can't be as bad as all that. We didn't do anything X-rated." Her memory rewound to the kiss. It had been hot—it had been Madras curry hot—but that was about all.

Jack still stomped, his eyes fiercely glued to the phone. Except for that explosion of heat when he dragged her into the bar corridor to show her his cave paintings and kiss her senseless, he had only ever projected a hazy sense of cool. Now he was acting so . . . Italian.

A couple of moments later, he took a time-out from his hissy fit and looked up. "I'm overreacting, aren't I?"

"Just a smidge, but it's very entertaining."

He plopped down next to her, flattening the heel of his hand to his forehead. "Take a look."

The recording started about halfway through, and if she hadn't been there, she wouldn't have recognized the participants. Jack's hand was already all over her butt—the small screen totally worked in her favor there—and her own hand gripped his silky hair. The distant soundtrack was provided courtesy of the boys from U2, and as the video played, her body anticipated the syncopated backbeat of moans and whimpers.

In the present, his thigh currently pressed against hers and she tensed while sexual awareness raced through her. On screen, it was a hot display of hands, mouths, and—*gulp*—other body parts all grasping and sucking and grinding. Idly, it occurred to her that kissing was rumored to burn calories and tone facial muscles. The Kilroy Kissing Workout. Finally, an exercise regimen she could get on board with.

"It's not exactly chaste," he murmured. Chaste it was not, more like smoking. They got to the point in the performance when she wrapped her leg around his thigh. Yum.

"Weak spot," she whispered.

"What?"

"When I did that, you moaned. It's one of your weak spots." She couldn't meet his eyes.

In the video, they parted, exchanged now-forgotten words, but almost immediately, they were kissing again. That's when her hand had started an unauthorized solo mission down his chest, his abs, past his waistband. Oh dear, she had gone *there* and someone had captured it frame for damning frame.

She covered her face, then splayed her fingers to find
Jack zoned in on her, his eyes dark with intent. Neurons
in her brain fired like a round of applause. Her nipples
beaded; her breasts ached. She had never wanted a man
with such desperate, taut need. The thought of being
kissed by him—or worse, not being kissed by him—
made her shake.

For a moment they did that age-old dance where neither could decide which was most compelling, eyes or
mouth. Eyes or mouth. Eyes or—oh, thigh. His sudden
move made her jump like water drops on a griddle or
maybe it was the distant thumping sound that jolted her.
The Ghost of Illicit Kisses Past. She could almost hear the
clanking of chains.

The pounding got louder. "Jack Kilroy, open this door
right now." *Cara.*

He frowned, then inhaled with a wince. "That's all
right. I don't need all that hair."

"What?"

"Chest hair. Some skin, too."

Lili looked down to find one of her fists full of Jack's
tee. Wonder when that happened. "Oh, sorry." She slackened her grasp but her fingers refused to open all the way.

Cara hammered again. "Jack, if you don't open up, I'm
calling nine-one-one."

Lili reluctantly loosened her hold on the bull's-eye
covering his chest and the Kilroy DNA she'd taken a
fancy to.

Rubbing his maligned pec, Jack dragged himself off
the sofa and made a subtle package adjustment. *Oh, yeah.*
He opened the door to admit an agitated Cara and waved
her by with a deadpan, "Please. Come in."

Her sister was dressed in lime-green Juicy sweats. Eight a.m. and she looked stunning.

"Are you okay?" Cara asked Jack. "I just got Lili's messages." Reaching out to cup his jaw, she got in close and personal. A potent surge of emotion waved through Lili, terminating in her brain with one word. *Mine.*

"It was nothing." He stepped out of Cara's grasp and Lili cheered a mental touchdown.

"*Grazie a Dio,*" Cara said. "Well, prepare yourself for a new heap of cray cray." She thrust her phone in Jack's face.

"We've seen it," he said, nodding over to Lili.

Cara's priceless expression was almost enough to procure Lili's forgiveness for her manhandling of Jack. Almost. "Lili! What are you doing here?"

"I stayed to make sure Jack didn't fall into a coma."

Cara cast a shrewd look at her star and his gorgeously mussed hair, then turned back to Lili and her mushroom-cloud helmet. "Did you know you're trending on Twitter, sis?"

"Christ," Jack muttered.

Twitter? That sounded...not good. "What does it say?"

"Just something stupid," Cara said, waving it away to a corner of the room.

Lili stood as quickly as her head daze would allow. "Cara, what is it? Tell me now."

Her sister flushed, a glow that only made her more beautiful. "Hashtag, Jack and the fat chick. But it's all one word, so you have to really focus to figure it out."

The fat chick? Lili buried her massive face in her gargantuan hands. Flashes of teenage wretchedness discharged in her brain, evicting all those happy spark-offs she'd felt moments ago while Jack's eyes feasted on her. In their stead, long-suppressed images of torment returned to taunt her. Pencils jabbing her fleshy back. Upset books as she walked from her locker to class. Macaroni salad splattered in her lap—she rarely made it through lunch unaccosted. She had joked with Tad that she should thank Diana Matteo and her clique for helping lower her daily calorie intake. The bully diet.

But as bruising as the physical teasing had been, it didn't compare to the jibes and sneers. Lardass Lili. Tubby DeLuca. Lili the Elephant. *Fat chick* was comparatively kind.

A voice called to her, muffled and far away.

"Lili, are you okay?"

She blinked to find Jack staring at her. Not so hot and needful now, just compassionate. Pitying.

"I'm the fat chick?"

"Don't be daft. You are not fat," Jack said sternly, sending a scowl Cara's way in a clear demonstration of shooting the messenger. His phone hummed again. "I need to take this." He treaded back into the bedroom, answering as he walked.

Cara smiled sympathetically. "Lili, don't worry about what they're saying online. Haters gonna hate." The benevolent grin turned saucy. "Damn, girl. You sure went for it with Jack."

"Cara, I—"

"Jack's agent is probably already working on a plan to spin this. We just have to be careful it won't affect the contract." Her sister patrolled the doorway, her ponytail swishing furiously behind her. With a graceful pivot borne of ten years in a tutu, she wagged her finger. "Jack wants me to produce his new show. It's my big chance and your little spectacle last night better not get in the way."

Cara had conveniently forgotten this was her dumb idea. Best to fess up. "Don't worry. Nothing—"

"I've already had Aunt Sylvia calling in a complete conniption. It was all the congregation at seven a.m. Mass at St. Jude's could talk about."

"Aunt Syl called?" Lili glared at her own phone, lying like a time bomb on the coffee table. Church bells chimed faintly in the distance, and her throat went dry. Her aunt was probably interrogating Father Phelan this very minute about the going rates for an exorcism.

A tremor started up in Lili's thigh, and not the sexy kind either. If Sylvia knew about Lili's fallen woman status, her parents were waking up to the joyful news right about...Lili's phone started to vibrate. Now.

"That's Mom," Cara said as her own phone rang out with Beyoncé's "Single Ladies," which meant Dad was leaving a message on Lili's phone. "*Ciao*, Mom."

Lili shook her head fiercely, the signal for *I'm-not-here-to-anyone-especially-parents*. Cara raised a razor-thin eyebrow and uh-huh-ed and um-ed through the conversation before ringing off.

"You need to call her. Il Duce's on the warpath."

"Who's Il Duce?" Jack's crisp voice penetrated through Lili's mental fog as his bare feet whispered across the plush carpet.

"My father," Lili said. "I've brought shame upon the entire family."

She stared at Jack, daring him to come up with some

smug, charming response so she could punch him in the arm. His face registered only concern. He slid an arm around her waist and slipped his fingers below the border of her cargo pants, caressing. A chef's hands, scarred and callused. She had never felt so grateful for the touch of another human being.

Moving behind her, he skated his hand beneath her tank top while his muscle-corded forearm banded beneath her breasts. Usually, when a guy cradled her, she felt big and graceless, but not with Jack. He was the right size for her, and dare she say it, she was the right size for him. She allowed her body to rest into Jack's hardness and strength, marveling at how quickly the tremor abated.

"It's going to be all right," he said, his lips tickling her ear. She didn't believe a word of it but her rapidly heating skin clearly appreciated the effort. If it had been Marco, he would have made some offhand comment about her loveable squishiness.

Cara's lips formed a grim seal; then she said, "Well, there's work to be done. Jack, you're still coming to Casa DeLuca for dinner tonight?"

Lili's discomfort zone expanded alarmingly. Her father and the man she had publicly groped, both at the same table with easily accessible steak knives, her matchmaking mother, and Aunt Sylvia wringing a novena out of the rosary beads.

"Counting down the hours," Jack said easily.

Cara's eyes scanned her phone, then squinted up at Lili. "Now, no more PDA, you two, especially during the taping. There's only so much we can edit out." Her sister left, leaving a blast of air in her wake that was completely disproportionate to her slight frame.

Jack still held tight, his strong arm feeling so good twined around her. Her body prickled with pleasure before ratcheting up to high alert. She told herself there'd be no more kissing. She was most insistent.

"How are we doing?" he asked, low and seductive.

The sheer absurdity of the situation crashed down on her hard. Was there such a thing as a sympathy concussion? Because if there was, she must have it. Considerable damage to her gray matter could be the only way to explain her presence in that video, in this man's hotel room, and in his solid, ripped arms.

She jerked away. "You just can't stop, can you?"

"I told you I can't help flirting with hot women. You're a hot woman, so you'll just have to put up with it. Most women would be happy to receive this kind of attention."

Perhaps, but in the cold light of day, when forced to address your panda eye makeup and the run in your stockings, clarity kicks in like a bitch. This was no longer a bar on a steamy summer night crawling with tipsy Frenchmen, stunning Brits, and oversexed Italian girls. This was the morning after the night before. The Brit was still hot. She was just a punch line on the Web.

"I'm not most women"—she was certainly not hot—"and right now, I'm more concerned with my reputation. And the fact I'm known all over the Twittersphere as the fat chick."

"You've changed your tune from ten minutes ago."

"Ten minutes ago, I was anonymous Kilroy bait in a bar. Now I'm famous."

He grunted. "You're not famous. No one knows who you are."

She wasn't too hopeful of that lasting long, not once

her cousins got involved, but they weren't here to blame and he was.

"This is entirely your fault," she snapped. "You and your grabby hands."

"I'd say *your* grabby hands are what's driving Internet traffic this morning."

"Oh, God." Both offending hands went to her burning face. How was she ever going to live this down? She met Jack's grin, now bright enough to power the grid for the Chicago Loop.

He rubbed his thumb and forefinger together. "Aren't you overreacting just a smidge?" Oh, that was classy. Throwing her words back at her.

"My life is ruined," she grumbled.

"Give it a day. It'll all blow over."

CHAPTER SEVEN

Jack should have been on his way to DeLuca's to start testing his dishes, but he felt about as useful as a chocolate teapot, so he took some time out after Lili left to clean up his phone messages. Today's special was schadenfreude. Evidently, news of the impending contract had made the rounds because most of the calls were dripping with malignant joy. Former cooking colleagues who considered him a sellout checking in to see if he was okay. Text messages with sad faces. Hushed voices with barely suppressed glee. Even Ashley had called, her breathy, Daytime Emmy–nominated gush letting him know she was here for him. He almost threw the phone at the wall.

At least he hadn't heard from *him*, and he offered up a moment of thanks that John Sullivan had heeded Jack's warning and stayed out of his son's life. Though once the man Jack preferred to call his sperm donor heard about the multimillion-dollar network deal, Jack expected he'd turn up again with his hand out. It would be far too good an opportunity to miss.

He wished Lili had stayed, but as soon as Cara dropped that Twitter bomb, she had shut down. All her sass and flirt stowed away as she drew a fireguard over her quick mouth. There had been an ease between them while they shared breakfast, like they had leapfrogged the getting-to-know-you phase and were hovering on the edge of comfortable. Flirting with trust. Which, given his experience scrabbling around the hamster wheel of fame, did not come easy.

Oh, and he was balls-deep in lust with her. Can't forget that.

Last night, those soothing tones and her fingers cooling his forehead made all his blood rush south. Never mind the ache in his head, it was a wonder he could answer anything she asked when all he wanted to do was pull her astride him and relieve the ache in his dick. Instead, he forced himself to watch her lush sway as she padded away from him. In his Black Sabbath T-shirt, no less. She had stood in the doorway, that banging body of hers silhouetted by a corona of light from the outer suite, and he had bitten back a moan. During all three visits.

Abstinence was a multihorned bitch.

The call he expected wasn't forthcoming, so he grabbed the initiative. Two p.m. in London, but it still took his sister five rings to pick up.

"Why don't you answer any of my texts?" he asked sharply.

"You know I don't text. It's better to ring." Jules was the only person he knew under the age of thirty who hated texting. When she bothered to answer his messages, it was with meaningless emoticons. When she bothered to answer his calls, it was usually obvious she'd just woken up. Like now. She worried him greatly.

"Saw you made the news again," she said around a yawn. "You really need to keep it in your pants, Jack."

"Less of that, you cheeky mare. Tell me about the interview." Deafening silence broken by a sniff and a cough greeted him. "Jules, tell me you at least called Corin. He promised to keep the job open for you." And Jack had promised his old friend at Ecogrand, the hot new organic food eatery in London, that his sister would be perfect for hostess. Jules's fresh-faced, willowy blondness screamed *salad-eater*, and Jack was sure she'd make a great addition to Ecogrand's front of house.

"Jack, I've told you a million times pub work suits me better."

"But it's so—" *Beneath you*, he wanted to say. Like him, his sister had dropped out of high school at fourteen, but she was smart, astute, and funny. Where her professional talents lay was a mystery to all and she didn't seem interested in finding out. *Bored with everything* was her motto.

"Degrading? Lowborn? Working class?" she finished archly. She knew exactly what he was thinking.

"I was going to say dangerous. I've worked in bars. They're filled with drunk people." Sometimes, amorous drunk people, but more often belligerent dickwads.

She ignored this, but then she always did. It was a regular game between them with ever-shifting goalposts. Years ago, he had abandoned her to the care of her aunt and uncle on her father's side after his death. At the time, he hadn't thought of it as abandonment; he'd been too excited about his big chance to work in Paris with Claude Marchon, who had spotted Jack during a visit to the restaurant of one of Claude's former students. That apprenticeship had started everything for Jack but sent his relationship with Jules on a downward trajectory with no course correction in sight. Now his guilt over his sorry lack of involvement in her upbringing turned him into an overbearing busybody.

Knew it. Owned it. Not changing it.

"When are you coming to London?" she asked after a long pause. "Or can you not pull yourself away from your latest floozy?"

Jules knew exactly how to poke him, though he usually found it easier to ignore her jibes about the women he dated. It was good practice for all the tabloid crap. His head had started throbbing again, matching the hastening uptick of his pulse.

"She's not a floozy," he snapped, knowing Jules had meant it in jest but feeling an irrational rush to blow it out of proportion. "She happens to be an amazing woman."

"All right, calm down, Cro-Mag. I'm sure she's out of this world."

Slowly, he counted to five. "I'll be in London the day after tomorrow and I'm taking you somewhere nice for dinner, not some fish-'n'-chips shop. A real place with tablecloths and stainless-steel cutlery. And we're going to discuss your future." *Young lady*, he may as well have added. Talking to his sister aged him ten years each time.

"Right, 'cause that went so well the last time. I've got to go."

Grimacing at the memory of their last fine-dining experience four months ago, he tried to breathe himself to calm. When she didn't hang up immediately, he asked, "Is everything all right, Jules? You seem out of sorts." Or more out of sorts than usual. Another elongated pause followed and familiar worry soaked his chest.

"I just woke up this minute, that's all. Next time, don't call so early." She clicked off.

He barely had time to process that before the call he'd been dreading flashed ominously on his screen. He got as far as "Hell—"

"You couldn't do as you were told, Jack," said Evie, his agent. Her smoker's voice scraped across his bruised brain like a rusty rake. "What did I say?"

"I know, I know. It just sort of happened." Jack picked up his Black Sabbath tee, the one Lili had filled out very nicely, and sniffed it. He'd gotten an uncommon thrill out of her wearing his clothes. Her scent was faint, but it was enough to tap into his sensory system and revive delicious memories of holding her. And kissing her. And running his hands—

His fantasy was interrupted by a lung-hacking cough and replaced by a Komodo dragon with red lipstick and pearls, lustily dragging on a cigarette. It was in no way a fair trade.

"Is there anything else I need to know about?" Evie choked out.

"No." He decided against telling her about collapsing on the street, his visit to the emergency room, or the fact that Lili spent the night playing sexy nurse. She might not appreciate the finer points.

"So who is she?"

"Didn't catch her name."

Evie cackled like a Shakespearean witch. She'd be

rubbing her hands in glee if she could ever relinquish the ciggie. "It's a little late for chivalry, Jack. I already talked to Cara. She doesn't look one bit like her, by the way. Been pigging out on the penne, has she?"

A red haze blurred his vision, and when he finally spoke, it was through gritted teeth. "She's a very nice girl."

"Nice girls don't do that with their hands, though the Catholics are always dark horses."

"Give it a rest, will you?"

"Oh, God, you like her." His agent was one sharp cookie. "She's the daughter of the Italian chef, right? The competition."

"There's nothing doing here, Evie. Don't even bother."

Seamlessly, she switched to spin mode. "The opposition. Food feuds. Good old Italian American family values meets British arrogance and decadence. Falling for a nice, plump, regular gal might do wonders for your image. Stone Carter at NBN will love that garbage."

At the mention of NBN's veep of programming, Jack felt the fear of failure fading. Stone Carter was a grade A dick of the Highest Order of Dicks but he had taken a liking to Jack and wanted him on the network, a steamy barroom grope notwithstanding.

"But, Jack?" Evie asked on a smoky sigh.

"Yes?"

"Tell your girl to stop being so handsy in public."

* * *

Walking into the kitchen of her parents' house, Lili exhaled a noisy sigh of relief at finding her mother alone at the table, her fork hovering over an Ann Sather cinnamon roll. She dropped a kiss on Francesca's head and feathered the wispy, baby blond growth at her temples.

"It's starting to come in thicker." Lili stashed her cheese purchases from the farmers' market in the fridge and poured herself a cup of coffee. Sitting, she carved out a sweet roll from the six-pack in the box, making sure she got an extra thick slice of icing. Still warm. Only after she'd let a healing bite of doughy goodness pass her lips did she look at her mother directly. Her bright blue eyes sparkled. Of course.

"So, how is Jack?" her mother asked with an impish grin to match the eyes. No beating around the bush with her, just a straight chop with a machete.

Lili pushed out a cautious, "Okay."

"Hmm, I had hoped a man as good-looking as that would be better than okay."

Clunk. That was the sound of Lili's jaw unhinging to the slate floor.

Her mother's grin pulled into a wide crescent. "I am glad you are having some fun with Jack. He is a very handsome man."

"Mom, you need to stop right there." Before Lili was forced to place her hands over her ears and repeat la-la-la over and over to block out the horror.

"All I am saying is that he is like the *dolci* for the eyes, and if I were twenty years younger, I would be very interested. Perhaps I should trade in your father for a younger model now that I have the new bosoms." Francesca arched a barely there brow. Those were starting to grow in as well.

Lili could feel a smile tugging at her lips at the sight of that inner glow lighting up her mother's translucent skin, stretched over still-pronounced cheekbones. The last eighteen months had been hell for Francesca. The surgeries and chemotherapy and radiation. The loss of her beautiful, fair hair. The days when she was so weak she couldn't raise a glass to her dry, cracked lips.

It was so gratifying to see her cheerful. Lili's imaginary sex life, entertainment for cancer survivors everywhere.

"It was just a kiss, Mom. Nothing more."

"I had hoped you might have met someone worthy of you." Her mother tolerated Marco insofar as he was her husband's business partner, but that was where her appreciation ended. "You have missed out on so much lately, Lili. I haven't told you often enough how grateful I am." The swallow in her mother's throat contracted Lili's heart.

Casting a sideways glance, because a direct one would result in a complete breakdown, Lili placed her hand over her mother's. "Mom, I'm glad I could be here for you. And don't forget I got plenty out of it, too. When else would I have had the time to watch the entire filmography of Johnny Depp?"

Francesca pushed Lili's impossible hair behind her ears. "You have always bottled things up, just like your father. Instead of talking, you make jokes and spend all your time behind the camera. That is all well and good, but there are other ways to express yourself."

Jeez, was her mother still talking about sex? "He's not interested, Mom. And I'm certainly not interested in him." *Liar, liar, thong on fire.* She left out the part where he'd asked her for a date. Best to attribute that to the brain injury.

Lili sipped her coffee and looked about the kitchen. Having run out of space in the living room, her mother had turned every available patch of wall into a display of her daughters' most embarrassing school-era memories. Cara sporting a retainer, reminding Lili that perfection took work. The two of them like oil and water at a family get-together. One in particular stood out now—Lili's tenth-grade portrait, still taunting her from on high above the back door.

It wasn't just the hair—not much had changed there— but the bloat, which no one could ever term as adorably chubby. Several thousand laps of the pool later, she had come to terms with her body and the fact she would never measure up to the media's ideal of feminine beauty. Only in the last couple of years had she dared to enjoy her curvier silhouette and how her love of food manifested in her shapely hips and voluptuous figure. But last night's events had pitched her back into that maelstrom of teenage torment. School had been a nightmare, and today she had felt like she was in Casimir Pulaski High's cafeteria all over again, ducking low and dodging mean-girl zingers.

"He looked very interested in that video," her mother continued, undeterred by Lili's protests. "And Taddeo said Jack could not take his eyes off you the entire night."

Francesca, the incurable romantic, believed there was someone for everyone. Her parents' marriage was the envy of all, a love story started on a playground in Tuscany and consummated with a teenage wedding as soon as they were of age. Their happiness was both an inspiration and a curse to their daughters, who could only dream of being that content in their choices.

"I can't believe you watched it, Mom. I'm so embarrassed."

"It came through very well on the new phone your sister bought for me." She held up the latest gadget de jour,
an extremely fancy example of communications wiz-
ardry. "And I've had your aunt Sylvia calling me every
hour to tell me how many times it has been viewed. It is
quite the hit."

Lili's sigh encompassed everything that was wrong
with her mother's statements. Cara, the video, Cara...

"Now, Lili." Francesca placed a cool-skinned hand
over hers.

"Now, Lili, what?"

"There is no need to get upset with Cara."

Mom was on fire this morning. "I don't mean to be—I
just wish she wasn't always copping out."

Francesca looked thoughtful. "Do not judge her so
harshly. Not everyone has your strength."

Lili would happily swap her much-admired stoicism
for a day in Cara's Manolos. She stood, feeling wearier
than ever. She really needed to lay off the morning carbs,
especially now that she required all her wits about her for
the coming hell days and the countdown to Jack Kilroy's
departure.

"Where is he?" Getting it over with sooner was best all
round.

"Where he always is on Sunday mornings."

* * *

She left her Vespa parked outside her parents' house in
the hope that the short, usually pleasant stroll to Andersonville Park, feet from the gray-blue Lake Michigan,

might will her pulse from a gallop to trot. No such luck. On arrival, Lili watched as her father stooped into the familiar huddle and carefully rolled the ball. When it landed at the far end of the boccie court, about ten feet away from its intended target, she winced. Tony's concentration was clearly off and she knew why.

His youngest daughter had let him down.

Unbending to just shy of six feet, her father scrutinized the arrangement of the balls. Lili shuddered to think what was going through his mind, though the fact that the target of the game was a little ball known as a *jack* gave her a pretty good idea. Likely, her father wanted to take that jack and dash it against the closest tree.

"Dad," she called out. He hesitated for a moment, then came over to greet her with a stroke of her unruly hair. He wasn't about to disown her in front of his boccie buddies no matter how shameful her behavior. The Italians had a code about this kind of thing. She'd hear it later.

"I thought I'd walk home with you when you're done."

"I'm done now," he said quietly, turning to signal his good-bye to the crew. A couple of the old codgers in tweeds snickered, and Lili felt that adolescent gloom all over again. Except instead of the high school elite poking fun at her turkey-thigh legs, her sexy hijinks were the talk of the assisted-living set over Jell-O surprise. She supposed that could be called progress.

They cut from the park onto Sheridan, and Lili took the change of scenery as her cue. "How mad are you?"

No response. Not even a sigh. So, as mad as all that.

She braved a look, noting the strain etched on his handsome face and the worry-crafted grooves around his mouth that hadn't existed two years ago. Instead of gratitude for her mother's survival, her father chose to see every passing day as a test of the family's fortitude, and Lili usually came up short. He studied the ground, taking each step with a careful calculation.

"I'm not angry, Liliana. I'm disappointed."

Oh, not that. She would rather he rant and call her out, but lately, his communication with her had devolved to cold silences interspersed with clipped expressions of censure. They had been close once, a love of cooking helping to forge a bond between them, and she knew he'd hoped she'd take over the restaurant. But those hopes faded when she had taken an after-school photography class in the eighth grade. As soon as she held that camera in her hands and felt its weight, it didn't matter that she was Lili the Lump—ha, she'd forgotten that one! In front of a camera, people changed into subjects, their focus turning to their own hair and smiles. Their visibility. Behind a camera, Lili became invisible.

She became free.

Her father hadn't liked it; photography was fine as a hobby but its practicality as a career was null. Never mind the strange types of people it attracted—deviants and misfits, with their elaborate body art and seedy, unhygienic piercings. Even getting her photos on the restaurant's walls had been a titanic battle, and he had only relented when she produced conservative portraits dripping in family values instead of the edgier explorations of beauty that had become her hallmark. Good girls don't take photos of naked people, he had said.

Good girls don't molest strange men in bars, either.

"It wasn't planned, Dad," she said. Not entirely. Sure, she had planned to seduce notorious man whore Jack Kilroy, and she had expected he would be a good kisser, a better-than-good kisser. What she hadn't planned on was the heat and the need, or how off balance she felt around him. She certainly hadn't planned on liking him.

"I hope not, Liliana. DeLuca's is a family establishment and that kind of behavior is bad for business."

"You'd be surprised but this is the kind of thing that's actually good for business. Along with the cooking show," she added quickly.

"My daughter acting like—" He carved his hands through the air, grasping for an appropriate descriptor. It didn't come. "In public is not good for business, no matter what you think." He stopped and finally looked her straight in the eye. "And I'm not sure this Jack Kilroy is good for anything."

She could take the unspoken hussy jibe like the hussy she was, but she didn't like the sound of his dig at Jack. As much as she'd like to blame him for that toe-curling kiss and its fallout, she was just as guilty. More so. She had challenged him to match her and he had stepped up, in more ways than one. For a few moments while they teased and flirted, while he spoke about his sister, there had been a spark of possibility. *Someone worthy of you,* her mom had said.

Pushing those thoughts aside, she steeled herself for an argument. The family's livelihood was on the precipice. They desperately needed Jack's show, and her father would have to put aside his disapproval for the sake of the greater good—namely, saving their pancetta.

"Dad, the show is going to be a boost. It'll open us up to a whole new audience—young professionals, foodies. I have friends who could help spruce the place up, and

Tad's got some great ideas for a new cocktail menu. We can jump-start a new, more modern DeLuca's."

"And what about our regular customers? Are we to abandon the people who have been with us from the start just to become fashionable?" A tired sigh slipped his lips, matching the slump of his shoulders. "I will see you for dinner tonight, and do not be late."

He stalked off into the house, his disappointment chilling her every cell despite the muggy heat. She tried to call on the moments when they had been simpatico—most of them involved the kitchen and a ball of dough—but the image of fear marring her father's face when he gazed on her mother during chemotherapy trumped the good times.

Fear had a habit of trumping everything.

CHAPTER EIGHT

Jack stood outside DeLuca's office, hand paused in mid-knock. Lili's voice, unusually somber, rang out clear. "I should have done this years ago, but I was too much of a chicken. We're finished."

He pushed ajar the door to the smallest office he had ever seen and the sight before him pulled a smile from deep inside. Lili sat at the paperwork-laden desk, tan legs bare, crossed, and tapering to short boots with cutouts for her toes. Her fingers curled around a glazed doughnut and she was glaring at it with a mix of lust and disdain.

"Are you breaking up with a pastry?" he asked. She was so bloody adorable.

Her eyes met his, half pissed, half challenge. All sexy. "I'm cutting out the bad influences in my life. And that includes you."

"Surely it's not as dreadful as all that."

"You want to know how dreadful it is?" she said, mimicking his accent. Terribly. "There's a Facebook page called 'I hate Jack's fat chick.' It's got over a thousand fans, Jack. A thousand."

Tension spread through his body like a series of clenching fists. "That'll be Min."

"Who?"

"She's the president of one of my fan clubs."

"You have more than one?" she blurted incredulously.

"Yep. But Min runs the most vocal one. They hate everyone I date. You should have read some of the things they said about Ashley." Of course, Ashley had scrutinized every single post like it was a criticism from her withholding mother.

"Well, we're not dating, but it seems everyone thinks we are—or worse." Her voice squeaked high in protest. "Someone posted pictures of us coming back to the hotel, and you look dazed and drunk while I look like I'm taking advantage of you with my big bear paws."

"I'm hard to take advantage of." Making light of it seemed like the best strategy here, though he was finding it mighty difficult to retain his composure. He plucked the doughnut out of her hand and took a bite. Cinnamon notes, the sweet glaze a little crunchy. Lili's lovely lips parted and her eyes took on a sweet glaze of their own. The familiar tug of desire tightened his groin but now it was mixed with two parts anger and three parts protectiveness. If that wasn't the recipe for an atomic fuck, he didn't know what was.

The cluttered desk was starting to look awfully inviting. Just move that stapler to the left and the pencil sharpener to the right—

"And that's not all." She stood, her gaze still fixated

on the doughnut. He bit into it again because she needed distracting. And he needed distracting from the way her skirt's fluid fabric clung fondly to her hips.

She tried to smile but couldn't quite make the conversion. "One of the hotel people took photos of the breakfast we ordered and now it's up on the Web with snarky comments like 'Jack's fat chick needs her vittles' and 'Feeding time for the fat chick.'"

His jaw tensed midchew. Heads were going to roll at that hotel once he got through going medieval on their oh-so-hospitable arses. "Sweetheart, I'm sorry. Any idea who posted the video?"

"No. I called everyone I know who was there. No one's owning up." Every breath of her distress was like a paring knife to his heart. "And you know what the kicker is in all this?"

"There's a kicker?"

Her eyes blazed and he knew he didn't want to hear it. "My butt is tweeting."

Okay, maybe he did want to hear it. "Come again?"

"Gina told me. My butt has its own Twitter account."

"How do you know it's yours?" he asked cautiously. "I'm sure there's plenty of arse on Twitter."

A couple of indignant taps later, she pointed at her phone. "Look at what it just said."

The latest tweet from @FatChicksAss read, *Wish Jack's hands were grabbing a meaty handful right now.* Oh, FatChicksAss, you have no idea.

There was nothing he could say that could make this better. Gamely, he tried all the same. "I'd follow your arse on Twitter any day of the week, Lili."

She socked him hard in the chest, which shouldn't

have felt good, but it did. Really good. "How can you make jokes about this?"

The crack in her voice hit him hard in the solar plexus as it dawned on him that for all her bravado, she was having a hard time holding it together. He was used to this, could weather the insults with the never-ending play-by-play analysis of his personal life. Hell, he had no personal life. Now she'd been caught up in his drama in the worst possible way.

He gathered her into his arms and stomped down on the hot charge that ripped through his body. Thankfully she didn't resist, but she didn't relent either. "Jokes are the only thing you can make. You've got to see the funny side or you'll never get through it. People have been slamming me for years, so I stopped reading it."

She held her body rigid, her forehead on his chest, her fists balled against his double-breasted chef's jacket. Through ten layers of Kevlar, he would still be able to feel her heat and the swell of her gorgeous breasts. Her disorderly hair begged for his touch, but he compelled his hands to play nice and rub her back benignly.

The sucking sound in his head told him what his brain thought of playing nice.

She peeked up, eyes wide and vulnerable. "When are you leaving Chicago?"

"Soon."

"Not soon enough," she muttered.

Reality poured over him like a vat of iced water. Last night leaching into this morning, there had been a wonderful stretch when he thought he had a real chance with this woman. She had shut him down, but he'd been confident he could persuade her to come around. Now they were irrevocably connected, yet further apart than ever.

He told himself it was for the best. He'd get back to his glamorous life and her amazing behind could return to obscurity. This existence he had chosen precluded normal relationships. He couldn't even take care of his sister. How in the hell could he protect a wonderful woman like Lili?

With a not-so-accidental lip brush against her forehead, he reluctantly let her go. He had a couple more days in Chicago. He could spend it moping about lost opportunities or he could spend it bringing pleasure to this woman without using the dick that was in danger of shriveling from disuse.

"Pity you've cut out all your vices," he said.

She arched a suspicious eyebrow. He'd never met anyone who projected skepticism quite like she could.

"Because I know what might make you feel better," he continued.

"Oh, please. Enlighten me."

"Food, Lili. Food cures all."

* * *

If the heady aromas hadn't tipped her off that Jack was making himself at home in the DeLuca's kitchen, the bass guitar riff of Iggy & the Stooges might have done the trick. Walking in, Lili was instantly transported to happier times. Meals at her nonna's in Fiesole. Family dinners before her mother's illness turned their lives upside down. Her father teaching her to cook when she was a kid. Cara had never been interested, and learning to love food with Tony was one of Lili's earliest and fondest memories. So much had changed in the last year.

Now the smell of her father's cooking conjured up disquiet and anxiety. She had always felt the equal tug of love and duty at DeLuca's, but since taking over as manager for her mother, duty was winning out. Not just winning, but morphing into an ugly bitterness. She didn't want to be the girl who whined about her lot but refused to throw off the shackles of her insecurity. She wanted to be liberated Lili, the girl who proudly stepped out in figure-hugging superhero outfits, told a gorgeous guy she wanted him in the clearest terms, and grabbed her future by the *coglioni*.

Look where liberation had got her.

She had shared only half the story of her sudden infamy with Jack. Some of the nastier comments about her size on Facebook were too embarrassing to mention, as were the hateful barbs about the audacity of someone like her hooking up with a god like Jack. *Fat chick* was about as nice as it got; the anonymity afforded by the Web brought every troll and hater out of their caves. Those defenses she'd carefully constructed in high school couldn't possibly stand a new onslaught. Worse, who would ever have thought she'd need them again?

Tamping down her emotions, she surveyed the kitchen, hungering for escape if only for an hour or two. Every burner held a pot of promise, merrily bubbling away in direct contrast to her foul mood. The counters looked like a futuristic garden out of a sci-fi movie, metal and glassware vying with vegetables and herbs for breathing room.

"When did all this happen?"

Jack leaned his hip against the far counter and folded his arms, causing those unreasonable biceps to push up the sleeves of his chef's jacket. "Cara took me to see some of your father's suppliers. We also hit that big farmers' market in the park yesterday morning."

"The Green City Market? I love that place." The largest farmers' market in Chicago, it was one of her favorite stops when she was in Lincoln Park. That he had shared it with Cara sparked a surge of jealousy so powerful she almost grabbed a bunch of carrots and dashed them to the ground. But Lili had no right to that feeling because she had no right to him. Instead of taking out her frustration on innocent vegetables, she completed a calming circuit of the kitchen, pausing at the stovetops to check out the sources of the delicious smells. Jack's tracking eyes made her itchy.

"What's this?" Holding her hair back, she bent over a pot of something stewlike and inhaled the generous scent. Her knees almost jackknifed with hunger.

"Braised rabbit with white wine and thyme. It should go well with pasta."

"*Coniglio*," she murmured appreciatively. Warmth flooded her body at the idea that Jack had cooked something that connected with her on such a basic level. Meanwhile, Jack's dizzying nearness was connecting with her on an even more basic level.

"But I thought you didn't get to choose your *primi* or *secondi*?" The wooden spoon on the adjoining counter whispered to her. She needed that stew in her mouth now.

"Yeah, I know. Your father's calling the shots there. But I could always turn it into an appetizer, too. Serve it over rustic bread."

"Hmm," she said, doubly distracted by the potted glory before her and the hard-bodied banquet at her side. The expression *food porn* came to mind.

"Want some?"

The rabbit? Yes, let's pretend they were talking about the rabbit. Her mouth watering, she dipped the spoon and pulled out a couple of chunks of meat with the thick sauce. She allowed the morsels to lie on her tongue for a few wonderful, anticipatory seconds, the liquid coating the inside of her cheeks. A single swallow. A satisfied moan. It tasted like the best Tuscan food should—rich, gamey, comforting. Life-affirming.

"You approve?"

"Not bad," she said evenly, then threw a light jab: "Although it's more of a winter dish."

She caught him smiling at the feeble attempt to dampen her enthusiasm and inwardly kicked herself for not doing a better job. Minimizing the mouthgasms would be a good start.

From the oven, he extracted a tray of what looked like mini-pizzas and moved them to a cooling rack. *Mini-pizzas? Really?* Any self-respecting Italian would be all over that, but she'd lost all self-respect last night when she goaded him in that bar and woke up to find herself clogging the Twittersphere. Besides, they looked oniony and cheesy, two of her favorite flavors.

He poured her a glass of wine, a Chianti she didn't recognize from their list. Humph. So DeLuca's cellar wasn't good enough for Lord Kilroy. There was something a little decadent about drinking wine at 11:00 a.m. on a Sunday, a twisted take on morning Mass without the sermons and smoky incense.

"What should we toast to?" he asked.

"The supremacy of Italian cuisine over all others?"

His lips parted on a sigh. "Must you be so competitive?

I was thinking something more pleasant...like new friendships."

Ah, the friend speech. The final breadstick in the basket. After all the drama of the past twenty-four hours, she knew it was for the best. But she couldn't help feeling that she had missed out on something special, and not just the potential of hold-on-to-the-light-fixtures sex.

Suppressing a sigh of her own, she clinked her glass against his. "To new friends...and may the best chef win tomorrow night." She sipped her wine and let it roll around her mouth like her father had taught her. It tasted thick and fruity.

Sparkling assessment, DeLuca.

"Where's Laurent? Shouldn't he be helping you prepare?"

"Couldn't get his sorry arse out of bed. He claims someone slipped him a Mickey at the bar." He added a curly leaf of arugula atop each of the little pizzas.

"Bowing to the porcelain god all night, was he?"

"Yep. And I heard the doorman at the InterContinental needs a new uniform."

Squashing a giggle at the thought of Laurent barfing all over some unfortunate hotel employee, she was about to offer up a witty riposte when she felt the ground fall away beneath her feet. Jack lifted her onto the counter, and shock, he didn't even grunt.

How ridiculous! Here she was melting in a girlish puddle because a big strong man lifted her a couple of feet off the ground.

Okay, she was thrilled.

His hands lingered lightly on her waist. "Now I'm going to feed you," he said in a rumble so low and sexy that her body translated it as, *Now I'm going to make love to you.* The cool, stainless-steel surface against her thighs did little to counteract the wildfire racing through her blood. Slowly he moved his palms down her hips and she parted her thighs in readiness.

"Comfortable?" he asked, his green-gold gaze locked on hers.

Her nod was a barefaced lie; she was the opposite of comfortable, but years of hiding had taught her how to train her expressions. He stepped away, taking his warmth and the scent of lemon-spiced skin.

Anticipation mounted even as the herby, heat-infused aroma of the cooling pizza diminished. Jack held the pizzette up, an invitation to eat from his outstretched hand. *Not a chance, mister.* She took it from him, anxious to avoid contact, anxious to suppress the memory of his talented hands. A memory still warm and present from last night's kiss and this morning's near miss.

A light bloom of flour on the underside of the crust coated her fingers and heat seeped from the mini disk into her skin. Little specks of green sprouted above the snowy, tan-freckled surface. It was just a squiggle of golden-brown onion topped with melted cheese, but right now she'd never seen anything so beautiful. Jack's gorgeous mug finally had competition.

She bit down, listening for the juice-crunch, that familiar sound of crust and squish. The dough base was perfect. Chewy in the middle, crispy around the edges. The candied tang of sautéed onions assaulted her taste buds, invoking all sorts of happy.

"What do you taste?" he asked.

"Hmm, caramelized Vidalias?" she ventured. He was

standing too close to her, his eyes searching her face for signs of yea or nay.

"And?"

"Oregano, for sure. Goat cheese?" He might have been sneaky and used feta, but she didn't think so. Not salty or tangy enough, and feta didn't look the same when it melted. She stroked her teeth with her tongue, relishing the creamy richness. "Definitely goat."

"*Oui, le chèvre.* Anything else?"

That little trill of French sent a quake of pleasure barreling down her spine. Not even Laurent's dulcet tones had such a devastating effect on her. Although, Jack could be talking about cleaning out the kitchen grease traps in English, French, or Klingon and she'd be drooling like a St. Bernard within seconds.

"Lili, are you still with me?"

She blinked to find him staring at her, the corners of his mouth tipped up.

"I can't work out that other flavor," she murmured thoughtfully, trying to cover her drift off to Jacklandia.

"Sarriette. It's called *santoreggia* in Italian. We use it in French cooking a lot, but it goes well with the oregano, don't you think?" He pronounced it ori-*gahn*-oh, and yes, that got her worked up all over again. *Get a grip.* "Actually, you should tell me if you think it goes well."

"It's good," she said, though he didn't need to hear it from her.

The assembly line of tastes continued, each more delicious than the last. A tomato consommé with plump, ocean-kissed crab, reminding her of summer visits to the Cinque Terre. Chicken liver crostini slathered in a fig marmalade that melted down her throat. A decadent, lush bruschetta with lobster crème fraîche and prosciutto. Turkey meatballs in a tomato cream sauce so divine she wished she could inject it straight into her veins.

All the while, he talked. Nonstop. About cooking and his favorite dishes and that spark he felt when he created something new. She usually disliked guys who gabbed constantly—heaven knows, she had dated enough of them—but this was different. It wasn't so much about him, but about his worldview and his quest to make haute cuisine accessible to everyone. He drew her in, asking her questions about flavors that resonated with her and ones that didn't (there weren't a whole lot in the latter category). At the hotel, she'd told Jack she liked food, which was a lie. She *loved* it, and talking about it was the next best thing to eating it.

Correction. Talking about it with Jack. Because she loved talking to him, more than any other guy she could recall.

A frisson of excitement fizzed through her, like the anticipation felt at the beginning of something new, which made no sense because it was coming to an end. Once the show was done, he'd be out of her life and regular programming would resume. Perhaps he'd pay a courtesy visit to her father when his Chicago restaurant opened, but the intimacy they had shared, the intimacy they were sharing right this minute, would be nothing more than an ancient memory. An all-encompassing taste that overwhelmed at first and lingered after swallowing but would fade as time passed.

He made her laugh, he made her feel sexy, and she would miss that.

It seemed incredibly unfair that she would *have* to miss that.

"Come here," he said, pulling her back to the reality of hot male at close quarters. At the stove, he tested a pan with a few drops of water, then a couple of shards of butter, eyeing it carefully while the fat melted and bubbled. His hands shaved garlic, working fast, and she imagined they would do wonderful things to her body. When he threw in the slivers, the aroma exploded, dragging her closer. By the time he'd added a chopped chili pepper and dropped in several jumbo shrimp, tails still on, she was practically on top of the stove.

Down, girl.

The shrimp pinked up perfectly, and he held one by the tail and bit into it. "Mmm, that's the stuff," he murmured as he offered the remainder to her.

"No, you're okay. Remember, I'm trying to cut out bad influences and that includes death foods like butter." *And you,* she thought, keenly mindful that letting him feed her would stir up all sorts of sultry sensations in the deep south.

He muttered something in French. She responded with her blankest, least-turned-on look, and silently congratulated herself. Mistress of her domain.

"Butter. Give me butter. Always butter," he translated. "That was the mantra of Fernand Point, a great French chef who died about fifty years ago."

"Let me guess. He keeled over after a madeleine binge."

The shrimp still beckoned, so she surrendered, placing her hand over his while she bit down on the chili-

and-garlic-encrusted crescent of joy. God, so good. A trickle of melted butter drooled from the corner of her mouth and his thumb was immediately there, sneaky-fast, wiping it away. He dawdled, dragging her bottom lip down gently. A wild yet insistent pulse started deep within her.

His eyes bored into her and she pulled away, but her retreat was only physical. Riveted, she stared, hunger gnawing at her that was completely unrelated to food. He licked the butter from his thumb. The same thumb she wished was jammed inside her mouth this very minute.

"It's okay to admit it, you know," he said quietly.

Her breath caught. "Admit what?"

"That you like my food." They both knew that wasn't what he meant.

She held his molten gaze. "We're in a contest tomorrow night and I can't be seen giving comfort to the enemy. It's best we keep this on a professional level, don't you think?"

"So, no flirting." He stepped in. Pretty damn flirty.

She backpedaled. "No flirting."

Two more steps to make up for her withdrawal, and he cupped her jaw. The spread of his warm fingers along the curve of her neck was unbelievably sensual.

"Or kissing," he said.

Her body acted fairly predictably to his provocation before what was left of her brain took over and insisted that her hormones would not be the boss of her. Little suckers refused to play ball but she talked up her best game.

"Especially not kissing." She moved out of his reach.

"Haven't you heard? You're bad news, Jack Kilroy. It's all over the Internet."

Discomfort brushed across his features. Her stomach pitched in guilt, but she made her back a titanium rod and steeled her resolve. Better a little upset now than a bellyful of heartache later.

CHAPTER NINE

Jack was living in a world of hurt. With each swallow beneath the golden skin at Lili's throat, a corresponding beat kicked up at every pulse point of his body. With every whimper of approval, he had become unbearably aroused. Lili was so turned on by food, was so turned on by *his* food, it was driving him insane. When a woman moaned like that and his fingers, tongue, or anything else wasn't already buried inside her, it got his attention. It got his dick's attention.

And he was finding it impossible to hide, salivating all over her like a dog tethered six inches from a T-bone. He needed to dial it down. It wasn't fair to either of them. He'd already cocked up royally when he lost all control and mauled her in that bar, bringing shame on her family and probably some gypsy curse on himself. Now she'd made it clear his advances were as welcome as sand in Blue Point oysters.

Hastily, he targeted a more neutral topic. "So, do you cook yourself?"

She shrugged. "Sometimes, but when you have a bossy master chef around, it's usually best to let him do his thing."

"Tony's a bit of tyrant in the kitchen?"

"Aren't all head chefs? Their way or the highway?"

"Not me. I'm more the nurturing type."

One of her eyebrows flew up, and he laughed. "Nah, I'm a tyrant, too, though it's been a while."

He wondered how the brigade at Thyme was getting on and felt that twinge of guilt in his gut, a far too common feeling these days. Clarence, his garde-manager who made the best duck-liver pâté Jack had ever tasted. Derry, his poissonier, telling dirty jokes while he filleted a trout in thirty seconds flat. Marguerite, his pâtissier, who'd just had her first child. She'd asked Laurent to be godfather, and while every irreligious bone in Jack's body should have been fine with that, his heart keened at being passed over for his sous-chef. His kitchen crews were as close to family as any man could ask for, but lately, those relationships had been tested as his life became increasingly centered around the TV shows and all the crap they entailed.

"I miss it," he said under his breath. He chanced a glance and found Lili staring at him. "I could do with your help," he tacked on quickly.

"Oh?" She tried to smile but it was as if the effort might do her some injury.

"Show me how a real Italian makes pasta."

She lasered him with an acute look that said she wasn't buying what he was shoveling. Any chef worth his salt knew how to make pasta, and she knew that, but her lovely shoulders sank in resignation.

"I'm nowhere near as good as my father, but my Italian genes can probably conjure up some noodle magic."

Within minutes she had assembled the ingredients—flour, water, salt, an egg—and spellbound, he watched her elegant hands as she expertly worked the dough in a startlingly erotic clench and unclench. The rolling and kneading action also did other things. Wonderful things. It made her body undulate in a sexy wave that plumped her breasts and rocked her hips. He gawked, fantasizing about how her fingers might clench a particular part of his anatomy. The one that was stiffening with every passing second.

Keep it together, idiot.

She took his hand and pressed it down on the dough. He almost had a heart attack.

"This is the consistency you're looking for." Her palm covered his knuckles and her slender fingers intertwined with his. "Sort of smooth and elastic. Better to knead too much than too little."

"Uh-huh." He had his doubts about the effectiveness of this two-handed strategy, but now wasn't the time to bring it up. Throwing a sneaky glance sideways, he found her staring at their joined hands, her lips parted, a watercolor pink bloom on her cheeks that was in no way attributable to the heat of the kitchen. So, not that pissed after all.

Her long fingers worked, but the dough was no longer getting the treatment. Their flour-covered hands hovered an inch above the countertop, fingers lacing, unlocking, exploring. Critics on three continents had described his food as sexy and sensual, and in his younger days he had banged more women against refrigerators than he'd had hot dinners, but this was, without a doubt, the most arousing experience he'd ever had in a kitchen.

I love your hands, and as she jerked away, he realized he'd spoken aloud. She wiped her brow, leaving a streak of flour that he longed to attend to.

"That was all you," he said, annoyed that he couldn't go ten minutes without running his mouth off about his attraction to her.

A smile threatened, but the blush suffusing her cheeks overcame it and spread across the exposed skin of her neck and, no doubt, to the other parts hidden by her clothing. Parts that pulsed and pinked, parts he wanted to kiss and lick. The nipples now straining against the unholy thinness of her blouse would be a dusky rose, maybe darker in keeping with her Mediterranean coloring. Across the curve of her belly, his mouth would suck while his hands would shape those tweeting globes of perfection. Moving to the southern trail, he would find her pretty pink, succulent sex begging for his tongue to taste and own.

Woman needed her own section in the Michelin guide.

"Jack."

"Hmm?"

"Are you okay? You look a little dazed." Her lips parted, revealing more luscious pinkness that would look so good wrapped around his—Dazed. Yep, dazed, confused, head-over-nuts in lust. He shook his head to clear it. If only a quick shake of his dick could have the same effect.

"We should finish this," he said inadequately.

They returned to the original plan—she kneaded; he stared longingly. It wasn't a bad plan.

"What do you miss about your restaurant?" she asked.

He hesitated, unsure how to answer because he missed too much. That first thirty minutes of service when he gauged the mood of the brigade and how each piece of the machine was operating that night. The haul-arse-hustle as everything came together like a symphony of gliding motion. Even the nights it all went wrong and the only option was to get wasted at the basement dive on Tenth while the postmortem was argued over well into the wee hours.

"The swearing," he said. "I miss the swearing."

Their gazes met. Held. She nodded, and relief that she got it drenched him.

"Kitchen crews tend to be close," she said. "Like family."

Yes, exactly like that. For someone who didn't have much in the way of family after his mother's death when he was barely in his teens, the camaraderie of the kitchen was the next best thing. Jealousy tweaked him that Lili enjoyed the best of both worlds—the restaurant and her big Italian clan.

"Everyone's in everyone else's business, that's for sure," he said lightly. "Weddings, kids' soccer games, who's banging who. My crew at Thyme is mostly Dominican. I'm telling you, if I never go to another *quinceañera*, it'll be too soon."

She laughed, a rich and robust sound that stroked his spine. "Liar. I bet you love line-dancing with all the teenagers. You probably think you're as good a dancer as you are a singer."

"Hell, yeah. I've got moves you've never seen, DeLuca."

That sent another flush to her cheeks that looked so

good on her he felt alternatively aroused and annoyed. He had never wanted something to happen so much, but he couldn't expect a woman as grounded as this to turn her life upside down for him. The stinking injustice of it all popped him in the gut.

Her smile was sympathetic, an acknowledgment that they had stretched the boundaries of what was possible. *Give it up, dude.*

They continued in silence, except for her instructions on how to make the *pappardelle* noodles as thin as possible using the roller. He'd already started the stockpot of boiling water—it came as no surprise that Tony DeLuca didn't use a commercial pasta cooker—and after a couple of minutes, Jack drained, then dressed the noodles with a quick waltz of the rabbit *ragù* around a sauté pan. Together, they carried the Chianti, plates, and a basket of truffle oil focaccia he had whipped up earlier out to one of the booths at front of house and settled in.

He swirled the coated pasta around the fork and slipped it between his lips. The world halted on its axis, then jolted awake as he swallowed. He had died and woken up in Tuscany.

"Oh, baby. This is absolutely amazing," he said. The pasta ribbons were the perfect size and consistency to pick up the rich, meaty rabbit *ragù*.

"You didn't just call me baby," Lili said.

"Correct, I didn't. I was talking to the food."

"You two need to be alone?"

"Maybe. I would have sex with this pasta if I could."

"With the way your love life is going, that might be your best bet." She licked her lips, catching some of the sauce from the corner of her mouth. Her hand hovered over the focaccia, but she withdrew breadless.

"There's plenty more."

"That's okay," she murmured, and something about how she said it sent a quiver of unease through him. Bloody Twitter.

Covertly, he watched her slurping the noodles, all while envying her fork. Damn if it wasn't sexy. He loved that she'd eaten everything he had fed her today and that she didn't have a weird relationship with food. So unlike most of the women he dated who were constantly whining about carbs and diets. He was suddenly aware of the irony, that his taste in women usually veered toward the ones who despised the very thing he spent his life's work on. It gave him a moment's pause. At the same time, another interesting thought lit up his blood-deprived frontal lobe.

Healthy appetites usually had universal application.

He loved cooking, women, and, since he'd moved to New York eight years ago, the Mets. In that order. And this season, the Mets couldn't hit for shit. He'd played sexy food games with previous lovers but it had always felt like a fraud, like he was going through the motions because eating involved mouths and tongues, ergo it was a natural complement to sex. But experiencing food with a woman had never felt like this. Sensual and visceral. Right.

Rein. It. In.

Needing to get his filthy mind off sex, he shifted his gaze to the restaurant's exposed brick walls. "These photos are good. Yours?"

She looked around as if noticing them for the first

time. "Yeah. I took some of them in Italy. Some of them in the parks around the city."

"Is this the kind of work you usually do?"

"No, this was just for fun, my take on Cartier-Bresson. Trying to catch people at a decisive moment. I'm more interested in posed portraiture at the moment, specifically the human body as text and narrative."

"What does that mean?"

She paused, probably trying to think of one-syllable words to explain it to him.

"Nudes, Jack." She gifted him with a lazy, devastating grin. "I work with my friend Zander. He's interested in the male form and the interplay of light on muscle, particularly when the body is under stress."

"Under stress?"

"Yeah, working out, tied up, that kind of thing. The tauter the muscle action, the better for Zander."

Jesus, only artists could get away with that kind of shit.

"Do you work with men?" The only taut male musculature he wanted to think about Lili seeing was his.

"No, I work strictly with the female body. As interesting as the male form is, a female's lines are much more beautiful."

"On that we can agree," he said, stupidly relieved. "Cara said you're planning to go to graduate school in New York. Which one?" *Real subtle, subconscious.*

"I had my eye on Parsons. They have a great photography program, but..." The pause stretched tight.

"You've been busy with other things," he finished for her.

A short nod, a quick blink, and she looked away. Her thoughts echoed loudly, so loudly they made his heart thud against his rib cage.

"Sounds like it's been a tough year," he said.

She made a gulping noise. "Tougher for my mom. And for Dad, too. He's crazy about her and I'm not sure he would have survived if she hadn't." She hesitated and rubbed the lip of her wineglass.

"Go on, love."

She took a deep breath. "It changed him. You'd think he'd be overjoyed, see every day as precious. Don't get me wrong, he was difficult before. Bossy, traditional, real old-school Italian, you know, just like the movies, but now he's even harder. He acts like we've only been given a reprieve, like the axe could fall any second." Her gaze panned over the restaurant, visualizing something beyond the space. "He can't see what a gift it is to have her with us still."

His chest tightened to the point of discomfort. He so wanted to touch her, but any overture might be taken the wrong way. And frankly, he wasn't sure he could trust his body not to want to go there if he laid a finger on her. He was such a dick.

"My mother died when I was twelve and my sister was just two," he said, drawing a jerky uplift of her chin. "My stepdad didn't handle it so well." That was a complete understatement. His mother's death from cancer had sent his stepfather into a spiral of neglect—of himself, his stepson, and his daughter, before he died a couple of years later with a bottle in his hand.

Liquid pain filled her eyes and she curled those long fingers around his palm. His whole body sighed into her hand's embrace.

"That must have been awful for you."

It had been hell but luckily for Jack, his own surly

teenage years had kicked in and created other distractions.

"And for your sister. She was so young. What about your own father?"

"He wasn't around. I met him once but it didn't go so well."

"What happened?"

"He wasn't interested." The father-son reunion had been a bitter disappointment, a forgone conclusion when reality overtakes hope. He shook off that dark memory and focused on a happier time. The happiest of times. "Not long after my mother died, I found cooking. Or rather it found me."

Her hand squeezed tighter, so he talked, knowing she liked the sound of his voice. Women dug the accent, for sure.

"I acted out, got into trouble. Fights, stealing, kid stuff. I ended up in a program for juvenile delinquents that taught me to cook. Apprenticeship in Paris at eighteen, my first restaurant at twenty-three, my first restaurant failure at twenty-four..." That netted him a wry smile. "More success, British TV. I opened Thyme on Forty-Seventh, conquered America, and here we are."

"Wow, just like the Beatles. The American dream fulfilled. And it's about to get better with your new show."

He wouldn't have put it in quite those terms but he could see why she would think that. Money and fame equated to better for most people.

"Nice switch," he said. "We started out talking about you and I managed to make it all about me."

"One of my superpowers."

A throwaway comment, but he suspected there was a lot of truth in there. Putting other people first was how she operated. Last night, she had taken a chance on him and he'd turned her down for his own self-flagellating reasons. Yep, he was a dick squared.

"What about your fairy-tale ending? Your mom's better, so you can kick-start all your grad school plans again." The thought of Lili living in the same city as him sent an unreasonable thrill through him. Curiously, it wasn't sexual...or not only sexual.

She released his hand and his stomach felt weirdly hollow despite being stuffed with pasta and bread.

"I have responsibilities here. Managing this place."

"Sounds like a lot of work," he prompted.

"It's not so bad. The killer is the early morning deliveries. I'm so not a morning person."

His head shot up so fast he almost got whiplash. "You handle the deliveries?" Most chefs or their sous took care of that. He had a team of people who took care of it.

"Dad's first mate, Emilio, lives in the suburbs, so it's difficult for him to make it in that early. We used to split it when I lived at home, but since I moved to the apartment upstairs a couple of months ago, I do it." There was a noticeable bite in her tone. The bonds of familial obligation had to chafe sometime.

"What else do you do?"

"Scheduling, payroll, ordering, the books." She smiled. "The usual."

Despite the brevity of their acquaintance, he recognized a forced smile when he saw one. "That's a lot for one person." All this and caring for her mother. Admiration got all mixed up with his libido, which was pretty much how one defined a crush.

"We all help out. It's a family operation."

Topic of conversation over. Time to try Door Number Two. "So you're too busy to date, or maybe you're just too busy to date me."

She tilted her head and gave him that look, the one that could cut him down at fifty paces.

"Tell me about the last date you went on," he said, praying it wasn't with that moron, Marco.

"The last date I had." She shook her head, then straightened, girding herself for…he didn't know what. "You want to hear about my dating adventures?"

"Only if they're entertaining. And, of course, embarrassing."

"Oh, I can guarantee that. How about the guy who collapsed in tears when the appetizers came out? The shrimp cocktail reminded him of his ex."

"Sounds like you dodged a bullet."

"Then there was the one whose Bentley broke down on Lake Shore Drive on our way to dinner. He asked if I could help change the tire. While he sat in the car, texting. In January."

His hand curled into a fist on his thigh, but he forced humor into his tone. "So you bring useful skills to a date. Good to know."

She laughed, the sound more heartbreaking than amused.

"What did you see in not-so-super-Mario?" It spilled out quicker than it took for the thought to form.

"His name's Marco."

"Whatever."

For a moment, he thought she was going to ignore him, but as before, she had evidently decided that humoring him was the best strategy to handle the idiocy.

"It didn't last long," she said, which came nowhere close to answering the question, or perhaps it did. A couple of bright spots lit high on her cheekbones. "I was at a point where I needed something, someone, to take my mind off things. It was never supposed to be serious."

"But…"

"Yeah." She raised those drown-in-me eyes to meet his. "Under normal circumstances, I wouldn't usually fall for a guy like that. Mr. Smooth."

Under normal circumstances. But her mother had been ill and Lili had been what? Looking to lose herself in the arms of some guy? Is that what she'd wanted from him last night? Some measure of sexual oblivion? The comparison may have been unintentional, but it hit him like a cricket bat to the kidneys. There was no way in hell he was like Marco or any of these cabbage heads she'd dated. Idiots who wouldn't appreciate a beautiful, funny, and sexy-as-all-get-out woman like Lili if she danced a cancan on DeLuca's bar.

What he wouldn't give to show her his appreciation. Touching her until she moaned like she had when she tasted his food. Discovering those spots on her body that drove her crazy. Making her beg him to plunge inside her and take her someplace she hadn't even known existed until she'd met him. Jesus, he wanted to shag her senseless, and then hold her so she wouldn't feel so lost.

So, that had taken what…five minutes to get back to sex?

Kudos, Kilroy.

He'd known this woman for less than thirty-six hours. A thoroughly pleasurable thirty-six hours colored by a brain injury, a rather girly faint, and a hospital visit. The bad publicity, the contract, the upcoming taping, how burned out and dog-tired he felt, it could all go to hell because with her, food tasted better and he wanted to grasp it and hold on for dear life.

They stared at each other for a long, expectant moment. Suddenly, this no-sex kick was shaping up to be the most ridiculous idea he'd ever had. His dick was never meant to be as useless as a white crayon. It was meant for pleasure. It was meant to pleasure her.

Her eyes darkened, like the pupils had swallowed all the blue. "You look weird again. Is it your head? Do you need your pain meds?"

Would the meds help the ache in his jeans, now building to an unbearable level? His hands twitched, ready to slide around her, under her, inside her.

"Are you still in love with Marco?" he bit out, surprised at his own sharpness.

She looked flummoxed. "I don't see how that's any of your business. Or relevant."

"It is my business but you're right, it's not relevant. A little time with me, you'll forget about him."

An amused smile curved her lips. "I've already explained why dating wouldn't be a good idea."

"Because we live in different cities? We can figure that out."

She rolled her eyes, but she did it patiently. He liked that. "Well, that problem has been superseded by a shit storm I'd rather not deal with."

"I told you it'll all die down, and everyone thinks we're together anyway. Why not give us a chance?"

"Clearly you're not used to taking no for an answer."

"Can't say I am. It's one of my most endearing qualities."

"Sounds annoying for everyone else."

The heavy clop of footsteps echoed behind them. Torn between irritation at the interruption and gratitude he was putting an end to the desperation portion of the proceedings, he looked up to find Lili's cousin, Tad, swaggering in from the kitchen.

"What's up, kiddos?" He placed a motorcycle helmet on the table and made a move on the focaccia.

Lili swatted at his hand. "Hey, try asking first."

He scoffed and snatched the largest piece in the basket. A single bite transformed his face into something close to an epileptic fit. Yeah, it was that good. Once recovered, he divided a look between Jack and Lili.

"How goes it?"

A slow, knowing smile lifted Lili's face. "Could be worse."

"Well, not to worry, *la famiglia's* on the case."

"No, no, no," Lili said, her smile evaporating as her hands white-knuckled the table's edge. "You are not to get involved in this."

"Too late. Gina's already mobilizing the troops on Facebook and Twitter. And if you want any input on the T-shirt design, you should get on the horn."

Lili pulled herself up. "I'd better call her." She lingered, her gaze locked on her cousin, sending wordless messages that only family this close could comprehend.

Irrational jealousy ripped through Jack as Tad enveloped Lili and whispered in her ear. It should be Jack's job to comfort her, and not just because he was to blame for her current predicament. With a deep exhale, she drew back, splaying her fingers on Tad's chest.

"Be nice," she said quietly.

Tad's face split into a grin. "When am I ever anything else?"

As she swiveled to saunter off, Jack urged himself not to look. *Ah, to hell with that.* He drank in that va-va-voom body with more curves than a winding Italian road, only stopping when Tad plunked down in the booth and leveled Jack with a stare of steel similar to Tony's storm front last night.

Busted.

"Don't hold back," Jack said.

Tad gave a press-on smile, but it made no impression on those flinty eyes. "She knew what she was doing. At the top of my list is the fucker who put up that video."

Jack nodded grimly. "You and me both."

"But that doesn't mean I think you're completely blameless. There's some rumor going round the Interweb that you've got a new show in the hopper."

"And?"

"And," Tad dragged out, "after all that Hollyweird shit with your skanky soap opera chick, advertisers might be more open to a guy with a regular girl from the hood, complete with a nice TV-friendly family." His mouth curled into a sneer. "Not that we're especially friendly."

Is that what people thought? More importantly, is that what Lili thought? Evie hadn't wasted a second. "That's a rather cynical viewpoint, and that video doesn't exactly fit the wholesome image so beloved of advertisers." He adjusted in the booth, the memory of her hand between his legs sending all his blood rushing hellward. Nope, nothing wholesome about that.

Tad smirked. "Maybe. But it's not going to do you any harm, is it? As long as we're clear, if I see you gaining an advantage at Lili's expense, you'll be moving to the top of my list. She's too good a person for that."

"I would never hurt her." Jesus, all he wanted to do was protect her from all that. Keep her safe from every hater with a camera or a keyboard. Sweat trickled down the back of his neck. He strummed the table and added, "I like her."

A slow burn of a smile animated Tad's face, and Jack immediately wanted to bite back his admission.

"Okay," Tad said, a million things hinted in that single word, all of them annoying as fuck.

They were bonding. Cute.

"Anyway, I'm not the DeLuca you should be worried about."

Jack knew it was coming and he almost welcomed the gut check. He needed to be brought down from this cloud he'd been floating on for the last day and a half.

Tad's grin turned to pity. "You might want to dust off your crotch armor because Tony's going to have your nads in a vise before the day is over."

CHAPTER TEN

Standing on the threshold of the DeLucas' brownstone in Andersonville on Chicago's north side, Jack immediately knew the pain of every randy teenage boy who had dared to take a DeLuca girl on a date. Tony loomed in the hallway doing his best Don Corleone. Hands clenched. Feet planted like sequoias. Mouth a gray slash. Lili fidgeted behind her father, looking like she wanted the hardwood floors to split at their seams and drag her to the earth's molten core.

"Jack, this is my mother, Francesca," Cara said. He took the hand of a beautiful, frail woman with elfin features and cropped blond hair. Sucking in a bolstering breath, Jack embarked on the grovel to end all grovels.

"Tony, Francesca, I'm so sorry about what happened last night." *But your daughter got me so riled up I had no choice.*

The muscles in Tony's face scrunched, mirroring the imminently dangerous situation with his fists. Francesca placed a hand on her husband's arm. No one spoke, so Jack did what he usually did when faced with adversity—tried to talk his way out of it.

"Your daughter's a lovely woman." *And I want her so much it hurts.*

Lili's eyes widened and she shook her head vehemently.

"My behavior was unforgivable." *But I don't regret a single moment.*

An imperceptible nod from Lili. Better.

"Jack, it is okay," Francesca said warmly. "You cannot be blamed for the kind of society we live in." She mashed her lips together in disapproval of the ravenous media and their appetite for the slightest scandal. Jack would have kissed her if he wasn't so worried about getting decked flat by her husband.

Tony wouldn't be so easily swayed, but after his wife squeezed his arm once more, the older man clasped Jack's hand. A reluctant détente, but he'd take it. Jack huffed out a breath and caught Lili's equally relieved expression.

"Well, thank God," Cara said cheerily. "I think we could all do with a drink."

Amen to that.

Dinner was served around a large communal table in the backyard, which was roughly landscaped in a style reminiscent of the gardens of an Italian villa. The aroma of lavender and basil from the herb garden scented the air. Terra-cotta planters, paving stones, and trees strung with twinkling lights all combined to create a little corner of Tuscany in the middle of the city. It was like something out of a fairy tale, complete with a modern-day Cinderella. Lili served and cleared, usually under Tony's barked instructions *en Italiano.*

It didn't take long for Jack to intuit that, while Tony was the consummate host, he wasn't about to give away any of his kitchen secrets.

"So what's in store for me tomorrow, Tony?"

Tony swirled his wineglass, watching as the legs of the Brunello Jack had brought dribbled dark rivulets down the sides. "I haven't given it much thought."

And I'm the Queen of England. Jack had seen enough of the Italian maestro's management style on his brief tour of the DeLuca kitchen to know he had his contest menu prepared, right down to how many leaves of basil he would use to garnish the pasta. Even tonight's simple meal of bruschetta, veal parmigiana, and homemade linguine was perfect. More saber-rattling. Now the man had the family honor as an extra incentive to nail Jack's arse to the wall.

For the rest of the meal, Jack underwent a barrage of questions from Tony's scary sister-in-law, Sylvia, and her towering bouffant. She had seen every one of his shows and grilled him like the head chef at Le Cordon Bleu would an unprepared student.

"In the episode where you killed that squid on the boat, it looked like a different squid in the next shot," Sylvia said, scarcely able to disguise her disgust at the deceptive practices of the editors.

"It might have been." He tried to trap Lili's gaze to see if she was even slightly amused, but she hadn't looked his way once since his arrival.

"So you cheated," Sylvia concluded sternly with a wave of her hand. Every time she gesticulated, his gaze rose to her hair, poised for something disastrous to happen.

"It's television. It's all cheating," he murmured, but she'd already transferred the Gestapo tactics to her niece.

"Cara, what time Mass do you attend in New York?"

"Nine-thirty, St. Patrick's Cathedral," Cara replied without missing a beat. Clever girl. No one but tourists attended St. Pat's, but Sylvia clearly wasn't in the loop or had any idea that Cara lived forty blocks uptown.

"Better than your sister. She can't be bothered," Sylvia said.

"Too busy with those atheists. Those artists," Tony snarled, to which Lili inhaled deeply and turned a dull shade of red.

"Tony," Francesca murmured. "Not now."

That would normally be a cue to let the uncomfortable moment slide but Jack didn't like how Tony's tone sucked the conviviality out of the proceedings.

"Atheist artists?" he asked innocently.

Tony delivered a pained expression. Shocker. "My daughter spends too much of her time with unsuitable people."

"Good for her." Jack met Tony's glare head-on. "Can't be any worse than restaurant folk. The people who work for me are a bunch of miscreants and reprobates. Probably the same for you, I imagine."

Tony's stone-faced expression didn't budge a millimeter. Francesca smiled at him brightly. Jack caught Lili's look of surprise and succumbed to a pleasurable dizziness.

Sylvia leaned in close and gave him a flash of crinkly bosom that turned his wash of dizzy to nausea. "Are you Catholic, Jack?" *Jesus Christ.*

"Sylvia," Francesca warned.

The Italian Inquisition flapped her hands. "They say most relationships start in the workplace. Where else is Cara going to meet a man?" Her eyes flashed with an oddly lascivious disgust that made him shudder. "Even if he's a *donnaiolo*, at least he's good-looking."

He had no idea what he'd just been called, but he needed to nip this in the bud. "Cara's the best producer I've ever worked with and we make a great professional team, but that's as far as it goes."

Cara winked and gifted him a wide grin. "Thanks, babe, your check's in the mail."

"We're very proud of her," Tony said with a genuine smile that completely disconcerted Jack, probably because it was the first time he'd seen the older man do it. "Plenty of time for her to settle down."

There was no missing how Lili's expression faded to hurt at Tony's words. Those bright eyes, that sunshine smile, dulled to dishwater in the face of some family dynamic Jack tried hard to grasp. Lili, loyal, hardworking, by all accounts a wonderful daughter, was on the outs with her father. Sure there was the video, but Lili couldn't be blamed for that.

"So, Jack, are you in the market for a wife and children?" Francesca asked, at which he almost choked on a ribbon of linguine.

"Mom!" Lili and Cara exclaimed together, echoing his own horror.

"I'm so sorry," Lili said, the first words she'd spoken to him all evening. "Ever since my mother beat cancer, she thinks it's given her license to say whatever the hell she wants."

"I don't want to die without getting all the answers,"

Francesca said with an astonishing smile that reminded him of Lili. *In twenty years, she'd still have that smile. Her kids would have that smile. Their kids...Hold your horses.* She has a nice smile. 'Nuff said.

Tony gave his wife a tender kiss on the cheek and muttered something in Italian.

At Jack's raised eyebrow, Cara repeated it slowly. "*Casa senza fimmina 'mpuvirisci.* It means 'how poor is a home without a woman.'"

How poor indeed. Lili's words about her father's devotion to her mother came back to him. The man might be a hard nut with his daughter but he clearly loved his wife with a frightening and enviable passion.

Lili spoke again, her voice as smooth as warmed butter, and he imagined that restful tone soothing him after a hard night or a bad day. "If Jack was to get hitched, I can see it now. Riots in the streets. Women the world over tearing their hair out. It would be best if he stays single. The fate of womankind depends on it."

"She's right," he agreed affably. "My public wouldn't stand for it."

"Never underestimate your capacity for marriage and parenthood, Jack," Francesca said sagely. "You may be surprised at how rewarding it is."

"Of course, Jack's had plenty of chances to father children," Cara said, knowing full well her words would cause a widespread halt to the collective chewing. It did. "He gets constant offers from busy career women and New York socialites who want him to be their baby daddy. I'm surprised he hasn't taken anyone up on it, if only to ensure the genius lives on."

Jack speared his producer with a murderous glare,

though his irritation stemmed more from the fact he couldn't flat-out deny it. He'd had several offers from women who wanted a child without the inconvenience of finding a husband first. *Note to self: tear the blabbermouth Frenchman limb from limb*.

"So, Jack, your DNA's a hot commodity on the New York baby market?" Lili asked.

"Too right. Women would kill to have kids with this bone structure," he joked, foolishly relieved she was speaking to him again, though the vapid topic could only further harden her opinion of him from sandstone to granite.

"Kill? Would they even have to bother?" Lili shot back. "I hear you're so virile you could probably impregnate a woman just by looking at her crooked."

Tilting his head, he slanted her a smile. "Let me know where to send the child support checks in nine months."

She burst out laughing and the current spread along a fuse, igniting and drawing him in. His laugh blended harmoniously with her opulent, full one and his chest contracted at the beautiful sound. *Yeah, this.*

Everyone at the table stared as if they'd never heard laughter. Jack knew how inappropriate this conversation was, but where Lili was concerned, self-control was as hard to come by as morels in the fall. She dipped her head to study her barely eaten veal, but not before he noted her lips still lifted in a sensual curve. Pride swelled his chest. He had done that. A fierce pulse thrummed through him, a biological signal telling him that he needed to be alone with her.

Now.

To hell with her family's gapes and to hell with Tony

and his tangible disapproval. He had kissed this woman thoroughly, not started World War Three. And he had every intention of doing it again.

Tony butted in, his tone stentorian. "Liliana, the dessert."

"Sure, Dad," Lili answered on a sigh, her bright aura muted once again as she swayed off to the kitchen.

* * *

On her way home from her parents', Lili cast out thoughts of Satan, aka Jack Kilroy, and tried to focus on the restaurant's troubles without wiping out on the Vespa. Last week, they'd had some Tuesday night success with two-for-one entrées, but her father hadn't approved. He hated sales gimmicks, which, in his words, "cheapened the integrity of the food." Jack's promise to have butts in seats for six months after the show aired was all well and good, but if her father insisted on running the restaurant like his personal fiefdom, any benefits to being featured on TV would disintegrate into dust.

She longed for the taping to be over. For Jack Kilroy to go back to where he came from so she wouldn't have to think about the smile that melted her insides. Or the beginnings of a five o'clock shadow that made her fingers itch to shape his granite jaw. Or how he had quietly challenged her father at dinner when the subject of her unsuitable friends came up. She didn't need anyone to defend her, but she had to admit it had been nice. Really nice.

Damn Cara and her crazy promises. And damn Jack Kilroy for giving her a glimpse of what might be possible. Today he had fed her food and chunks of his life story and had stood up to Il Duce. He had overwhelmed with his charisma and culinary chops. It wasn't fair of him to instill such hope and want and need.

It wasn't fair of him to be so dazzling.

After parking the Vespa, she trudged the block home, her precious veal parmigiana leftovers swinging in a plastic bag at her side. Playing catch up on *The Bachelor* with a limit of one fat-free yogurt was the tantalizing menu for the rest of the night.

"Mow any innocent bystanders down on your way home?"

She looked up, only to be leveled by a brash grin and moss-green eyes. Jack was draped against the wall of her building, all feline grace, looking every inch like he belonged there. Annoyance and attraction battled for space in her head. As usual, attraction won.

"Just a couple. Slow night," she said, feeling a smile building inside her. She pushed it down but it burbled up like a crude oil spurt.

He unhooked his thumbs from his jean pockets and pushed one of her uncooperative locks away from her face. She resisted the temptation to fold into his hand.

Focus, Lili. It's just the dazzle.

"We didn't get a chance to talk properly at dinner," he said. "You were so busy playing at serving wench."

She took a mock bow. "You honored us greatly by eating at our table, my lord."

His laugh was warm, enriching the air around her. Making him laugh pleased her more than it should have. Had Ashley brought a smile to his face? No matter, undoubtedly she had other talents.

"What are your cousins up to these days?" he asked.

Lili was currently last in the TMZ poll on Jack's Gallery of Bangable Broads but, with the help of her posse, was closing in fast on the actress Jack had been wearing to film premieres a few months ago.

"Oh, a Facebook page called 'Jack's Fat Chick Rules,' a Twitter war with my butt. You know, the usual."

This time she laughed with him. It seemed churlish not to be a good sport about it.

"And your dad? Did he give you a hard time about the video? He seems to be"—he paused in the act of measuring his words—"a total hard-ass. Pardon my French."

"It's not the dream most guys have for their daughters. Millions watching her get busy with a strange man's wedding tackle. All class."

He grimaced. "Right, I can understand that. I'm sorry—"

"But you're not." She could hear his lack of remorse slicing clear through the unresolved sexual tension.

"I'm sorry you feel embarrassed and it's put you in the doghouse with your father. But I'm not sorry it happened." He waited a couple of beats so she could absorb that declaration, or kneel in gratitude, perhaps. "So what else is going on with your dad?"

"Isn't that enough?"

He folded his arms like he was in for the interrogation long haul, and his sleeve hems pulled tight against his biceps. He really should cover those things up. "That stuff about atheist artists. Il Duce not a fan of naked women?"

Il Duce wasn't a fan of Lili. "He has that old country, immigrant mentality. Art's for recreation, not for real life." She waved her hand in explanation but really to calm her rising emotions. "He doesn't understand how something so intangible can be worthwhile. How it can put bread on the table."

"But producing food television rates highly?"

The derision in his tone made her bristle. He didn't get to mock. "Cara's done well. My parents are very proud of her."

Those green-gold eyes, all knowing and sharp as a cat's, softened. "I'm sure they're proud of you, too."

Her mother was grateful for Lili's help, but proud? That wasn't a word she heard often, not in a house where duty was a given and her father's precise definition of success colored everything. Cara's glamorous career represented the pinnacle of achievement in her family's eyes, and all that go-getting and high-flying put Lili's ambitions in the shade. Not that she could expect someone like Jack Kilroy, with his far-reaching empire, to understand. Her father might not be as successful as Lord Sexpot, but they were cut from the same dough. Arrogant, bossy, and terrifyingly certain.

But right now those certain Kilroy eyes were drilling into her, loaded with compassion. She hated how he made her feel, that potent mix of vulnerable, hopeful, aroused. His chest looked so strong, his shoulders so welcoming, falling away to strong arms that could banish her problems in one fell swoop. Last night, she had wanted a one-way pleasure ride with a modern-era rake. She'd wanted to get so lost she wouldn't know where she ended and he began. Now she wanted to be held and soothed.

This was not good. Not good at all.

He picked up a shopping bag near his feet, one she recognized by the red thread twist on the handles as being from the doggie-bag stash at the restaurant, and pulled out a Tupperware container.

"I come bearing gifts. Gelato."

Did he think she was that easy? Through the container, she spied something creamy shot through with what looked like caramel swirls. Okay, so she was that easy.

"Do you keep a freezer in your trunk for occasions such as this?" she asked.

"No, but I usually scope out the freezers of local restaurants so I can have something sweet on hand. For when I need to impress a girl."

Laughing, she took the bag from him, careful to avoid his skin. "Thanks," she said, and gave her jauntiest swivel away to her front door.

Quickly, he relieved her of the bag. His fingers lingered over hers. "Not so fast."

Freeing her most bored sigh, she aimed for nonchalance, though all the heat in her body was focused on that slight touch. She needed to take control of her emotions and she had the perfect solution. Something she had wanted the moment she'd looked up from her flat-on-her-butt position on the DeLuca kitchen floor and locked eyes with six foot two of rock-hard sin.

"Okay, you can come up. On one condition."

An arrogant smile touched his lips. "What's that, then?"

"Let me photograph you."

He hadn't expected that, which was evidenced by how thoughts chased each other across his face. He looked as though he would have preferred another skillet to the head, and his reticence, if that's what it was, suddenly made him fascinating. Dangerously so.

He's a glazed doughnut, a bundle of empty calories, a walking tabloid, she told her weakening resolve. Think

of the models and actresses—and photographers!—
scattered like human rubble in his wake. She could treat
him like any other subject. Cool, clinical, dispassionate.

"This wouldn't be another ploy to get me naked, now,
would it?" he said, his dancing expression settling for
aloof.

"Sounds like you're worried my camera will hone in
on your imperfections. Or maybe you just don't like photographers?"

His face exploded in a smile, changing him so much
that once more she felt the heady pull of its tractor beam.
Must resist the dazzle.

"Go ahead," he said. "Do your worst."

CHAPTER ELEVEN

They were supposed to be sharing a bowl of gelato, pressing thighs together, accidentally brushing fingers, while Jack wore her down and got her to agree to a date. That had been the plan, anyway.

So why was he now standing in her tiny living room, as skittish as a lobster within kissing distance of a stockpot? It was only a bloody photo. Shoots for magazines and show publicity never failed to bore him, but they didn't make him nervous. The thought of Lili pointing her lens at him made him sweaty-palms, pulse-pounding nervous. As if she needed another weapon to get past his rickety defenses.

The weapon in question, a complicated-looking piece of equipment, lay on a scarred mahogany credenza, exuding menace. Reminding him that he was here because he made a promising subject for her art. An arrangement of facial features that conformed to someone's standard of handsomeness.

He didn't want to be a pretty face in her viewfinder; he needed her to see past his image and understand that putting up with a few nasty comments was worth it. That he was worth it.

While she puttered in the kitchen, he perched on the edge of the plush, well-worn sofa, his body taut as bamboo, and cracked his knuckles. The room was chockablock with funky art pieces. An industrialized bronze angel loomed in the corner with metal fan blades for wings. To its right, some weird shit that looked like carpet remainders and shellacked eggshells left Jack floundering for adjectives. On the opposite wall, a photo collage sprawled like a half-finished jigsaw puzzle. He recognized Lili's cousins and servers from DeLuca's, all beaming and at ease. Not a single photo of Lili, which didn't bode well for their future in the public eye.

She appeared at his side and handed him a bowl of gelato, the spoon standing to attention in the center like a…Shit, he really needed to get laid.

"That's cool," he said, nodding at the collage. He suspected it was all cool, but he didn't feel qualified to discuss the more abstract works. "Why aren't there any pictures of you?"

"I prefer to stay behind the camera."

His follow-up query died on his lips as her low moan transmitted right to the receiver in his boxer briefs.

"Sweet baby Jesus, is this goat cheese?" she asked.

He nodded. More specifically, goat cheese gelato with caramel. The result was tangy like cheesecake; it needed the sweetness of the caramel to even it out.

"I've never tasted anything like it." She plunked down

on the sofa as if her legs might buckle any second. Her thigh brushed his. Excellent.

Her eyes crinkled in a smile as she licked the spoon, and that made his heart flutter right there. Cooking was about crafting an experience, bringing pleasure, creating emotion. Cooking for Lili, cooking *with* Lili, had given him more joy than anything in recent memory. Jack rarely cooked in his restaurants anymore, and it had been a long time since he'd witnessed such genuine reactions to his food. Cooking show guests didn't count.

I'm no longer a chef. I just play one on TV.

Her tongue skated a slow slide across her bottom lip and her shoulders danced a shiver before she put the bowl on the coffee table. She leaned over to the credenza behind her and picked up her camera.

"Ready for your close-up?" she asked, turning her sharp gaze on him. All business.

"Let's do it."

She started out slow with mid-distance shots like she was warming up the camera or maybe her artist's eye. Jack watched in fascination as she stepped outside the woman he had been getting to know and transformed into another person. Focused, absorbed, all her concentration on the task.

"Should I be doing something special?" he asked after a couple of minutes of silence, punctuated by hushed clicks and her soft step as she moved around seeking out new angles.

"Just relax."

Relax. He rubbed his damp hands against his jeans and flexed his fingers. After a few more torturous minutes, she slid in beside him and pressed some buttons on the screen, grimacing as she scrolled through the images.

"Am I a difficult subject?"

"No." She squinted at him, then back at the screen. "You're coming off as a bit tense. Is something wrong?"

"I'm just tired. Some harpy kept waking me up every five minutes last night and I didn't get a wink of sleep."

"Next time I'll let you fall into that coma."

He smiled. "Could we talk while you work or would that upset your focus?"

"Oh, sure." With a quick breath, she raised her camera again and restarted the assault. "How's your new restaurant coming along?"

"Good. Most of the basic construction is complete. I'm hoping to get started on design in a couple of weeks after I get back from London and the next shoot in New Orleans." The excitement of launching a new venture sent a surge through his blood. It had been two years since he'd opened his place in Miami and he longed to bury himself under that weight again.

"The life of the jet-setting chef. Sounds glamorous," she said with that same teasing disdain she used when talking about his sought-after sperm. An image of slowly throttling Cara flitted agreeably through his brain.

"It's not so glamorous. There are media junkets and parties but it's more business than pleasure. I spend most of my time traveling to a show shoot or checking up on my restaurants."

"But it has its compensations, right? The places you go, the people you meet, all that hobnobbing with the rich and famous."

Still with the attitude, but he couldn't deny his enjoyment when he'd got his first taste of that scene. The parties, the people, the adulation. Hanging on the arm of a beautiful, successful woman. It had been quite the head rush, until his career started to overshadow Ashley's and her tantrums increased in direct proportion to the interest of entertainment reporters in the Jack Kilroy brand. Thinking on it now filled him with embarrassment at his embrace of that phony world.

"Sure, but it gets old. To be honest, I'd prefer to be in my restaurant cooking."

Lowering her camera, she regarded him speculatively. "Did you cook for Ashley?"

Promising, promising.

"Not when we were together." As if that would have ever happened. "Ashley came into my place in New York once before I knew her. Someone told me she took two bites, said it was divine, and that she couldn't possibly manage another morsel."

"Oh, how dare she? So you got your revenge by dating her and pushing her into that swimming pool."

"Don't believe everything you read."

"Hmm," she hummed, back behind her camera. "That didn't happen? Ashley was very vocal on the subject in all those interviews after you broke up. And then all the details about how insatiable you were in the bedroom. Don't disappoint me and tell me that wasn't true."

He deep-sixed his irritation. "Ashley was bombed and standing too close to the edge. Do you really think I would do something like that?"

Her camera mask never moved and the futility of persuading her otherwise sat like a jagged boulder in his belly. So much for thinking the photographer-subject experience might be conducive to intimacy. Instead, he got this alien feeling of being invaded and probed and found wanting.

Minutes later, the siege ended. They checked the photos together, arm against arm, skin blistering skin. She had captured his variable moods—wariness at first, then reluctant acceptance, before the big finish with him taut as an arrow. Almost reverently, her fingers traced the images on the small playback screen. He knew better than to take it personally.

"But you definitely hit that photographer. It was all over the news," she said, picking up where her internal checklist of his crimes had left off. Determination to prove he was a blot on society was etched in the grim set of her mouth. "I'm sure your date appreciated the macho defense, though."

Every cell in his body ignited into rage, though he was unsure if it was because of what happened that night four months ago or because of the casual way she tossed out her conclusion. Anger clogged his throat, stifling any effort to speak.

He knew what she was doing. She wanted him. He'd seen it when they cooked together. He'd seen it in how her lust-stoked gaze raked him, lingering like a kiss on his mouth. How that body-made-for-pleasure beveled his way when she talked about her father's disapproval. The DeLuca family rock needed to be touched and ravished and held, and she needed someone to tell her that she didn't have to do it all on her own. And evidently, that someone wouldn't be him.

She'd decided to create a wall for her own protection, a wall that bruised when he banged up against it. If she couldn't fight him off with logic, she'd construct her own truth to push him away. He was a fame whore, a star fucker, a juicy cut of tabloid meat. Placing him into these shallow categories was a hell of a lot easier than trying to see what lay beneath.

"You don't think much of me, do you?" Draping it in the casual wrap she was so expert in weaving didn't work; it still came out bitter. He picked up the bowls and marched into the kitchen, defeat and need cramping his chest.

Maybe she was right. Maybe Jack Kilroy, superstar chef, was as deep as it got.

* * *

"Jack," she called out softly as she followed him into the kitchen. Mountain-strong, he stood, those broad shoulders she had longed to sink into an hour ago immobile with anger. Was this what she wanted? To poke him with her camera and harsh tongue until satisfied that he was less than the man she knew him to be?

"Not that it's any of your business," he said to the countertop, decked out with her nonna's vibrant cookie jars, "but I was having dinner with my sister in London and this photographer prick got up in her face as we left the restaurant. I politely asked him to stop and he didn't."

Oh God, his sister? A vague memory of some shaky cell phone footage filtered through her haze of shame. A lissome blonde being pushed around while Jack shielded her from a vampire's prying lens. Capturing his first date post-Ashley had been quite a tabloid coup, and Lili recalled that furtive, vicarious thrill she had felt because of Cara's new connection to him. She even joked with Gina about Cara needing hazard insurance if she was ever seen in public with her hotheaded boss.

But the devil was in the details, and the details had been lost in the aftermath of yet another tawdry example of celebrity versus paparazzo. Just one more round in the ever-escalating appetite for intrusion into lives over which the public feels some measure of ownership. Here she was, as bad as those bloodsuckers. No, worse, because she had seen it from the other side. She had been called horrible names, insulted to the point of tears, and she still thought it fine and dandy to look down her nose at him. All because she was afraid of how off-kilter she felt in his dizzying presence.

"They never said it was your sister. I didn't realize." Every word felt like a mouthful of cement, dragging her under like a cement-weighted body.

"No, you didn't." He spun about to face her. "To people like you, I'm just a collection of sound bites and video grabs and prurient headlines, all grist to the celebrity industrial complex. Admit it, you assumed I'd sleep with you because apparently I'll shag anything that's not pinned down. You can't even fathom the idea of dating me because I'm not a real person to you. I'm just a player on your fantasy-fuck list."

That's exactly what she had thought. It was easier to label him a pretty boy charmer who had his uses but wouldn't be around for the long haul. The luxury model you take for a test drive before you settle for the Honda Civic. Easier, but wrong.

"Jack, I'm so sorry. I did make an assumption about you."

"Doesn't matter," he said gruffly. Showing no surprise

at her apology, his face descended to a blank slate. Usually he wore his emotions freely, and the new look didn't suit him.

"It does matter," she insisted, to probably deaf ears. "I have this tendency to get smart when I'm nervous. I'm not used to this—"

"Used to what? Seeing beyond the surface?" He coughed out a caustic laugh. "I imagine that must be problematic for an artist."

If he had slapped her, it wouldn't have hurt as much. Since finding her home behind the camera, she had used it as both her sword and her shield. In the space between her lens and her subject, she was untouchable. Unbreakable. Ancient slights and cuts vanished into the ether with an open shutter and a definitive click. Framing people in her viewfinder allowed her to box them up, all neat and tidy.

But the flat, shiny planes and darkened contours of her work were two-dimensional, and not much else. Art was neither neat nor tidy; it was messy and deep and, most of all, human. Tonight there had been a brief moment when she held him captive in her lens and saw something beautifully honest in his fatigue. *I have it*, she thought, but a click of her Leica later, the moment was gone. Never good enough.

"I need to go," he said, rough and deep.

Her throat had closed up, but she believed she nodded.

He stared at her with those unfathomable eyes, the exact color of which she could never accurately apprehend with her camera. "Lili, I have to leave."

She gulped down her regret and curled her hands into fists at her sides to stop the imminent shake. "I know," then when he still watched in harsh silence, she offered a more resolute, "Just go."

He didn't budge. He just stood in her cramped kitchen, eyes judging, taunting her with his vitality. Reminding her of everything she couldn't have. Through his tee, she imagined she saw his heart as it pumped his life force to all the pulse points of his body.

"This is just too frustrating for me," he said, his voice barely above a whisper.

Her breath stopped, momentarily shutting down her lungs. She could not have heard that right. It was like he was continuing a conversation in his head and her words had made no impact. By now, he should have been halfway to his hotel, but he chose to stand in her kitchen telling her...

"Frustrating for you?"

"I'm in physical pain here," he said, his voice strained.

"*You're* in pain?"

This is what he had turned her into, a simpleton who parroted ridiculous male declarations. At what point in the history of gender relations had women decided that flipping a guy's statements into questions was a valid argument strategy?

He looked to the ceiling and appeared to be marshaling his strength. "Lili..."

She had given him an out. She had treated him shabbily and had her apology grudgingly accepted. But *he* had started this thing between them with every hot look he blasted her way since stumbling out of her fridge. Last night, she had offered herself on a silver platter, and her reward was a one-way ticket to Foolsville and the public scorn of his fan club. Tonight he had shown up at her door with his goat cheese caramel gelato and his fucking tractor-beam smile, continuing his mission to plow soul-deep ruts in her mind. And now he had the gall to tell her he was frustrated?

An anger bomb exploded in her chest, hurling bitter shrapnel to every nerve ending. "Jack Kilroy, you do not have a monopoly on frustration. I'm frustrated, too."

More of the gimme-patience look. "Sweetheart, it's different for a man."

"Are you saying it's worse for a man?" she demanded in a tone that said he'd better not be saying that.

The man smirked. Smirked! "Yes, I am. It's much worse."

"That's bullshit. You're prancing around, kissing me"—she jabbed him in the chest, gratified when his eyes flew wide and dark—"teasing me, and I'm not supposed to be affected by that. My whole body is aching."

Oh, dear. *Inside thoughts, Lili.*

"Aching?" he asked, a bourbon-laced rasp.

Squeezing her eyes shut, she tried to will away her admission, but she would have more success stopping her heart from beating. She couldn't stand the thought of him leaving without a kind word or a soft touch. Just a whisper of his hand to ease the pain, a light abrading to return her to sanity. That's all she needed; then he could go on his way.

"Tell me," he urged. "Tell me where it hurts."

In for a dime . . . Brazen hussy that she was, she opened her eyes and pulled his hand to her sensitive breast. Sexual awareness tinged then bloomed into full-scale knowledge as a branding heat rocked her. In that same moment, she realized her error.

One touch could never be enough.

CHAPTER TWELVE

He should have been out the door, on his way to a bottle of scotch and a good night's sleep. Should have walked the minute he realized this whole night was one gelato scoop short of a catastrophe.

Getting angry with her, watching her grovel had felt so...shitty. He hated seeing her upset, pouting those bee-stung lips above that stubborn chin, her big eyes, wide and glazed with hurt. More than that, he hated being at the root of it.

As for the killer bod, vibrating with sex and need? Didn't hate that so much.

And the soft breast cradled in his hand? No hatin' here.

You know how it goes. One minute you're whining about how rough it is because you're so bloody famous; the next you're feeling up a beautiful woman in her kitchen. After the initial shock of finding his hand exactly where it needed to be, millions of years of evolution kicked in. He had a gorgeous woman's breast beneath his fingertips—even better, she had put his hand there—so he'd damn well better know what to do with it.

He let her weight fill his palm and when that wasn't enough, he massaged through the thin layers of blouse and bra, insanely happy when his touch turned her nipple into a pebble of hard candy. She arched and thrust against his hand.

"Please, Jack." Her eyelids fell to half-mast, her breathing turned shallow.

His fingers felt thick as they fumbled with the buttons of her blouse, desperate to get it off so he could get her off. Damn things fought him like an obstacle course but he overcame. *Veni, vidi, vici.* He didn't even have to help her out of her top. A slight shrug of those sexy shoulders sent it drifting to the floor, and now she presented herself for inspection, her breasts barely cupped and spilling out of sky-blue lace.

Fucking beautiful.

He slid her bra strap off her shoulder and slipped his palm under the scalloped edge of one of the cups, releasing one breast, then the other. A quick flick of his fingers and her bra met the same fate as her blouse. She was as spectacular as he'd expected, times infinity.

His fingertips returned to one dusky, puckered nipple. His other hand encircled her waist and pushed her back against the kitchen table. "Better?"

She parted her lips, but nothing came out, and somehow that was sexier than if she'd spoken. His pulse beat an insistent tattoo. *Touch, feel, taste. Repeat.* On the table sat the remains of the gelato, now softened to a semi-frozen soup. He placed the flat side of the spoon against her breast and watched as rivulets of dairy dripped, catching in beads of sweetness on her lovely peak.

"Oh," she said as he traced circles around her ruched nipple, captivated by how her breasts heaved with every sinuous slide of the stainless steel. Her breaths came in short tugs.

"Too cold?" he asked gently. Her fingers splayed at the nape of his neck and she jutted her breasts toward his waiting mouth. Her eyes widened by slow degrees and pleaded with him to give her what she needed. What they both needed.

He licked her breast, a long, lazy ice-cream-cone lick, and vaguely registered her soft gasp followed by a heartfelt moan. The gelato tasted great. She tasted better.

The clatter of the spoon hitting the floor set off a vibration in his marrow, and deep-seated hunger skyrocketed inside him. He plumped her breast with his hand and took it in his mouth. He licked, sucked, and owned one hard peak, then switched to the other. Gotta play fair. Her taste, along with every one of her moans, traveled a direct route to his thrumming erection.

Panting, he traced his tongue along the soft hollow of her throat. "Where else does it hurt?"

She grasped his hand and pressed it between her legs, over her skirt. He pushed the heel flat and her legs parted, the warmth of her sex pulsing through the fabric. Not enough. He needed skin. He bunched her skirt up and, slow as cold honey, glided his hand along her thigh.

"Please," she moaned.

"I know, love. I'm going to take care of you." As he stroked over her undies, they dampened under his touch.

He slipped a finger past the edge and a strange sound that had caught in his throat croaked out.

Christ, she was so wet.

The urge to be inside her, to feel her muscles grasping and milking him, almost undid him but he tamped that down. This wasn't about his needs. He had little to offer her beyond his smile and his clever hands, but he could give her this even when he wanted so much more.

"Lili, you are the hottest thing I've ever seen," he murmured against her lips, wishing desperately that it was a lie. He wished there'd been past lovers who got his engine running like this, other potential bedmates he could anticipate with pleasure.

He wished it wasn't her because it felt like he'd already lost.

* * *

Lili loved Jack's hands. How their coarseness rasped her nipples. How their calluses imprinted against the soft skin of her thighs. And how those rough-cast fingers were causing a well of liquid trouble in her panties. With just a couple of delicious strokes, the pulse between her legs had boosted from dull to knife-sharp. She wondered if there was anything those talented hands couldn't do.

Her eyelids felt heavy and she fought to keep them open. Holding on to his penetrating gaze was as sexy as what he was doing down below. She had never experienced that kind of intensity in a man. He burned her alive with every look.

"Jack," she whispered, shifting her weight to allow him access. She needed the full Jack experience, which meant her underwear had to go. *Please say I didn't wear one of my granny pairs.* Through eyes blurred with desire, she caught a glimpse of her lace-trimmed hipster as Jack pulled it down past her knees, and she kicked them off. Not her sexiest pair, but phew.

He pushed her skirt up around her hips, giving them both a front-row view. *Yes.* Battling to focus, she watched as he coiled a finger in her curls, soaked with anticipation. He ran a solitary finger through her slick heat. Just one, a tease to let her know he was in control, that he had her pleasure in the palm of his hand. A shudder of pure bliss coursed through her, then more fingers, rubbing and caressing. She moaned, deep and primal, because she had lost all self-restraint and it was pointless to pretend otherwise.

"Yes, yes. So good." It was about to get more so. He slipped a finger inside her and hooked it, honing in on her spot. A wave of lust slammed her. After a minute of searing heat, he pressed another finger and slid it in, stretching her exquisitely tight. And yes, two fingers were most definitely better than one. His thumb feathered her clit. It felt so right, his fingers sliding in and out of her, his thumb creating delicious friction, his dark eyes wide and watching her like he was afraid of missing something. And watching him watch her was the biggest turn-on of all.

Until he started in on the French.

She didn't need to understand it to know he was telling her things he might never say in English. Maybe they were romantic. She hoped they were filthy.

With every motion, with every secret word he whispered, her skin tightened. Blood rushed from her head to below her waist. Spirals wound down her belly. She screamed his name, begging him to finish her, but he drew it out, slowing and teasing, stopping short of that peak she was so desperate to reach.

She dug her nails into his tattooed bicep, desperate to make her mark as indelible as the ink on his skin. He wouldn't forget her. Still, he taunted her with those slow fingers. Slow, slow, so damn slow. Fisting his hair, she yanked it hard and was rewarded with a grunt, but no upping his pace. The bastard's mouth found hers again, hot and demanding, stealing her breath. A blast of sugar and summer heat that sparked her ecstasy and ignited her frustration into fury.

So she bit him.

He didn't make a sound, but his mouth, the bottom lip pink and slightly swollen, curved into a carnal grin. He liked it. Oh God, he did, and she liked that he liked it.

Her hips thrust forward in blatant appeal and everything slowed and then sped up again. So close. He withdrew his fingers and applied them where she needed it most, sliding through her wetness, stroking her harder and faster. Her blood pounded and surged, sending her lurching out of control. Jack's devil smile widened. A smile made for her. A smile that made her come so hard, she kicked his shin. He yelped.

Good.

Despite the violent conclusion, his hand cupped her gently, absorbing her shivery shudders, shocking her with his tenderness. Hot tears sprang unbidden, and she buried her face in the warmth of his shoulder, trying to hide her churning emotions. He kissed her hair. He held her tight. He gave her the time she needed to descend.

The tide of their breathing rocked in a rhythmic whisper, just the two of them distilled to this single moment. She couldn't remember the last time an orgasm had been that explosive. Probably never, but she preferred the illusion that it had been so good it had messed with her recall. The alternative—that the memory of every man before him had crumbled to dust—was just too much to comprehend.

Eventually he raised her chin with his finger and dropped a kiss on her nose. "I know it's been a rough day, love."

In his voice, she heard compassion she didn't deserve and kindness she had never received from any other man. Jack Kilroy might have just performed a miracle for her physical well-being, but he was big, bad, and dangerous for her mental state.

"I'm not used to being the center of attention," she said. "It doesn't sit so well with me."

A flicker of something hard gave way to a smile that would make the angels sing. "Well, since about three a.m. yesterday, you've been the center of my attention. And I intend to keep you right where I can see you."

Her heart lifted clear through the roof, and she couldn't let such a lovely declaration go unrewarded. Her lips brushed against the hard planes of his face, taking momentary rest stops on those rock-hewn cheekbones. Twelve freckles—no, thirteen—lay scattered like a starry constellation across his nose. She wanted to memorize every beautiful smudge and contour because, after tonight, she would only have souvenir snapshots. Minutes passed while they slanted to find the best angles, exploring earlobes and eyelids, necks and jaws, and each time their mouths crossed paths, they whimpered in surprise that a kiss could improve with practice.

She combed through his silken hair until she found the ridge of his welt. "How's your head?"

"Muddled."

She traced a finger along his swollen lip. "And this?"

He smiled. "That was hot but in the future, we'll have to negotiate the rough stuff. I can't risk anything happening to my face. It's my ticket to fame and fortune."

"Bighead," she said gently, and kissed him to stop any more talk about the future.

Moving his hand back under her skirt, he shaped her butt, his calluses brushing fiery tingles across her skin. "I adore this sweet arse of yours."

Arse. Why did that word sound hotter and dirtier than *ass*? It must be down to the lips that formed it, the sonorous bass that spoke it. He squeezed one sweet arse cheek, making her mewl. She loved when a man gave her booty the attention it deserved, though with the kind of women Jack dated, she wouldn't have had him pegged for an ass, or arse, man. For some reason, that made her giggle.

"What's so funny?" It came out garbled because his hot mouth was sucking on the pulse at her throat, but she got the gist.

"I'm not exactly your type," she murmured in his ear.

"This should be good. Tell me what's my type, then."

"Hipless, top-heavy blondes with sticks for legs. That's your usual diet."

"Well, mine eyes have seen the glory of one curvy brunette with a body that won't quit and a mouth made for sin."

She chewed her sinful lower lip and drew back to face him. "So you'll have doubled your options. Just think of all that ethnic skirt you've been missing. Italians, Latinas, Jersey housewives..."

"Not interested. I've got all the ethnic skirt I want right here." His words sent stiffness to her spine. He must have felt it, too, because his brow crimped into lines like a corduroy swatch. "Do you really want me to see someone else? Why are you raining on this?"

Because a little rain now was better than a torrential downpour later. Saddling his hot-as-Hades ass with her was not going to help his brand, and neither would it do a solid for her self-esteem. One kiss had turned her into Celebrity Enemy Number One. A relationship with this guy would put her on every gossip shit list until the end of the decade. Improving the forward momentum of her life precluded detours to her chunky teens; she had come too far to risk a revival of that insecure blob inside her.

She let out a long, shuddering breath and broke out her most reasonable tone. "Jack, you know I can't date you."

Pressing her hands to his hard chest, she pushed him away and slipped to a stand. With trembling fingers, she wrenched on her blouse and grappled with the buttons. They ended up in the wrong holes. Typical.

"Can't or won't?"

She whirled on him in all her disheveled magnificence. "That concussion must have caused brain damage. There's the little matter of your rabid fan base."

"I'd protect you."

"How? Are you going to punch everyone who says something mean about me?"

"No one messes with what's mine."

That, and the accompanying unyielding gaze, turned her legs to swaying reeds. *Mine.* Had one word ever sounded so wrong and so right?

"I'm not yours."

"Not yet."

Sweet bursts of pleasure exploded in her chest at the thought of Jack claiming her like a piece of Victorian-era chattel, but as much as her inner girly-girl loved it, she couldn't allow his outer caveman to distract her from the real problem. The fallout from dating him would set back her recovery, a risk she was unwilling to take. She dug her nails into her palms to kick-start a return to the twenty-first century. And her very twenty-first century needs.

"I can't date you but I'd still like you to stay." She hoped she didn't sound overly eager to get them back to the business at hand, specifically her need to be tuned up by a guy who knew his way around a woman's body without having to program a GPS. Waking up with those beefy arms wrapped around her was secondary. It was on the list, too, but farther down, after orgasms and foot rubs.

He struck a challenging pose, real cock-of-the-walk stuff. They stood facing each other, the tension delicious and strung between them on a wire. Determined to hold her ground, she stared, unblinking, until his bright eyes dimmed, and she knew she'd won.

"No," he said quietly.

"What?"

"No," he repeated.

By the time she'd mustered her wits, he was already at the door. "That's it? You're...you're leaving?"

"No, I'm fake leaving." He turned, his face a mix of

disbelief and frustration. *Right there with ya, bud.* "I told you I don't do one-night stands."

"I've seen you with women in magazines and on TV since Ashley." He had told her about his sex drought, but it was hard to reconcile that with the parade of beautiful women he escorted to premiere parties and glittering galas. Of course, she was nothing like those women. Her gaze fell to her underwear, mocking her on the tile floor. Turned down twice by the same guy in less than twenty-four hours... A horrible thought poked at her.

"Was this some pity-the-big-girl thing?"

Uh-oh. Colossal mistake.

He marched over, his expression so stormy that the room skewed and she backed up against the edge of the table. Roughly, he grasped her hand and mashed it flat against his hard chest, vibrating with a thunderous beat.

"Don't ever say anything like that again. How can you even doubt my attraction after what just happened here? When all I can think about is burying my body inside you?" Still covering her hand, he dragged it against his rock-hard abs and finally, his erection. She gasped. He was firm and hot beneath her palm. He was huge. "Feel that? I'm so fucking hard for you that it hurts, but I'll suffer because I don't want to be with a woman who doesn't want to be with me. And I mean really be with me. Not just in my bed."

Her mind flailed as his words thunked against her skull, their mix of certainty and entreaty shaking her to the core. *Really be with me.* He wanted someone to see him for who he was, not Jack Kilroy the icon, just Jack, the regular guy in her kitchen. Tonight he'd offered a glimpse of his soul, and though she was drawn to him like no other man, there was no escaping the fact he was indeed like no other man.

He released her and stepped back out of her greedy reach. She hugged herself and tried to hold on to his heat in her still-tingling hand.

"Yes, there have been women since Ashley but I haven't slept with anyone. I'm tired of using and being used. The disrespect. This last year has been…" He paused and scrubbed a hand through his hair, leaving it adorably mussed.

"It's been what?" What she saw in his face devastated her.

"Forget it."

"You mean with Ashley and all the interviews?"

"That, my sister, my father—" He shook his head as if he had remembered who he was talking to. The woman who was only interested in getting a dirty thrill. The woman who didn't merit his confidences.

"Lili, I don't know you very well but you're clearly not ready for this. Maybe this Twitter crap is too hot to handle or since your mother's illness, you can't even recognize what you want anymore." He gave another head shake, sadder now. "I thought there was something here, but I was mistaken."

Her heart splintered at his words. He was tired of her excuses and she couldn't blame him. She deserved his contempt.

Dazed, she followed him to the door, her limbs as leaden as sacks of flour, numbness stealing across her body. What was wrong with her? She got her earthshattering orgasm and she didn't even have to touch his penis. Not officially. For a lot of girls, that was a win-win.

Damn, but she wanted to touch his penis.

She wanted to give him what he'd given her. A little joy, some shared comfort, because he needed it as much as she did. And yes, she was selfish and wanted more. She didn't know what exactly, she just knew she wanted.

He already had one foot on the stair to the street. In two more seconds, he would be gone from her life. Steeling her spine, she swallowed and spoke to his departing back.

"I was the fat chick."

He halted, a wall of stock-still strength, and her breath trapped in her chest. That checked breath gushed out when he turned to reveal an inflexible expression.

She heard the anger in his breathing before he spoke. "I won't stand for you putting yourself down like that."

Rubbing her collarbone as if it could grant her three wishes, she reached back to the most painful period of her life. "No...no, I don't mean now. I mean then. Past tense. In high school, I was *that* girl, the fat girl, the one people laughed at. Body by Tortellini. I was bullied every day because of how I looked and was made to feel worthless. It took a couple of years but I eventually shucked the fat suit and put it behind me."

Had she put it behind her? Clearly, not far enough. So what if she had a little junk in the trunk? Her curves were a helluva lot more reliable than any man in keeping her warm at night.

"I've got a big butt and big boobs and I know I don't square up to society's ideals of perfection, but I like it. I like how I look."

In place of the pity and platitudes she expected, she got his raw, consuming stare filled with some unnamed emotion. Annoyance or disgust, perhaps. His eyes, ice-frozen during her speech, watched her with uncompromising focus.

"You're not the only one who likes it." Voice low, heated, he stalked her. Slow and predatory. Pure, unadulterated sex.

She beat a hesitant two-step retreat, but her back met the door frame. "What I'm trying to say is that it was a tough road, but now I'm fine."

"So fine," he murmured as he closed the space between them. Oh Lord.

Passing over his compliment, she also tried to pass over just how small she felt in his potent presence. He was so big. So vital.

"Dating someone like you would leave me exposed to all sorts of hate I don't deserve." Her voice spiked on "exposed" like she had spoken a word she'd only ever seen in print and was unsure of its pronunciation. Under his hard scrutiny, she felt exposed, more so than when he had brought her to scorching release. More so than when she had read the hateful comments of strangers. "I can't go back to feeling like that girl. She's in the past."

The muscles in his jaw tensed. "So because of who I am, we don't have a shot? Who cares what people say? Isn't it enough that I think you're beautiful and sexy?"

This is what she hated about hot guys. That warm and fuzzy feeling she got when one of them anointed her as worthy. Well, she was supposed to get the warm-fuzzies, but right now, she was pissed at herself, at him, and the whole effed-up situation.

"I don't need you to tell me I'm beautiful and sexy," she lied, her throat burning with unshed tears. "I know

I'm beautiful and sexy, and I was doing just fine before you crashed my life party." At his stricken expression, she realized how accusatory her outburst sounded. "I didn't mean that the way it came out."

To the rigid jaw, he added a healthy muscle tick. "You were doing just fine until I showed up and put you in the middle of a media tornado you don't want or need."

Maybe she *had* meant it the way it sounded. Had she been doing fine? Darn tootin'! She'd been chugging along at an even keel, no muss, no fuss, and then Jack Kilroy did a hatchet job on her cozy existence.

He crossed his arms, drawing her gaze to his thick, muscled forearms. Very underrated eye candy, forearms.

"So let me get this straight," he said. "If I hadn't been in that walk-in minding my own business or you hadn't been strolling by that alley at three a.m. wearing a Wonder Woman costume or you hadn't pitched that skillet at my head—"

She opened her mouth and he gave her the hand. The hand!

"—or you hadn't provoked me into kissing you in a public bar with half of Chicago watching or I hadn't spent every moment since I met you imagining you naked"— he paused to take a breath and she matched him—"your life would have been just fine."

She snapped her jaw shut, shocked at how he had reduced the last forty-eight hours to its essence like one of his sauces. But the take-home was clear. She was just as much to blame. In his immediate orbit, she had no control, so the sooner she escaped this magnetic pull he had over her, the sooner she could get back to her just-fine life.

"Yes, it would have been, and once you leave—" She turned up a shaky palm in query.

"Day after tomorrow."

So soon? A burning, tight band of steel wrapped around her chest. Somewhere along the pause, he had moved in, putting oxygen at a premium. Butterflies took flight in her belly. "Day after tomorrow, I'll be fine again."

"Fine," he said, his face now so close she could lick her lips and simultaneously swipe his hard, angular jaw.

"So fi—"

Before she could finish, his mouth fitted over hers. It was that easy. Her eyes shuttered on his kiss and in no time at all, his sweet assault became more sure. He followed her Twitter rep's advice and played glorious grab-ass with her notorious booty. Oh, she loved how he made her feel. So beautiful, so sexy, but also special. His intimate taste enveloped her until it was only him and her heart, now beating wildly.

Stay, she urged with her tongue as she mapped his mouth. *I'll be anything you want, everything I can.* Her fingers licked the nape of his neck and they both shivered. *Hold me,* she spoke with her hands. *I want to wake up to your warm laugh tickling my ear.* The kiss deepened and curled inside her, finding private and untouched places. *Love me,* she thought as her breath mingled with his. *I don't want to be alone tonight.*

Knowing her pleas would go unheard, she took from it everything she needed to tide her over for the long night ahead. At last, he released her with a soft "damn," and they retreated to scant inches apart, a little dazed, a lot dissatisfied.

Neither of them moved for several seconds.

Then the edge of his mouth lifted in...was that cockiness? "Now, don't you think the finer things in life are worth fighting for, sweetheart?"

He wasn't giving up! This tenacious, infuriating, beautiful man wasn't giving up, but there was no missing the underlying dare in his tone. If she wanted this, she had to woman up.

Like a sleepwalker, she shuffled back and shut the door. Through the spy hole, she watched him linger, his expression half swallowed by the shadow in the dimly lit hallway. She knew he was smiling because she was smiling, and if any kiss deserved a joyful reaction, it was that one.

It didn't last. Well, it couldn't, could it? Smile vanishing, she sank to the floor, her body a spineless mess, her stomach knotted so tight it hurt. The challenge had been thrown down; the choice was a minefield. She could get what she wanted and lose him, or give him what he wanted and lose her heart. Either way, it was going to be wonderful.

And then it was going to suck.

CHAPTER THIRTEEN

It's *me-ee*."

Through the intercom, Cara sounded more shrill than usual, or maybe it was just the indecent hour that made her voice resemble a velociraptor giving birth. She breezed in. Eyes bright and perfectly lined. Check. Killer gams tapering to four-inch Manolos. Check. Blond chignon à la Grace Kelly. Check.

Chilled, chocolaty, caffeinated beverage, which she handed off to a grateful Lili.

After making a five-course meal out of surveying Lili's apartment, with its mismatched thrift-shop furniture and cluttered art arrangements, she delivered a love-what-you've-done-with-the-place simper. They settled in at the kitchen table, last night's scene of the crime. Lili suppressed a yawn. Her sleep had been restless, her dreams steamy and all Jack.

"So, how famous are you today?" Cara asked.

Lili was beginning to think she had some sort of self-obsession disorder. Wake up. Shower. Google herself. How did famous people ever get anything done when there was so much being said about them online?

"Shona Love, the entertainment reporter for Channel Five, wants to interview me."

Cara frowned. "Probably not a good idea. If she calls again, direct her to me. Let's keep this about the show. Anything else?"

Lili sighed heavily. "My Twitter stand-in, FatChicks-Ass, says it hears beeping every time it backs up. But on the plus side, I'm getting plenty of offers on the Facebook fan page Gina created."

Cara's lovely pout stretched to a grimace. "Do I want to know?"

"Apparently I have a great future in carnie-themed pornos. Fat ladies and Siamese twins."

"Is that even a thing?"

Lili sighed. "Jack says I shouldn't read it."

"Well, he's right." Cara giggled, all sugary wickedness, and leaned in, ready for confidences. "Now spill. I want to hear every smutty detail. Is he as good as he looks?"

"I wouldn't know."

Cara's mouth dropped open in a most unbecoming way, which pleased Lili much more than it should have. Ah, the little things.

"Shut. Up. What about all that malarkey in the hotel?"

"He was just kidding around. We never did anything."

Her sister pursed her lips like a prim schoolteacher, contemplating this revelation. "Did you try to be funny? Guys don't like girls who are too funny."

"Oh, he found my seduction attempts to be the height of hilarity."

Cara had a multitude of rules for dating—don't make stupid jokes, never pay for a meal or finish said meal, and don't put out for anyone who makes less than $500K a year—which probably accounted for the fact that her love life was about as successful as Lili's.

Her sister huffed out a disapproving gust of air and eyed Lili's hair as if it were the culprit. "The girls are going to the salon to get all gussied up before the show. Maybe you should go. Gina wants to get vajazzled."

A mouthful of coffee trickled into Lili's lungs, and she spluttered to recover. "You'd better not let her. She'll need to show everybody, and your cameraman will have to gouge his poor eyes out."

"Oh, nothing throws Jerry. But I won't have time to babysit them with all the prep I have to do. The production crew is already downstairs, I've got the menus to finish, and I have a million other things to sort out."

"I can take care of the girls. Just tell me what else you need." Lili's stomach growled and her mind replied, *Leftovers.* Veal parm for breakfast might not be acceptable in other cultures, but it was more than acceptable in the DeLucas'. "Is Jack at the restaurant yet?" she asked oh-so-casually.

"He went to the meat supplier with Dad. Speaking of Il Duce . . ."

"What about him?"

Lili could see Cara picking her words carefully. "He seems even more dictatorial than usual, if that's possible. I don't know why you put up with it."

So you don't have to. "He's worried about the restaurant."

"Is it really so bad?"

"It's not good. I mean, the show should help and all the current drama is good for reservations, but that can't last."

"Could we borrow money?"

Lili smiled at the cozy use of *we*. Nice to know Cara wanted to include herself in the family's crisis. At least this one.

"No go. We remortgaged the house three years ago, but we're still losing hand over fist. That's not the solution, anyway. We need to make changes, redesign the menu, appeal to a more diverse customer base." Lili stood and wrenched open the fridge door. A solitary fat-free yogurt cut a lonely figure on the bottom shelf. "Dad's clinging to a way of doing business that died out with Betamax. Cooking for the same few customers who show up like clockwork once a month. He thinks if we change anything, we'll lose them."

"Well, business was never his forte, Lili. Food's his religion. When we were growing up, it sometimes felt like he was chef first, father second."

Startled, Lili turned back to her sister. That was a curious way to put it together. "Food's important to him. Like any chef."

Cara shrugged. "Remember when Dad was worried about something, we would wake up to find the kitchen full of meals he'd worked on all night? Lasagna and chicken cacciatore as far as the eye could see. You know how he is—cooking is his touchstone; the kitchen is his cathedral...Hey, I need to write that shit down. That's going to sound great in publicity for Jack's new show." She extracted her phone from a slouchy red hobo and started tapping.

Lili had completely forgotten about Tony's all-nighters when he was upset. That cooking allowed him some measure of power over a life that had spun out of control when Mom became ill made a strange kind of sense. She'd always thought she could read him, but Cara's keen insight surprised her. Didn't sit so well, either.

"And he's worried about Mom," Lili continued, getting back to familiar territory. "Her checkup is next week." Three months cancer free if everything went well. Cara probably had a gift basket ready for distribution.

"About Mom." Cara's voice wavered as she placed her phone down on the table. "I know I suck."

Oh hell. Lili squeezed her sister's shoulder, immediately feeling guilty about the snide thoughts twisting her brain. She never used to be this bitter. Envious that Cara had got away, but not bitter. "Cara, it's okay."

"No, it's not. When Mom first got sick, it was tough, but when she started the treatments, it near killed me. I know I haven't been there for you, but I just can't handle seeing her like that. All skin and bone. No hair. It's incredibly selfish, but...I don't know how to explain it." Cara's voice hitched high in her throat.

Hearing Cara describing her reaction slammed Lili's heart to the back of her rib cage. It also felt like she wasn't getting the whole story. "Why didn't you talk to me about it?"

"I don't know. Every time we spoke on the phone, I could feel this judgment coming off you in waves. Or maybe it was my terrible phone service. Freaking AT&T." She laughed, but it got snagged on a sniffle. "And I didn't know what to say when you were doing all the work."

Recognition welled up in her throat as Cara's words

fisted Lili's heart. Maybe she'd been enjoying the view from up on her high horse a little too much. And not just with her sister.

Cara's eyes met Lili's, so blue and stunning. "Sis, you've always been the strong one. When we were little, nothing fazed you. Remember when you broke your leg after you climbed into that tree because Tad dared you?"

"I couldn't do anything for weeks. Worst summer ever." Lili sat again, her hollow stomach forgotten. "And you fainted." Cara had earned as much attention for hitting the deck in a swoon as Lili had for breaking her leg in two places.

"You didn't even cry. You just lay there quietly waiting for Dad to take you to the ER." Cara wagged her finger. "And I fainted because your bone was poking out and it looked like something out of *Alien*." Even now, her sister's face turned chalky at the gruesome memory.

Lili gave what she hoped was a sympathetic smile. "We're just different."

"I know you think I'm a princess."

"Well, you are."

"All right, I am," Cara said, stubborn chin up. "But I still think you're the most beautiful, kick-ass person I know."

Guilt and regret fought for space in Lili's chest as she was reminded of how they used to be friends. She longed for that closeness once more, and making a joke seemed as good a way as any of finding the way back there.

"So, throwing me at your boss was your version of penance?"

"Seemed like a good idea but…" She gave Lili a half-smile, Cara style. "Forget about Jack."

Say what, now? Lili's mouth went slack-jawed, shaken by the brusque declaration.

"I'm beginning to think it's for the best nothing happened. I should never have encouraged it."

"I know he's out of my league."

"That's not it."

Lili readied for the worst. He frequents swinger clubs or his tastes stretch to weird, New York–style kink. Or any style kink. The tabloids had been long on innuendo and short on cold, hard facts.

Cara raised both perfectly plucked eyebrows. "You're not out of his league. He's out of yours."

Oh…say double what, now? "Why would you think that?"

Cara shot Lili through with that know-it-all look she brandished like a weapon, and Lili braced for one of her "here's how it works in the real world" speeches. "Jack's hotter than a jalapeño and he's got charm up the yin yang, but there's no depth there. All he cares about is cooking and fucking. He's good enough for a one-night stand, but don't rely on him for anything long-term. He'll break your heart."

All that time working with Jack, and Cara hadn't learned a single thing. She had bought into his media image just like everyone else. Just like Lili had at first. Within minutes of meeting him, she had smirked her disapproval and called him awful names because she'd thought herself so above him and his trivial existence. She had always considered herself a giving person. An unselfish person. But last night, Jack had given and she had taken, proving herself no different than the vultures who wanted a piece of him.

She liked him better when she thought he was a man whore. She liked herself better. Now she wanted to know more about the man lurking behind that PR-crafted façade. The man who didn't seem all that at ease with his fame.

"After everything you went through in high school, I don't want to see you getting hurt. By Jack or the haters. Just be careful, 'kay?" Cara smiled, putting the unpleasantness behind her.

That's exactly what she would be. Careful. With her heart, and with Jack.

"Now to the important stuff," her sister said, and Lili was ninety-nine percent positive she wasn't talking about food. "What are you wearing for the taping?"

* * *

DeLuca's was bustling, with the production crew going through their paces, setting up what Lili could only assume were harsh, unforgiving lights and boom microphones that picked up every traitorous whisper against the Dark Lord. Off in the direction of the kitchen, Cara's strident voice barked unrecognizable orders. Not quite ready for that level of participation, Lili headed underground before the festivities really got going.

She wasn't avoiding Jack. No, not at all.

DeLuca's wine cellar was more of a basement than a proper cellar, but in the last couple of years, Tad had spent time building it up into something any top-notch dining establishment could be proud of. As Lili descended into the cool cavern, she took in the wall-to-wall racks, the temperature panel that looked like it could program a spaceship, and her cousin, now hunched over as he examined a bottle on the bottom shelf.

"Any chance we have something hidden in here that's worth a fortune?" she asked, not entirely joking.

Tad looked up and gave that lopsided grin he used to great effect on the opposite sex. "If there was a bottle of 1787 Château Lafite knocking around here, I'd be lying on a beach with one of Kilroy's lingerie models instead of trying to decide what wine recs we should have for the taping."

Too much to hope for. She drew a heart inset with a *J* in the dusty film of the nearest bottle, then quickly swiped it clean.

"The show's not going to help much, is it?"

Tad straightened to his full six feet two and rolled his shoulders until his spine cracked. "It won't hurt, but we need a more long-term strategy. Tony cutting the menu would be a start."

Having had this argument with her father over the size of the menu and how stock mountains inevitably led to waste, she knew it was a losing proposition. Dad's kitchen was off-limits and he refused to listen to any suggestions that would interfere with his royal vision.

Tad shrugged in response to her silence. He knew it was a dead end. "But why are we focusing on imminent financial ruin when there's scuttlebutt to be discussed? Saw something *molto interessante* when I was leaving work last night."

Lili felt like a bird was trapped in her chest and she fought to keep her reaction light. "Oh?"

"Do I owe you a solo spin on the Harley?"

"I just took his photograph."

"The old 'come up to my studio to see my negatives' trick? I haven't tried that one since freshman year in college." He laughed. "Even I could see that Cheshire grin of his from forty feet out. He is so warm for your form."

That Jack was still smiling when he hit the street gave her an unreasonable burst of hope. Lili studied the racks taking up the entire west wall of the basement, then looked at her cousin squarely. "I know."

"Why so sad? I thought that's what you wanted."

"He wants to date me." Or he wanted to date her, past tense. "No nookie until I agree."

"Weird strategy to bag chicks, but okay. And that's a problem because...?"

"Have you not been paying attention to what's gone down in the last twenty-four hours? I told him it wasn't happening and he backed off."

Tad snorted his disbelief. "So, you trot out a bunch of excuses and now you're annoyed that he's not down on bended knee still begging for the chance to be your arm candy?"

"No," she said uneasily. Was she annoyed? When had she become that person?

"Women. You have no freaking clue what you want. Kilroy does, though." Tad's lips turned up in a shade of a smile. "I bet I could learn a thing or two from him."

"So I should date him so you can have a bro-mentor?"

"You should date him because he likes you and you like him. Quit overthinking it."

Quit overthinking it. A hot prickle crept up her neck at the thought of how much Jack desired her, and how, unlike Marco, he had no problem showing it. His probing gaze touching every part of her. His dirty (she hoped)

French talk. His large, manual labor hands on her, inside her, setting off fires in places that hadn't seen that kind of heat since the Bronze Age.

Tad regarded her curiously. "I don't even want to know why you've turned that very bright shade of red."

Flustered, she forced her body to calm. She had very good excuses—reasons, dammit!—for not dating Jack Kilroy. If people were already wielding the bitch forks after one hot smooch, a relationship would whip up some sort of fan club bitchery frenzy. Setting herself up for online target practice in the cruel, unwinnable court of public opinion sounded like social suicide. She refused to become that girl again.

"It's not as simple as liking someone. You've heard what people are saying. He's the worst possible person for someone like me."

Tad looked affectionately bored. "Remember when you used to come crying to me because Diana Matteo said your body was sixty percent pasta instead of water?"

She shut her eyes as images of Diana and her cronies squirting packets of ketchup in Lili's hair streamed on the backs of her eyelids. Three years older than her, Tad was closer than a brother and had always been around to pick up the pieces. He knew it hurt then and that it still did.

"What did I tell you to do?"

"Ignore them. And stop taking third helpings of Mom's lasagna."

"Well, perhaps that wasn't the best advice."

"I know, I love lasagna."

"I mean about ignoring them, wiseass." He pulled out his phone. "Look at this."

It was the "Jack's Fat Chick Rules" Facebook page,

and though the name made her cringe, secretly she was thrilled at how her family had rallied around to defend her.

"What about it?"

"It's more popular than the 'I hate' one."

"Okay," she said slowly, trying to rotate her brain to comprehension.

"People are identifying with you, Lili. This page Gina created has almost nineteen thousand fans and it's gaining every hour. Don't shy away from this. You should be embracing how freaking gorgeous you are." He turned on the DeLuca smile that looked ten times better on the males in the family. "Just sayin'. And anyone's better than Marco Rossi."

"You don't like Marco because he's fond of helping himself to your precious..." She waved around the space her ex considered his personal wine supply, much to Tad's chagrin.

"I don't like him because he never treated you the way you deserved. All that crap about how cuddly you were and how he loved having something to hold on to. Asshole." Tad's mouth was set in a grim slash. Always indefatigably good-humored, it was a shock to see him as anything else. Marco's careless "compliments" had wounded, but Lili had always considered them the necessary trade-off in dating a hottie. Now she wondered if she'd been selling herself short all these years.

"He lives thousands of miles away," she said, getting back to Jack.

"Two-hour flight. Phone sex."

She'd be lying if she said it hadn't occurred to her. Dirty weekends in the Big Apple. Delicious phone sex.

And then a scandal when their spicy sexts got hacked—because knowing her luck, that was the most likely outcome.

"He's kind of intense. It's hot and all, but I don't know if I can be what he wants." Jack's need couched as a command still haunted her. *Really be with me.* How could she keep a man that passionate satisfied and, above all, interested? He wanted a woman who could match his appetite and drive, not a sharp-talking mouse.

Tad heaved a long-suffering sigh. "I know what the real problem is."

"Of course you do."

He brushed her forehead with a kiss, and when she wiped it off dramatically, he grinned. It was a thing they did. "Listen to your favorite cousin. I've never steered you wrong. You're afraid."

"Stunning deduction. Absolutely stunning."

"No, listen, not just about this online shit. You have it pretty cozy here. Sure, the business is headed to the crapper and Tony could give Genghis Khan a run for his rubles, but you've got a niche. You took over as mother hen when Frankie became ill. You're the person everyone relies on, and that can be comforting as hell, but it can also be confining. Time to bust out of those chains, babe. Learn to fly."

He flapped his hands like wings, and she slapped them away. Learn to fly, her ass.

First Cara, now Tad. Everyone was an armchair psychologist. "What do you think I was doing in O'Casey's with Jack? I tried to bust out of my comfort zone and take a chance. He made promises"—she flapped her own hands now—"with his eyes! He promised me a one-night stand with all that hot-'n'-heavy smoldering and then he changed the rules. And I'm the one who ends up trending on Twitter." With her comfort zone shattered and no longer showing up on any known maps.

Tad blinked at her outburst. "Jesus, you really need to get laid. So Jack challenges you. Very positive start." He returned to dusting off a couple of bottles of a nice Super Tuscan she was rather partial to and set them on the bottom step.

"You're such an ass," she said, not unkindly. Jack Kilroy liked her and she liked him. It was silly to feel such hope, but strangely easy in this cool, darkened room insulated from the world above her head. But more than hope, she felt one step closer to the person she had dreamed of becoming back in those harrowing days. Cool, poised, forward-thinking Lili. Her blood surged like the first time she picked up a camera and realized there were myriad possibilities.

"Go make him an offer he can't refuse," Tad said with a straight face.

She groaned. "How long have you been waiting to use that one?"

"All my life, babe."

CHAPTER FOURTEEN

Jack was officially in the ninth circle of hell. Not knowing how the original circles of Dante's *Inferno* were actually populated, Jack invented his own occupants. The seventh circle was for guys who hadn't got laid in months. The eighth was for idiots who were sex-starved and had a sizzling woman raring to go but still chose to wait it out in the hopes of getting a date. And the ninth was for the suckers who had the same problems as the ones in the seventh and eighth circles but had to suffer through it all while listening to opera.

Jack loathed opera.

But Tony's kitchen meant Tony's rules, so Pavarotti or whoever the hell was shredding Jack's nerve endings while he prepped his *mise-en-place* would be the musical accompaniment for the day and probably the entire evening. Laurent had muttered something about how it lent a sorely needed gravitas after Jack's seedier exploits.

He was running on a couple of hours of ragged sleep,

his every cell consumed with Lili and his aching need for her. He could still feel her kiss on his mouth, the imprint of her nipples on his tongue, her slick warmth coating his fingers. Holding her last night while she shattered against his hand had been so arousing that even giving it a flickering thought made him hard enough to pound nails.

Calling her out on her bullshit had seemed like such a smart idea until his dramatic exit had been cut short by that disclosure about her high school suffering. His heart hurt that she would ever have to endure that pain. Then it thundered furiously that she would allow it to create this barrier between them. Wasn't it enough that no other woman could hold a candle to her hotness, that he wanted her more than was truly good for him?

Right, because *his* opinion was all that mattered. Bighead.

He had always considered his life becoming public property the necessary saddlebags to his goal of taking his brand to the next level. Any woman in his life would need a thick skin to withstand the barbs of twenty-first-century fame. He couldn't ask Lili to upend her existence for him, and the express train to his next conquest, network television, had already left the station.

Still, even if they had no chance, he wished she could see herself the way he saw her. Funny, loyal, beautiful, sexy. Christ, so sexy. He rubbed his lip, still marked with her passion. When she bit him, he had almost come in his pants for the first time since he was a pizza-faced teen. That's how she made him feel. Like an infatuated teenager with perma-wood.

"What are you smiling about?" Cara's brittle voice arrested his fantasies while her glacial eyes screened him carefully. He needed to stop grinning like a half-wit. It would not do.

"Nothing." He snatched one of the menus she'd brought and scanned for errors. He had decided to open with a bruschetta trio—mini-helpings of three toppings served over his own toasted, rustic bread: tomato-basil-fresh mozz, the braised rabbit stew, and prosciutto and lobster crème fraîche. Working with the contest twist, Tony had chosen a risotto for Jack and gnocchi for his own menu. Not being able to serve pasta had immediately put Jack at a disadvantage—risotto could be tricky—but he had been more concerned about the choice of entrée. If Tony had picked something that needed to be slow-cooked for hours, Jack would have been screwed.

Thankfully, the host chef had gone easy on him with lamb chops, leaving Jack to choose a sauce. Jack had spent the entire morning creating something new, and he was pleased with the outcome, a salsa verde that brought out the meat's flavors to perfection. The finishing touch was another mini trio, this time sweet—a Valrhona chocolate torte, salted caramel gelato, and zabaglione with fresh seasonal berries.

All good, but he'd be hard-pressed to beat last night's feast and the sweet taste of Lili's plump, luscious breasts. He bet she tasted amazing all over.

"Listen, we need to talk," Cara cut in. Hands cupping slender hips, she balanced her slight weight on one precarious heel and eyed him like she'd caught him looking at smutty photos.

"Shoot."

"Just what do you think your end game is?"

His brain stutter-stepped, baffled by her choice of words. "My end game?"

"I was watching you last night at dinner, how you couldn't take your eyes off my sister. I won't have you screwing Lili over. When I suggested she indulge in your services, I never expected you'd get all"—with an arc of her hand, she swiped the air near his face in a threatening manner—"smitten."

"Back up a second," he said, scooting uncomfortably over the "smitten" bit. "When you suggested she indulge in my what?"

She tapped her foot. "Jack, did you, for one second, think my very young, very inexperienced sister would go for you without a little encouragement? She's had a bad year between my mom and Marco and slaving away at this place for my father. I promised her you'd be up for some fun and games." She looked to the ceiling and shook her head in disbelief. "And you couldn't even do that."

Well, he was with her on the disbelief front. In fact, he was more surprised that he was surprised at all. Lili had made it clear from the beginning that she was interested in one thing, and it wasn't what was going on between his ears, but last night, she had shared an important part of herself. Her fragility had blazed through his veins and clamped his heart in a vise.

Shit. Three days in and his heart had entered the equation.

Luckily, he didn't have time to inspect that because Cara was bringing her rant home. "I don't know what you expect to get out of this, but you are not good enough for my sister, Jack."

Cold fury grabbed him by the throat. "But I'm good enough to service her?"

She blanched. "She's not like us, Jack. If you hurt her—"

"Cara, mind your own business." He and his producer had butted heads before, but it had never gotten personal. Hey, it still hadn't. In her eyes, he was a meal ticket, a vessel she could pour her ambitions into, not a real person with, God forbid, feelings. Had it occurred to no one that *he* might be the one at risk of getting his supposedly bulletproof heart stomped flatter than a veal cutlet?

Again with the heart stuff. That needed to stop. Stat.

"You hurt her," Cara repeated, the ice coming through clear, "and I'm going to cut off your *coglioni* and feed them to tree squirrels." With that, she strode out of the kitchen in a tornado of indignation.

What. The. Fuck.

All he wanted was a date. Just a little quality time to get to know this woman. He shook his head, trying to clear the shock. Didn't work.

He needed to forget about loco DeLuca women and nails-on-a-chalkboard arias and get his mind in the game. A run might clear his head. Or whacking said head against the Dumpster in the alley for an hour.

"I'm taking a break," he snapped at Laurent, who had been too busy flirting with one of the scarier big-hairs to notice Cara's flip off the rails. Crashing through the kitchen doors, he bumped into that other infuriating DeLuca. Lili.

He frowned, then frowned harder at the way his heart boosted at the sight of her. "What are you doing here?"

"I work here." She tilted her head, taking in his fierce scowl. "What's wrong?"

"Nothing." Of course she was killing him in hip-hugging jeans and a wispy excuse for a top that barely contained her everything. Killing him.

"Okay," she dragged out. She peeked around his shoulder through the window panel into the kitchen. "Is Cara about?"

"No. I expect she's off shouting at someone and making them feel very, very small."

"I've always wondered what a food television producer does."

He shoved his hands in his pockets for safety and his own sanity. "You sleep okay?"

"Fine. You?"

"Like a baby," he lied.

"Wake up every two hours, wet?"

"How did you know?" That netted him a raspy laugh and went some way to defrosting his chill. It wasn't far from the truth, either.

"Jack, about last night..."

He held his breath. Nothing good ever started with those words.

"I just wanted to say...well, *grazie*."

That was a first and it eased a smile from him. "You liked my gelato?"

"Yeah, you give good gelato," she said, her color rising while her gaze dipped. He loved that. "How's the prep?"

"Menu's set. Your father breezed in for the beauty shots and then took off, so he must be feeling confident."

"Beauty shots?"

"The final dishes, perfectly styled. They cut them in during editing." A thought unfurled in his brain. A brilliant, sparkling thought. "I want to show you something."

"Sounds promising."

"You wish." He took her slender-fingered hand into his. *Zing.* Every bloody time. Her nipples poked through the devilishly thin material of her top, all hard and pouty. And now his dick felt all hard and pouty. Wonderful. "Let's get out of here for a while."

A nose wrinkle preceded a furtive look over her shoulder. "I really should find Cara. I said I'd help."

Farther along the hallway, a door banged open and out thundered Gina, closely followed by a bent-out-of-shape Cara. Both were far too involved in their drama to notice anyone else.

"Cara, I'm not taking it off," Gina said, puffing out her ample chest. It strained against a sparkly pink T-shirt adorned with the words TEAM FAT CHICK.

"You cannot wear it," Cara countered emphatically. "We need to show the restaurant in the most professional light possible. This is too important."

"Oh no," Lili murmured. She took a step forward, with the clear intention of doing what she did best—smooth and fix. His hand tightened around hers and willed her still.

Gina jutted her chin to match her chest. "Oh my God, Cara, you're such a spoilsport. Even when we were kids, you always had to be the queen freaking bee. We just want everyone to know they can't mess with the DeLucas." She flounced off to the front of the house to Cara barking her name.

Taking it as a sign that the gods were finally working in

his favor, Jack nodded toward the kitchen and whispered, "How about the great escape, alley-style?"

Ten minutes later, he parked his rental outside a nondescript building on Fulton Market, the West Loop street that hosted many of Chicago's finest dining establishments, art galleries, and high-end lofts. He'd made sure the car's air-conditioning was on full blast because apparently it wasn't sufficient that he couldn't have her—he needed to torture himself with the sight of those beautiful, erect nipples.

His jeans were not loose enough for this.

Her face lifted as they approached the entrance to the building. "Is this your new place?"

He smiled back, feeling unaccountably proud at her enthusiasm. "Yep. I've got six weeks to get it into shape, but I can do it." The mostly Polish crew was working on the electrics today, and every ripped-up wall was awash in a spaghetti wiring explosion. Lili stepped forward and he body-checked her back into the foyer.

"Best not to go any farther. It's easy to step on something you shouldn't and get hurt."

Smaller than his usual restaurant footprint, the space's eighty-year-old ornate tin ceiling and the warm firehouse brick lent it an intimacy not usually found in a Jack Kilroy outpost. As she peered in, he spent a few minutes pointing out the planned locations of the kitchen and the dining room. It was still unformed but he itched to know what she thought.

"Nice, but what about the food?" Of course his girl would focus on the essentials.

"It'll be new American with country French influences. Lots of small plates, no entrées over fifteen dollars."

"Will you have that chicken liver crostini dish?"

"With the fig marmalade? You liked that?" he asked, knowing damn well that she did but needing the boost only her validation could give.

"Hmm." Her eyes glazed over.

He spoke at length about his ideas, upping the ante with each subsequent dish, and watched carefully for her reaction while trying to control his own. Each description produced a sexy hum of approval or a flash of her tongue that aroused him intolerably. Why did his food sound so much better with her breathy endorsement? Cooking for her, then taking her while he tasted his flavors on her lips was about as good a date as he could imagine.

He snapped back to reality. His real life where dating this woman was no longer an option.

Somewhere along the way, her expression had faded to solemn. "Why do you do it?"

"What? Cook incredible food?"

"TV. The celebrity industrial complex." She stared at him with such intent that his body tightened like he was being grill-pressed against the wall. "You said you'd rather be cooking in your restaurant. That you miss it. Except for all those annoying *quinceañeras*."

The twinge in his belly acknowledged the truth of that. He did miss it but it wasn't as if he could stop moving. Success addiction was about the sweetest feeling, almost as good as sex, and the way his sex life was panning out lately, it was his only reliable high.

"I do it because it's never enough and I'm greedy."

Her tongue darted and licked her lips. Pink, wet, making him hard. He stared, telegraphing exactly how greedy he was.

She didn't back down, just hitched that skeptical eye-brow. "I thought you were going to say you owe it to the masses to share your genius."

"That too." He shrugged and the moment passed, as they always do. "I'm also providing significant employment. Publishing, television, tabloids. Cara's coming with me to NBN, you know."

"Good to know one of the DeLucas will still be employed by year's end."

Alarm pinged him. "What do you mean by that?"

"Nothing." She knuckled the corner of her eye and turned toward the exit. "We should go."

Not so fast. He snugged her close and breathed her in while he still could. "Sweetheart, tell me."

She didn't speak, so he rubbed her back. Holding her felt comfortable and right, like the first bite of a warm bread pudding. They stayed like that for a few minutes until she murmured against his chest, "We're in trouble. DeLuca's is in trouble."

"What kind of trouble?"

"My mother's medical bills left us pretty strapped. And you saw it on Saturday night. We're not exactly raking it in." She peeked up, her eyes shining. "But the show should help, right?"

The show might generate some interest, but he doubted it would solve anything over the long-term. Jack had enough experience to know that brief spurts of publicity were exactly that. Brief.

"What about Maximo?"

That made her smile. "Marco."

"Whatever."

She shook her head. "He's practically broke himself.

He spends a lot of time in Vegas and he has the worst poker face. My eight-year-old cousin, Freddie, could run rings around him."

Huh, just one more reason why Marco needed to be high-fived in the face. Taking her hand in his, he rubbed his thumb along her palm. "Do you mind me asking how much?"

"Marco loaned my father fifty grand for my mother, but we're bleeding money every week and the lines of credit are drying up."

His mind whirred. That was doable, but throwing money at it was just a Band-Aid. Her eyes, as big as blue headlights, found his again and it felt like minutes passed in her gaze. He released her because it was starting to feel a little too good.

"You've got something to say," she said, reading something altogether different into the fact that he had practically shoved her from his embrace.

"It's not really my place." A chef's kitchen was sacrosanct, which is why Jack despised those makeover shows where some mouthy big shot overhauled another chef's menus.

"No, go on. I'd like to hear your opinion."

He thought about diplomacy, then figured she was a big girl. "You're overstaffed, overpriced, overstocked, and your menu's too big. You have at least one line cook too many, maybe two, and your father would probably be better off running the kitchen instead of ambushing poor, unsuspecting, brain-injured chefs at the bar." He tried to soften it with a smile. "But I think you know all that."

"My father is old school. There are so many changes we could make to economize and draw in new customers but he won't hear of it. And he likes to keep his hand in everywhere."

Iron fist, more like, but Jack held his tongue and sucked in a speech-countering breath. Besides, he understood that instinct to control your environment. The position was called head chef for a reason.

She smiled. "At least you don't have to work with your family. As much as I love them, it can be trying as all get-out." The words were hardly on the air before discomfort marred her features. "I'm sorry, that was insensitive."

"It was?"

A flush of red crept up her chest. "Yesterday, you mentioned trouble with your sister and something about your biological father. About how he wasn't interested."

He'd forgotten he told her that. Next time he had a concussion, he needed to refrain from the vino while knocking back the narcotics. Despite being a chatterbox, as Jules was fond of telling him, Jack didn't usually lay out his life story on the first date. But hey, this wasn't a date and the likelihood of it developing into one was slim to crapola because after the taping—in, oh, three hours— he was never going to see this woman again. Why, then, was his mouth itching to spill? Maybe because she had cracked open that steadfast façade of hers and he knew that had been difficult for her. More likely, he wanted to make the moment last and ride this wave of intimacy until he wiped out.

He must be starting to enjoy the hospitality in the ninth circle of hell.

"Until I was ten and my mother married my stepfather, it was just the two of us. She was Irish and she emigrated to England when her family threw her out at sixteen for getting pregnant. She went into labor with me on the Liverpool dock."

Her eyes enlarged in surprise. "A dramatic beginning. How apt."

He smiled, appreciating her effort to make it easier. "She never talked about him. Maybe she thought she'd have more time. She was only twenty-eight years old when she died." A brief, painful memory of her brassy personality deadened by a faded hospital gown and an ill-fitting wig flashed across his mind. He blinked it away. "When I started getting spots on British morning TV about nine years ago, he came out of the woodwork looking for money."

"Oh." She rubbed her neck. "What did you do?"

"I paid up. Then I told him I never wanted to see him again."

The low whine of a drill made the perfect soundtrack to the maudlin atmosphere. She stepped close and slotted her hand into his. "What happened, exactly?"

"Exactly?" He squeezed, taking strength from her warmth. "I'd hoped to show him my new restaurant in Covent Garden, but he had a same-day return ticket to Dublin and didn't have time. Instead, we met in a bar at London Paddington." The clarity of that day struck him anew. The bustle of the station, the departure announcements ringing reedy over the PA system. Jack had arrived a half hour early and knocked back a double scotch, then shredded countless napkins while he waited for the express train from Heathrow. A flying visit, his father called it, flashing that smile, a funhouse mirror image of Jack's. No time to tour his pride and joy. No time to talk about his mother or why the man whose genetic material he shared had been absent all these years. Only a few rushed moments to clink whiskey glasses (both rounds on Jack—*sláinte*) and cut to the meat course.

"He led with 'Jack, son, I've had a run of bad luck...' He called me son. It was a nice touch, I suppose." Learning his father's true intentions had crushed him, but better he know than hold on to childhood fantasies of starcrossed youth ripped apart by their censorious families.

"He's rung a few times since but I never call him back." The most recent time six months ago. His assertion of illness hadn't moved Jack in the slightest. He met Lili's glossy blue gaze, challenging her to judge him. "I know that must sound harsh to someone for whom family is everything."

Her hand tightened in his. "You did what you had to do, Jack. Sometimes you have to cut out the toxic elements. For your own sanity."

He couldn't help but read doom into that. It's what Lili had been trying to do since that video came out. Weed him out before he poisoned her life any further.

Telling her should have made him feel better, especially as it opened up the possibility of sinking into that soft womanly body for a sympathy hug. There would be no more of that nonsense. He broke their connection and returned his gaze to the restaurant's embryonic interior.

"There I go again, making it all about me."

"I could listen to you talk all day," she said, her voice thrillingly compassionate.

His chest tightened and he cleared his throat like he could dislodge the annoying constriction. "I'll probably need art for these walls. Interested in picking up a commission?"

At his abrupt halt to the intimacy, her mouth quirked but she didn't question it. "I'm not sure my work would be suitable. It's—"

"Porny?" he cut in, aiming to lighten the mood.

That got him a cuff in the arm and they were back to the playful vibe between them. Not entirely, but he faked it. He'd learned a few tricks since climbing the ladder of fame.

"No!" she said. "I was going to say far too sophisticated for new American with country French influences. Though I suppose you could get some nice pics of farm girls doing chores."

"Virginal milkmaids with big buckets?"

"The farmer's wife with her husband's huge...knife," she said with a naughty laugh that did wonderful things to his brain, and surprisingly, not the one in his jeans. The tension of last night and the previous few moments had faded only to be replaced with a sweet ache somewhere in the vicinity of his lungs. A ground-rumbling sound started up at the back of the site.

"We should make a move," he said, resolved to keep a cool head where Lili was concerned from here on out. Just a few hours to go.

"We have some time, don't we?"

"Depends on what you have in mind."

She brushed by him toward the exit. On purpose, the little minx.

"Well, I figured you showed me yours, so now it's time I showed you mine." Those pool-deep blues gaped wide, an innocent coda to her flirty words.

Not. Buying. It.

Heat burned a molten trail down his spine. So much for keeping it chill. He followed her out to the street.

CHAPTER FIFTEEN

There was no respite from the heat inside the fourth-floor studio of the Flatiron Arts Building in Wicker Park. Not that it would have made a blind bit of difference. The studio Lili shared with Zander was small and stuffy, but still large enough that she should have been able to keep a sane, chilled distance from Jack.

Seemed they both had other ideas.

Gravitating. That's what they were doing. No touching, not since he had held her during her meltdown back at his restaurant, but a couple of circuits of the space seemed to exert a curious animal magnetism. If he wasn't standing next to her, she came to him. If she found herself alone, it didn't last. He would slide in by her side, swarming her senses.

He tilted his head while examining one of Zander's very earthy male nudes, hung, ahem, on the studio's north-facing wall, and did a marvelous job of keeping his upper lip stiff.

"This guy sells?" His gaze skimmed the $3,000 price card, tucked discreetly at the corner.

She nodded. "Quite well. He was part of the New Artists exhibit at the Museum of Contemporary Art last fall."

He arced around her and moved to the next one. Every hair on her neck stood to attention as he passed. "I'm going to go out on a limb and say you didn't bring me here to look at photos of naked men. Not that there's anything wrong with that."

She swallowed past the lump in her throat. There was no reason to be nervous; he'd already seen her more conservative photos on DeLuca's walls and the collage in her apartment where everyone but Lili took a starring role. It was just that she rarely showed her real work to anyone but her artist friends. The unsuitable people who understood the beauty and the pain.

Jack understood beauty, and from what he'd said about his father, he had more than a nodding acquaintance with pain. Back at his restaurant site, she had wanted to draw him into her body and hug away his hurt. Assure him she was worthy of his trust. But he had slapped on his emotional armor and shut her down. After how she had treated him, could she blame him?

Fingers shaking, she yanked open the top drawer of the corner file cabinet, acutely conscious of the stunning hunk of male at her shoulder. *Which first? Which first?* Her mind raced as fast as her deft fingers raked through the prints, passing over the luminous black and white close-ups of her mother, starkly beautiful during her treatment. Lili's delicate emotional state meant those photos would have to wait for another day. Today, she would show the work that made her smile. She plucked out one of her favorites. *Sadie Number Three.*

She held it for Jack and smothered her surprise when he took it from her. No need to tell him to be careful about smudgy fingerprints. A man with hands like his knew exactly how to hold a photo. Like he held a woman. Gentle and sure.

He gave it a long beat of his attention, then walked the couple of feet to Zander's drafting table, where he placed it in one corner.

"More," he said, his eyes still glued to the photo. *More,* he'd said when he kissed her that first, pulsating time. Until now, she'd forgotten that brief exchange, that moment when they made the leap from testing to knowing. He hadn't waited for her answer then. He had taken because he wanted.

She loved that about him.

Pulse quickening, she mined more prints from her catalog. On the table, she positioned them in a grid and stood back, waiting.

He switched a couple of them around. She sighed and earned herself a quelling look. *Quiet. Genius at work.* A couple of tight minutes passed, the hum of street traffic below providing inadequate cover for her thundering heart.

His brow crimped. "Why aren't you selling these?"

The manic giggle she loosed did nothing for her nerves. "Do you know anything about art?"

"No, I don't. I usually have to have it explained to me very slowly." *Touché.* "But I know what I like."

"Photos of half-naked women?" Damn, she had a serious case of foot-in-mouth disease today.

"*Your* photos of half-naked women, though really the way you've composed them makes them more *Vanity Fair* than *Playboy*. These are beautiful. You should be selling them or showing them, not hiding them away in a drawer." He shook his head, bemused. "What are you planning to do when you go to grad school? Lock yourself in a garret and never exhibit your work?"

"Of course not. But I'm not at that stage yet. I've so much to learn."

He frowned. "You need to put yourself out there and be ready to take your lumps. It's all part of the creative process. How about explaining to this Philistine what he's too ignorant to see?"

"It's supposed to speak for itself," she said, flustered by his challenge. "Like your food." That was so dumb. As if her work could exist at the same stratum as Jack's culinary artistry.

"I describe my food on my shows and in my cookbooks all the time. And MFA students have to defend a thesis, don't they? Orally." He rolled the word *orally* around his mouth like he was tasting it, and her breasts tingled in memory of his hungry mouth devouring her last night. Doubly flustered, she averted her gaze and studied the floor.

The pause stretched like a rubber band.

"So, Rock Chick Red." He pointed at *Sadie Number Three*. "What should I be seeing here?"

Lili wasn't sure why she loved this photo so much. Sadie, the cashier at Classic Trax Records two blocks over, was an indomitable redhead with more curves than the Indy 500 racetrack, so there was that. There was also the elaborate cluster of blue roses that inked up most of her right side, its curly vines snaking down her shapely leg. With her arms strategically placed, the side angle was still more suggestive of her beautiful curves than any full-frontal nude photo.

Exquisite. Breathtaking. A feast made for Lili's camera. These were all good reasons but not why she loved it.

"Power." She coughed, peeked sideways, looked down, and stumbled on. "In her eyes, she's got this look of power. This 'I'm fucking beautiful, so bow down before me' look that's impossible to fake." Even now, that power radiated through Lili's body and made her proud to have witnessed it in person. To have captured its spark through her lens.

Out of the corner of her eye, she saw him nod. Unable to meet his direct gaze, she told him what else she saw. Jenny, shot from the neck up, with eyes so fierce they could fell the college quarterback. Kayla, her skin glowing with freckles like a connect-the-dots puzzle, her gaze self-aware and sure. Details of Lili's favorite spots on a woman's body: the seductive hollow at the base of the throat, that vulnerable spot behind a knee, the swell of a generous hip. Close-ups of shoulders that bore the weight of families, lovers, and lives well lived.

Each woman was a prime example of female magnificence and strength. Every one was proud of her body, whether it was petite or large, skinny or ample. What she didn't say was that all of them were braver than Lili, who faked bravado in her superhero costume.

She'd always had little confidence where her work was concerned, though she could occasionally get enough distance to realize it might be good. After all, she had saved for graduate school, hadn't she? But she never took the next step to apply. Her mother fell ill, her father fell silent, she was needed at the restaurant…excuses, excuses, excuses.

Because it's never enough and I'm greedy. That's what Jack had said when she asked why he continued in TV. Why he wasn't satisfied with what he had. If only she could inhabit for a moment that aura of certainty he projected, feel a sliver of the confidence he exuded, one iota of his raw passion. She laid her head against his strong shoulder and made a wish.

He slid an arm around her waist and grazed his lips against her temple. "Stop hiding, sweetheart. Your work is amazing and so are you."

Jack Kilroy, woman whisperer.

She wanted to take a chance. She wanted to look at a photo of herself and see the power and pride. Be more like Sadie Number Three instead of Little Miss Do Nothing. Panic at losing this opportunity overrode her cowardice. Faint heart never won fair beefcake.

A murmur, so indistinct she was unsure words had formed, passed her lips.

"Didn't catch that."

"I think we should go out on a date," she said quickly before the true scale of it all could kick in.

He released her and took a couple of steps away, his face strangely impassive. Not exactly the reaction she was expecting. Fear that she had made a huge mistake rocked her, but she'd already come too far to bow out gracefully.

"I mean it," she protested.

"What changed your mind? My erudite opinions on modern art?"

"Let's just say I didn't sleep well last night," she said, hoping he understood.

"I haven't had a good night's sleep since I met you either, Lili." He looked perturbed. "And the online stuff? You're all right with that?"

Hell no. "I want to do this."

He hauled a deep breath and stared at her, his eyes stark and unfathomable. Still no smile. If anything, he appeared relieved. "I can't guarantee that being with me will be a walk in the park, Lili. But know that I'll do everything in my power to protect you."

"Do you promise?" she asked, not because she needed confirmation or even because she believed he could possibly do that. No, she wanted to hear how his voice roughened when he got his caveman on.

His eyes darkened and her panties dampened. Oh, yes.

"Anyone who fucks with my woman will have me to answer to."

She had a mini-orgasm on the spot.

His face was awash with fluttering thoughts as he worked something out. "I have to travel for the next few days, but for our first date, I'll take you anywhere you want. London, Paris, Rome. You name it."

London, Paris, Rome...oh, my. "Well, there's this hot dog place I know," she said.

His mouth twitched. "Sounds classy."

"Sometimes I'm so classy I can't stand myself. Best chili dog in Chicago. Duck fat fries. All-night bar."

"So you liquor me up and ply me with encased meats, and I suppose you're expecting to get lucky?"

Leaning in, her lips brushed against his stubbled jaw on the way to his ear. "It's a pretty awesome hot dog, Jack."

He laughed, a deep rumble that heated her blood and

made her heart brim over. This was the Jack she was crazy about. Plumb crazy.

Now that they were dating—oh God, she had agreed to this madness—she felt it was within her rights to touch him freely. Mimicking the guided tour he had given of his body last night, she trailed her hand against his chest and paused as his nipple stiffened under her touch. When she bordered his waistband, he halted her explorations with a hand tight over hers and raised her wrist to his lips.

Hallelujah.

"A little self-control, sweetheart." He placed a scorching, openmouthed kiss on her pulsing wrist.

Every cell in her body sparked to life and warmth rushed to where his mouth lay. Tingles fired down her arm. Heat raced to her cheeks. The whole shebang.

"I love when you blush, Lili. When your lips part—" On cue, they did just that and she sucked in an emergency breath. "I can't stop thinking about how beautiful you looked when you came for me last night."

Speaking of coming… "When does the taping start?" she asked. Begged.

He made a low, needy sound in her ear. "Not enough time, love."

"I don't mind if it's fast. Fast can be hot." Desperate much? She flicked her tongue along his jaw. "So hot."

More sexy rumbling noises ensued. "What I have in mind for you is going to be torturous and slow and will take the whole night. In short, we're going to need a bed."

After a mind-blowing kitchen table orgasm with gelato as foreplay, now he was reverting to traditional? "Beds are overrated," she murmured.

"You won't be saying that after you've spent a night in one with me."

Sweetly struck darts of pleasure shot straight to her groin and she matched his now ragged breathing with her own short tugs. He scraped his jaw against hers, the scruff hiking her desire to urgent. Last night, he had taken care of her. Surely, she could do the same for him?

"You've already made me feel so good, Jack. Let me touch you. Please." She placed her hands on the hard plane of his chest and crept lower. Her hip rocked against the hard ridge of his erection. Wrapping her hands, her mouth around him was all she could think about.

He closed his eyes, evidently rallying his strength. When he opened them again, she read determination. Damn.

"Hands off the goods, DeLuca." Quickly, he manhandled her shoulders into a turn toward the studio's exit. "We've got a show to get through."

"Sadist."

He sighed. "This is—"

"So much harder for you than it is for me. I know. Tell it to the judge, tough guy."

She made sure to infuse some sway into her step as she headed to the stairs. His deep groan was her reward.

On the short walk back to DeLuca's, Jack demonstrated steely self-control with hands in pockets and subduing glares whenever she strayed into his orbit. Gorgeous, infuriating man. Inside, Marco and Tad were talking at the bar, or rather Marco was sounding off about something to a silently skeptical Tad.

"Lil," Marco said chirpily; then his face blackened on noticing Jack. His heavy gaze ping-ponged between the two of them, assessing the situation. "Out and about in public, you two? The rumor mill will be in full swing before the day is through."

"Marco," Lili said, exasperated.

Her ex held his hands up in a conciliatory gesture, but the goodwill didn't quite reach his eyes. His gloomy, sneering gaze told Lili something unexpected—Marco was jealous of Jack. It seemed there was nothing more attractive than being attractive to someone else.

"Not that I'm complaining," Marco continued, his voice dripping with sullen incredulity. "You two are great for business."

Something that sounded like a growl came from Jack's direction; then she felt his hand splay possessively on her hip. Seemed touching was okay when a woman needed claiming. Men.

Cara stuck her head around the corner of the short side of the bar, her judgmental gaze immediately shooting to Jack's hand. "Where the hell have you been?"

Unsure of her sister's target, Lili looked at Jack only to find him glaring at Marco, a muscle pumping at the edge of his mouth. Oh, boy. Any moment now, they'd be whipping out the tape measures. Last night's brief hand inspection told her Jack would win. By far.

"You said you'd help, and you"—Cara pointed a peremptory finger at Jack—"need to be in the kitchen. Now. Laurent is having a Gallic fit over the salsa for the lamb chops."

"I'd best go," Jack said. Before Lili had a moment to gather herself, he clamped his hand on her butt and drew her close for a kiss that she couldn't have said no to even if she wanted to. Fairly safe to say that she didn't want to.

It lasted mere seconds, an infusion of hot, scorching roughness. His lips cut a path of sweet torture across her jaw until coming to rest at her earlobe.

"Tonight, Lili DeLuca, you and that sweet arse of yours are mine."

Wow, oh wow. With a gentle squeeze of said sweet arse, he strode toward the kitchen, indulging in a clearly calculated shoulder bump against Marco. Tad gave a low whistle while Cara scowled and flounced off to shout at someone else. Heaven help the first person to cross her path.

At Marco's grim smile, the line from the Grinch song about termites popped into Lili's head.

"Nice job. Maybe you've managed to throw Kilroy off his game."

Lili considered her ex and flattened her lips. Jack thought she had a beautiful figure. He said she made him so hard it hurt. He wanted to jump her bones in assorted European capitals.

Marco had called her body "comfortable."

"Tosser," Lili muttered.

From behind the bar, Tad's cough sounded suspiciously like, "Awesome."

Marco frowned. "What's that?"

"Nothing," she replied with her most saccharine smile. While she would like nothing more than to stand around telling off her ex for his various dating crimes and misdemeanors, she had better options for channeling the power flooding her veins. It was only a date, but it felt like so much more. A new beginning, a fulfillment of all she had to offer. Tonight, the taping would propel DeLuca's Ristorante into prosperity and later...later, she would have Jack.

CHAPTER SIXTEEN

Showtime!

The restaurant had never looked better, and even if it was on the Cooking Channel's dime, a full DeLuca's was about as gratifying a sight as Lili could have wished for. And while she knew Jack was the main attraction, the curious looks she got confirmed that she was a draw in her own right. Two guys had passed her their numbers. One woman had asked if she was bicurious. Maybe there was something to Tad's theory of Lili as poster woman for curvy gals everywhere. Have the hot guy and eat your cake, too.

Ducking the television camera that seemed to be stuck to her butt like white on rice, she recapped her father's menu. Veal meatballs followed by his famous gnocchi with brown butter and sage. For *carne*, he offered juicy bistecca, and Lili almost pitied Jack, who was left serving lamb chops to the steak-loving clientele they had lined up for the taping. The coup de grâce was creamy hazelnut gelato and raspberry sorbetti for *dolci*. It was the ideal menu to showcase her father's cooking.

It might even be enough to win.

Lost in her thoughts, it took a few moments to register Tad calling her over to the bar.

"Take a gander." He inclined his head in the direction of the water station.

Her gaze alighted on Gina, whose furtive hunch made it clear that customer hydration was the furthest thing from that girl's mind. Lili turned to Tad and got an eyebrow jump in return. Her thoughts exactly.

Marching over, she tapped Gina's shoulder and was rewarded with a guilty hop.

"Jeez, Lili, could you not do that?"

Over her cousin's fuzzy veil of hair, Lili spied a plate of Jack's lamb chops with rosemary-truffle oil potatoes. "This had better be good."

Gina blew out her cheeks like a pissed off chipmunk. That's when Lili noticed the large container of sea salt behind the plate.

"Don't tell me you're sabotaging Jack's dishes!"

She got the distinct impression that Gina would have placed her hand over Lili's mouth if she thought she could get away with it. "Shut up, would you? It's only a couple of dishes here and there. Just leveling the playing field."

"What possessed you to do this?" Lili surveyed the room in a panic, seeking out Gina's evil conjoined twin, Angela. Her pliable cousin wouldn't be acting alone.

"It's no big deal. Marco said it would be better for business if we won."

"Marco!" Lili gasped. Sweat trickled between her breasts and a cold weight settled in her belly. Grabbing

Gina by the shoulders, she pressed down, forcing her stunted cousin even shorter than her five foot two inches. "How many dishes have you ruined?"

Her cousin squirmed, but Lili dug into her flesh, willing her to answer. She was prepared to resort to slaps if necessary. "Two or three. But nothing's been sent back. Nobody knows."

"You stupid, stupid girl." Which sounded ridiculous because Gina was four years older than Lili. "Have you any idea of the position this puts us in with Jack? He could have picked any restaurant and this is how we repay him."

"Oh. Em. Gee," Gina drawled. "You're on Team Jack now because you guys swapped fluids? How about some respect for how we defended you online?"

Lili imagined steam coming out of her own ears. There had to be a better way to make a living. Gina's piss-poor attitude and sorry dearth of skills had meant she was flying close to the sun for a while now. There was only one possible way to handle this.

"You're fired."

Her cousin squeaked in amusement and her hair bobbed in unison with her shoulders. "Good one, Lili."

"I'm serious. Give me your apron. I'll take over your station." She thrust her hand out stiffly, readying for the tremor she could anticipate rolling a tsunami down her arm. "Now."

Like something out of a children's book illustration, Gina's big eyes flew even wider. "I...I can't believe you're taking Jack's side against the family. I was going to ask you to be my maid of honor!"

Aw, that was so sweet, and it would be so much fun

to see the look on Angela's face...*Stand your ground. Do not let her play you.* "I don't want you anywhere near food or the customers." When Gina still didn't make a move, Lili added, "Don't make me get Dad out here."

At the mention of Lili's father, her cousin's face collapsed. With her parents passed on, Gina's closest male relatives were her brother, Tad, and her uncle, Tony, whom she adored. The foolish girl might think she was doing the family a favor, but the mere mention of its patriarch was enough to shake loose the realization that she had screwed up. Spectacularly.

Slowly, she handed the apron over. "Everyone's been served their entrées. Desserts should be up in ten."

Feeling wobbly, Lili donned the apron and tried not to melt at the sight of her cousin's rapidly welling eyes. For the love of Frank, the bitch knew Lili was a sucker for the waterworks.

"I'm sorry, Lili. Honest to God." Her voice broke on *honest*, which Lili reluctantly admitted was a nice touch.

"Me too. Just get your stuff and go home."

Gina pumped out another glossy-eyed stare, blinked a couple of times, and trudged off.

Lili returned to the bar and gave Tad the scoop. Thankfully, he took her side, though she wouldn't have blamed him for trying to throw a good word in for his sister.

"You know what you have to do, right?" he asked, his expression troubled.

Her head felt too heavy for her neck. How she wished the night was long over and she was safely wrapped in Jack's arms, but after what had transpired, she couldn't stay silent. The taping might grind to a standstill, her family's reputation might be shot to hell, but if she kept this from Jack and her father, it would be so much worse.

"Well, it was nice while it lasted," she said miserably, her limbs as limp as noodles. The firing squad awaited.

Then she spotted a woman barreling toward her on her way to the restroom. Model tall with long, blond, I've-just-been-ravished hair, she wore the kind of casually put together outfit that took hours of effort and cost hundreds of dollars. However, it wasn't her stunning looks or fashionable threads that immediately struck Lili, but her ground-eating stride once she hit a clear path. Even with giant sunglasses obscuring half her face, she radiated self-possession.

The woman bumped against a chair at the bar, and the huge caramel-hued hobo slung over her shoulder plopped to the floor, spilling its contents.

"Let me help you with that." Lili squatted to pick up the detritus—a phone, makeup, tissues, an airline baggage receipt—and took note of Blond Sunnies' shaking hands. Not so cool, then.

"Are you okay?" Lili asked, taken off guard by the woman's familiarity. Those cheekbones, that chin...

Ignoring Lili's question, she grasped her leather goods possessively and lurched off.

"Be still my beating dick. Who's that?" Tad asked, his keen gaze following his next ex-girlfriend.

They watched as those long stems took her past the restrooms on a collision course with the kitchen. Lili locked eyes with her cousin. They both took off in hot pursuit.

* * *

The night was turning into a complete and utter cluster fuck. Dishes that had left the kitchen perfect returned destroyed. Jack had bungled two servings of risotto and the salsa verde for the lamb chops tasted like vinegar. He preferred to blame the minute space for the less-than-stellar performance instead of the fact that Laurent was just helping the show as a one-off and the usually-in-total-sync chefs hadn't actually cooked together in over a year. They had no communication. No rhythm. Nothing.

But none of it mattered because tonight, dessert would take the form of a hot, curvaceous woman. Just the thought made him jittery with need and carved out a big, foolish smile on his face. Next stop, Half-Wit City.

"Hullo, Jack."

His meat tongs slipped from his grip and clanged to the floor, vibrating like a tuning fork through his bones. He blinked a couple of times, as though that might work to sharpen his muddled hearing. On any other day, Jack might have thought he was dreaming, but this was just the glacé cherry on top of the turd that was tonight's dinner service.

"What the hell are you doing here?" he shouted at his sister.

Juliet propped her sunglasses up on her head and dumped her purse on the counter like she was planning to stay awhile. An entourage of sorts materialized behind her. Concern sketched on Lili's face, amused interest on Tad's.

Everyone had frozen upon hearing Jack's roar, but started up again like a wonky carousel when Tony commanded them to get back to work. Even Laurent obeyed. Jack threw down a towel and marched over to Jules. The same aquiline nose, the same cheekbones, the same green eyes. The only difference was she was as blond as he was dark. Her likeness to their mother struck him like a baseball bat to the gut.

Taking her arm, he steered her away from the alley and out of the servers' path. "Jules, I told you I'd be in London tomorrow."

"This couldn't wait." Her voice was graveled like she had just woken up.

His grip slackened as concern replaced his surprise. "Are you all right? How did you even know where I was?"

"It's not hard to find out. Your fans report your whereabouts constantly." She combed through her hair, knocking her glasses to the ground. "Oh, God," she muttered, her eyes glowing with incipient tears.

Alarm rocked him with the realization that something was seriously not right. "Jules, love, what's wrong? Are you ill?"

"I've messed up," she said on a strangled sob.

A preternatural awareness told him the next words out of her mouth would be the last ones he wanted to hear. *Don't say it. Don't fucking say it.*

"I'm pregnant." Her words escaped in a gush, stilling the air around them.

Jesus H. Macy. He had known something was amiss when he spoke with her on the phone yesterday, and now he felt like that baseball bat had stopped by for another round of shit-kicking. More roughly than he intended, he walked her back to the office and deposited her in one of the swivel chairs.

"How did this happen?"

"Well, insert Tab A into Slot B—"

"Don't even. Who did this to you?"

She barked out a hysterical laugh. "No one did it to me. I screwed up all by myself."

Oh, great. An immaculate conception. "What do Daisy and Pete have to say?" Her aunt and uncle might not be the most devoted guardians, but they were all she'd known since his stepfather died when she was five years old and Jack was fifteen. While content to take in the angelic blond offspring of her dead brother, Daisy had been less receptive to his stepson, or "the bastard son of that Irish slag," as she'd referred to Jack when she thought he was out of earshot. Over the next three years until he left for Paris, he spent more nights on friends' sofas than under Daisy's roof, though they'd all become great friends once Jack's financial contributions to his sister's upkeep tipped the scales. His first lesson in the purchase of affection.

One of Jules's slight shoulders lifted in a half-shrug that contrasted with the downturn of her mouth. She picked up a stapler from the desk and proceeded to pull it apart. "They don't care. They're on their annual pilgrimage to ex-pat-landia on the Costa del Sol."

"I'm calling them now," he threatened, eager to take out his frustration on the people who were supposed to be responsible for her. Acknowledging Jules's adulthood had always been nigh on impossible for him, between her irresponsible attitude and her recalcitrance whenever he offered help. That she was here at all meant she was in serious trouble, and maybe more than just being pregnant.

"You can't reach them. They don't have international mobiles." That sounded plausible—he usually phoned them at home—but he couldn't be certain. His sister had a tendency for an excessive liberality with the truth. She lifted her eyes, his mother's eyes, to meet his. They were wide with confusion and fear. His heart sank further, if possible. The confusion might be out of his wheelhouse right now, but he could do something about the fear.

Shifting her head slightly, she addressed a spot behind him. "You look skinnier in person."

He turned to find Lili hovering in the doorway, Jules's purse dangling in one hand, a glass of water in the other. She deposited the bag inside, gently, as if running a military stealth operation. Now he absorbed the rest of her appearance. Something black and Audrey Hepburnesque covered by a server's apron. Her legs were sheathed in shiny boots on spiky heels, and he felt the now-familiar hardening of his body. Could that be any more inappropriate?

He spun about to face Jules. "Who is it? Do I know him?" Anger mounted in his throat and he fought to suppress it before it turned into a full-on rush.

"It's no one you know," his sister muttered.

"I know a lot of people. Try me." This dickhead was on the hook for knocking up his sister and he'd better be prepared to take full responsibility.

"Eight million people in London, Jack. Even you can't know everyone." She squinted up at him like Clint Eastwood.

Lili set the water down on the desk and wheeled out another chair, hitting the back of his legs. He supposed that was an invitation to sit. As soon as he did, Jules's slender shoulders slackened, and he realized that standing over her, he'd been scaring her. Worst brother ever.

"How do you feel?" He looked up at Lili, who had backed away but halted at whatever she saw on his face.

"A little tired," Jules said. She grasped the water glass with trembling hands.

Once she had taken a sip, he took both her hands in his. Really, he wanted to hold her close but she wasn't one for big displays of affection. Where he preferred to rant and rail and hug it out, she turned her focus inward and shut down shop. But for the physical resemblance, he might wonder if they were related.

"Baby girl, we're going to fix this." He tried to remember the last time he'd called her that and came up empty. A stab of pain lacerated his lungs.

"I'm not going back to London, Jack," she said defiantly, withdrawing her hands from his. She knew that would be his first suggestion. "I'm sorry about barging in but I couldn't wait."

He didn't have to look behind him to know that Cara and assorted crew were strafing his back with visual gunfire, willing him back to the kitchen.

"Can you wait here while I finish up?" Not that she had anywhere to go. She had always been tall, but now her body looked boneless and small and nowhere near ready for the burden of a child. His heart exploded with his love for her and his fervent wish she was anywhere but here. He nodded to Lili to follow him out and headed through the door.

Outside the office, they stood facing each other, trying to craft a moment of quiet above the metallic clinks of the kitchen a few feet away. She brushed his hand, testing, and they exhaled as one, then took a long breath together. He was relearning to breathe and she was his teacher.

With soft fingers, she stroked his forearm, rhythmically, tracing a path from elbow to wrist. She hadn't said a thing, but he felt soothing words in her touch.

He longed to slip under cool sheets, wrap his body around her, and sleep for a week.

"What a fucking mess," he finally grunted out, because they couldn't stand here all night and it was true. "She hates me."

"Because it's all about you, Jack Kilroy."

Ouch, a low shot, but thoroughly deserved.

She pressed her soft hand into his. "She's in trouble and she came to see you. Her big brother."

He shuddered out a begrudging breath, reluctant to acknowledge that might be conceivable. "Could you sit with her? I don't want her to be alone." The fury and frustration had simmered to helplessness, such an unfamiliar feeling. He solved problems and no situation was ever too broken for him to fix.

The compassion in Lili's eyes almost undid him. "Sure. Go finish up the show. I'll take care of her."

"She should eat something," he said, grasping at the one thing in his control. Jack, provider of sustenance.

A slight smile touched her lips. "I'll get her some gnocchi. She should have real Italian food, not whatever hash you're slinging in there." That tugged a half-grin from him. "And I'll get someone to take her home to my mom."

"To your parents' house?"

"Jack, she's just come off a long flight, and she's tired and emotional. She needs a bite to eat and a good night's sleep."

She needs her mother. Her aunt had never been the

most maternal type, though she had convinced him otherwise years ago. Right about the time she told him he was out of his mind to think a cocky eighteen-year-old could ever be a proper parent to an eight-year-old girl. She had persuaded him Jules would be better off with them. He had been easy to persuade.

"I don't want to impose on Francesca," he countered halfheartedly, knowing all the while that placing his sister in her care was the best solution for now.

"It's not imposing. Italian mothers live for this. And when she's rested and"—she fiddled with a button on his chef's jacket—"and you're calmer, you two can sort it out."

She was right, of course. He was in no condition to talk to Jules, and any conversation between them would quickly descend to hurling insults and pulling up past slights. He moved closer and the scent of vanilla and hibiscus, the scent of her, made him dizzy. Even now, with the proverbial shit pummeling the fan, he reveled in the rush that proximity to her always gave him.

"Thanks," he said, relief and pleasure flooding him equally. He pressed her palm flush to his chest and her fingers spread, their warmth seeping through the starched cotton. It made no sense, but somehow he knew he could handle Jules with Lili in his corner.

"Jack, there's something you need to—"

"Hate to break this up, people, but we do still have a show to finish." Cara appeared at his side, eyes flashing in warning. *Bugger.*

Servers walked by carrying dessert plates of Tony's gelato and sorbet combo. Behind those swing doors, Laurent was likely having Siberian tiger cubs. In leaving the cocoon of warmth that radiated from Lili's body, Jack immediately felt bereft. Perhaps this was how it would always be when he couldn't be near her. Wanting something this much couldn't be right; it could only end badly.

"Good thing this night is almost over," he said, wiping his damp brow. "Everything's gone pear-shaped in the kitchen. Dropping stuff, dishes coming back. We taste everything before it goes out, so I've no idea what's happening. It's like we're complete amateurs in here."

She wrinkled her nose. Laurent was spot on. Cute as hell.

"Well, about that. We have a problem."

A shot of alarm buzzed his brain. "What kind of problem?"

"Gina got a little carried away. She added salt to a couple of your dishes." She gave a sympathetic mouth twist. "Misplaced family loyalty."

Oh...His stomach plummeted to below floor level. "How long have you known about this?"

"I was just coming to tell you when your—"

"Because we started getting dishes back about forty minutes ago."

She managed to pull off baffled pretty well. "It was only supposed to be a couple. I was told nothing had been returned."

"You were told wrong." Only supposed to be a couple? There had to be at least ten returns and those were just the ones who had bothered. Add to that the overly acidic salsa for the lamb chops, which could just as easily have been sabotaged with a quick flick of the wrist.

"As soon as I discovered Gina with the salt—"

"You mean one of your well-trained girls? Don't blame it on her, Lili. You're in charge out there. The least you can do is own up to it."

Her face underwent a run of diverse movements. She was struggling to change gears, grasping for spaces. A couple of the waitstaff halted to watch the sideshow. Jerry, cameraman-gone-rogue, had decided the action outside the kitchen was hotter than whatever was happening on the line. From the corner of his eye, Jack caught Tony peeking through the kitchen's doors. He looked concerned. He bloody well should be.

"What the fuck is going on here, Lili?"

Her tongue darted out, wetting her plump lower lip. She blinked rapidly and her gaze flicked over his shoulder. "Could we go somewhere quiet and talk about this?"

"No, we cannot. I want to know why your family felt it necessary to screw with my service. No matter who wins, the restaurant still gets publicity. This didn't need to happen." He had to be missing something. He drew closer and crowded her, then cupped her chin. "So Gina came up with this all by herself, did she?"

"Jack—"

"Leave her alone," a deep voice cut in.

He turned to the source, surprised to find Marco invading his body space, his grasping gaze on Lili.

"Stay out of it, Rossi," Jack ground out.

"Marco, it's okay," Lili said in that soft salve of a voice she had used to calm Jack five minutes ago.

"Yeah, Marco, it's okay," Jack mimicked, not caring that he sounded childish.

Marco's gaze narrowed to snakelike slits. "Quit bullying her, Kilroy."

"I'm not bullying her. I'm trying to have a private conversation here."

"Nothing you do is private." He waved his hand around the semicircle of spectators comprising restaurant and TV crews that ended at Jerry, who with his shoulder-held camera captured Jack's meltdown frame for frame.

That's when a different blast of technology glinted and caught Jack's eye. Raised phones in the hands of those well-trained girls, each one grabbing footage for their next upload. Not just the girls. Marco held his mobile at thigh level but Jack knew in his heart of hearts where it had been a moment before.

"Were you filming us? Did you film my sister?" These people would stop at nothing. His vision went dark around the edges and before he even realized it, he had shoved Marco in the chest. A testing shot.

"Jack!"

Lili laid her hand on his arm, and he jerked away. Marco's lips curled up in a condescending smile like the fucker had been proved right before he moved in farther, sucking the air Jack needed to breathe.

"The universe doesn't revolve around you, Kilroy. You're beginning to sound paranoid." He caressed Lili's forearm. "Come on, Lili."

Jack blocked him, rage coursing through him in a torrent. "So help me God, if you don't take your hand off her—"

"You'll what? Pound me like you did that photographer?"

"That would be too generous."

"Jack, stop," Lili said quietly.

Anger surged in a flood, closer to the surface because

of what he had thought he'd gained. "You're taking his side now?"

"Of course not," she said, but her eyes betrayed her. Something passed between her and Marco, and she colored as deep as a habanero pepper.

He tried to swallow, but his throat felt like it was filled with broken glass. He had misjudged the situation completely. This was Lili's life, her family, her raison d'être. Marco and his gambling problems. Lili and her chronic case of familial devotion. Former lovers, maybe current lovers, working together to get publicity for their baby. Working him.

He'd had his suspicions about the DeLucas involvement in the video, but Lili had dismissed them as crazy talk. *Oh no, Jack. My cousins would never do a thing like that.* He knew better now. Someone had done exactly that. A wave of emotion careened through him, leaving him nauseated, like he'd eaten a clutch of bad clams. Had Lili known all along? Had she encouraged it? Cara's words returned in an icy rush. *When I suggested she indulge in your services…* And her cousins, with their T-shirts and their Facebook pages and their media campaign worthy of any New York or LA PR outfit had capitalized on Lili's fame faster than you can say "Jack and the fat chick." The sickening conclusion slammed him so hard his chest caved.

Hello, baseball bat, welcome back.

Everyone watched, eyes stripping them bare. Servers, kitchen staff, and show crew waited on the balls of their feet. Cara towered in an angry shimmer with hip cocked and lips puckered.

"Can we please finish this effing show?" she called

out, and it was enough to shatter the tableau everyone was frozen in. It was also enough to loosen the clog in his throat.

"Show's over."

Silence reigned and vacant expressions greeted this pronouncement. For fuck's sake, his own crew didn't even take him seriously.

"Jerry, turn off the camera. Now."

"Yup," was his cameraman's laconic reply. He flipped a switch and the red light above the lens dimmed, then died.

"Jack, I'm sorry," Lili said, a tremble in her voice.

What exactly she was sorry for was of no interest to him because he was already heading for the kitchen, pushing the pain away with every step.

"So am I."

CHAPTER SEVENTEEN

Jack leaned against the counter in DeLuca's kitchen and rested his eyelids. Better that than watch Cara tallying the votes. Better that than watch Lili drawing ever-decreasing circles on the weathered countertop he had admired so much three nights ago. Had it only been three nights? Near the burners, Tony exuded enough negative vibes that there was a fair to middling chance their respective energy fields would clash and detonate. He hadn't said a word so far, but Il Duce was primed to go ballistic. Jack wouldn't have blamed him one bit.

His muscles ached. His bones felt like they'd been squeezed through a pasta roller. His nerves were blunted to the point of numbness. Jules was going to have a baby, and for some messed up reason, she'd decided he had to know this very minute instead of waiting for him to get to London tomorrow. And Lili had pushed a shiv between his ribs, suddenly and without warning.

Cara had begged him to finish the service (*for the cus-*

tomers, Jack) and until Laurent stilled Jack's arm while he was plating the desserts, he had assumed it was all going without a hitch. Spaced out, he had created a pyramid of gelato scoops so high, that if toppled, it could have leveled Moscow.

Cara smoothed out the ballots and raised her ice blues to Jack. "Forty-three in favor of Chef Kilroy. Sixty-two for Chef DeLuca. Jack, it's your call. We can do a little creative editing with the reaction shots…" She snuck a glance at her father, who wore an expression like a smacked arse. Quality reaction shots there. "And declare you the winner. You *do* have final edit."

"Or final say on whether an episode airs at all," Jack said.

Cara's mouth registered a pained patience, like he was being the difficult one here. This family didn't just take the cake; they ransacked the entire bloody bakery.

"Of course, if that's how you want to play it," his producer said, but he'd worked with her long enough to recognize the skitter in her voice when something bothered her. She was scared. The success of the show, her job, and the future of her family's restaurant were all on the line here. No pressure.

Lili rubbed her collarbone the way she did when she got distressed. Her gaze met his, willing him to understand. To accept that her family had good reasons for what they did. Tough, he had already run out of fucks to give.

"Is my sister all right?" he bit out.

Lili nodded and hugged herself, protecting herself from the chill he projected. "Mom came by and picked her up. She's probably asleep by now." The heat and humidity of the kitchen had expanded her hair and painted a sheen of perspiration on her face. Looking at her was like staring into the sun. He still wanted her, all of her, and he hated himself for that.

Anger solidified into a hot, raging mass beneath his breastbone. Someone had taken advantage of his sister, and the woman before him had tried to take advantage of him. He had worked in this business long enough that he shouldn't have been surprised when users latched on to him for personal gain. His ex had wanted only the blistering flash of their grease-fire celebrity pairing. His sister sought him out only when she was up a creek, paddle AWOL. His father... Christ, John Sullivan emerged from his whiskey-sodden haze only when the barrel ran dry. And now Lili and a murder of scheming DeLucas, not satisfied with the free publicity they were already getting, had determined that humiliating the notorious chef would make a nice notch on the marketing campaign bedpost.

Tony stepped away from the stove. Nuclear fission imminent.

"I knew this was trouble from the beginning," he said, his gaze passing over Jack. "We did not need the publicity. We did not need this show."

Tony had finally elected to grace them with his two lire. Good thing Jack clenched his fists right then; otherwise he might have started a slow, sarcastic clap.

Lili's expression resolved to panic. "Dad, there's already been a ton of publicity." *Sure has, sweetheart, and how much of it was crafted by la famiglia and co.?*

"Everyone knows the episode was taping here. If it doesn't air, there'll be questions, rumors about what happened. It would be a PR nightmare. We need the show, but Jack should win the challenge, of course."

"Brava for coming up with a solution that lets me save face, love," he murmured.

Hurt she had no right to blemished her face, making him angrier.

Tony's color had darkened to aubergine. "You are not in a position to make decisions, Liliana. I do not know what has got into you lately. This would never have happened when your mother was in charge or if you had been keeping your eye on the staff instead of otherwise distracted."

That was a more colorful version of what Jack had said an hour ago. The discomfort on her face deepened to a pain that seared his soul. *Toughen up, Kilroy.* He refused to care if she came apart.

Cara chimed in. "Dad, she fired Gina the minute she found out what happened."

Jack's head snapped back so hard a nerve in his neck pinched. "You did?"

"It doesn't matter," Lili said dully, eyes on the floor. All the spirit had left her body at Tony's reprimand.

Cara squeezed her sister's arm. "Lili did what she could to contain it, but that won't stop me from murdering the poisonous dwarf when I see her next. Now, I think we can all agree that it's been a very unusual evening." She delivered a pointed look at Jack. Apparently he should accept a portion of the blame because his sister had elected to put in a show-stopping arrival. "Jack, babe, it's down to you."

Her usual cajolery was not going to fly. "Cara, don't think you can produce your way out of this. You dumped me into this situation and neglected to mention your family's financial problems or how desperate you all are to get your fifteen minutes." He left out the gem about how she had set him up to service her sister like he was a prize stud horse. Tony already had the shotgun; Jack wasn't going to offer to load it.

"Jack, the show was in a fix," Cara said, still with that easy soothe no different from Lili. This woman was skating close to the drop. "We needed another location stat."

"You think I don't know a slew of chefs in Chicago who'd drop everything to be on *Jack of All Trades*? I trusted your judgment, Cara, but hey, I have my uses, right? Doesn't matter what I think."

"I do not care who wins," Tony interrupted. "I only care about what is right."

All eyes shifted to Tony. Jack couldn't blame the man, who was just as much a victim in this ambush. His excellence in the kitchen was matched only by his honor and his love for his family. Tonight, Jules slept in a DeLuca bed, no questions asked, and as much as Jack despised the younger generation's intrigues, he couldn't take it out on their father. Hell, he admired him too much.

"The result stands," Jack said. "Tony's the winner."

He insisted the decision had nothing to do with how his heart scrunched at Lili's clear anguish in the wake of her father's scolding. Nor how the same maddening muscle lifted when he heard she'd sacked Gina. Tomorrow he would pick up his sister, shake the pasta flour off his feet, and forget the whole freaking lot of them.

Tony threw his hands up in air already thick with tension. "No! I will not accept the benefits of my family's disgraceful behavior."

"Dad, it's Jack's decision to make. He's in charge," Cara said wearily, gathering up the ballots quickly before the boss could change his mind. "We've already kept everyone waiting long enough. Let's not make it any worse than it already is."

The relief on Lili's face infuriated and pleased Jack in equal measure. He might say he was doing it for Tony, but they both knew differently. Shit was messed up but that's what happens when you're so bowled over you can't even think straight. When you're in love.

Holy fuck.

That was...damned inconvenient.

And impossible. Not after three days. Not after less than three days. Infatuated, yes. Sexually obsessed, definitely. But in love? Not bloody likely.

Ker-ist. All he'd wanted was a date.

"This is not acceptable," Tony said to no one in particular, eerily echoing Jack's sentiments. Being in love with this woman was in no way acceptable.

"Tony and I need a moment alone." What Jack really needed was to get away from *her*. His skin felt too tight; every breath felt labored. He slid a sharp glance to Cara, who nodded and steered Lili toward the dining room. As she left, Lili sent him a look of gratitude he neither desired nor needed. He fought to get control of his emotions. *You are not in love, dickhead. You just need to get laid.*

"Tony, you deserve this win. Your menu was superb and to be honest, that gnocchi should win an MVP award. Most valuable pasta." His words spilled over each other in a nervous tumble.

Tony's mouth twitched. *Almost, almost...*nope, the threatening smile never materialized.

Il Duce wouldn't be swayed by compliments, so Jack took a calming breath and sought safer territory. "I don't like what your family did, but I know who won here. And believe me, people love when the famous chef is taken down a peg or three. For me to lose on the premiere episode of my new show and to the father of—" He tripped up when he realized where *that* was going. *The father of the woman I ... shut the hell up.* "It'll make for great ratings. Sure, you're doing me a favor."

He was buying stock in his own hype now, showing Tony he was exactly what the man despised. A fame-hungry megawhore who had dragged his daughter's reputation through the mud. It's all about the ratings. But Jack would not back down from his decision. Having some say in how this played out was about all he had left.

Tony unfolded his arms and laid his palms flat on the abraded countertop, the one Jack had caressed the first night he met Lili. He should hate this kitchen, but for a reason he couldn't fathom, his affection for it had only increased.

"Thank you, I will accept your decision. On one condition," Tony said, the words incisive jabs to Jack's thumping head.

Unbelievable. How did they get to the point where Tony could impose conditions? Jack sighed.

"Stay away from my youngest daughter."

It shouldn't have hurt, but Tony's demand gouged a pit where Jack's heart usually lived. What had he expected? Gratitude that he had stopped a shit storm from plummeting down on this man's livelihood? Acknowledgment that Jack's decision might have actually saved their business? Tony was looking out for his family and Jack had no choice but to respect that.

Besides, the older man's sparse request would be a snap.

"Won't be a problem."

* * *

Lili wasn't sure how much time passed once the restaurant emptied out the crews, both television and DeLuca. Everyone had descended on O'Casey's Tap to celebrate the outcome. All she wanted to do was creep upstairs and crawl inside a tub of Cherry Garcia.

What a fiasco. Her father's admonishments about her managerial inadequacy were tough to take, but she couldn't blame him for being upset. She had been playing hooky with Jack when she should have been keeping her finger on the pulse and ensuring the girls toed the line. Tony would eventually come around, with the turning radius of the *Titanic*, maybe, but they'd get through it.

Jack, on the other hand…oh, Jack. The hurt on his face had sliced her through and made her heartsick, and then his incredibly honorable and unselfish act to let the vote stand had smashed her to the ground. He had held her family's future in his palm and come down on their side, even when they had betrayed the man and made him angrier than a bull battling a bee swarm. Angry enough to leave without saying good-bye.

Her one comfort, for she had to grasp on to something, was that she had stopped him from punching Marco, because she had no doubt that Jack had been about to clean her ex's clock. Not that the scumbag deserved a reprieve but any more negative publicity would endanger Jack's huge network deal. A few more seconds and there would have been a whole new video stealing focus from that infamous kiss.

Left alone, she made her usual pre-close walk-through and noted the long, weathered bar, the undressed tables that looked more modern without linens, and the leather banquettes fraying at the edges. A scrap of silver duct tape scarred the floor, the only evidence the show had been there. That and the dull ache in her heart.

Until a crash from the kitchen broke the stillness, she had assumed she was flying solo with her misery. Cautiously, she stole a glance through the kitchen door's window, expecting Emilio or one of the line cooks making a final round of checks.

She didn't expect Jack.

Her heart rate sped up to dangerous levels, not unlike three nights ago when she crept down that alley. He should have been gone, but he was here, and she luxuriated in a moment's hope. She used that moment to watch him secretly. No longer in his chef's togs, he wore faded jeans and an even more faded Pink Floyd T-shirt that molded the flexing contours of his broad back. It went without saying that he looked hotter than hell, but she told herself the news all the same.

"You're here," she said stupidly.

"Just finishing up," he said without looking at her. He returned to his task of scrubbing something the kitchen crew could handle tomorrow.

"Can we talk?"

"I'm all talked out." He looked up and met her gaze. His mossy eyes had turned to hunter green, dark buttons in his tired face. There was none of the heat and intensity she had come to love, only cold reproach and a hardness that shocked her. She wanted him to warm her with his gaze, soothe her with his touch. She wanted *her* Jack.

"Jack, I can't thank you enough for what you did tonight. You have no idea how much it meant to me."

No response, just the scratch-scrape of the steel wool against the pan. She took a wonky step, hoping that inching closer to him might help dissipate the animosity crackling through the air. Might help to ease him as it had done after Jules's bombshell. He scrubbed harder.

"I can only imagine what you must think of us."

He set the pan on the dish rack to be run through the next dishwasher cycle, then fixed her with a stare of such flat rage that she recoiled.

"I don't think anything."

She doubted that very much. "You have every right—"

"Because I'm not supposed to think, am I? I'm just supposed to shut up and play my part. At least, now I know why you didn't want to date me. It was easier to string me along until I leave. Keep me sweet while you played me like a fiddle."

"Jack, I haven't been playing you. I wanted to date you. I want to date you." Her words sounded too small for the moment, not urgent enough to repel his accusation.

"Oh, really? Have you finally worked out that being associated with me is good for your business? I've had people try to work me for a profit, but I never would have expected this from *you*."

He said it like he knew her. She had felt as though he did. Hurt rolled off him in waves, lapping at her heart.

"I told you things, Lili. Things about my father, about Jules. Stuff I've never told another living soul." He threw a dishtowel at the sink. It missed and sailed sadly to the floor. "Have you gathered enough information for when the gutter press come knocking? Should be quite the exclusive. You've got all the up-close-and-personal shots on your camera and now some juicy human interest gossip to round it out. His father's not interested and his sister will only talk to him when she's hit rock bottom. Shit writes itself. Jack Kilroy, good in the kitchen, good in the sack, not so good in real life."

Realization warmed the glacial air and pricked her skin. This went so much deeper than the show. She wanted to curl her body around him and tell him he was mistaken. Tell him he could trust her just like she knew she could trust him.

"Jack, I haven't been playing you. You've got to believe that. I know we got off on the wrong foot, that it looked like I wanted you for one thing, but it's different now. I swear."

But hours of simmering had stewed his anger into something sour. Fury sharpened his features to granite, and when he spoke, it was rougher and less cultured than usual.

"I felt sorry for you. I thought you were actually upset about that video. About all those mean things being said about you. You offered up your sob story and I fell for it hook, line, and sinker. But no, you had a completely different agenda and it doesn't matter who gets hurt. I'm just a guy with hot hands and a hard-on, a narcissistic fame whore primed to lose his ever-loving mind when a sexy girl comes onto him in a bar. A bar filled with your friends and relatives and coworkers all ready to get the money shot."

The cold dread chilling her veins hardened to ice. Back to that ridiculous accusation? "You've got this all wrong, Jack. I already told you my family wasn't responsible for the video." But even as the words slipped past her lips, doubt assailed her. She just didn't know anymore.

"Tell me, was the video a spur-of-the-moment thing or were you and Marco in cahoots all along? And when that wasn't enough to guarantee full houses, you thought having your father beat the famous chef might be better all around."

Mind flailing, she battled to process this latest punch. Jack thought she planned that video—with Marco? He thought she purposefully made herself a laughing stock and invited a storm of torrential hate to rain down on her. And for what? A few extra bookings for her family's restaurant.

That was wrong on so many levels she didn't know where to start. She didn't have to. Suddenly he appeared taller, larger; then she realized it was because he was closer. Looming over her with those green-gold eyes dark as burned caramel. The freckly smudges she had worshipped with her mouth, all thirteen of them, were practically transparent against the high color in his face.

Trying to parse gradations of the truth would be futile. She had stopped Gina—she had fired her—but the actions of her cheating family were down to her. The buck stopped here, she thought grimly, like she was the president or something.

"I had nothing to do with that video. My family made a mistake and I take full responsibility for it."

In his fury-stoked eyes, she thought she saw a flash of the Jack she knew, but it vanished before she could grasp it.

"Which part, Lili? Which part was a mistake?" A couple more steps and he had sealed them together, his forearms trapping her against the countertop. All banked heat, his body vibrated raw power, a contrast to his unyielding mouth, cruel and unforgiving. Still beautiful, though. Always that.

He rubbed his thumb across her lip, soft, devastating, and she gasped at the tenderness, another electrifying difference from the hard, unbending lines of his face. It shamed her to admit it, but that simple touch was enough to rev her body up to all systems go in zero point zero seconds flat.

"Which part was a mistake, Lili? Kissing me senseless in that bar? Playing hot nurse at my hotel? Letting me stroke and tease you until you could barely stand it? Biting me when I wouldn't fuck you fast enough? Was that a mistake?"

He pushed his thumb past her lips and the heat in her belly turned to want. And the want turned to need. And the need turned to heat again. She moaned.

At the sound, he dropped his hand from her face as if her touch made his skin crawl. His eyes dimmed, like all the lights in the city had blacked out in one fell swoop.

"I think the mistake was that you were found out. I've just been a pawn in your games. Promote the restaurant. Win back Marco. Take your pick. And if you get your rocks off along the way, that's a bonus. Cara told me all about the plan. How I was brought in to show you a good time."

Now her gasp was from shock instead of pleasure. She couldn't get a full breath. Only useless little bursts of air made it to her lungs.

"We could have been so good together. So damn—" He raked his hair fast, but not so fast she missed the tremor in his hand. "I should have just screwed you when you threw yourself at me."

A choked sob caught in her throat. Whoever said words could never hurt hadn't the first idea what they were talking about. She felt hollowed out, her chest a large, empty cavity. No heartbeat, no breaths, nothing.

Then he was gone.

She wiped tears from her eyes with shaky hands and slumped against the countertop. Her skin still burned from where his thumb had branded her.

A few hours ago, she had felt she could do anything because being with him had that effect. She could get the restaurant back on track and finally apply to grad school. She could fix things between Jack and his sister. She could give herself to the most exciting man she had ever met and revel in his naked desire for her. The thought of seeing more of him had scared her, but she could withstand a lot, even insults and jibes from people she had never met. But not from him. She was strong, but not that strong.

Because if she were stronger, she wouldn't be feeling like her entire world had crashed around her ears and the one person who could make it better despised the floor she stood on.

CHAPTER EIGHTEEN

This hotel suite is too bloody small, Jack decided.

And there was nothing on TV. A *Kilroy's Kitchen* episode sighting resulted in a resounding strike of the Off button on the remote. At the moment, he couldn't stand his real self, never mind that impostor on the small screen.

Since stalking out of DeLuca's a couple of hours ago, he'd fought an internal battle, trying to push from his memory Lili's injured expression when he'd laid out his indictment of the DeLucas. Either she was good enough to give Meryl Streep a run for her Oscars or he'd got it so wrong he had destroyed everything.

But damn, he wasn't wrong. A mistake, she'd said about her family's cheatin' ways. Sure was. One big mistake, yet somehow he was the one left feeling like shit. That kind of math made no sense. Not getting laid for months, that was the kind of math he understood because when you haven't had sex for an eternity, it blocks up your brain. Lili was the first woman to spark his interest since he'd started this ludicrous sex fast, and he had let her burrow under his skin.

No.

More.

He should watch porn. That'd teach her. But even though he'd demanded the indiscreet, snap-happy employee who had uploaded photos of his breakfast banquet be gifted his pink slip, Jack still couldn't be sure that tasty morsel wouldn't get passed on to the press. *Jack Kilroy watched* Busty Babes of Baja Beach. *Twice!* Anyway, who needed porn when his brain was jam-packed with one gorgeous Italian girl wearing a come-hither smile that guaranteed a permanent hard-on? Oh, and he was clearly a masochist because the object of his obsession didn't just despise him—she'd flat-out used him. Just like Ashley with her tell-all. Just like John Sullivan with his upturned palm. Those heart-crushing disappointments should have taught him to calibrate his hopes.

But she sacked Gina.

Big deal. She protected Marco. No doubt she was enjoying the comfort of his Armani-suited arms right this minute.

Arms you drove her into.

Didn't have far to go, though, did she? She had run to that rat-tailed d-bag when her mother was ill and now…now he needed to drown his chatty conscience in a vat of scotch before he did something stupid like race to her apartment and sing to her. Maybe something from *Les Misérables* this time.

His skin felt like he'd peeled back three layers to the blood-saturated sinew underneath and scoured it with bleach. In his mind's playback of the night, every word, gesture, and nuance stroked him raw. Had he screwed up? If he had, it wouldn't be the first time. Jules leaped to the forefront of his guilt-ridden mind. Always Jules, with his mother's eyes drowning in accusation.

Only one time had his stepfather brought him to visit Mum in that run-down hospital, the walls and people worn and sagging like something out of a Dickens novel, the stench of disinfectant doing a miserable job of masking the cloying smell of sickness. Angry with her for some childish reason he could no longer recall, he had refused her pleas to hug him. At twelve, he was too old for maternal affection, too self-absorbed to care for her needs. If he had known it was the last time he would see her, he'd have clasped her frail, cancer-ravaged body to his until they pried him away screaming.

Look after your sister, Jack, she had said in her soft Irish burr to his retreating back. When his stepfather passed a couple of years later, Jack still had some fuzzy notion of becoming Jules's guardian once he was of age, but he'd had things to do. Trouble to find and a life to plan when trouble found him. The new freedom he felt in the kitchen had trumped duty and a mother's wish. Wasn't he doing his sister a favor by putting her in a two-parent home with Pete and Daisy? His peripatetic lifestyle couldn't be adapted to the needs of a kid.

Now Jules was here to cash in on all those broken promises and she'd come armed with a doozy. He had felt so useless until Lili stepped in. Calm, competent, no-fuss Lili with her sultry voice set to salve. A woman who knew the meaning of family and could help translate the code. With her, he felt like he could be a better chef, a better brother, a better man. Just better.

Yeah, she knew the meaning of family all right. She would cheat and lie and use for them. And his nitpicking conscience answered, *What about Gina, idiot?*

Two a.m. in the middle of a vibrant, cosmopolitan city. There must be a bar open nearby, something seedy that might turn the boiling self-recrimination in his belly to a surly simmer. He dragged himself off the sofa, wrenched open the door, and got the surprise of his life.

Lili.

One hand clutched her scooter helmet beneath her heaving breasts like a talisman, the other paused in mid-knock. The forbidding set of her full, lush mouth signaled purpose, and combined with her cotton-cloud hair and orange flip-flops, it made her look like a fiery goddess. Her eyes blazed volcanic, sending trails of lava through him that blew hotter than the ninety-five-degree air outside.

Hungrily, he surveyed the rest of her. A turquoise bra strap drooped off her shoulder, a clashing contrast to the yellow sundress that hugged her curves and revealed about ten inches of glorious thigh. As usual, gazing on her legs inevitably led to how they were attached to her other luscious body parts, firing his body like a kiln from the inside out. But flip-flops? They seemed like the least appropriate footwear for riding a scooter. Maybe she should wear a sweater in case she caught a cold.

Stop worrying about her, you moron. Because she was clearly capable of taking care of number one.

His hazy focus trickled upward, giving way to a chest pang with a revisit to her face. No more thunder, just her heart, big and beating in her eyes. She bit down on her lip, a move he knew she didn't intend as erotic but that registered as unbearably so.

"Lili—" The words clotted in his throat. Never tongue-tied, he always knew what to say. His hands were his tools, but words came a close second. He was British, for Chrissake.

Finally he managed, "Why are you here?"

"Because I need to fulfill my quota of Brit-accented insults." She jabbed her helmet into his chest. Hard. "Why do you think I'm here? You got your divo on and accused me of some pretty heinous crimes. We need to sort this out."

"There's nothing to sort out. You used me. End of." He clenched his teeth so hard he risked grinding them to bony fragments. Less than twenty feet away, a well-dressed couple stood by the elevator, craning their heads, looking suspiciously like opera lovers. It would be all over the hotel, or worse, in minutes.

He yanked her inside and slammed the door. For privacy, he told himself. But now she was close enough to taste, both of them trapped in the small entry about two feet apart. Since meeting her, he'd fooled himself into thinking his body was the traitor, which he now knew was a blatant fallacy. All the treachery could be laid squarely at the door of his mind. The mind that wanted a woman who didn't want him.

"You took Marco's side. He put up that video and he's guilty of God knows what else."

"You don't know he's behind that." She didn't sound convinced. "The salting, yes, but—"

"Still defending him, I see. Still madly in love."

"I'm not in love with him," she said, her voice louder, clearer. "I don't think I ever was. Not really."

Relief bubbled through his veins but it couldn't quite overtake the nice head of righteous anger he'd worked up. "Tell that to him. The way he looks at you—"

"I can't help how he looks at me," she said before adding softly, "How does he look at me?"

"Like he can think of nothing but stripping you and stroking your skin. Exploring your body. Making you his."

Hands trembling, she folded her arms beneath her breasts. Good to know he wasn't the only one having trouble keeping it together.

"That's not how he looks at me. That's how you look at me."

His body caved with the weight of her accusation. The undeniable rightness of it. Her eyes bored into him, broadcasting her need, dragging him in.

"I wasn't working with him," she said. "I swear I had no idea what he or Gina were up to, and as soon as I found out, I stopped it. I was coming to tell you when your sister showed up and everything went—"

"Pear-shaped?" he finished on a sigh.

She nodded. "It might have looked like I took his side but I was worried you were going to go all ultimate fighter and drop-kick him into the middle of the next millennium."

A conclusion that was fairly well founded. Deep down, he knew what she said was true and damn if he didn't hate when unassailable logic butted up against his more visceral impulses.

"I know that the life you lead means you have a hard time trusting people, Jack. Half the world wants to sleep with you and the other half wants to be you. You're richer than God, ten times as arrogant, and everyone wants a piece. But I don't care about any of that. I'm not interested in what I can get out of you, Jack. I'm only interested in you."

Her words humbled him. This was Lili, *his* Lili. The woman who never hesitated to put everyone else's needs ahead of her own. Who chose him over her family when she sacked Gina. Shit, she had actually done that. Shame eddied through his gut that he could ever have doubted her.

She edged closer and, incrementally, he matched her moves. At this rate, they might be within touching distance by Christmas.

"Do you mean that? You want me…not…" He couldn't finish for feeling foolish. *Not Jack Kilroy, not his image, not that other guy.*

"Yes. Just you." She stretched out her hand. Christmas had come early.

He grasped it for the lifesaving device it was and bound her to him. Her helmet hit the carpet with a soft thud; her arms twined around his waist.

"I know I've made mistakes but I'm only human." Her cheek felt wet against his throat. "And you're here with your blockbuster chest and your hot mouth and all that terrifying certainty. I don't want the man I see on billboards and magazine covers and TV. *They* can have him. I want the man who makes me feel like anything is possible."

His heart clicked into place like the final puzzle piece. Did she not realize that she already had him?

"Forgive me, Lili. The things I said…I was out of my mind." He clasped her close, all while murmuring words

of affection and apology and biting back the one thing
fighting to find voice.

I love you.

He didn't kiss her yet or scare her, or himself, with
crazy declarations of love. Plenty of time for that later.
Minutes passed as the tide of their breathing slowed to
semi-normal.

"I can't believe you canned Gina."

Her eyes welled with tears, crumbling what was left of
his internal organs to dust. "It had to be done. Girl was
out of control." Sniffling, she swiped at her cheek. "And I
can't believe you were jealous of Marco."

Strangely, hearing her acknowledge it relaxed him. "I
really should be more evolved than this."

"The Neanderthal thing works. You're pretty hot when
you get all shouty."

There she was, his beautiful smart-mouth.

He cupped her cheek and glided his thumb across her
quivering bottom lip. That tremble was all the invitation
he needed. Their mouths searched and queried, frantic
for each other's attention. All his problems faded away
in her kiss. Urging her closer, he pressed the hollow of
her back, and her heat seeped through his denim-covered
thigh, shiver-shocking him until he forgot his own name.

She pulled away from his hungry mouth long enough
to ask, "Jack, are we dating again?"

He parted from her long enough to chuckle at her less-
than-subtle plea for sex. "Yes, yes. We're dating again,"
and then it hit him and he detached completely.

"I don't have condoms."

He had stopped carrying months ago so he would be
more likely to think before he had heedless sex with

a production assistant or anyone who fit the bill for a no-strings lay. Could he order condoms through room service? Was that even possible? Of course it wasn't possible. And if it was, it wasn't smart. He would have to go out. Leave her again.

Slowly, languidly, she dipped into the pocket of her dress and pulled out a square-shaped, shiny blue wrapper. He almost fell to his knees in supplication at the most beautiful sight he had ever seen. After her, of course.

"Hmm, you think one's going to be enough?"

"A girl who carries more than one risks getting a bad reputation." With a sensuous slide of her tongue across her bottom lip, she drew out another and held it up with its mate like a winning poker hand. Her hand foraged again and retrieved more, which fell to the floor in a cascade. She had enough condoms to suit up an orgy.

"I lost the other half when the Vespa hit a pothole on Michigan Avenue."

It took him a full seven seconds to recover.

She covered her mouth like a naughty child, new color brightening her cheeks. She was embarrassed, but in that moment any doubts he'd had about her vanished. Love couldn't describe what he felt right now. More like ruination.

"You're pretty confident," he pushed out, trying to make light, impossible when his heart felt too full for his chest.

Brushing by him into the suite, she slipped a couple of condoms into his pocket. "Just a cock-eyed optimist. I figured after turning me down twice, third time's the charm."

That it was. He was the luckiest man alive.

"Lili," he said, searching for the right words. "*Grazie*."

She greeted that with an eyebrow jump. "Show me."

Peeling off his shirt rendered him blind for a few precious seconds, and when he found light again, she was walking away from him, pulling her dress up over her head. Strip-walking. Jesus, she was strip-walking and how she was able to get that hip sway without heels was doing strange things to his brain.

She turned to present those mouthwatering breasts falling over lacy cups and generous curves filling out underwear that looked like shorts. Speaking of *Busty Babes of B—*

"What's wrong?" she whispered, all humor drained from her face.

He tried to catch his breath. "You're so gorgeous, Lili. Your skin, your breasts, your—"

"Are you just going to stand there talking about me all night?"

He could stand and look at her all day, but his dick would not be down with that plan. The rush of desire drowned out the thump of his heart. The suite he had thought too small ten minutes ago was suddenly too big, and before she could react, he had hoisted her up so she was curled around his hips.

"Oh," she gasped. "Jack, you shouldn't—oh, God, I love how strong you are."

He pushed through to the lamp-lit bedroom while she pressed her open mouth to his neck and sucked at his pulse, making his skin sizzle. Tossing her onto the bed, he got another approving "oh" while he stood back to assess his options. So inviting, yet he had no idea where to start. He needed more hands, or better yet tentacles. He needed to be Octo-Jack.

Forward momentum met unexpected resistance when she placed her foot flat against his stomach. "Wait," she said. Standing, she spread her hands over his chest, her touch cool on his scorching skin. "Let me look at you first."

That was code for slow down. Slow was good. Slow was very good because he was ten miles past desperate here, and if he didn't ease up to at least five, he was going to make a fool of himself. Avidly, he watched the leisurely but measured path her hands took.

"Do I make the grade?"

"Hmm, B plus."

"I'm improving," he said, remembering how she ranked his kissing technique that first night.

She slipped around to his back, the raspy caress of her bra's lace shooting tingles through him. Her hands appraised lovingly—over his drum-tight skin, circling his shoulder blades, his knotted muscles, trailing fire down to his hips. She ran her fingers to his stomach, tracing the hair above his navel, and it took all his strength not to push them down to his cock.

Crackling-hot kisses dripped down the ladder of his spine, sending every nerve into meltdown. He felt her sigh, a warm flutter as she placed her cheek against his back.

"Jack," she whispered, scarcely audible above his serrated breathing.

"Yes, Lili?"

"What do you like?"

His skin prickled and his erection bulged hard against his zipper. He needed to free it, but the anticipation was so downright enjoyable and exquisitely painful.

"What do I like?" What did he like? Her. This. *Her* and *this*.

She curled back around to stand before him and cleaved her body to his. "Yeah, what you like. Don't you like certain things?"

The metallic scrape of his descending zipper almost unraveled him. His cock stretched against his boxers, pushing into her belly and willing her to provide the resistance he needed.

"We can get into specifics later. Right now, I just want to slide into you and never leave."

Her eyes grew wide like what she was seeing wouldn't fit in them. "I thought you'd want something—" She clamped down on her plump bottom lip.

"Kinky? Not for our first time, sweetheart." A stray thought needled through his lust haze. "Lili, you know all that online stuff about my sex life was rubbish, right?"

"Sure, I knew that," she said, sounding a trifle disappointed.

He laughed and kissed her deep. "We're going to figure this out. What you like. What I like. What we both like. There's no one else in this room but you and me." Having to live in the shadow of his tabloid reputation was bad enough; he didn't need its long fingers in the bedroom. He pushed his jeans and boxers down in one fluid movement and kicked them off. No slouch, she plunked down on the bed, shucking her panties as she went.

"Wow." Her eyes widened on seeing his erection, now cocked and aimed right at her mouth. She slanted her head to a couple of different angles. He felt like her next art project or a *Playgirl* centerfold.

"That's what I've been putting up with since I met you, Lili."

"Poor Jack," she murmured as her soft fingers wrapped around him. At the slight touch, he groaned, the satisfaction of her finally holding him saturating his senses. But there was apprehension mixed with the desire. He was nervous, something he hadn't experienced since he was a kid. She had this surreal effect on him.

"I can't believe I'm finally getting to touch it," she whispered in mock awe. "Jack Kilroy's illustrious member."

"My what?"

"It's just that you've been so stingy. Not letting me play with it, telling me I had to wait. I assumed it must be gold-plated or bejeweled—"

"You've got a cheek," he spluttered while her hands did wicked, wonderful things.

Her thumb glided along the bulging head, spreading the moisture that had beaded at the tip. She bent forward and delivered a chaste brush of her lips that surprised him so much he jumped, but then she raised those killer blues to him, and chaste was nowhere in evidence. Only naughtiness.

An unhurried glide of that luscious pink tongue across her lips, sheened with his precome, produced a hum of pleasure from deep in her throat. She liked how he tasted and that turned him on so much he started to shake. She was a chef's wet dream. His wet dream. A woman who enjoyed the salt and the sweet, the taste of his food and the taste of him.

His dick grew an extra couple of inches on the spot.

She fell to her knees and something inside him broke.

She could have stayed sitting on the bed but that simple act of kneeling did it for him right there. She owned him now.

Sweet butterfly kisses were the opening course along his thigh; then her tongue licked higher with rich, velvet strokes before she took him in her mouth. Christ Almighty, it was all he could manage not to shoot off like an uncapped blender. A recipe. Run through a recipe. *Gougères*. Combine butter, milk, salt—

"Lili." His hands cradled her head, intending to push her back to retain some grip on his sanity. Instead, he held her steady and planted his feet, digging his toes into the soft carpet. Anything to stop from thrusting because if he started, he wouldn't stop and he needed to last. To make it good for them both. Her mouth, wet and warm, slid along his dick in a delicious rhythm. He swept her riotous hair back so he could get a better view of her lips and cheeks as she sucked. So damn pretty. His balls tightened with every draw but he forced his pleasure deep.

"That's it, love. Just like that."

He still couldn't believe she'd chased him down, that she'd been brave enough to see past his bullshit and meet it head-on. Because let's face it, a relationship with him was no pleasure trip along the Seine. He didn't do anything by halves, and he needed a woman who was willing to travel that road with him. A woman who understood that he demanded a similar energy and passion because that was the only way he knew.

It was going to kill him if this wasn't real.

Real or not, he knew how he wanted their first time to be, and as much as he loved what her mouth was doing, there was no way he was getting off like this. Fully primed and teetering on the edge, he coaxed her head back.

"Sweetheart, I need to be inside you." He grabbed a condom from the pocket of his discarded jeans.

"Let me." She took it and encouraged him to lie on his back so she could straddle him. Her assertiveness astonished him, turning his arousal up to a level he didn't think possible. Any higher and his balls might never recover. Deftly, she rolled on the condom.

"I thought it had been a while," he said, his tongue thick and rubbery.

"Oh, I've been keeping my hand in. Practicing on bananas."

He laughed loudly, so at odds with what they were doing. Until Lili, he'd never wanted to laugh and fuck a woman at the same time. That quiet, dry humor of hers gave him as much pleasure as her clever hands and her lush body.

"Take off your bra."

Eyes never leaving his, she unhooked and released her perfectly sculpted breasts.

"Look at you. So beautiful." And she was. Achingly so. He ran his hands over her breasts, loving how responsive they were to his touch.

"Oh, Jack," she murmured with a vulnerability that knocked his heart clear across the room.

He propped up on one elbow and gentled her head toward his. She needed to understand what was happening here even if he hardly understood it himself. "You slay me, Lili DeLuca. Utterly, completely."

He heard her breath catch in her throat. Tears pooled in her eyes, flecking her lower lashes like diamonds when she blinked, but then she regrouped. Those shiny blues now blazed, fired with desire and longing and maybe some of that confidence he had to spare.

"Jack, I need you." And with that, she lowered herself onto him slowly, so slowly he feared his brain would melt. He grasped her hips and pulled her down a couple of magnificent inches to the tune of her satisfied sigh.

"Don't stop," he said. "Feels so good."

She took him in a little farther, panting while her body softened and adjusted. His cock thickened beyond what he thought possible and a winding pressure built at its base. Her tight, wet heat wrapped around him. Her fire, her body, his Lili. All wrapped around him.

Anchored to her, he knew that finally he was exactly where he was meant to be.

CHAPTER NINETEEN

Lili's body was hyperaware, every nerve teased and tensed. She had never felt so desired. So powerful. Jack had gone months without sex; he could have any woman he wanted, but he had held out for her. Okay, he'd held out three days for her but still.

Her planned outrage had fizzled the moment he opened that door and she saw a hollow-eyed Jack staring back at her. Hurt made people act ten kinds of crazy, and while she was the kind of person who internalized her pain, Jack wore his emotions on his sleeve, then wanted to talk about the soiled shirt. Passion that raw scared the hell out of her, but she knew she was the person to fill those deep pockets of sadness he wore, to give him what he needed and get what she needed in return. This time, this place, they could do for each other what no one else could.

As she rolled her hips, he arched to meet her, his fingers digging into her flesh so hard she suspected she might have bruises later. She contracted her muscles around his length, muscles that hadn't been used in a while, and imagined they would have something to say about that later, too.

He lightly brushed his knuckles against her breast. A shivery tease, but she needed it rougher. She leaned into his touch, urging more pressure, and his thumbs dragged over her nipples and rolled. She almost died from pleasure. He slid his hands under her famous butt and raised it a couple of inches, reminding her of where she was. What she was doing. Jack was buried inside her, and a man's hardness had never felt this good.

"Move with me," he panted.

Slowly, she slid up, down, accelerating the pace in rhythm with the urgency of his hands. Every motion was slick and wet, pulsing through her with fluid heat.

He cupped her neck and drew her close. Their mouths joined hungrily, tongues meeting and getting along like a house on fire. She licked his stubbled jaw, his scar, his gorgeous, crooked mouth. Her own personalized tasting menu. Jack à la carte. The brush of his chest hair tickled and warmed her breasts, a strangely comforting sensation in the midst of all this down and dirty lust. She continued to slip up and down, her clitoris getting the love against his sleek, thick length. Arousal, sharp and urgent, surprised her and she moaned softly.

"Better," he said. Not a question, just a statement of fact.

"Yes."

He knew the right angles, the right moves, the right pressure. He knew her body and what she needed. He was in her head, reading her lusty thoughts before they could fire. *Yeah, just there. Baby, so good. Never, never stop.*

She loved the feel of him, the silky slide of his skin against hers. Being on top, getting that deep, deep penetration. It had always been a favorite position but self-consciousness usually prevented her from enjoying it fully or even asking for what she wanted. But not now. In Jack's eyes, she saw unguarded appreciation of her shapely, sexy body. She saw everything she had been missing.

His thick girth glided in and out of her, every downstroke caressing her core until her vision hazed. Such a simple motion, Jack filling her up, again and again, but it was too restrained. Too…British. She needed more. She needed to be broken open.

"Jack?"

"Yes, sweetheart?" His fascinated gaze lifted from where their bodies joined. Halting the show for a moment, she settled and leaned in so close she could count every beautiful eyelash.

"I'm a big girl. Don't be gentle."

A very male sound rose in his throat, barely human but unmistakably Jack. He flipped her on her back and still managed to stay inside her. Not expecting that. Neither was she expecting his hot, deep reach as he impaled her to the root. She grasped the tightly loomed muscles of his excellent ass. She scratched and clawed. She might have hurt him but she didn't care. His moans as he pounded her said he didn't care all that much either.

She loved a man who could follow instructions.

She rocked with him as his powerful hips thrust him farther into her and he speared her with long, rhythmic strokes. Every motion generated waves of pleasure, starting with where their bodies connected, radiating through her belly, her rear, her breasts, and her toes, and back down the spokes again.

"Yes, that's—ah, yes," he moaned, and her body pulsed in agreement.

It's never been this hot it's so hot this can't get any hotter. And just as those thought fragments bonded, he hooked her leg up, creating an angle that had her close to losing the will to live. His other hand gentled her jaw, coaxing her to face him and meet that intimate green-gold gaze.

She resisted. She had to, knowing that as soon as she went there, she would come and it would be over. And *she* would be over because one look from Jack would confirm it had never been like this with anyone, and likely never would be again.

"Lili, please."

His vibrating voice reached inside and laid siege to her heart. She was used to being needed but not like this, and that need in him jumbled with her need for him until they were entangled in a crush of mindless want. She opened her eyes and surrendered her fate to this man. Her man.

Her arousal heightened and a keen pleasure swept over her, around her, inside her. Thought, speech, none of it was necessary as her brain switched off and her blood and skin and nerve endings took over. Slowly, he raised his body up but his gaze never left hers, and she wanted him to look at her like that forever. She hit that flash point, wailing while her body convulsed and flew apart in pure sensation. Depth charges exploded at every nerve ending.

Shards of pleasure lingered at each for a moment before returning to their source.

As she rode the dying shudders of her pleasure-drunk haze, he gave one final thrust. His jaw clenched; his neck muscles strained. Simply watching him was its own high. She felt him rattle and release before he went rigid and collapsed on top of her.

Quietly, she lay there, loving the weight of him and how he smelled and sweated and breathed. The natural fit of him in her body. Moments passed while he remained lodged deep, branding her from the inside out until he shifted them both on their sides to face each other. Hating to leave the heat of him, she inched back, but he clamped a big hand over her butt and draped her leg over his.

"Stay." He was still wedged within, firmly filling her and my God, that was sexy. Most guys would be creeping to the other side of the king-size by now.

Forever, she almost said. With a purr of assent, she slipped into a dreamy doze, loosely aware of his lips rasping her jaw and his hands roaming her curves. Learning her shape, making plans for later. When she opened her eyes again, he had left her body, but she didn't feel cold. Light from the bedside lamp threw eyelash-smudged shadows on his cheeks, illuminating his big, dopey grin.

Blinking, she took a candid for her memories, then curled into his side.

"What are you smiling about?" Yep, she was shamelessly fishing.

He squeezed her tight to his chest. "I just got laid and it was damn near perfect."

"Only near perfect?"

"Well, it was a little fast, but that's understandable considering how desperate you've been. Next time, we'll take it slower."

She pinched his biceps to punish his cheekiness, but he didn't even flinch. Ridiculous, hard muscles.

"Seriously, though," he said. "I can't remember it ever being this good."

"Abstinence makes the penis grow fonder."

"It's not a line."

She lifted her chin to study him. No, it wasn't a line. He was more honest than anyone she knew but she refused to get caught up in his postcoital hype. Someone had to keep a clear head.

"You must have slept with—" Lots? Best to stop there. "Lots of women. You can't possibly think that."

"You're the hottest, sexiest woman I've ever seen, and I love how you make me feel." He swept her hair from her eyes and gifted her a wicked burn of a smile. "I'm not saying it to drag some matching confession out of you. It is what it is."

Stunned, she laid her cheek against his chest and listened to his heart, the ultimate lie detector. It clacked along like a galloping horse, finding a rhythm with the hammering pulse all over her body. She felt the same way, though she didn't have to dig deep for comparisons. No one had ever wrung this much pleasure from her. No one had ever made her feel this special. No one had ever cared enough to.

She traced a finger around his nipple and kissed it when it popped up to say hello; then she kissed lower. Over the most open heart she had ever known.

"Have I freaked you out?" he asked.

She nodded, but it turned into a sensuous cat rub against his delicious fur. Laying bare was so not her forte, and years of avoiding attention had produced coping mechanisms Freud would have a hard time unraveling. In spite of those guardrails, her heart rolled over, revealing its underbelly.

When she looked up, his burning gaze met her head-on, all artifice stripped. Only Jack and those eyes that held no secrets.

"Lili, when I want something…well, you've probably noticed I can be a bit intense. I know that scares you. Am I right?"

"Yes," she said, her voice barely registering in the cavernous suite.

"Good. Scared is good." He nodded a few times, and then a few times more. She wouldn't have thought it possible for him to be more attractive, but here he was, naked and vulnerable in every way. It toppled her.

Three days ago, Jack Kilroy had been the designated fling. The sexy rut to get her out of her boring rut. The guy to turn her on and turn off that blinking "Service engine soon" light. It was supposed to be a one-night stand, a temporary mantidote to her problems, yet here they were, scaring the hell out of each other. And oh, was she terrified.

Lili had made some big decisions these last couple of days—hitting on *Bon Appetit*'s Sexiest Chef Alive, agreeing to date a guy who should have been all wrong for her, coming after him because the idea of losing him made her physically ill—but even those crazy moments paled in comparison to what she needed to do. Tell him that he slayed her, too. Completely, utterly.

"Jack," she whispered.

No response. She raised her head and lapsed into a smile.

The rise and fall of his warm chest and the steady sough told her the afterglow soul-baring would not be happening tonight. After several sleepless nights and a very satisfactory orgasm, Jack Kilroy had finally fallen asleep.

So, mortal after all.

* * *

Jack was trying not to shout at his sister partly because being pregnant gave her a pass, but mostly because Francesca and Tad were hanging on his every word not ten feet away in the DeLuca family kitchen.

Out on the patio sofa, Jules folded her long legs under her body and set her jaw. "I told you I'm not coming to London with you."

"You can't bury your problems, Jules."

She gave him an oh-yes-I-can smirk. "Francesca and Tony have offered to let me stay for a while," she said, unable to keep the triumph out of her voice.

Irritation notched his throat, though he was already privy to her scoop. On his arrival, Francesca laid her hand on his arm and said, "She's safe with us," and he almost tackled her to the ground in a hug of gratitude. Now he was having second, third, and fourth thoughts.

"You can't stay here. They're complete strangers."

"Really, Jack? Complete strangers? I'd say you know one member of the family quite well." Her eyes glittered like golden coins, a light that spread to her smart-arse smile. She was enjoying this. Pregnant in a strange city with people she met five minutes ago and she was enjoying it.

Still didn't stop him from smiling back. Yes, he knew Lili quite well and the memory of her coming apart for him so many times would have to fuel him for the next few days. She had wrung him dry and left him boneless. He would sleep well on the plane.

"So Lili seems nice. Did you have fun?" she asked, still with the impish grin.

"None of your business. Back to you."

"I'll be here when you return." She left this suspended between them, the implication being that he would whisk her away to New York in some fairy-tale resolution to all their problems.

"You know how busy I am. How much I travel. Wouldn't it be better to stay with Pete and Daisy? They can look after you." He sure as hell couldn't. So proven multiple times over.

"I know you think I'm a burden," she said, scoring a direct hit on the guilt center of his brain. "But I can get a job."

"You're not even legally able to work here. And you need to stay off your feet."

Her mouth wobbled. "Jack, I'm not a little girl anymore. I can look after myself, but I have to get out of London."

Again, that ominous dread trickled through him. "Why?"

She looked shifty. "I just do. I need the change."

"Is the father—" He gestured to her stomach, still not quite believing the magnitude of her situation. If he said it a million times out loud, it would take him an age to comprehend it. *Pregnant*. His baby sister was going to have a baby. "Is he giving you a hard time?"

"I haven't told him."

Of course she hadn't. "Who is it?"

"I told you it's no one you know."

"Jules," he warned.

"He's married," she pushed out quickly, then held up her hand in a calming motion that had the opposite effect. "And before you ask, I didn't know."

"Married? Oh, Jules." His skin prickled at the thought of his sister with a taken man and this piece of shit getting off scot-free. "Married or not, he needs to take responsibility."

Her face shuttered to blank, a vacuous expression she'd perfected when she was a teen. When she pulled that one out, he knew the conversation was over. Maybe she'd be okay here with a generous, loving family who could do for her where he was incapable. The bitter tang of failure oozed from his overheated skin. Rage seething through him, he stood to leave and barely restrained himself from kicking a large potted plant on the deck.

"Let's talk in a few days, Jack," she said, sounding like the mature one. That was just perfect. "And bring back some decent tea. The stuff here tastes like cat piss."

CHAPTER TWENTY

Lili's eyelids were stuck together, but finally they cracked apart. A flick to the clock on her nightstand. Late again.

She searched for clean panties, but nothing was doing, not even the old-lady ones she usually shoved to the back of her underwear drawer. That's what happened when you ignored laundry for three weeks. Wrenching on a crumpled tee and skirt, she bounded to the door and almost collapsed with pleasure.

Mouthwatering scents filled her apartment. Wow, that gorgeous Brit knew how to hit her where she lived. He'd gone all out this morning with not just her favorite lemon-ricotta pancakes, but also the apple-smoked bacon she'd picked up at Green City Market yesterday morning. Delish.

Rounding the corner, her breath caught as it did every time she found him standing at the stove. While there was nothing sexier than a man who knew his way around a kitchen, this was just ridiculous. Faded blue denim, slung dangerously low on his hips, skimming the floor around his bare feet. Back muscles rippling—not too much, but rippling all the same—while working the bacon. And just about the sexiest ass she'd ever seen on a man.

She would never get sick of the view.

Though he could only manage a couple of days in between tapings, the last two weeks had lived up to their billing. Mornings were spent like characters in a sixties New Wave French movie. Eating, making love, planning bank heists. Well, not the criminal conspiracy part, but it was just as thrilling and more than a little terrifying.

He wanted to hear all her stories, from anecdotes about her embarrassing relatives (a bottomless well) to her inspiration for her upcoming art projects (he thought sexualized vegetables had a certain *je ne sais quoi*). On his trips away, he called, smugly announcing he had won the *Jack of All Trades* challenges in New Orleans and Austin. Seemed only the Italians played dirty. And while the phone sex was off the charts, it couldn't replace the man himself. Waking up with Jack sliding into her was the hottest alarm call a woman could want.

The singing still left something to be desired. The man had to have some fault. Now his voice cracked as he stretched for one of those notes that even a Bee Gee would have trouble reaching. Squashing a giggle, she grabbed her phone off the cracked granite countertop. Just the twentieth voice mail in the last two weeks from Shona Love, entertainment correspondent at the local news affiliate, but otherwise, nothing.

"Where do you think you're going?" he said without turning around.

"I missed the meat delivery. Sal's going to kill me." The meat guy was the least of her problems. That honor went to her father if he found out about her tardiness.

"Sit, Lili. I already took care of it."

"You did?" Last week he'd risen at six and lolled beside her, sleepy, bed-headed, and so damn sexy, while she inspected the meat and signed for it. Now she knew why.

Tears threatened and she blinked to force them back, conscious of how easily she'd fallen into relying on him for her comfort and well-being. Her startling need for him was bad enough; she didn't have to turn into minestrone soup over it.

Covering her sudden wave of emotion, she snaked her arms around his waist and laid her cheek against the smooth planes of his back. At her fluttery breath, his body sighed back, and yet again she marveled at his reaction. The same every time, like he was surprised and would never tire of her touch. She wondered if that was true or even possible.

"I must have been good in a previous life." Her throat felt raw and scratchy.

He turned and gathered her close. "Yeah, 'cause you're certainly not good in this one."

She breathed him in, absorbing the beat echoing like a drum beneath his skin. Fast and vital, like her own. He smoothed her hair helmet, a futile gesture given the time of day and the heat of the kitchen.

"You may not be aware of this, but I've accepted a few deliveries in my time. And it shouldn't always be down to you. Tad should do more, your other cousins." The unspoken, *your father*, hung in the air. Competition between Jack and Tony had picked up where it left off at the taping. When not trying to one-up each other with tales of who had eaten the most disgusting thing to date—Jack was leading with fried water bugs, a Thai delicacy—they continued to square off in the DeLuca kitchen, pushing each other to create as Jack waited for his Chicago kitchen to be finished and planned his new menu. And while they kept their interactions painfully civil, Lili sensed Jack itching to be her champion in everything, including her strained relationship with her father.

"Jack, it's my job. It's my family."

He raised an eyebrow.

"And we're not taking your money," she added, knowing that was next. Jack had broached the idea of helping out financially, but Lili had instantly shut down that line of thinking. Accumulating more debt wasn't the solution, and they both knew it, not while her father refused to make the wide-sweeping changes necessary. Neither did she want her rich and famous man bailing them out; her list of online soubriquets was insulting enough without adding "gold-digging whore" to the mix.

Thankfully, interest in Lilack—her girlhood dream to be one-half of a celebrity couple mash-up checked off the list!—had simmered down in the last couple of weeks, largely because they were being discreet. Not hiding, just not shouting it out to the hills. They'd hit a summer street festival in Old Town and attended a DeLuca family picnic at Grant Park for a free performance of Puccini's *Tosca*, a favorite of her father's. In between grumbles that it was two hours he would never have back, opera-hating Jack had kept her entertained with his own bawdy translations of the libretto.

Gently, he shoved her toward the table with, "Just let me take care of you. I want to."

She wanted that, too, but wanting wasn't going to make the fantasy into reality. Jack in her life for a couple of days a week was so much more than she could ever have wished for and she had to constantly remind herself that he was a loaner. Just a supernova fling. At this stage, checking her heart at the door was a downright impossibility, but she was trying to be cool about it. Any day, his network deal would be inked, beginning the countdown to the end of Lilack, but for now she just wanted to relish this unspoiled bubble of sex and comfort.

Gladly, she sat and relieved her jellied legs. A cup of coffee materialized, and Jack glided in by her side, distracting her with his monumental chest. He insisted on cooking breakfast shirtless even though he risked grease burns and singed chest hair. He said it was worth the sacrifice to keep her in a constant state of sexual red alert.

They dug into scrambled eggs with fragrantly wafting truffle shavings and expelled a soft "hmm" of unified satisfaction. Lili sipped her skim-muddied coffee. One and a half Splendas. Perfect.

"Jack, thanks for the delivery. For this." *For everything,* she wanted to say. For coming into her life and making her realize that life is so much better when someone has your back, like he had hers.

He bestowed on her one of those Special K stares that was hot enough to burn calories. "Come here," he said, his tone sexy-serious.

She'd given up protesting whenever he insisted she sit in his lap and just let herself enjoy how his body reacted to her weight. He liked how her butt spooned against his crotch and she liked how his breathing started to come in jagged jerks.

"Did you get a chance to look at the prospectus I brought back from Parsons?" he whispered against her neck after she'd settled in.

Reluctantly, her gaze veered to the glossy booklet on the counter near the sink. She had yet to decide if his act of picking it up on his last visit to New York was sweet or manipulative. Knowing Jack, probably both.

"Those brochures support the murder of trees," she said, smiling. "You know there's this thing called the Internet and it's got all the information you could ever want on it."

"The Internet. What's that ever done for anyone?" Given her adventures over the last month, that was true to the last drop. He gave her waist a gentle squeeze. "Sometimes, holding something solid in your hand makes it seem more real. More within reach."

Holding Jack didn't make it seem more real and he was about as solid as they come. She had enough reality outside her apartment. Tracing the tattoo on his bicep with her finger allowed her a moment to gather her thoughts. "I've told you grad school is off the table for now. With the restaurant's fortunes still up in the air, it's not a good time."

"I know you're scared, sweetheart, but you've got to take that leap sometime. You're using the restaurant as a crutch so you don't have to make a decision."

Am not. She examined her nails, but he called her on it by tilting her chin to face him. No avoidance stratagem was safe from his scrutiny.

"Dreams don't come true by themselves, Lili. You've

got to work at them. You think I wasn't scared to go to Paris, to open my first restaurant, to jump into a new venture? You have to take what's rightfully yours and the first step is acknowledging your needs."

How had she ever thought Jack Kilroy was just a charming rogue with depths as shallow as shoreline pools? With that all-knowing gaze and terrifying confidence, he had a way of wrong-footing and challenging her that had her seriously wondering if she could keep up with him.

"Luckily, I have you on hand to fulfill all my needs," she said, infusing her voice with a healthy dose of sultry. It was a cheap play, but she wasn't above a little manipulation of her own. She was just getting accustomed to how much power she wielded over him.

He frowned in response. Damn. She squirmed in his lap. He hitched a querulous eyebrow. Double damn.

"Stop pushing, Jack." She made to get up, but he held her fast in his sure grip, a place where she usually felt only safety. Now she felt pressure to perform, to live up to Jack's expectations of balls-out passion. To say his faith in her potential touched her was an understatement, but she wasn't ready to throttle up to Jack's speed and grab the wheel. Mute with emotions she couldn't name, her throat sealed up.

"Sweetheart, I don't like when you go all quiet. I prefer it when you're shouting at me and telling me what a dick I am. At least then I feel like we're communicating. You spend far too much time inside your head."

"No, I don't," she protested feebly.

"Yes, you do. And you're not one for visitors. Talk to me."

She wanted to be honest with him because his amazing forthrightness deserved that respect. Those eyes filled with a heaping spoonful of compassion and intelligence made it not exactly easy but a touch less difficult.

"Jack, these last few weeks have been some of the hardest and most humiliating of my life."

His face fell. "Lili, love, I know it's been rough for you and I'm not the easiest person—"

She stopped him with a touch of her fingers to his sensuous lips. "But they've also been the hottest and most exciting. I'm loving this time with you, but *madre di Dio*, could we just take it slow?"

"I'm not so good with slow," he said. "Except where it counts."

Yes, Jack knew how to take it slow when it suited him, and she gladly reaped the benefits of his consummately torturous skills between the sheets.

"We're not finished with this conversation." He hadn't gotten his way, but he was being magnanimous about it. His lips curved up in that killer smile and all the tension uncoiled from his body, except for a lovely, gratifying pressure against her butt. Her reward for winning this round.

"So what's on the menu for today?" she asked, relieved to have escaped a brewing argument.

"Milk-braised pork shoulder with garlic mashed potatoes," he said, laying shivery kisses along her collarbone. "Spring peas with lardons and mint." Kiss. "Portabella stuffed with apple chutney." Kiss. Moan. That last one was her.

"Stop, you're turning me on."

He nuzzled her neck. "I know, you're so easy. As my

official taster, you must stop by later to give me your approval. What'll you be up to?"

"Yoga class, sex, staff schedules, paperwork, sex, more paperwork..." She grinned. "I thought I'd take Jules shopping. Hit some of my favorite vintage stores."

"I really appreciate you making the effort with her. She needs a friend right now." His body drew taut once more. "Will Tad be sniffing around as usual?"

"He can't help having a little crush. The Kilroy gene pool is irresistible."

Her light tone made no impact on his dark expression. Whenever Jack visited Jules at Casa DeLuca, invariably he would find Tad had got there before him. He hated the idea that Jules might be confiding in a guy she barely knew instead of the brother who had her best interests at heart.

"Your cousin better not take advantage," he said gruffly. "She's vulnerable right now."

Lili could see how off balance Jules was and was trying to get to know her, even so far as gifting her a couple of pregnancy books, but she barely glanced at the covers. Her lackadaisical attitude to the most momentous thing to ever happen to her worried Jack. The contrast between the siblings was startling. Jack was so open and emotional compared to his closed-off sister.

"Something, or someone, happened to her in London," Jack went on, his frustration plain. "I'm not sure why she's here if she won't talk to me about it."

"Give her time. She'll get there." Patience was the least of Jack's virtues, and his propensity to think everything could be fixed, usually with sheer Kilroy will, had put his relationship with Jules into a curious holding pattern.

Jules stubbornly resisted and refused to be specific about her needs; Jack got frustrated and pushed, and the cycle started all over again.

She nibbled on his ear to ease the strain in his rigid body. It was one of the areas she'd committed to memory as a Jack weak spot, and that, combined with a butt wriggle, got the response she required.

"Lili." Low. Lusty. Then, "Evil woman."

His hand slipped under her skirt and trailed a sensuous path up her inner thigh until it reached—oh, yes, that felt so good. She melted like butter in a hot pan.

"No underwear? This is how you planned to meet this morning's delivery?"

She adjusted, ensuring more friction where she needed it. "Gotta pay those invoices any way we can." Of course she was kidding, but Jack's brow furrowed all the same. He still projected His Royal Broodiness whenever another man was mentioned, not that Sal, with his beer gut and eight grandchildren, even qualified as a man. Knuckle-dragging Jack turned her on to an unreasonable degree. Her head did not approve but everywhere else was fairly okay with the situation.

Speaking of knuckles, he slid one inside her sensitive, quivering flesh. "Time to schedule the next meat delivery."

She burst out into a laugh. "That's terrible, even for you." But soon her amusement fell away as his eyes shifted to that smoky hunger she loved. Reaching behind her, he pushed the dishes out of the way and hoisted her onto the table in one fluid motion. Like she was a slip of a thing. His strength always unraveled her.

He stood, and with a stretch of his ropy-muscled arm

opened a countertop cookie jar, the one with the blue iced snowflakes ringing the rim. She didn't even keep treats in there because why create more dirty dishes when her cookie habit was strictly of the box-to-mouth variety? Bafflement boosted to pleasure when he pulled out a condom and slipped it on in a practiced motion. Such clever hands.

"My nonna's cookie jar, Jack?"

"Great chefs are all about the preparation," he murmured, right as he plunged into her and everything glittered.

God, she loved this table.

* * *

Jack's mind buzzed with all he had to do. Finalize the decor on his new place. Finish interviews for the Chicago brigade. Complete negotiations on a multimillion-dollar network contract. Repair his frazzled relationship with his sister. And save DeLuca's Ristorante without pissing off his girl.

Easy as *un, deux, trois.*

He had slotted neatly into Lili's life, her long-distance lover who showed up to fill a need and take her mind off her problems. That wasn't going to fly for much longer. She might want to keep things on a low simmer, but Jack was ready to plate and serve. The sooner he could get the monkey of her restaurant's troubles off her back, the sooner she could start focusing on her own needs. And on them.

So this morning, when Jack entered the DeLuca restaurant kitchen and found Tony standing at the sink wearing a face like an overwound clock, he thought checking off the hardest thing on his to-do list would be a great way to start the day. Or second greatest because his mid-breakfast sexcapade with Lili was going to be tough to beat.

Tony glowered.

Dirty mind wipe, activate.

"Tony."

"Jack."

They clasped hands with manly firmness; then Tony slid several sticks of celery and a knife across the counter. Jack started chopping but could feel Tony's scrutiny even as the older man's hands made fast work of dicing an onion for what Jack assumed was *soffritto*, the Italian version of mirepoix. Three weeks in and he still felt like a horny teenager who was about to get the third degree from the overprotective father.

A problem for later. Today he just had to appeal to that other part of Tony's personality. The vainglorious chef part.

"So, you probably know I have a cookbook."

Tony looked up from chopping, eyes narrowed to slits as thin as the blade in his hand. "You have some good ideas, though you do not simmer your veal stock for long enough. It should be sixteen hours, not twelve."

Okay. The prickle of pleasure Jack felt that Tony had actually read one of his recipes went some way to minimizing the underlying tone of Tony's backhanded compliment. Sort of. "I have another one in the works and I wondered how you'd feel about a collaboration."

The older man pursed his lips and resumed the whip-fast knifework. "And what would you possibly gain from that?"

"Doing it by myself, it gets stale. I think you're a great chef and I'd like to work with you on this."

Tony heaved an audible sigh like he'd been unaccountably insulted. "Do you think you can buy my blessing?"

"I'm not trying to buy your blessing, Tony," Jack said, surprised at how quickly he had lost control of the room. Why did the man have to make it such hard work? "I thought you might be interested in sharing your recipes with a wider audience."

"Thank you for the offer, but I would rather not encourage your connection to my family. I am fine with allowing you to use my kitchen in a professional capacity, and my wife enjoys the company of Julietta. She is a lovely girl. But that is where it ends."

So much to enjoy in that little speech. Jules had already been christened with an Italian name. Bully for her. Neither could Jack fail to miss that undertone of pity for the sister who was saddled with a piece of bad news like Jack for a brother. But best of all was the jibe about not wishing to encourage Jack's connection to Tony's family. That one had *score* written all over it.

"I'm really grateful to you for taking my sister in while I travel. I intend to pay—"

Tony waved his knife magnanimously. Or maybe it was more of a threat. "Keep your money for the next time you get sued for that temper of yours. My daughter has a lot of responsibilities and all these distractions take her away from what's important. The restaurant, her mother."

"And her art?"

For his impertinence, Jack got a shoulder lift that might beat Laurent in a Continental shrug-off. "It is good for her to have a hobby, I suppose."

"It's more than a hobby, Tony. She's very talented."

"I do not need you to explain what my daughter is. I have known her all her life. You have known her for a few minutes."

A fizz of annoyance arced through Jack. "You expect too much of her. She's your daughter, not your servant. It's not like you listen to her, anyway."

Tony's hand stilled in midchop. He placed the knife down carefully, as though concerned it might suddenly develop a will of its own.

"And you should mind your own business," he said, his voice injected with steel. "Think about putting your own house in order before you start interfering in mine."

Okay, he deserved that. No one knew more than Jack how much he had failed Jules, and a reminder from the DeLuca paterfamilias knocked the wind out of him. Tony picked up his knife and sliced through an onion so quickly that Jack felt a squirm of discomfort in his crotch.

"Do not cut the celery so thin," he added without even looking up.

Keeping his knife in a kiss with the board, Jack shifted his chopping from mincing to coarse. Had he somehow wandered into Tony Soprano's kitchen instead of Tony DeLuca's? The kind of women he usually dated didn't have wise-guy relatives who would break his legs or encase him in concrete if he didn't treat their clanswoman right. He'd already suffered through this shit with Tad and Cara, and while he didn't need this guy's say-so to see Lili, it was rather early in the game to descend to rudeness about it.

"Tony, I understand I might not have been your first choice for Lili."

Tony scoffed. "You understand, yet here we are after you agreed to stay away from her. This video business, the cruel things that are being said about her. None of this would have happened if you weren't in my daughter's life."

Jack's heart squeezed. Not usually this slow on the uptake, it should have occurred to him sooner that any father would suffer on his daughter's behalf even when he was pissed at her. Alternating between injury and offense pretty much described his relationship with Jules, and if that video incident had happened to his sister, the fucker responsible would have needed a very deep hole to hide in.

"Tony, I know you only want to protect her."

"Someone has to." He turned, about as agitated as Jack had ever seen him. "This isn't the first time people have bullied and taunted her. Her schooldays were a nightmare, and this has brought it all up again. What are you doing to keep her from being hurt?"

Maybe not enough, but at least he was holding her and telling her every day she was amazing instead of acting like a bloody martinet.

"Tony, I love your daughter and I will stop at nothing to keep her safe." It wasn't a real answer to Tony's demand for assurance, but as Jack heard the words coming out of his mouth, quiet and steady, he knew it was the only answer. First time he'd said it aloud, too, and it didn't sound as odd on his lips as he would have expected. It sounded brilliant.

There had been so many times it had been on the tip of his tongue to tell Lili, usually while he was buried inside her, drowning in those shotgun blues, every part of his body so recklessly happy. She owned his heart, but until she was ready to open hers to him, he'd use his time wisely to curry favor with the people she cared about. Starting with the man before him.

Your move, Il Duce.

Tony raised his eyes to Jack's. There might have been respect lurking there, but it could just as easily have been Tony musing on the best way to chop up Jack's body. Several strained seconds ticked by before the maestro spoke again.

"The moment I saw Liliana's mother, it was *colpo di fulmine*." He looked down, focused on a knot on the chopping board. "Love at first sight."

Jack swallowed. Loudly. Were they having a moment?

"Of course, I was only ten years old at the time." Alrighty, then, so much for bonding. "And my daughter feels the same way about you?"

The sixty-four-thousand-dollar question. "No bloody clue."

Tony smiled. The bastard actually smiled. "I see."

Jack wasn't sure what had happened here, but the relief at being able to express his feelings publicly made him giddy. Pity he'd wasted it on the one guy who thought Jack and Lili were the worst idea since New Coke.

His balls were still hiding somewhere up around hip level, but Jack no longer gave a toss. He was too busy trying to keep a foolish grin from conquering his face, but it slowly built and he turned away so Tony wouldn't see. He wanted to shout how happy he was and tell his future father-in-law—he'd come to that stunning conclusion as well—that he envied Tony his life and his family, and he wanted to make something like that with Lili.

He settled for, "Celery."

Tony grunted and handed the remaining stalks over.

* * *

Once it had been his favorite place in the whole world, and as Jack crashed through the doors of Thyme on Forty-seventh, he waited for the familiar magic to wash over him. Opening it ten years ago had signaled his arrival in New York, a kick to the establishment that said French food couldn't be simultaneously high concept and accessible. Now the only thing stopping that elusive third Michelin star was his spotty presence over the past year, or so he liked to think. Chefs had their fair share of conspiracy theories.

Laurent sat at his usual table in the corner glued to his laptop, espresso cup at his wrist. Jack assumed he was planning a menu, and knowing his friend, it would be the winter menu. In the middle of July. Jack strode over, only to be practically sacked by a man who sprang like a mountain lion from behind the bar.

"Jack, it's great to see you," the stranger said in an Irish-lilted trill. He pumped Jack's hand and held on. Tall and lean with dark brown, messy hair, Irish had the hungry look of an apprentice, though he had to be at least midtwenties.

"Have we met?"

"Ah, no, we haven't." He released Jack's maligned hand and looked over at Laurent as if he might find support from that quarter. Jack caught Laurent's smirk. No help there, rookie.

"I'm Shane. Shane Doyle. I just wanted to say hello."

The new pâtissier. Laurent mentioned he'd hired him

after the guy had sent his résumé once a month for the last year. Five years as a pastry chef in restaurants in Ireland and the UK. A stint at Lenôtre, the culinary school in Paris. Eighteen months with Anton Baillard at Maison Rouge on the Upper West Side. He was more than qualified, but Thyme hadn't had an opening for years until his junior pâtissière, Marguerite, went on maternity leave a month ago. Add to that the work visa hassles for non-U.S. citizens. But the guy had been adamant about working here and not at Jack's place in London.

"Hope you're settling in," Jack said, trying to put the poor guy at ease just as he realized the kid didn't need it. His eyes sparkled, making Jack wearier. Damn, he couldn't remember the last time he'd been so excited to meet a fellow chef.

"Yeah, everyone's been wonderful," Shane said with a cocky eyebrow lift for good measure.

"Well, it's great to meet you." Jack nodded over Shane's shoulder to Laurent. *Move along, kid.*

"Oh, yeah, sure." He held Jack's gaze and smiled, wider now and with a touch of insolence, before heading out to the street. In under sixty seconds, Shane had gone from newbie eagerness to brash cockiness to something along the lines of "huh?" Maybe the great Jack Kilroy hadn't lived up to the iconic image in the younger chef's head. Jack slumped into a chair beside Laurent, his muscles duller because of Shane's whatever-the-hell-that-was.

"*Viande fraiche*," they said together. *Fresh meat.* Jack hadn't spoken to Laurent in a while. The Frenchman hadn't been his sous for the last few episodes of the show, preferring to get back to his duties in New York, so it was a relief to fall into their usual easy camaraderie.

"Remember when we were that young?" Jack asked.

"Younger. That one's ambitious like you. He's already making suggestions." This last statement was underlined with disapproval; Laurent was old-fashioned and preferred the greenhorns to be seen and not heard for at least a year.

During the early days of his apprenticeship in Paris, Jack had barely known béchamel from caramel and thought a mother sauce was some weird French street slang, but he fronted it out with a nice line in chat and a cocksure grin. Back then, he'd never met a situation he couldn't talk or screw his way out of. If only it were that easy now.

"I was an arrogant little bastard," Jack said wistfully, feeling pleasantly warm at the memory.

"True, but you could back it up. Running stations by three months with hardly a word of French to your name. Your accent is still *merde*, by the way."

That pulled a laugh from deep in his belly. He'd missed his friend.

"I didn't expect to see you today," Laurent said. "The charms of Chicago have lost their appeal?"

"No, still charming as ever."

"So this is it. The great Jack Kilroy brought to his knees by the cloud of big hair and the cute nose wrinkle." A sigh escaped his lips. "And she could so easily have been mine. We were getting along very well in that bar until you swooped in."

"You snoozed, *mon ami*."

Laurent narrowed his eyes. "So where is she today? I thought she would be with you."

He thought right, but he was beginning to wonder if

Lili would ever truly be with him. If she would ever make the leap necessary to meet him halfway or if he was no more than a prop to her fragile ego. He knew she cared up to a point but all the noise—her family, her history, her fear of change—was drowning out the possibilities for their future. At the mere mention of anything related to what comes next, she shut down emotionally and became Lili the temptress. *Think of your needs, sweetheart.* Her hands turned into weapons of sensual torture. *What about grad school?* Her lips nibbled and grazed, advance scouts for her warm tongue.

Shucking off her insecurities would take more than Jack whispering sweet-nothings through the voluminous hair that drove him lust-wild. He wanted it settled before he signed the contract; otherwise she'd use that as an excuse to retreat.

Irked at himself, he picked up the paper Laurent was making notes on, his large expressive scrawl barely legible. "Duck à l'orange? I know retro is in, but they can just as easily take away Michelin stars as give them."

Laurent's mouth tipped up in a grin. "Trust me. I have something special in mind."

Jack knew better than to doubt it. Laurent's brand of genius was quiet and methodical, and Jack often wondered why he stuck around all these years instead of branching out on his own. He would readily invest in any venture led by his right-hand man, but luckily for Jack, he'd always seemed happiest at Thyme.

Feeling nostalgic, Jack cast his eyes about the room, drinking in the polished wood and gleaming brass finishes, all molded in the style of a nineteenth-century Parisian brasserie. He and Laurent had planned it together down to every last detail, from the copper pans imported from Marseille to the antique light fixtures, exact replicas of ones they'd discovered gracing the walls of a run-down Pigalle bistro. It had been their baby, their big splash in the Big Apple, but as much as he loved it here, Jack knew in his marrow it didn't belong to him anymore.

Laurent must have noticed something in Jack's expression. "Lunch starts in thirty minutes. Did you want to run the kitchen?"

That too-familiar twist of apprehension wriggled in his gut. He hadn't run a kitchen, a real kitchen, in over a year. "I'd love to, but I have a meeting with my agent."

Laurent raised an eyebrow, resulting in a parallel rise of Jack's defensive hackles. His friend had never begrudged Jack his success but tended to be amused by it all instead. The look he was giving Jack now was on the other side of diverted.

"You should be here, Jack." Laurent's usual blue twinkle had suddenly acquired bite. "You don't enjoy the current show. Why would you enjoy this new one?"

Jack harshed out a laugh that rang hollow against all that shiny brass. "What makes you think I don't enjoy it?"

"Because the Jack Kilroy I know would never have lost that cook-off with Tony DeLuca."

Jack stared. Blinked. Stared some more. "You were fairly hungover during the taping, but surely you recall our hosts engaged in a spot of cheating."

Laurent made a sound that could only be described as "French." "You are the best chef I have ever worked with, but you've lost your edge. None of your dishes that night were half as good as you're capable of. You've been coasting for a while now. Cheating or not, Tony deserved to win, but a year ago there would have been no contest."

Where the hell had that come from? Jack readily acknowledged that cooking had ceased to be an enjoyment since he'd swapped his chef's toque for the bright lights, but he didn't think the work had suffered. Not really. Knowing his diminished passion manifested where it counted—the fucking food, stupid—flicked his ego like a rusty nail over a raw wound. But in the last few weeks, he'd felt that passion's joyful return as he planned his new Chicago menu. As he fed Lili and fell in love.

"Thought you liked it when I'm gone. Gives you a chance to boss all the young bucks," Jack said, half in jest but really to cover his discomfort about his best friend's annoyingly pointed conclusion.

Laurent gave one of his trademark Gallic shrugs. In truth, he was the executive chef at Thyme except his name wasn't on the menu. He'd never ask outright, which was part of his problem. No drive. Too much of a dreamer.

"You don't need the money and you certainly don't need any more reason to attract women," Laurent said in a seductive cajole, more like the easygoing Frenchman he knew. "Come back to what you love."

Come back to what you love. Food, Jules, Lili. These were the things he loved and he would fight to his last breath to have them all.

CHAPTER TWENTY-ONE

So the advice of your elders means nothing?" Cara traced the rim of her martini glass and tilted those accusatory sapphire blues up.

Lili hid her smile in the mouth of the microbrew bottle she'd never heard of and looked around the chic bar, another recent addition to the neighborhood. Scattered throughout were gamine pixie dream girls and bearded hipsters wearing bowling shirts and trilby hats because it met their weird definition of irony. Trendy watering holes usually left Lili cold, but Cara only frequented places where the bar staff had advanced degrees in mixology. And she was buying.

"I'm not seeing Jack to annoy you. I happen to like him."

Cara's expression became so inflexible it could rival Botox as a beauty regimen. "How much?"

She imagined stretching her arms out to their full span.

This much. Clearly, the pause had gone on too long because Cara jumped in pout-first.

"Oh God."

"This was all your idea, Cara."

"A hot and sweaty one-night stand, I said." She inclined her platinum crown and the muted light from the wall sconce caught it just right, giving her a halo. So freaking beautiful. "Hot. And. Sweaty. Not our-second-car's-a-Volvo. Not don't-forget-to-pick-up-little-Emily-from-violin-practice. You've gone and done exactly what I said you shouldn't do." She lowered her voice. "You've fallen for him."

Duh. Of course she had fallen for him. She was crazy in love with the guy, but she was trying not to be a dumb-ass about it. He might say he wanted her in his glittering world, but she knew this relationship had an expiration date that was fast approaching.

"I'm not stupid. I went in with my eyes open, and while I like him more than is probably good for me, I won't collapse in a heap when it's over."

"Wait a sec—over?" Cara's smooth brow pinched as she tore her gaze away from the dregs of her adult beverage. "Is that shithead acting chilly toward you or something? You don't still think you're out of his league?"

Sexually, no. Emotionally was another thing altogether. "No, he never stops telling me how hot I am. He makes me feel more desired than any guy I've ever been with."

"As he should." Cara tilted her head. "So what's the problem?"

Lili smiled thinly at her sister's show of support. "It just doesn't feel real. It's like some fever dream that I haven't woken up from yet." But she would soon enough if Jack didn't first, because if she'd learned one thing from her time with Marco, it's that the axiom *Hot guys got bored* was self-evident. When it came to men, past performance was definitely indicative of future results. "We'll go our separate ways and life will go on as before."

There was no missing the concern that flashed over Cara's face. "You spent the last couple of years running around after Dad, looking after Mom, making the rest of us look like pigeon crap—" At Lili's mouth opening in dissent, she held up a calming hand. "For which I am eternally grateful, so isn't it time you thought about yourself for a change? Grad school, all the hopes and dreams bit, and if that includes Jack, then you need to go for it. No one expects you to put your life on hold any longer, Lili. It's your time."

That's what she had been telling herself since high school, but the chasm between telling and believing was as big as the gulf between old, insecure Lili and that brave, liberated version of herself that always seemed out of reach. When life remained as hopes and dreams, then there was still the chance they might turn out okay.

Unable to voice her fears, she fell back on what she knew. "Thought you didn't approve. What did you say about him? All he cares about is cooking and fu—"

"Maybe I was overly critical," Cara interrupted with a smirk. "I have to say that since you've been knocking boots with Jack, you seem more confident. More assured. And he's definitely a lot less of a divo these last couple of tapings, which I suppose we should attribute to you. You're good for each other." Sighing, she tipped her empty glass by the stem between her thumb and forefinger. "I assume he lights up your hoo-hah like a Christmas tree."

Lili bit down on her lip. "Not going there."

"Damn, girl, I'd tell you."

"Liar. You never tell me anything about the guys you date. All that prime man candy in the Big Apple and your conversation sorely lacks for filthy details." For all Cara's rules about men, she never shared her adventures in Big City Singledom. It occurred to Lili that all might not be as perfect in Cara's glamorous world as she had wanted to believe. The mere fact that she had graced Chicago with two visits in a month was indicative of some sea change in her sister's life, though Lili couldn't say what.

"Dating's impossible in New York. Everyone's too busy and they all think they can do better." A brief flicker of discomfort passed over Cara's face before she dialed up the sun in an instant. "Of course, with the new show, I'll be working eighteen-hour days and wrangling a staff the size of the DeLuca clan. No time for men, so I need to live vicariously. Throw your old maid of a sis a bone and tell me about the lady boners."

Lili leaned in and licked her lips. "I will say he talks a lot."

Cara rolled her eyes. "Now why doesn't that surprise me? The guy never shuts up on the set. Of course, he's going to be a chatty Cathy during sex."

"French, sometimes. It's so sexy. And then he does this thing with his—" She took a long pull of her fancy beer, trying to regulate her hot and bothered temperature. "Oh, you wouldn't be interested in that."

Her sister's mouth fell open. "Yes, I would. I'd be very interested."

Lili burst into a laugh, Cara joined in, and for a moment, everything was A-okay. Her family's business was on the brink of failure, Jack Kilroy's fan club was probably taking bids from hit men, but otherwise, her life was not too shabby.

"Another round?" Lili raised her bottle to finish the last couple of fingers of her beer, but before Cara could respond, a shadow fell across the booth. She lifted her eyes to the smoking hot face of her dirty-talking boyfriend. A swig of beer spurted from her nose. Elegance personified.

A move that classy should have earned her a smile. All she got was Jack looking tall, dark, and pissed.

"Hey," she said, to which he delivered a short nod. Still pissed.

Warm, itchy panic sloshed over her as she wiped the beer from her nostrils with the back of her hand. He took a seat in the booth, his body emitting dangerous, wavy vibes she could practically see.

"I didn't expect you until tomorrow," she said cautiously. "How did you know where to find us?"

"I stopped by the house to see Jules. Francesca told me you were here."

"Is Jules okay?"

"I suppose," he said, resigned, and her heart scrunched on seeing his pain.

"Are *you* okay?"

He picked up her beer and studied the label. "I'm fine."

The last time he said that, he collapsed on the sidewalk outside her apartment. It felt like something similarly ominous loomed on the horizon. A voice at the next table whispered Jack's name and a smidgen of anxiety flared in her stomach. Lili sensed rather than saw the wave of nudges as news of Jack's arrival spread like a rash across the bar.

"You don't seem fine."

"Is it the contract?" Cara asked.

He glared at her. "Contract's fine." Okay, so banter Jack was all boxed up.

"I'll get the next round in," Cara whispered loudly, raising a dramatically arched brow at Lili that said she was doing them a huge favor and giving them some alone time. Lili cut a nervous glance around the bar. Alone time. Like that was possible.

"Did something happen?" Lili asked once Cara had left.

He answered with a kiss. A hot, demanding tongue sweep that made her thankful she was sitting. When he released her, they were both out of breath.

"I needed to see you. Just you." The rigid set of his jaw paralleled the tightness of his hard torso, now encroaching on her body space. "How soon can we leave?"

Over his shoulder, she watched Cara's tottering approach with an appletini, its contents flirting dangerously with the rim of the glass.

"Twenty minutes?"

"Ten. Then we go home and fuck each other stupid."

That eased a smile from her, but it vanished immediately under his insistent gaze. A gaze filled with intent and need and all the things she wasn't brave enough to say.

Cara had barely sat before she started peppering Jack with questions about the new show. The size of the studio, crew members she had in mind, foreign broadcast rights. Jack's monosyllabic answers kept Lili on edge, and as the

conversation slackened, she tried to will a similar loose-
ness into his body. Her hand found his under the table and
he grasped it tight in return. None of that dead fish grip,
either. This was a fully paid up registration to the hand-
holding convention.

It worked. He relaxed, and she relaxed enough to get
lost in the normality of it. The nearness of Jack, the
weight of his body practically curled around her in the
booth. Again, she marveled at how big he was—
physically, intellectually, emotionally—and how right she
felt in his powerful presence. She'd heard of this, how
being with that special someone could make you feel as
though you were the only two people in the world. That's
how Jack made her feel when he was with her. Like she
was the only girl in his world.

Cara was babbling about convection ovens when Jack
cut her off. "Cara, you think Lili should apply to graduate
school, don't you?"

Lili almost choked on her beer. They were doing this
now? "Jack."

He turned his I'm-not-messing-around-here gaze on
her.

Cara divided an astute look between them. "I think it's
up to Lili."

Jack scoffed. "If we were to leave it up to Lili, it would
never happen."

"This isn't your call, Jack. I've already told you I can't
think about that." She extracted her hand from his controlling grip.

Fast as a cat, he stood and held out his hand to her.
"We'll talk about it at home. Come on."

Hesitant at first, she only got up because she didn't

want to make a scene, but she made a stand for the sisterhood by ignoring his proffered hand. *Take that, bossypants.*

Then she heard it. The titter.

It could have been from anyone about anything but she knew better. The hip-looking couple at the next table, the ones who had mentioned Jack's name earlier, was all agog. The girl, a streaky blonde with an eyebrow ring, made no effort to hide her phone with the camera lens facing them.

Jack placed a hand at the small of Lili's back, an intimate gesture that she might have read as just another assertion of Jack's control if she wasn't so concerned with getting out of Dodge tout de suite. She took a quick step forward, her worried gaze trained on the exit.

Walk past them. Avoid eye contact. Don't acknowledge it.

"Fat cow."

It was muted, a tossed away statement that struck hard in her breast and registered stranger still because it was said in a male voice. Online hate against women was usually fueled by other women, and Lili had always assumed the people who cared about this kind of thing were female and middle-aged and likely to be found dead after a week of no contact, welded to their La-Z-Boys while cats nibbled on their extremities.

Jack halted and spun around. So close. "What did you say?"

"Jack, let's go." She snagged his wrist but he held his ground, an immovable object. Mules had nothing on him.

The guy, a shaggy-haired surfer type, sneered. "Nothing, man, it's all good." His fingers nudged his phone provocatively on the table, while the girl plastered on a brittle smile. All for Jack.

"Did you take a photo of us?" Jack asked, his tone even to normal observers, but Lili detected the underlying turbulence. What had started out as cloudy with a chance of hot caveman sex was now turning into a cat-five hurricane about to make landfall in some idiot's face.

"No," the blonde said at the same time Surfer Dude said, "What if I did?"

Lili tugged again, but Jack twisted out of her grip and stepped forward and sideways to block her. Protecting her. She tried to shrink her body behind his but peeked around his arm, keeping a line of sight open on the couple.

"Whatever you've taken, I'll need you to erase it. And apologize for what you said." Jack's voice dripped polite menace, like a gangster in one of those British Quentin Tarantino rip-offs. His smooth accent might fool someone into thinking he was weak. It was the perfect disguise.

"I don't think so," Surfer Dude said, taking a sip of his imported beer. CLYDE was embroidered on his two-tone shirt, but Lili doubted that was his name. Blondie's face slipped into panic. Maybe she was able to read Jack's body language better than her friend. Women knew these things.

"I'll ask one more time. Delete whatever you took and say sorry."

That edge in his voice jangled Lili's nerves. "Jack, it's okay. Let's just go."

"It's not okay," he said, his eyes still zeroed in on the guy.

"It's a free country," Clyde said.

"No, it's not." Jack moved so fast Lili felt her skirt rustle as if a rush of air had blown through it. With one quick thunder crack of violence, he grabbed the phone and slammed it against the edge of the table, then threw it down, shattered screen up. There were probably ways to retrieve stuff off phones with broken screens, but the message was crystal.

"Man, what the fuck's your problem?" the guy yelled, his voice pitched high enough to attract the rubbernecking attention of bar patrons in a three-table-deep radius. Lili slid a furtive glance to Cara, whose expression screamed, *Leave!* Leave before Jack beats the tar out of some bigmouthed moron in front of an avid audience with twitchy fingers hovering over their Send buttons.

Jack turned his imperious gaze on the blonde, who fidgeted with her phone and held it up, screen forward. "Deleted, I promise." She looked at Lili and bit her lip. That was her apology, Lili supposed.

He jammed his hand into his pocket, peeled a couple of hundreds from his billfold, and threw them down with the same vehemence as the phone. His eyes, as murky as impenetrable night, sliced through Lili. That was a whole other level of scary.

"Now we can go." With his hand grasping her arm tightly, he steered her toward the door.

CHAPTER TWENTY-TWO

Outside, a wall of oppressive July heat rose up to meet them, but it still registered cooler than the stifling atmosphere in the bar. Slipping Jack's severe grip, Lili retreated to several feet away from the bar's entrance, her heart pounding so hard she worried her chest might explode.

Ohgod ohgod ohgod.

Once, she had asked Jack if he would punch everyone who said something mean to her. She'd thought it was sweet when he said yes. Be careful what you wish for.

Cara paced, phone surgically attached to her ear, muttering "shit" over and over, and something about how they needed to get a statement out to the press. Her whole posture spoke to caged chaos as she got to work on saving her job and the television future of her boss.

Dazed, Lili turned to find Jack crowding her. "Sweetheart, are you all right?"

No, no, no. "You shouldn't have done that." She

squeezed her bottom lip between her thumb and forefinger. "You really shouldn't have done that."

People streamed out of the bar, their noisy laughter strident and probably unrelated to what had just happened. Lili's cheeks blazed hot all the same and she tried to walk away, but Jack commandeered again and directed her to his car. He felt too big, too potent, the power she envied barely leashed. Not that she was afraid of him, but she saw now that he had good reasons for ignoring the trash that was written about him.

Seconds later, they were making their getaway through the side streets of Wicker Park. An eerie calm descended, as if the farther away from the bar she got, the easier she could breathe. But it was just an illusion, another segment of her fever dream. She hadn't even said good-bye to Cara. At last glance, her sister had been eating the sidewalk in her Manolos, hands sculpting the air furiously as she did what she did best. Managed and controlled. The network deal might survive the night—no one had been hurt physically—but how long before a smashed phone turned into a smashed jaw?

Looking out the window, she saw they had slotted into a space right outside DeLuca's. Long past closing, the lights were still on, which meant Tad was likely mangling the cash-out. Holing up in the back office with her Mount Everest of paperwork until the storm passed by was starting to look like a very attractive option.

She jumped at the warm brush of his knuckles on her arm. "Lili, are you all right?"

"You shouldn't have done that," she repeated, feeding him a sidelong glance.

"He deserved it."

"Maybe, but have you given a single thought to how this affects your contract?"

The corner of his mouth twitched. "Can't say I have. That's typically how mindless rage works."

"This isn't funny, Jack."

"I agree. Someone calls you names, disrespects you, and I'm supposed to just stand by and take it?"

"You're supposed to use your common sense and think about what's best for your career. Your reputation. I don't care what people say about me," she said, stunned at its truth. The insults might pierce for a moment but she could learn to tune it out. Not so sure that Jack could, though.

He snorted and muttered something she couldn't make out.

"So, the next time something like this happens, off come the gloves again?"

She could see his mind whirring, computing the implications before dismissing it to the other side of the street. "Well, I've been informed by my lawyer that the First Amendment prohibits me from getting cease and desist orders for Facebook pages and Twitter accounts, so I'll just have to take care of it the old-fashioned way."

"Cease and desist orders? You mean you tried to get the pages taken down?" She struggled to get the words past her rapidly constricting throat. "Jack, you can't stop the Internet from existing!" She had completely underestimated his need to protect. It was Jules and the paparazzi, a disparaging remark in a bar, a nasty comment in 140 characters or less.

Guilt and love collided in a fiery pileup in her chest. He had stood up for her and put everything on the line, behavior that was crazy and stupid and struck every emotional chord in her body. How could she not love a man who was willing to risk everything to protect her? And how could she love him and let him do that?

"Jack, this can't go on."

"Don't worry. It'll all blow over."

"That's what you said after the video and it didn't. The Internet exploded like a confetti bomb. My father practically had a coronary."

"And your father will know now that I can protect you. Anyone who tries to hurt you will have me to deal with."

It would never end. Jack would wage a full-scale war on anyone who crossed her. Living with that responsibility, and the dread fear that he would begin to realize what a liability she was, would crush her. She wasn't worth this depth of fervor. She never could be.

"I'm not a damsel in distress. I don't need you to fight my battles."

"Really, Lili? Because the way I see it, you spend so much time taking care of everyone else that your battles—your needs—get pretty short shrift. You can't stand up to your father. How are you going to stand up for yourself?"

Shock rolled over her at the way he pieced that together. "This...this has nothing to do with my father," she spluttered.

"Yes, it does. You let him tell you what to do, with the restaurant, with your life. Even now, you're only concerned with what he thinks."

There was truth there but hell if she was going to let it muddy the waters. "So I should just substitute one tyrant for another? Because that's what you are, Jack. You expect everyone to fall in line with your worldview and to hell with the art of compromise. That's what families, friends, lovers do. They compromise."

That muscle near his mouth was in full throb. "You'd know all about compromises. You've compromised so much you've forgotten what you want. Who you want to be."

She swallowed back the hurt of yet another pointedly accurate blow. "I'm trying to make sure your career doesn't explode in your face."

He made a sound of scorn. "No, you're not. You're looking for the easy way out. You're afraid of what you feel. You're afraid of trying and failing. Hell, you're afraid of trying and succeeding. You'd rather let your own dreams die instead of rocking the boat. With your father, your art, with us. I know exactly what you're thinking, Lili. I always have."

A tremor rattled her thigh and she fisted her hands in her lap to force it to calm. No go. Where did he get off being so intuitive and handsome?

"Let me tell you what I think. You weren't protecting me back there. You were just marking your territory."

"I prefer to think of it as branding you as my own, but you can phrase it in those terms if you like."

He talked like she was an acquisition for his empire, and she was glad because it gave her the fuel she needed. "From the minute I met you, you've done nothing but bully and make demands. If it's not me you're trying to bend to your will, it's Jules and probably a million other people you expect to kowtow to the great Jack Kilroy. Veiling it in charm and that stupid accent doesn't make it any less manipulative. I told you I wanted to take it slow but all you do is push and push."

His face stormed over. "Better that than standing still."

The words sliced through her like blades. Her distress wound a path from gut to chest to throat and she swallowed hard to force it back. She'd always known she wasn't slick enough for Jack's world, where he hurtled along at the speed of light, forever chasing some textbook vision of excellence.

"Sorry I can't move fast enough for you."

He laughed, short and bitter. "Oh, you moved pretty fast in that bar, Lili. And you were certainly no slowpoke when you came to my hotel room after the taping. Seems you're happy to take risks for certain things, like sex, but when shit gets real, up go the walls and out come the excuses."

Lili couldn't conceal her astonishment. "We're not all as sure as you, Jack. Not everyone comes out of the womb with a fully formed plan for world domination."

He leaned in close, his mouth as hard as his gaze. "At least I'm not afraid of admitting what I want. What I need. I'm not going to beg, Lili. Either you're in or you're out."

"How could I refuse such an attractive offer?"

"That's right, smart-mouth. Make a joke." A half-sneer curled his lips. "Whatever you need to keep it simple. I'm coming on too strong and you can't stand to be pushed. Or you're making this huge sacrifice so I won't be forced to rip anyone's head off and ruin my career. Let's just go with one of those, shall we? Either way, you come off looking pretty good."

His vicious grip on the steering wheel drew her dizzy gaze to the pale knuckles of those strong, blunt hands. She didn't have to look to know his jaw was set in a hard line, his lips thinned to invisibility.

"Jack, you want too much," she said to the window.

"And you don't want enough." He spoke, not with rancor but with a tired resignation that sent a bolt of alarm through her chest. He had reached an impregnable wall and no longer had the energy to break through. Those well-crafted defenses of hers were too entrenched, those bone-deep fears impossible to overcome. And the worst part was that she knew it and couldn't do a damn thing about it.

"Did we ever have a chance, Lili? Did you ever see a future for us or was I always meant to be the good-time guy to make you feel wanted, a stopgap to go with the half-life you're living? Well, go find someone else to use because I deserve better than that. I deserve more than you're willing to give."

She felt as though her heart and lungs were about to fly apart. He was right. She could never be the woman he deserved. Fumbling, it took her a moment to find the door handle, never mind that she was looking right at it.

"I need to get out," she gasped, but it didn't open until she heard the click of the lock. It would be stupid to read anything into that, such as Jack releasing her from her bond to him. Really stupid.

After slamming the car door, she expected him to drive away, and it took her a moment to realize he was waiting for her to get inside her apartment. Protecting her to the end. Once sequestered, she gasped and hauled in oxygen to the heart she could feel blackening with hurt. When it didn't help, she realized the muscle was damaged beyond repair.

* * *

"Jack, wake up."

He jolted and almost fell over because his left side had

decided to stay in the land of Nod. Apparently, a Mack truck had run over his head, then backed up to finish the job. And he was drooling. Bloody brilliant. He peered up and Jules peered down, her face pale and concerned. Huh, there's a switch. She was worried about him for a change.

Then he realized the incongruity of their positions. She stood over him, and he was puddled on the floor of his new restaurant kitchen. Stiffness had snarled his back muscles into a slab of frozen beef. Par for the course when you fall asleep with your back to a refrigerator door.

"How did you get in?" he croaked while he swiped at his mouth. He strained to lift his head. Any more than an inch would require coffee or a crane.

"You left the door open, idiot. I called your mobile but you didn't answer."

"Because I was asleep." His head snapped back and a painful wince answered. "So you walked into an empty restaurant in a dodgy neighborhood on the off chance I'd be here?"

"Don't worry. The sprog kicks up whenever it suspects danger. Like baby spidey senses or something." Bending over, she extracted a quarter-full bottle of Johnnie Walker from his hand, subbed it with a cup of coffee, and looked around. "You've been busy."

He followed her gaze. Pots begat pots, skillets had birthed skillets. All the countertops bore evidence of last night's surge of creativity-slash-destruction.

"I was trying to get something right."

She squinted. "Did you?"

"I don't know." The entire night had been spent on one thing: the risotto from the taping. It wouldn't make an appearance on his new menu, but he was determined to perfect it or die trying. After pan number fourteen—or was it fifteen?—his numbed taste buds won over his judgment and he packed it in. That's when his friend Johnnie Walker stopped by for a confab.

"Aren't there health codes against drinking and cooking?" She placed the whiskey bottle down on the counter with a disgusted nose wrinkle.

"I cooked, then I drank. No chefs were harmed in the making of this mess." Much.

With her sandaled foot, she gave his thigh a gentle shove. "I remember you used to stay up all night cooking when you were hacked off about something." *Before you left,* she didn't add.

He had no desire to take a trip down memory ditch. Besides, more recent events took precedence in his overcrowded brain. "How bad is it?"

"Not so terrible. You're top of the video charts, but this time, someone got your good side."

Unfolding to a stand, he stretched the pins-and-needles away, wishing it were that easy to shove aside the pain in his head, his chest, his...hand? He turned over the palm of his right hand in response to the throbbing call of a burn. How the hell had that happened? Michelin-starred chefs, or the executive chefs of restaurants that earned Michelin stars, weren't immune to the odd burn here and there, but usually he remembered how he acquired a raw welt that stretched from pinkie to thumb. The memory-numbing effects of alcohol, he supposed.

He took a sip of coffee, surprised that it was just how he liked it. That was immediately replaced with guilt. He had no idea if his sister even drank coffee.

Spanning his forehead with his injury-free hand, he

shielded his vision for a needed moment and tried to recall the events of last night. All day he'd been pissed off—at Laurent for his know-nothing Frenchness, at Tony for his lack of trust, at Jules for the mixed-nuts messages, at his useless lawyer who had no legal solution to the online bullying. But mostly he'd been pissed at Lili, and going Jack-smash on the first person to look at him crooked seemed like a marvelous idea. The details were foggy. His gaze drifted to the bottle. He was fairly positive the fireworks had culminated in property damage but no fisticuffs. For months, his policy had been to let it ride so it didn't acquire power, but he refused to stand by while someone took pot shots at his woman. And then to have her use his ham-fisted heroics as an excuse to bail . . . well, wasn't that just the funniest cosmic joke? Protect her. Ignore it. Damned if he do, damned if he don't.

Everything he was feeling must have been visible on his face. Before he knew what was happening, he found himself locked in Jules's tight, and frankly unfamiliar, embrace.

"What's that for?" he asked, ruining it.

"You looked like you were about to drop," she said, making up for his crankiness as only family can do. "Heard about Lili. She didn't like Tough Guy Jack?"

He drew back. "Don't stop there. She doesn't think all that highly of Bully Jack and can definitely do without World-Dominating Jack."

When Jules didn't jump to his defense, he stared. And waited.

Unfazed, she gave the slimmest of shrugs. "Well, you can be a bit over the top."

He remained silent. There might have been glowering.

"That's all well and good with your kitchen slaves, but it can be tough for the rest of us."

"So, I'm a bully?"

"Not exactly. It's more..." She pulled a breath from somewhere deep. "You're like this force of nature, this bright star. Everyone wants to please you and you know that and expect it, so when they don't, you get disappointed. You're a fierce optimist, the most optimistic person I know, actually. You see all this promise in people and when they don't live up to your expectations, it frustrates you. A lot."

Stunned, he blinked at her because that was about the longest speech he had ever heard pass her lips. "But just to be clear, I'm not a bully?"

That earned him an indulgent smile, a blast of sunshine as rare as steak tartare. He loved when she turned it on for him. "Bully. Optimist. Perpetually disappointed. Which do you prefer?"

He preferred whichever one got him Lili, but there was only so much his overworked heart could withstand. Teasing her to distraction when she wanted sex and he wanted more was one thing. Bullying—no, convincing—her to date him was another. But he was damned if he was going to beg her to love him. He was flat-out, knockdown in love with a woman who wouldn't, or couldn't, match his raging appetite for her.

Fucking depressing.

And now Jules. How much of that sharp observation applied to their hell-in-a-handbasket relationship? The perpetually disappointed tag, on both sides, sounded most apropos. Even though he felt like tiny people with tiny hammers had taken up residence in his head, and his heart sat in his gut like a lead balloon, there were still enough caffeine-activated neurons to recognize that Jules and he had just had a moment of honest-to-God communication.

"Thanks for checking in on me," he said, meaning it. Needing it.

At this, her face crumpled like she'd just tasted vinegar. He pointed. She bolted. Looked like Baby's spidey senses recognized the imminent threat of sibling candor and kicked off. He considered following her to the bathroom and holding back her hair while she threw up, but they weren't quite at that level yet.

On the nearest counter, his phone lay in the shadow of a bowl of shiitake mushrooms, and he turned it on for the first time since he'd parted ways with Lili last night. Seventy-three messages. Forty-four from Evie. Thirty-odd from Cara, Jules, and assorted well-wishers. Zero from Lili. That about summed up his life.

He bit the bullet and made the call. She answered on the first ring.

"Jack," she dragged his name out to ten syllables. "You're killing me."

"Pretty sure your three-packs-a-day habit will get you first, Evie. Worried about your fifteen percent?"

A lung-stripping cough rattled the line, and for some reason, it cheered him. The world might be collapsing around his ears but Evie was still Evie.

"Fifteen percent of nothing is still nothing," she husked out. "But all is not lost. They're meeting right now and my source at NBN says Stone Carter had quote, unquote, a twinkle in his eye. Fat old fart. The ratings for *Kilroy's Kitchen* reruns are better than the original broadcasts, and with the premiere of *Jack of All Trades* moved up to next week to capitalize on your current popularity, interest in the Jack Kilroy brand has never been higher. People can't wait to see your great Italian love affair told with real production values and commercial breaks."

His cells tingled with a pain he couldn't ascribe to his hangover. It was looking increasingly likely that he'd be getting reacquainted with Johnnie W. the night of the premiere.

"But?" he prompted, because he could hear it as clear as if she were blowing smoke in his face.

"You're going to have to cool it. Defending your Rubenesque girlfriend might appeal to the horny housewives of Middle America, but it can't last. Once or twice is heroic. Any more will be seen as downright moronic. They won't tolerate it in the long-term."

Jack was well aware of that. On cable, he could be humping goats and roasting them on a spit afterward and no one would bat an eyelid. Network, as everyone insisted on telling him, was more suited for eunuchs. He'd been called a lot of things but testicularly deprived was not one of them. Anyway, the woman he would happily surrender every one of his Michelin stars for had no more use for Jack Kilroy's personal bodyguard service, so Tough Guy Jack could officially retire.

"The cookware people phoned again—they want to set up a meeting this week. And Random House needs to nail down the proposal for the next book." She coughed long and hard. "Relax, Jack. Everything's coming up roses."

The countertops, dappled with the remains of his elusive search for perfection, screamed back their dissent. His hand started to throb again.

Bloody roses with a mess of fucking thorns.

CHAPTER TWENTY-THREE

For the second time in as many weeks, Lili almost crashed the Vespa. The first time she had been thinking about dinner and had failed to notice a car door suddenly opening along Ashland Avenue. Luckily, her hunger meant her usual carb-dazed reflexes were nowhere in evidence. Now she was on her way to her parents' and had just swerved out of the way of an SUV that decided to do a last-minute lane change without signaling.

That time she'd been thinking about Jack.

Her chest hurt something awful with a pain she hadn't experienced since she'd first heard the news of her mother's cancer. Back then, after a couple of days spent wallowing, she'd put that behind her and got on with the business of living, or more specifically making sure her mother lived. Getting past Jack should be easier than that. There was nothing life-threatening about a broken heart.

Every night since he'd left, she'd tossed and turned, her body aching. Aching for the one person who could put her straight and do her right, the man she missed more each day instead of less. The smile that scrambled her brain; the sexy, lickable scar; even the atrocious singing, all part of Jack's armory of slash-and-burn. She needed to force herself into a place where Jack didn't exist, which was near impossible when every thought was filtered through her time with him. Every word she hadn't said. Every decision not taken.

Once, she had threatened to leave all she knew, move to New York, live her life at full tilt. Francesca's illness had changed all that and not in the way she liked to think. She might have fooled herself that the relief she felt when she spent her savings paying those medical bills stemmed from putting her mother onto the road to recovery, but it was just as much about helping herself. Giving Little Miss Do Nothing an exit strategy so she wouldn't have to take that chance. She hadn't even tried to find another way.

For the longest time, she had been stuck in a shell of her own creating. The overweight teen who lost the pounds but not the baggage. The artist who lived in the space behind her camera because the shadows felt safe. The good daughter who used her family to keep her grounded, and caged. She knew that. Hell, she lived it. Because no matter what way she parsed it, she *was* afraid of trying and failing.

Or trying and succeeding.

When she got to her parents' house, she slipped around back to where they sat with Tad—and sigh, Marco—at the outdoor table, already set to bursting with a glorious spread. Without asking, her mother piled a plate high with ziti and put it before her.

After the taping, Marco had gone missing for several

weeks, ducking all the burning questions Lili longed to ask about moonlighting as viral video producer and saboteur. Now her self-loathing kept him safe as she internalized all her anger and tried to focus.

"Well, where are we at?" Marco asked, glancing at his watch.

"We've definitely seen an uptick in reservations since news of the show taping got out." Lili slid an oblique glance to her father, who sat stoic and unyielding. "With the broadcast of the show next week, we'll probably see some additional business for a short time but it won't last."

"Unless we find a way to hold on to them," Tad chimed in.

"If they like the food, they'll come back," her father shot back, his refrain familiar but tired. "We have steady customers now who return monthly, sometimes weekly."

"Right, Dad, but we're not getting any new blood. It's not just about the food. It's an environment, an ambience—"

"So, we should play loud music and baseball games over the bar?" Her father made a disgusted noise. "Those are not the type of customers we want."

"Dad, we're a neighborhood institution, but there's a lot of competition, and we look like old hat. Tad and I have some ideas for a design makeover, maybe trim the menu so it's not so overwhelming. Just a few touches to make it more modern. Appeal to how the neighborhood has changed."

Tony's gaze grew narrow and hard. "When you are in charge of the business, Liliana, you can make these decisions. Until then, you must abide by my rules."

"Then why am I even here? You asked me to take over as manager when Mom became sick, but you second-guess every decision I make. Every suggestion I offer. There's no trust there."

"This is not about trust. It is about what is best for the family, something you don't seem to know anything about."

"Tony, don't." Her mother laid a soothing hand on her father's arm, threw Lili an affectionate look, and dipped her maternal gaze to the ziti. *Eat up, that'll fix it.* Lili had already lost her appetite. A heart-rending breakup and parental recrimination beat Atkins every time.

"Dad, if I could go back to that night in O'Casey's and do it over, I—" She faltered. What would she do? Not goad Jack into losing control? Ignore that surge of power she felt when he looked into her eyes with such hunger? No, she wouldn't change a thing. Kissing Jack in a crowded bar would remain with her as one of the most precious experiences of her life. It was the first step toward becoming New Lili. No one could take it away from her, least of all her father.

"Well, we cannot turn back time, Liliana."

"No, we can't, Dad, but we can move forward."

"Tony, she's right," Marco said, sounding bored. "These days, it's all about social media, online promotion, tapping into new user markets. Lili's shenanigans have brought us a lot of attention. We need to build on that."

Oh, that was just too much. Lili turned on him, fury finally overriding her sense. "Yes, let's build on it, Marco, but next time, I'd appreciate it if you ask before you turn me into a marketing sensation."

The atmosphere at the table frosted over as both Tad and her father ossified, their glacial gazes zoning in on Marco.

"Marco, explain," her father said.

Throat working convulsively, he raised his hands and looked around. "You think...? No way. I didn't put up the video."

"Then who?" Lili asked, baffled.

"No idea. I might have encouraged the girls to be a little overzealous during the TV taping, but that was it." His eyes locked with Lili's, pleading for understanding. "Honestly, Lil. I'd never have done that. I mean, we're friends. We're more than friends."

Her mind floundered and tears smarted her eyes. Down was up; east was west. Nothing made sense anymore. Swallowing her emotion, she forced her thoughts back to the present, aware that her father was watching her closely.

"I need a glass of water," she mumbled, and fled to the kitchen before she lost her composure completely. She gripped the sink to prevent her body from folding in half.

Jack is gone.

Since driving him away, her heart had been stuck on a frenetic techno beat. Cardio without the fat-reducing benefits. Now it felt curiously dead, like it had given up the ghost after all that effort. She missed the pain.

A heavy footfall echoed behind her and she turned, expecting Tad leading the charge on Operation Comfort Lili. Surprise at seeing her father made her gulp.

"*Piccola,*" he said.

Just that one simple word and she burst into tears. No one called her that anymore. The nickname that meant "little one" lost its cuteness factor somewhere around the sixth grade. Her father's hard strength enveloped and soothed her through her crying jag. For a wonderful, long time.

"Say the word and I will kill him. I know a guy."

A semi-hysterical laugh ripped from her. Above the stress of her mother's illness, the restaurant, and her strained bond with Tony, she had forgotten he had a sense of humor. How close they had once been and how alike they were.

"Dad, it's not his fault. I know you didn't think much of him, but he loved me very much. More than anyone ever has."

"Not more than anyone." He dropped a light kiss on her forehead. "If he loved you so much, why is he not here fighting for you?"

She couldn't quite summon her usual front-it-out smile. "Maybe you scared him off."

"He did not seem the type to scare easily," he said. "I tried my best but he insisted on defying me."

How could she possibly explain how inadequate she had felt in the face of Jack's all-encompassing passion? Her father would dismiss her fears, saying they made her unworthy of being a DeLuca, though his tacit dismissal of her ambitions had gone some way to keeping her wounds festering for as long as they had. Still, blaming her problems on her daddy issues was a little too movie-of-the-week for Lili's taste.

Her father picked up the conversational slack. "He said I'm too hard on you."

Even now, an allusion to Jack defending her made her tingly and aware, like he was in the room supporting her in everything she did. Her champion, standing at her shoulder, encouraging her to be strong. She parted her lips to disagree, but her mouth had other ideas.

"You are."

He gave her a long look and she held his gaze.

"Please, Dad, talk to me."

His eyes turned rheumy. "When your mother became ill..." He coughed. Started over. "When your mother became ill, I was not the husband she needed. The thought of losing her almost destroyed me, but you, Liliana, you were so strong. Managing everything, keeping us all on schedule for your mother's doctor appointments, taking over at the restaurant. I could not—we could not—have survived these last two years without you. I do not mean to be hard, but I have been so afraid of how my life would be if neither of you were here." He paused, taking a deep breath. "I know the restaurant has suffered while I have been so weak. But the kitchen, it is where *I* feel the strongest, where I feel like myself. And to realize I have failed there, too, shames me. *La cucina Italiana* is my life and I couldn't even win against Jack without cheating."

He sighed so wearily that her heart listed.

"Dad, you haven't failed. All our lives you've provided for us. Mom is better. That woman is not going anywhere and you're going to have to get on board with that." She rubbed his strong arm, the one that had never failed to comfort her as a child. "You are a great, great chef. The best. The problem is not the food. It's just in the details. There's so much more we could be doing. An on-line takeout menu, a food truck, drink and meal specials, small improvements that won't change the fundamentals of who we are but that would keep us competitive."

Head dipped, he placed his hands on the sink and took a moment. "Liliana, as well as failing as a husband, I have failed you as a father. I wanted you to always be here, working by my side, but for a while now, I've known you were meant for better things. You are far too beautiful and talented to be stuck in the restaurant."

Her numbing heart sparked, and the pain of the past week lessened by the faintest degree. Now would be the time to lay it all out, dissect every hurt, revisit every sharp comment, demand satisfaction. But being held in her father's unconditional grip was enough, his acknowledgment of her worth the satisfaction she needed.

"What do you want to do?" he asked, and she gulped because it was the first time he had ever asked.

"Make sure everyone knows how amazing the head chef at DeLuca's in Wicker Park is and then"—she inhaled deeply—"graduate school, Dad. I don't know when or where or how I'll pay for it, but I'm going to do it. I have to. I'll always be your daughter. Wherever I am, my heart will be here with you." She had a life to plan. A life without Jack, but she could make it the life she dreamed of before she met him. Their time together had crystallized the realization that she deserved good things.

"I think your heart is somewhere else, Liliana." He considered her carefully. "He asked me to collaborate with him on a cookbook."

"Jack?"

He gave the barest shrug, the embodiment of Continental nonchalance. "Do you think he meant it or was he doing it to for other reasons?"

She supposed it was possible, but... "He meant it, Dad. He really admires you. And he's too much of a perfectionist to risk attaching his name to something he doesn't believe in. Kind of like you." A wisp of hope blossomed in her chest. "You should do it. The world should have a chance to cook your fabulous gnocchi."

Her father's mouth turned up in a hint of a grin. Chefs were an egotistical bunch, and Jack Kilroy, crafty and not a little egotistical himself, knew that better than anyone.

"Tell me more about your ideas," Tony said.

An hour later, a blueprint for survival was in place: Tad would draw up a stock inventory and control plan, Lili would get to grips with staffing and decor, her father would tackle the menu, and Marco would work on publicity. So much to do before the premiere of *Jack of All Trades*, but keeping busy would keep her idle heart from veering into devil territory.

The weight was lifting slowly from Lili's shoulders, though she wasn't sure she was ready to let it go. A burden can ground you just as much as it can weigh you down. Sometimes, it's the only thing stopping you from flying away.

* * *

There was no answer to his knock at the DeLucas' brownstone, and for a moment, Jack was at a loss for what to do next. The last couple of weeks had seen a distinct deterioration in his mental faculties. He would walk into the fridge in his new kitchen and forget what he needed. He would scroll through his phone contacts without a clue who he had planned to call. Some weird form of dementia had ravaged his brain. Breakup senility.

The sweet murmur of voices carried on the warm air, and he followed it through the side path to the back of the house. On the deck, his eyes fell on Lili's bare, golden legs stretched out in front of her and his heart wrenched a response. Damn, he hadn't been expecting that. As he rounded the railing, Jules spotted him.

"Hey, Jack."

"Hi, Jules."

He felt like he was walking through treacle, every step a dead weight. Nothing dead about his heart, unfortunately. It bounded about his chest like an excited puppy that had just spotted his owner. Fan-freaking-tastic.

The light from the twinkling tree lights cast an unearthly glow over Lili's face, highlighting her discomfort. She pulled up to a stand and carefully backed away toward the house, as though worried he might force her into conversation.

"I'll leave you two alone," she murmured, barely audible above the twang of the screen door.

He sat on the patio sofa and let his hands stray to the warmth of the fabric where Lili had sat. Her lingering vanilla fragrance joined with the herbal scents from the garden, an olfactory salve that complemented this quiet haven in the middle of the city. In London and New York, there was no escaping the noise, but Chicago, a city of neighborhoods, offered pockets of peace for anyone who searched for it. No wonder his sister liked it here.

"Thought you were in Miami," she said, breaking the silence he had been enjoying.

"I was. Now I'm here." He settled back with an exhale and let his eyelids shutter closed. The idea of falling asleep under the stars appealed so much he opened his eyes before the wish came true. "At least I will be off and on for the next few weeks until the restaurant opens. Then

I'm back to New York." And she would be tucked away in London if he had his druthers.

She didn't react. Just sat there with her hands clasped in her lap like they weren't talking about her future. He didn't know how to bridge the yawning emotional distance between them. The whispering night breeze and the rest should have conspired to make this the perfect spot for him to have a calm, reasoned conversation about her situation. Of course, she chose to deflect and talk about his situation.

"Lay it on me, big bruv. I'm all ears," Jules said with not the least bit of irony.

"Pot, meet kettle."

"You're my brother, Jack. My overbearing, know-it-all brother. I can't always talk to you, but you can talk to me. Let your lady feelings out."

That dragged a smile from him, the first in a couple of weeks. His mouth hurt with the effort all the same. "You're a cheeky little tart, you know. You've got a gob on you just like Mum."

He knew she'd appreciate that, though that wasn't why he said it. In the last month, he'd spent more time with Jules than he had in the last year, and he had forgotten how much he liked her. Lili had said to give her time, let her come to him, and he was trying. Really trying.

He took a good look at her for the first time since he'd sat down. Her face had filled out, evicting the wan, haunted appearance she'd sported on her arrival in Chicago. A steady diet of pasta and DeLuca TLC had done wonders. Moments ticked by in stultifying silence, which only worked to make every cell bubble in irritation. To hell with pussyfooting around the rusty can of worms. They were both going to need tetanus shots after this.

"Jules, all I've ever wanted was to be a good brother." He could prod the guilt centers as well as anyone.

She looked surprised. "Jack, it's okay. I know you feel like you owe me. When you left, I sulked and made you feel like crap."

"Well, that's what eight-year-olds do."

"And I was a brat for several years after. I just missed you. You said you were going to apply for my guardianship when you turned eighteen and when you didn't"— her voice stumbled on her emotion—"I thought you had given up on me."

Those words corkscrewed into his heart. "I truly believed you were better off with your aunt and uncle. After your dad died, you needed stability and I couldn't offer that, but there was never any question of how much I loved you."

Her condemning silence punched him hard in the gut, and he struggled to recover his calm. And he thought he could beat her at the guilt game. Amateur. He couldn't change the past, but he could fix the future. "The jobs, Jules. The rut you seem to be stuck in."

"We can't all be big shots," she said impatiently. "You'll just have to face it that you have a dud for a sister."

"Why do you say that? You're sharp as a tack. I don't get why you don't want something better. By this point you must have some idea what you want to do with your life."

She made a hand-shrug. "What's better than free drinks, no responsibilities, and getting to sleep in till three in the afternoon?"

Was she trying to send him over the precipice? He stared at her until she dropped her gaze.

"I'm not cut out for those jobs in fancy restaurants," she said quietly.

"Why? You take reservations on the phone. You show people to tables. Maybe you jot down some drink orders. What's so hard about that?"

She ignored him and studied her tightly clasped hands.

"What's so hard about it?" The exasperation in his voice was intensifying, and he tried to dial it down. Be patient with her. Don't bully her. Especially don't argue with her about getting a suitable job when they both knew he was going to do his damnedest to pay for his sins and keep her job-free for the foreseeable future. It was the principle of the thing.

Still freezing him out, she knuckled the corner of one eye. There was something important here and he tried to grasp on to it without losing his cool.

"Anyone can do that job, Jules. I know I push, but surely you don't hate me that much."

Finally, that elicited a response that wasn't blasé. "Jack, I don't hate you."

"It certainly feels like it sometimes. I've no idea why you came to me. Why you left London in such a hurry. You won't tell me anything. I set you up with interview after interview. I try to help and you throw it back in my face."

She gripped the arm of the sofa. "Like I said, I just can't do those jobs. I'm not good enough."

If she had told him she was thinking of joining a nunnery, it wouldn't have shocked him more. "Good enough? You could do those hostess jobs with your eyes closed."

"They may as well be closed for all the good they do me."

"What does that mean?"

Her swallow was so hard it sounded like she had gulped down a golf ball. "I need to pee. I need to pee all the time." She stood, tears streaming down her face. All hopped up on baby hormones was his best guess.

"Jules." He reached for her but she skirted him like his touch could burn and headed into the house. Something about what she'd said poked at him, the important thing he was missing just on the edge of his consciousness.

With purpose in his stride, he followed her. This ended here, or it would if he could get by Lili, who stood sentry. Her raised hand stopped a couple of inches before his chest.

"Give her a moment. She's been pretty emotional the last couple of days."

He looked over her shoulder into the inviting, homey kitchen, the heart of Casa DeLuca, where his sister's heart felt at ease. Another few steps and he would feel the warm splay of Lili's palm on his chest. For some reason, that enraged him beyond all sense.

"I know I can't possibly compete with the DeLucas when it comes to happy families," he said, unable to keep the vitriol out of his voice, "but that's my bloody sister and she's going to talk to me whether she wants to or not."

"Of course," she said in a reasonable tone that immediately deflated him. She stood back to let him by, and he walked in, feeling like a prize idiot for getting his nose out of joint. Despite the knock-back, he loved that about her. How she held no truck with his moods, how a single look could cut him down to size.

"Slow down and listen to her. Getting frustrated is not going to help," she said, still as reasonable as all get-out.

"Oh, shut up," he jabbed back, just to see if he could still make her smile. He could and that knowledge pierced like a knife in his heart.

"How are you?" she asked.

Oh no, they were not doing this.

"Busy with the restaurant." He waved a hand to fill in the rest. Full sentences needed full breaths and he was having a hard time inflating his lungs to speaking capacity. The two women he loved more than life itself didn't need him, and hell, that hurt like a mother.

Unable to look at her, he turned away from the pain to find Jules in the doorway to the living room, her eyes red-rimmed and going back and forth between them. Lili offered her a glass of water and Jules accepted it with trembling hands.

"I'd sell this kid for a vodka martini if I could." At his raised eyebrow, she rolled her eyes, then finished off the water in a couple of swift gulps.

"Tell me what you meant about your eyes being no good." He held back, his arms taut at his sides instead of crossed, trying to project nonthreatening body language. He'd read it in a book once.

"Just my usual backchat," she mumbled.

"No, it wasn't."

She rinsed the glass in the sink and cast her nervy gaze about in search of a dishtowel. Or a way out of this conversation. With care, she turned the glass over on the draining board.

"Jules, he only wants the best for you," Lili said.

He could feel Lili's pitying gaze prickling his cheek,

but he refused to look at her, preferring to focus on his sister. "Talk to me, baby girl."

The endearment softened her face but all the tension transferred to her hands, now grasping the edge of the sink. The silence sat weighted but he let it ride.

"I can't read all that well."

"Because you need glasses?" he asked, confused. She did squint a lot.

"It's not my sight. I wish it was." She ducked her head and her speech streamed in low tones. "I stare at the words and sometimes I can see a picture of it. But other times, it means nothing and it takes forever to figure it out, if I can at all. The worst is names because I can't imagine anything. By the time I work out what table to bring someone to, they'd be dead from hunger."

He swore the room tilted. This could not be...His next words sounded like they came from a spot two feet to his right. "When did this start happening?"

She gave a defeated shrug. "It's always been like this. I muddled through in school until I was old enough to leave."

His sister couldn't read.

She hated texting. She didn't have an e-mail address. How had he not known this?

"Did you know about this?" he asked Lili, who shook her head slowly. The surprise on her face confirmed her response.

"Why didn't Daisy and Pete tell me?" In answer, Jules dragged her teeth along her quivering lower lip. "You mean they don't know?"

"I could get by with copying other people's work in class. Badly. I'd usually fail all the tests." He had known she never did well in school but her aunt said it didn't matter. The world can never have enough hairdressers, she'd announced in that malevolent East End accent. He had despaired but then bought into the presented narrative that she was lazy because it was easier than making the effort. The failure he had felt then rose up to choke his throat now.

All his pain—and hers—reflected back from her shining eyes. "So, it doesn't matter how many interviews you set up or how many jobs you try to get for me. I'm too stupid."

His heart, lately fragile at best, broke at last. All this time, she had been alone, coping with this terrible burden. If only someone had paid more attention to her in school, if only he had visited more often, if only she had asked for his help.

If only could take a running jump. From here on out, there was only Jules.

He wrapped himself around her, willing her stiff frame to relax into him. "You are not stupid, baby girl. You're my amazing, gorgeous, funny, clever, and incredibly annoying sister. You can do anything you want."

"Except hold down a decent job or read a book without giving up two sentences in or have sex without getting preggo." With every self-accusation, he grasped her tighter. "Oh, God, Jack. I was on the pill, I swear. But sometimes I get confused and miss a day. I'm so ashamed."

"I wish you had told me. Everything."

She didn't answer, just sank into him more. This is what comes of being a bloody optimist. He expected so much of people that his own sister couldn't confide in him, fearful of his disappointment.

"Jack, I'm worried about the baby. What if he's got th-this same thing I have?"

"What if he does?" It sounded like a learning disability, dyslexia perhaps. He would get her diagnosed and hire tutors or whatever was necessary to make this better. Make it right. Drawing back, he cradled her face in his hands.

"Now, I know you don't want to hear this, but for the love of everything that's holy, would you please, please let me help you?" He just wanted someone he cared about to let him love them. His world had been upended by her revelation, then righted again as he realized what he was dealing with. He would fix this because that's what he did, but for the moment he would give her what she needed most. He would hold her and never let her go.

"Jack, you don't have to—"

"I know I don't. I want to and you know what I'm like when I don't get what I want."

Her eyes flew wide, shiny and filled with something he hadn't seen before. Hope.

Supporting her would be his highest priority, and his thoughts tumbled over each other, his mind racing with everything he needed to do. First on the list, a chat with Evie.

"And you won't send me away?" she whispered against his shoulder.

"No, you're stuck with me. Wherever you are, I am."

Turning his head, he sought out Lili, but the spot of tile she had occupied a moment ago was empty. She had stepped up to the plate to help, then receded back into the shadows. Just like always.

CHAPTER TWENTY-FOUR

The message from his sister had said Tony would be cooking at DeLuca's tonight and that he wanted to talk about the cookbook offer. To say that astonished Jack would be a massive understatement, but then his life over the last month had been a cavalcade of surprises, most of them at the hands of a certain Italian family. And now, just as he had cut his ties to Lili, the man who was adamant he didn't want to encourage Jack's connection to his family was holding out his hand.

Hell if he could figure out those crazy DeLucas.

The restaurant was closed on Mondays, so she wouldn't be here. Still, as he approached the large oak doors, his body primed in anticipation of seeing her like it knew she was nearby. Upstairs watching those trashy reality shows he teased her about. Or over at the studio on the next block, cataloging her secret photo collection. Crossing paths at her house had only made his need burn hotter, and now, almost three weeks without her, he was like a junkie jonesing for his fix. A clammy, jittery bundle of nerves.

More likely, he was nervous about Tony. Sure he was.

He stepped inside to find the place was hopping. And filled to capacity. And different.

He tried to put his finger on it.

The tables looked to be in the same configuration, but gone were the crisp white cloths, revealing lacquered tops that took it from staid to hip. The ceiling was still frescoed, but the imaginative drop-bulb lighting over the bar looked like something out of a modern art museum. The walls were still exposed brick, but the art—

The art. The swanlike curvature of a neck, the subtle arc of an inked calf, the graceful taper to a well-turned ankle. Sensuous, quirky, but tasteful enough so as not to scare away the regulars. Something unfurled inside his chest, a tentative curl of warmth and hope that he stamped down before it could race to the photo finish.

He blinked, and a blond, cherubic vision materialized before him. Francesca. Her serenity faltered for just a moment before she made a smiling recovery. Clearly not expecting him.

"*Ciao*, Jack. It's good to see you." She leaned up, he leaned down, and they did the Euro double-kiss exchange.

"New hours, Francesca?"

"No, just a special occasion." The smile stretched wider now and his heart turned over. Looked like he didn't even need Lili's presence to get the yen. "We are showcasing a new menu and, well, you see…" She gestured to the end of the bar where a large flat-screen TV had been placed kitty-corner to give everyone an unobstructed view. Even from a distance of thirty feet, Jack could see images of cookware carouseling across the screen.

His heart swooped to his stomach. Commercials. Cooking Channel commercials.

Ad break over, the volume was unmuted and the graphic he had okayed six months ago came into focus, the lead-in for the premiere episode of *Jack of All Trades*. Pulse accelerating, he looked around, his brain finally catching up to his vision. This was a viewing party.

"Quiet, everyone. It's starting up again," Cara called out, waving the remote control. A hushed awe descended across the room. Jack hadn't exactly forgotten that it was broadcasting tonight; he'd just preferred to ignore it. Maybe watch it later and wallow a bit. He had assumed Tony's wounded pride would demand he forget about it, too.

He knew it was a long shot, but what the hey. "I got a message saying Tony wanted to see me."

Francesca's brows dipped in a chevron and Jack cursed his meddling sister.

"He is rather busy now but let me get you a glass of Brunello. Would you like to see the new menu?" she asked, as cool as the other side of the pillow.

"Sure," he mumbled, taking it from her. Then he looked down, surprised at the weight in his hand, or lack thereof. Just a single page on quality cardstock. A few appetizers and salads, the best pastas and entrées. The veal meatballs. The gnocchi with brown butter and sage. Clean, inviting, fresh.

The cutting-edge art. The scaled-to-superb menu. His girl had won.

Damn if that didn't excite the hell out of him.

At the bottom of the menu, a line proclaimed the chef would prepare any Italian specialty and that patrons only had to ask. Jack couldn't hide his smile. He supposed that was what's known as a compromise, the art of which he supposedly knew nothing about.

Francesca had moved off to talk to someone who was clearly related—he still hadn't met them all—and Jack rested against the hostess podium, trying to blend in. All eyes were riveted to the screen, their attention only interrupted by brief dips to shovel that kick-arse gnocchi into their mouths. Everyone, that is, except a severe-looking blonde in a tight skirt and tighter blouse, who fiddled with a microphone and whispered to the guy with the video camera behind her. Local news crew, from the looks of it. Jack scanned the room and tried to convince himself disappointment felt close to relief when his search for the manager came up empty.

From what he could gather, the thirty-minute episode was at the business end. He didn't have to watch it to know it had followed the standard play: the setup of cocky arriviste versus traditional by-the-book, something going terribly wrong, in this case, Jack overcooking a risotto to a mushy glue, cut with images of diners lamenting a missing flavor or waxing as lyrical as the editing allowed. The point wasn't accuracy but to tell a tale in twenty-two minutes. In one shot, Tony was captured in that scowl the DeLucas had a patent on; then Jack was shown at the burner, competently managing several orders at once. Spliced together, it looked like Tony was envious of Jack's flair, which he was damn sure was not the case.

Aunt Sylvia had the right of it. Television *was* cheating.

"Hi, Jack."

Glancing down, he encountered four feet of attitude, topped with one foot of bird's nest.

"Hey, sweetheart," he said to Gina.

She fidgeted, opened her mouth, closed it, then blew out a long sigh. "I'm sorry about the salt in your dishes."

"Forget about it." When she still looked woebegone, he squeezed her shoulder. "It's all vino under the bridge."

"It was Marco's fault, really, and I just wanted to make everything better after"—she delivered a furtive over-the-shoulder glance and mouthed—"the video."

"The video?" he repeated, feeling sluggish.

"Of the kiss. It was me," she said in a torrent. "It was supposed to be a joke, but then Angela started sending it to everyone she knew and it just snowballed. And then Uncle Tony was mad, and Lili was upset, so I tried to make it up to her with the Facebook page and the T-shirts. And then I thought if Uncle Tony won the contest, it would cancel out some of the bad publicity."

Jesus. "Does Lili know?"

Gina shook her head despondently, her eyes big and glossy. "I'm trying to persuade her to give me my job back and if I tell her, she'll kill me."

"Probably." Kissing her on the cheek would require more knee-bend than he was willing to give, so he dropped one on the cotton-candy crown of her head. "It's all right, munchkin. No hard feelings."

"Aw, thanks, Jack. You're a real star and absolutely gorgeous." A melancholy sigh escaped her lips. "I'm getting married in a while and you would have looked so good in the wedding party. Can't think why Lili dropped you."

She flashed a smile, adjusted her breasts, and bounced off, conscience cleansed. Oh, to be that young and clueless.

Back on *Jack of All Trades*, the drama was ratcheting up and now played to an audience with eyes out on stalks. He'd known that Jules's dramatic arrival and anything that hinted at the cheating would grace the cutting room floor, but surprise rolled over him at seeing him and Lili taking that moment of comfort right before the second coming of hell broke loose. The hairs on his arm spiked in memory of her soft hand stroking him to calm. His lips twitched in remembrance of how near her mouth had been to his. His whole body ached like it had done that night when he'd realized he needed her more than he needed food or air.

The crowd cheered as Lili and Jack almost kissed on camera, then booed as Cara broke up the party and ordered everyone to get back to work. In good-humored acceptance of her role as stage villain, his producer stood up to take a bow. He cast about again, noting the healthy mix of young and old, including the trendy, professional kind of clientele Lili had said the restaurant needed to supplement the regulars. More DeLucas crowded his vision, laughing, living, and loving. People he wanted to know better. Aunt Sylvia, with her hirsute tower, partially blocked the view of the poor souls sitting behind her. Jules and Tad, whispering like coconspirators. His sister felt his gaze and grinned at him with his mother's smile, and he remembered that he loved her very much and that it might be bad form to throttle her before the baby was born.

And then he saw her. The euphoric surge of electric that coursed through his body felt like that first time when he stumbled out of a walk-in fridge and found a spread-eagled vision in red, gold, and blue.

She stood off to the side near the corridor that led to the kitchen, separate, presiding. Dressed in a drape of shimmery silver that kissed every curve, she looked like she'd been dipped in something precious. Her hair was piled up high but even from his distant vantage point, he could see a couple of wispy strands had formed an escape committee and were making a break along the elegant curve of her neck.

He moved to a seat at the side of the bar so he could covertly watch her. She lifted her high-heeled foot and rubbed her ankle, a move that hitched her dress up so far he had to close his eyes to harden his mind against the on-slaught of golden skin. Didn't help his body any, which had turned to granite the moment he saw her and stayed that way.

From the TV, the announcement that Tony had won sent a wave of applause and cheers undulating through the room. Shouts of *salute* and *il cuoco, il cuoco* filled the air, drowning out the closing interviews and the theme of *Jack of All Trades*. It took a moment for Tony to make his appearance, and he clearly did so under sufferance as Tad strong-armed him from the kitchen to take a bow.

Jack found Lili again, and his heart reeled at the sight of that upward tilt to her lips and those clever eyes watching the proceedings from beneath her dark veil of eye-lashes. Tony was saying something about how pleased he was that people were here to celebrate the new DeLuca's. Still, Jack could see only her. Vaguely, something registered about Lili's art and Tony's pride in his daughter's accomplishments. She smiled, looking both teary and a whole lot happy. And Jack was truly happy for her.

The claps and roars faded into the painted sky above his head. He closed his eyes again, but she was still there, imprinted on the backs of his eyelids like a tattoo of his personal heaven and hell.

* * *

Content to keep a low profile and let her father enjoy his moment, Lili held back against the arch that separated the two dining rooms and inhaled the nerves away. They had done it. Okay, so they weren't exactly out of the woods, but there was sunlight streaming through the trees. She was under no illusions that a few cosmetic changes and a couple of arty photos would heal all their ills, but her father had listened to her for the first time in forever. And that felt immensely gratifying. Not quite enough to ease the Jack-shaped ache in her chest, but that would come.

Marco had wanted to invite him, of course. Squeeze every last drop out of the Kilroy-DeLuca connection, but thankfully, the family had vetoed that idea. They'd gotten their pound of flesh from Jack; there was no need to be tacky about it.

Tell that to the local news.

Brief interview with her father complete, Lili found herself in the inquisition circle with Shona Love, Channel 5's entertainment reporter. Before Lili could take a fortifying breath, the cameraman, wearing a Canadian tuxedo and a mustache that Burt Reynolds might want back, counted a silent three-two-one with his fingers.

Shona's face transformed into showtime. "We're here

at DeLuca's Ristorante in Wicker Park, a twenty-two-year veteran of the neighborhood that, tonight, was featured on über-chef Jack Kilroy's newest hit cooking show, *Jack of All Trades*. We just heard from Tony DeLuca, chef/owner, who won the cook-off against Jack. Now we're talking with his daughter, Lili, who manages the restaurant." She wheezed after the fast-talk introduction. "So, Lili, you must be pleased with the outcome of the contest."

"Well, it's a testament to how great my dad is and how his food can rival that of any"—she almost said *idiot box chef* but caught herself—"any of the greats."

"Of course, Jack Kilroy *is* one of the greats," Shona said with a wink for Lili that would be missed by the camera. *Amirite, sister?* "It must have been tough for you to keep your composure with your father and your man going hammer and tongs in the kitchen. And some of those shots of you and Jack getting cozy were hot enough to get us all steamed up out here." She added another provocative wink.

"Is there something wrong with your eye?" Lili asked, amazed at how calm she felt.

Shona's perfect eyes widened, the epitome of coy. "What we all want to know, Lili, is the skinny on you and Jack." On *skinny*, Shona's sloe-eyed gaze lowered imperceptibly to take in Lili's formfitting dress, all drapes and dips, and damn, didn't she look fine in it. In fact, Lili would bet dollars to doughnuts the bony-assed bitch didn't realize she did it.

"We're so grateful to Jack and the Cooking Channel for giving us a chance to remind everyone that DeLuca's in Wicker Park is the go-to place for Italian in Chicago."

Shona wouldn't be put off so easily. She smiled, but it was as if she had to consciously rearrange her facial muscles in the appropriate pattern.

"And will Jack be eating Italian anytime soon?"

That just about ejected Lili's hard-fought-for equanimity. Was this the local news affiliate or Skinimax? She couldn't be rude, though this woman deserved to be taken out into the alley and introduced to the side of the Dumpster. Struggling for a response, Lili squeezed her eyes shut and held on. She just needed to get through this night . . . and the next night, and the next. Keep going until the Jack-shaped ache faded to dull, and the dull faded to numb, and the numb faded to nothing.

She was Tony DeLuca's daughter. She could do this.

Her eyes blew open and she saw him. She blinked to make sure it wasn't some desperate hallucination she'd conjured, but no, he was still there. Sitting about thirty feet out at the short side of the L-shaped bar. He looked so good, so Jack, that her heart flip-flopped like a dying fish and her hormones rioted in agreement.

"Jack is always welcome at DeLuca's," she said, her gaze zeroed in on his. He had seen her—he must have seen her first—and the ache in her chest turned blade-sharp as the drugging effects of the hormonal rave wore off. That it hurt even more now to look at him shouldn't have surprised her. Beauty like that bruised, but it was his gentle handling of Jules last week that had crushed her soul. Avoiding TV, magazines, the Internet, and her sister for however long it took to get over him was going to be really freaking hard.

Still, she couldn't tear her gaze away. It may have been her imagination, but every hellish minute of their time apart was as evident on his face as she was sure it was on hers. That's when another realization assaulted her.

Small-screen Jack might be a god, but real-life Jack, the brand made flesh, was *hers*, pain and all.

"He has a special place in our family for all he's done." She hesitated, then looked into Shona's face with her cheekbones so sharp they could cut tin cans. At the bar, Jack's intensity ringed him like a force field, repelling everything in its vicinity, or maybe it was an invisibility field because no one seemed to know he was here. There was something a little ironic about one of the most famous guys in the country, sitting anonymously at a restaurant bar while a media typhoon centered on him barreled through.

"Of course, when I first met him, I didn't really see the appeal, to be honest."

Shona did a cartoon double take and looked at her microphone like it might offer an explanation for what she'd just heard. "You didn't?"

"Don't get me wrong, he's gorgeous. Right, Shona?"

"Um, yes, he is." Shona giggled nervously, both aghast and thrilled at the intimate tone the interview had taken.

Lili leaned forward, her round shoulder brushing the bony one of her new gal pal. "Anyone would be lucky to have him, but you know, there was a time I didn't even think he was all that."

"You didn't?"

"No, I thought he was just one of those guys who charms his way through life. Getting by on his looks. Not much going on upstairs. In fact, you're not going to believe this. He's not all that great..."

Shona's upper body moved in, and Lili sensed the

whole crowd cant forward by degrees, proxies for the TV-viewing public.

She paused long enough to work it. "… a singer."

Somewhere behind her, Cara's singular laugh, that naughty, girly gush, tinkled above the swelling murmurs of the throng.

"Oh." Shona looked puzzled, like she'd just missed the punch line to a joke. Jack rubbed his mouth just then, and Lili knew he was concealing a smile. A seed of hope took root in her heart.

"Something else you might not believe, but in high school, I was overweight." Shona's expression changed to the phony sympathetic one she used when interviewing people about their missing cats. "I was bullied, physically and emotionally, and while I eventually got comfortable with my body, it wasn't so easy to change the mind-set that stays with being a victim. I guess I've always aimed low because I wondered how any gorgeous guy could really be attracted to me. All of me. And even when there were no doubts on that score where Jack was concerned, I found other reasons to doubt him. To find fault with him—and with me."

Shona looked like she was in media hog heaven, visions of sugarplums and local news Emmys dancing in her head. "And now?" she prompted hopefully, because this was the good stuff. The hearts-and-flowers, give-'em-what-they-paid-for, where's-my-promotion-to-E! gold dust that the public demanded of its celebrities, even transient ones like Lili. Besides, the segment probably couldn't go longer than three minutes, and Shona, like the good little reporter she was, needed to get to the bottom line.

Lili's heart thumped a rabbit's beat in her chest. Holding her breath, she spoke over Shona's shoulder to the one person who needed to hear this.

"Jack is the smartest, funniest, most challenging and demanding guy I know. From the moment we met, he supported and pushed me to be better, and then he risked everything to defend me. I didn't think I had the *coglioni* to deserve someone as awesome as him. I'm still not sure I do, but I need him to know that he rocks my world and I love him."

Jack's broad shoulders lifted on an inhale. Shona's mouth dropped open. A collective sigh of relief swished through the room.

"Well." Shona fanned herself with the microphone before realizing it needed to be stationary to pick up the audio properly. "I think after tonight, he'll definitely know."

"Not sure I can wait that long, Shona." Lili sidestepped her and stole her way to the bar, dimly aware of a platoon of indulgent DeLuca smiles flanking her journey. Others, too, but the gantlet was a blur, like a Vaseline-edged lens with a single point of clarity in the viewfinder.

Jack.

It took forever to get there and he made no effort to meet her halfway. That was okay because she owed him the trip. Behind her, she heard Burt Reynolds shuffling into position at Shona's blatant urging.

On reaching Jack, he turned in his seat to face her with legs apart, almost in invitation, his gaze viciously hot. Just like the man. Only sheer willpower prevented her from slotting in between those mouthwatering thighs and snaking her arms around his strong body.

"You get all that?" she pushed past a lump the size of a ham hock wedged in her throat.

He paused long enough to irritate. "Well, I've never been known for my brains." His voice rumbled too low to be picked up by Shona's microphone or the easily scandalized ears of her older relatives. "Are you telling me you love me so I'll sleep with you?"

She gave a half-shrug. "Thought crossed my mind. Would it work?"

"Maybe. I'm sort of superficial that way."

She moved as close as she could without touching him. Not yet. *Please, soon.* "You going to make me beg?"

He shook his head, but with it he gifted her a contrary smile, one of those smiles that lit him from within and coated all her nerve endings. She couldn't think or speak, but that didn't matter. All she had to do was rip a leaf from the Book of Jack and take.

She took what belonged to her, moving her mouth softly over his until the hunger overtook them both and their cores imprinted on each other. She fit just right, but then it had always been that way. Her body registered a throaty Jack sound and her ears registered the cheers and if her eyes had been open, she would have been rolling them because it was just so cheesy and gosh-darn-romantic.

"You never had to beg, sweetheart," he murmured against her lips. "I was yours from the start."

Somewhere deep inside, that knowledge had resided and of course she hadn't trusted it. It wasn't every day a commoner receives the favor of royalty. Tears stung the backs of her eyelids and she didn't even have a Jack-made orgasm to blame. At least, not yet.

"I always suspected brain damage," she rasped while the tears made good on their threat and rolled down her cheeks.

He shaped her jaw, stretching his thumbs to catch her saltwater leak. "Sure, how else could you land a catch like me?"

"Arrogant, conceited, impossible"—*Gorgeous, perfect, my*—"man."

His hands fanned her hips, levering her body flush, though it wasn't really possible to get any closer. Not all that advisable either, judging by how his hardness was making her damp, and she was about to burst into an inferno. She so wanted him to cup her, to squeeze her booty and worship it like he used to in private, but he kept it clean. When it came to lewd groping in public, he'd always been the one with more self-control.

She couldn't move, and not just because his thighs had scissored her in their muscular grip, but she thought that maybe she could live here for a while. Safe in the cradle of Jack's body. Great for her work commute, too.

Seemed he had other ideas. He could be so difficult.

"That little performance of yours was enough to get you to first base, but I'm going to need a lot more before I let you slide home." Slipping off the stool, he enfolded her hand in his warm, male grip. "Let's go, Lili."

He led her through the crowd, holding tight while people alternated between slapping him on the back and clasping her arm affectionately. Her mother beamed, Gina's eyes looked suspiciously shiny, and Cara gave her a dirty wink.

Then they ran into Obstacle Number One. Her father.

Tilting his head, Tony considered her for a heartbeat

before kissing her on the forehead. *"Mi mancherai tantissimo, Liliana."*

A too-full feeling ruled her chest and she nodded, not trusting herself to speak. She would miss him, too.

Her father turned to Jack, but before he could say a word, Jack squeezed her hand. "Lili, could you give your father and me a minute alone?"

"Sure," she murmured, taking a couple of surprised steps back.

Jack leaned into her father and spoke in too low a voice for Lili to hear. And she tried, she really did.

"Nice to see you finally taking my advice," Tad whispered in her ear. "Though I wonder how Jack would feel if he knew the real reason you made a play for him. That all you wanted was a ride on the chopper. *Tsk, tsk.*"

"Oh, shut up," she said nervously as she watched Jack and her father finish up and exchange what looked like bone-crushing handshakes. It must be about the cookbook. Let the fun times begin.

"Any time you want to ride the hog, babe, it's yours." Tad kissed her on the temple. "I think you earned it."

"Oh…" But that thought would have to wait because she was on the road again with her own personal thrill ride, Jack dragging her toward the back office…no, the restroom…oh, the kitchen. A mercifully empty kitchen, now that service was over and the crew was out celebrating with the revelers. Finally alone with him, butterflies collided in her stomach and she felt ten times more nervous than she had in front of the news camera and the entire restaurant of customers.

"What's going on with my dad?" she asked, stalling.

His smile was a warm secret. "Just very important chef

stuff. Nothing for you to worry your pretty little head about."

"Jack!" Why, that arrogant... At his sly grin, it dawned on her that he was trying to get her riled up to move her into communication mode. Clever, clever.

Her heart zigzagged in her chest and she rubbed her collarbone, seeking calm. "I'm no good at this. I'm Italian and I know I should be better at all this emotional stuff, but we've never really been like that in our family. So, I'm sorry if I get it all wrong, but I'll try not to make any jokes."

He bestowed on her an encouraging smile. "You're doing fine."

She ran her fingers along the nearest scratched up stainless-steel countertop.

"Lili," he said, not ungently.

She swallowed past the lump of emotion. "I used to be fat and I used to be scared. Then I was no longer fat, but the fear stayed. Yeah, I took edgy photos and attacked would-be burglars dressed as Wonder Woman and made shocking passes at TV idols in bars, but I was determined not to allow any of those dalliances out of my comfort zone change who I truly was. Lili DeLuca, stoic restaurant manager, martyr daughter, all around chicken. I was all those things and I had every intention of staying that way."

"Ah, sweetheart."

She shot him her most condemning look. "Don't interrupt. You wanted this, so you're going to damn well listen. Besides, you'll like the next part. It's all about you."

He raised his hands. "Please. Continue."

"Then you came into my life. Well, the coming part took a frustratingly long time because first you had to needle and get under my skin and tell me I had potential and could do anything. That was pretty overwhelming for me. To have someone as amazing as you care about me that much—" She flapped cool air at her face, hating herself for acting like such a girly-girl and loving how the weight she'd carried for so long seemed to lift with every word. "I wasn't sure it was real. I wasn't sure you were real because let's face it, you're the fantasy. So yes, I panicked because that's a hell of a lot easier than trusting my heart to what might be a figment of my imagination."

"But I'm very real." His voice was heartbreakingly compassionate.

Yes, he was. He was flesh and blood and fantasy, all rolled into the sexiest, most awesome package of male she had ever seen. No wonder she was confused.

"I'm sorry I didn't trust us, but mostly I'm sorry I didn't trust myself. I'm just getting used to being a superhero, you know."

He kissed her, slow and sensual and so, so hot. "All right, that wasn't half bad. There's hope for you yet. Think we can move to second base now." Sliding his hands up along her ribs, he thumbed her already-primed nipples. Bones and other important body parts went with the flow and liquefied in pure pleasure.

"Lili, I walked in here tonight expecting nothing, and I got everything I needed. Seeing your art and all the changes, I'm so proud of you. And then to put yourself out there on camera. Woman, you've got balls."

"Yes, but I needed a push, someone who saw me. Really saw me. It's scary when someone can read you that well, can understand what you need better than you do yourself." She gulped. "I applied to graduate school."

His thumbs stopped that lovely plucking at her breasts. Damn, she needed to time these revelations better.

"Atta girl."

"And I sold a picture."

His eyes went as wide as charger plates. "Which one?"

"Sadie Number Three." When his brow furrowed, she translated, "Rock Chick Red. For twelve hundred dollars." Her hand flew to her mouth, still not quite believing *that* had happened.

"One of my favorites. Sounds like some perv got a bargain."

She socked him in the chest. His rock-hard, wonderfully touchable... *Focus, girl.* She placed her hands flat on that same chest, like she meant business. "I'm still worried about something."

"What's that, sweetheart?" He laid molten kisses along her jaw, getting a head start on smoothing away the worry.

"That hot head of yours. I don't want you going off when someone says something. You can't. Not with all you could lose."

"Well, that's no longer a concern. You're looking at the guy who will *not* be the next big thing in daytime TV."

She knew her features must have shuttered to blank because her brain had ground to a halt and he was looking at her strangely.

"I'm not signing with the network," he explained. "And I'm not renewing with the Cooking Channel, either."

This time, when she thumped his chest, sexy muscles

were the last things on her mind. Lightning fast, he covered her body with his and caged her with his palms to the refrigerator door. Lord, she had the reflexes of a two-toed sloth.

"Before you call me an idiot, hear me out."

"Okay," she muttered mutinously, like she had a choice with all his hard parts clicking like LEGO into her soft parts.

"I want my life back. I want to wake up on lazy Sunday mornings, screw you breathless, then think about which of the farmers' market ingredients will make the best special at the restaurant that night. I want to cook for people instead of viewer demographics. I want to be the best brother to Jules and the best uncle to her kidlet. I want my own kids to value family and food and know they are loved to an embarrassing degree. And I want them to stay virgins as long as possible, and frankly, that can only happen if we're sitting down at the dinner table and talking like real families do." He put a finger to her lips because she must have opened her mouth to interrupt. "I know you're concerned about keeping all this culinary genius and sex appeal under wraps, but I can still spread the Kilroy gospel with books and Web videos. Or something." He punctuated his speech with a brazen grin.

"World domination ten minutes at a time?" she asked when really she wanted to say, *Kids, Jack? You're already talking about kids!* Unavoidable images of emerald-eyed, dark-headed tykes tugged at her ovaries, though she suspected a lot of teenage angst might be avoided if the girls inherited Jack's lustrous locks instead of her obdurate mop.

"I'll still have businesses," he said. "I'll have to travel, but not as much. My life will be with you, wherever you want that to be. Here. New York. Anywhere."

"You'd move here?"

Cue another heart-fracturing smile. "As long as I have a sharp knife, a place to chop, and my woman, I can live anywhere. Turns out Laurent has been filing away the significant coin I pay him in some nefarious plan to usurp my throne, so I'm selling him a half-share of New York and making him executive chef. I could work there but I'm not very good at taking orders." He brushed away the hair that had fallen over her eyes. "I know you have your heart set on Parsons..."

"The School of the Art Institute is also on my list."

His eyes sparkled. "Interesting. You might not have heard, but I'm planning to open a restaurant in Chi-Town. And my sister seems to like it here."

Or rather she liked a particular person here. Rather than let Jack's boxer briefs get in a twist about the threat her man-slut cousin presented to Jules, she focused on the positives. "She'll never want for a babysitter."

"A ready-made army of child minders." His face lifted in a grin. "That kid's going to be so lucky."

A wave of unease rolled over her. "What about Cara? Does she know about the show?"

His brow crinkled. "Not yet. In a couple of days, there'll be a carefully worded announcement from the network about creative differences, but I still have to talk to her. Don't worry, she's the best at what she does and she won't have a problem finding some other poor sap to order about. Come the zombie apocalypse, I want to be on Team Cara."

"Jack, are you sure?" She had to ask, though she could

tell he was decided. He might be impulsive when provoked to kiss or defend women in bars, but he wasn't one to take a business decision, or a family one, lightly. And knowing that Jules figured largely in his thinking made her heart expand in love even more.

"I am. So sure. Now, do you think you could be with a once-famous, now-ordinary guy, who in a couple of years might be featured on one of those 'Where are they now?' TV shows?"

She rose up on her toes with a little help from his hands, which had now slipped to cup her toast-of-the-town behind. *At last.* Her lips baited his, and her tongue swiped the seam, teasing and tasting.

"You know I was never interested in your fame."

"Right, just my body."

"Hell, yeah." She nuzzled his nose and kissed him softly. "Jack, I know you're joking about me wanting you for your big, manly muscles, but I need you to know it really is so much more than that. You and Jules are family now. Welcome home."

She heard his swallow, felt the tremble of his body. All his gratitude, his need, his love. Blinking, he buried his face in her neck. Underlying all that ambition lay a man more Italian than any guy she knew, who needed a family and heart big enough to embrace him and his. Her family, her heart. That Jack and Jules had found each other here in Chicago and now would be welcomed into the DeLuca clan swelled Lili's chest with yet another upsurge of love. A few moments passed, the hum of the kitchen appliances providing backing vocals to the thud of their hearts.

"I love you so much," she said, relishing how those words tasted on her lips.

Drawing back, he coasted his hands along her arms. "With no show, my huge ego is going to need to hear that a lot. Tell me again."

"I love you, Jack Kilroy. I love your cocky smile, your pancakes, your terrible singing, and how you never gave up on me." She tilted her head. "Hey, aren't you going to say it back?"

"No chance. You can suffer for a while."

"I think I've suffered long enough." Hooking her foot around his thigh, she dug into that sensitive area she knew so well. She wandered her greedy hand down that wall of muscle to his belt buckle and lower, to a bulge—*yes!*— with a hard-edged shape. Huh?

"What's this?"

"Oh, a pocket-sized pity party." He fished out a robin-egg-blue box—Tiffany blue, but a little squashed—and flipped it open, revealing the biggest diamond she'd ever seen, with a yellowish tint that made it look like a very pricey Jolly Rancher. Her head spun and her heart jumped clear into her throat.

"But, Jack, you came here tonight with no expectations."

"I've had it for a while and until I left Chicago, I suppose I wanted to hold on to something." His throat worked through his emotion, his eyes shimmering. "I've known from minute one this was it for me and I wasn't ready to let that go. So what do you say?"

"About what?"

"Try to keep up, DeLuca. About being my wife."

"You're asking me to marry you?"

"You're not usually this slow on the uptake," he said, vaguely exasperated. "I'll assume that not seeing me for several weeks has dulled your wits. Now, before you answer, you might want to take it out." When she looked pointedly down, he added wearily, "The ring, you guttersnipe."

Laughing, she obeyed and examined it from all angles. It felt light and oddly...sticky. "But this isn't a real diamond."

"Nope. It's made of sugar."

Molecular gastronomy—science and food run amok. "You made me an edible ring." Oh, this man knew her so well. Ferran Adrià and his elBulli minions couldn't have done a better job.

"We'll go shopping for a real one, but I like the idea of getting you off the market sooner rather than later, especially now you're so famous."

In a tremble, she put the ring on her wedding finger, feeling like a kid in the candy jewelry store. Another perfect fit. She gave it a tentative lick. "Tastes like chicken."

"I should hope not or else I've really lost my touch." He flashed that bone-melting smile and her heart pumped harder. "I love you, Liliana Sophia DeLuca. Now marry me and finish what you started when you clocked me with that frying pan."

"Yes, Jack, I'll marry you," she said, trying desperately to sound like saying yes to a proposal of marriage from the hottest man on the planet was part of her usual skill set when really, her heart was in danger of bursting out of her chest.

"Thank Christ." He kissed her hard, the relief ebbing and flowing between them like a tide. "Maybe Tony will finally forgive me for corrupting you."

She caught her breath. "Let's not run before we can walk, Jack."

"You might be surprised. I asked for his blessing before we came in here. I figured after everything I put him through, I should do it properly."

"Smooth move, Kilroy." Wow, he would never stop surprising her. "You were positive I'd say yes, then?"

"Well, you've always been a sure thing." He swept his fingertips along her jaw, against the wild pitter-patter at the base of her throat, and brushed her collarbone with a whispering touch. In his eyes, she saw right into his heart, the one that belonged to her. Completely, utterly.

She ran a lazy finger over the handle of the walk-in fridge and pulled it ajar. "How about we see how long it takes to heat things up in here?"

His expression registered mock shock. "Evil woman. The last time I was in there, it didn't end so well."

"Oh, I wouldn't say that, Jack." And to prove how evil she was, she pretzeled herself around the man she couldn't get enough of and made him growl. "I'd say it ended very well indeed."

Things get hotter in Kate Meader's
sizzling new novel...

See the next page
for a preview of

ALL FIRED UP.

CHAPTER ONE

It was the most beautiful wedding cake Cara DeLuca had ever seen. Three architecturally perfect layers of frosted purity designed to make the guests drool as soon as it was rolled out on a wobbly serving cart to the center of the harshly lit ballroom. Of course, a slice cost thirty, maybe forty-five extra minutes kicking the bag at the gym.

Cara checked that thought to the tune of screeching tires in her head. In a previous lifetime, she had measured every bite in push-ups and treadmill minutes, piling on more to punish the slightest infraction. Old Cara would be looking for an excuse to slip out of a wedding reception before the cake so she could work off the chicken or fish entrée, and she had several options for how she did that. New Cara—*healthy* Cara—didn't need to count every bite and worry if she had passed over onto the wrong side of the fifteen-hundred-calorie border.

But only an amazing cake could tempt her.

Cutting into the slice on the Limoges porcelain dessert plate, Cara slipped it past her lips, chewed slowly, and swallowed. *Ugh.* Dry, pedestrian, uninspired. No one knew better than Cara the truth behind that old adage about looks being deceiving. This cake might have been the bride's dream, but a single bite confirmed the suspicions Cara had formed the day she was roped in to salvage her cousin Gina's wedding. About ten minutes after the official planner had finally thrown up her hands in despair and gone running to the nearest sanatorium—read, palm-tree-lined sandy beach.

This wedding was cursed.

It wasn't so much the bride's insistence on the stab-your-eyes-out pink, fishtail-hemmed bridesmaid dresses or her requirement that she must have both a Neil Diamond string quartet for the cocktails *and* an all-girl Neil Diamond tribute band, the Sweet Carolines, for the dancing. Neither did Cara mind having to organize last-minute fittings for a wedding party of twelve or a reception for two hundred ravenous Italians. As for corralling the ovary-explodingly cute ring bearers? Child's play, though Father Phelan had drawn the line at chocolate Lab pups traipsing down the aisle behind ankle biters who could barely stay upright.

No, all that was manageable, and managing was what Cara did best. Where it all went undeniably south was at the joint bachelor-bachelorette party in Vegas. This type of thing had become de rigueur, and as much as Cara would have liked to put down the poker chips and back away slowly, she'd felt it incumbent on herself to manage that, too. A gaggle of drunk-off-their-butts DeLuca women needed her superior wrangling skills to make sure they had a wild and crazy—but safe—time. Unfortunately, her usually sober view had been crusted over by one colossally stupid mistake. A six-foot-tall, amber-eyed, mussed-up-haired mistake.

She should have stayed home in Chicago.

Slowly, she surveyed the room and tried to breathe herself to calm in the face of the happiness onslaught. Her father—*Il Duce* to his daughters—held court at the elders table after spending most of the meal bounding in and out of the hotel kitchen. Ensuring his menu was followed to exact specifications, no doubt. His queen, Francesca, rocking regal now that her corn-silk blond hair had returned to its pre-cancer glory, wore a familiar upward tilt on her lips as she viewed the dance floor hijinks. Cara tracked her mom's gaze to a flash of flailing arms among the writhing bodies. *Oh, you've got to be kid—*

"I'm beginning to have second thoughts." A crisp, British voice intruded on her internal scold.

Jack Kilroy, her boss and future brother-in-law, wrinkled his patrician nose and laid down his fork primly as if it might be radioactive.

"If you can't even get the cake right, Cara, I'm not sure I should be entrusting you with the most important day of my life," he added with just enough of that divo tone to remind her why she was glad he was marrying her sister, Lili, in six weeks and not her. Having worked with Jack as his TV producer when he was *the* Jack Kilroy—ragingly successful restaurateur, cooking show icon, and tabloid meat—and now, as the private events manager for his Chicago restaurant, Sarriette, she was comfortably familiar with his moods and tics. Jack was almost as controlling as Cara, and that type never made it onto her dance card. The one that had turned yellow and dog-eared from disuse.

"The cake was a done deal before I got involved, but don't fret your pretty head," she said, enjoying immensely how his face darkened at her patronizing tone. Gun. Fish. Barrel. "You've requested the most spectacular, stylish, knock-'em-dead—"

"Artistic, poetic, avant-garde," Lili picked up, a little breathlessly.

Cara smiled up at her sister, newly arrived after cutting a rug on the boards. "Wedding to end all weddings," Cara finished while Jack pulled his fiancée into his lap despite her whiny protests. It was a cute playact they did that would have turned her stomach at its sheer preciousness if it had been anyone else. The ache she felt in her belly could only be that cardboard cake talking.

"You shall have the wedding you've wanted since you were a little girl, Jack," continued Lili, touching his forehead in the style of a fairy godmother before dropping a kiss on his lips.

"You're so cheeky," Jack said, though there was little heat there. "Engaged for almost a year and still no joy. I'm told I'm very eligible, you know."

"Been reading your old *Vanity Fair* fluff pieces again, Jack?" Cara asked. There was a time when you couldn't turn around without seeing Jack's handsome mug on a magazine, billboard, or TV screen. Cara wondered if he missed it. Achieving her goal of becoming Chicago's Events Queen depended on him missing it.

"Most women are dying to walk down the aisle—" He ran a hand along Lili's thigh, clearly appreciative of her va-va-voom figure. Even in the bridesmaid dress from Hades, Lili looked like an advertisement for real women with those generous curves. *Thin women are just as real*, Cara's inner therapist whispered.

"But this one has no interest in the fairy tale."

Lili rolled her eyes. "I'm happy to go quietly to city hall, but if you insist, I'll indulge you."

"Sweetheart, indulge me a little now," Jack said, and pulled her in for a kiss.

Cara loosed a sigh and tried to reel in her envy at how Lili and Jack stared at each other to the exclusion of anyone else and their unmistakable joy at being in each other's company. Just seeing how much Jack loved her sister made Cara's cynical heart grow larger. Not three times, but maybe one and a half.

If anyone deserved the fairy tale, it was Lili. Her younger sister had carried the weight of family obligations during their mother's battle with breast cancer while Cara had folded up like a Pinto in a head-on collision with a semi. Cara owed Lili, and she was going to repay a fraction of that debt by planning her dream wedding down to the finest detail.

"How's the cake?" Lili asked Cara once Jack let her come up for air. Her gaze slid to the slice, lying listlessly on the scallop-edged dessert plate.

"Not so great," Cara said. "Don't worry, we'll have something much better for your big day." She already had an artiste in mind, and if he was good enough for Oprah's farewell do—

"Cake's sorted," Jack announced.

"What?" Cara asked, but the tingle she felt as the word spilled out told her she should be asking "Who?" She didn't even have to hear his name; her traitorous body was already on board.

"My secret weapon." Jack chuckled and nodded to the dance floor.

Cara followed his gaze, and by some Moses-like miracle, the tangle of bodies parted to reveal the weapon himself.

Shane Doyle. He of the Irish eyes, devastating dimple, and incredibly dorky dance moves.

The Sweet Carolines were playing the eponymous tune, and Shane was waving his hands in the air, alternating between an interpretive dance featuring a tree and Marcel Marceau trapped in a box. Maisey, a server at Sarriette and Shane's dance partner, was holding tight to her side because apparently Shane wasn't just bustin' moves—he was bustin' guts as well. From twenty feet away, Cara could hear him hollering about how good times never seemed so good.

Don't look. Don't give him the satisfaction.

She was gearing up to drag her eyes away—any moment now—when a rather daring pivot landed him in a face-off with their table. One eyebrow arched. He held her stare. And then he winked. Which he had no damn right to do after what had happened between them a week ago in Sin-Freaking-City.

"No," she said firmly, turning away from those chocolate-drop eyes set in that ridiculously fine face. Not just fine, but friendly and cheerful and oh hell, mostly fine.

"No, what?" asked Jack.

"No, we can't use Shane." When Jack's expression turned curious, she hastily added, "He's too new and he's got far too much on his plate trying to get up to speed at the restaurant. Let me remind you that you've given me a very tight timeline here. Less than two months to plan the kind of shindig you want means I can't leave anything to chance." Though Jack and Lili had been engaged for close to a year, Lili had only recently pulled the trigger on the wedding planning now that she was well and truly settled into her MFA program at the School of the Art Institute. Jack was champing at the bit like a prize racehorse to make Lili "Mrs. Jack Kilroy," but her sister refused to be pushed. That summed up their relationship in a nutshell.

Jack and Lili shared a meaningful glance. Cara hated when they did that.

"Something happened in Vegas and it clearly hasn't stayed there," Lili said. "We all know you slept with him."

"I didn't know." Jack's brow knitted furiously. "Cara, tell me it's not true."

"It's not true," Cara repeated, sort of truthfully. She hadn't slept with anyone in over a year, and even then, she—or he—never stayed overnight. It was one of her rules, or it had been until a week ago when she woke up with a screaming hangover and a big lug of an Irishman twined around her body.

"You destroyed my last pastry chef," Jack said. "Shane's been here only a couple of weeks and you've already got your hooks into him."

"Now, now, Jack," Lili chided, flipping on the calm. "You can't tell your employees who they can and can't be with."

"Oh yes, I can. She made Jeremy cry. The poor guy left because Cara stomped all over him."

Cara bristled, then covered with a languid wave. "Don't be ridiculous. Jeremy and I went on one date and it didn't work out. I can't help it if you employ weak-willed, mewling kittens just so you can surround yourself with yes men who'll bow down and kiss your ring."

He *had* cried, though, the wuss.

"Well, Shane's off-limits," Jack said, still peeved. "That guy's a genius with a pastry roller and I'm not losing him. Don't make me choose."

Cara caught Lili's eye and they both fought back laughs. Jack's dramatics were a source of great amusement for the women in his life.

"So if you didn't do the deed with him, what happened? You hightailed out of the hotel like you were auditioning for Girl Being Chased Number Two." Lili's unearthly blue eyes zeroed in on Cara, making her shiver with their perspicacity.

"Nothing happened. We just had a few drinks and that's it. Nobody got stomped on." Much. She felt her head cant slightly in Shane's direction. It completely sucked to have no control over her body.

And then as if she had summoned him out of thin air, he was there. The distance from dance floor to table should have given her a decent interval to adjust, but Shane had bounded over like a big Irish setter, throwing Cara off-kilter. Any farther and she'd be listing like the *Titanic* in its final moments. His hip-shot loll against the table's edge made his ancient-looking jeans cleave fondly to his thighs, prompting Cara's own thigh muscles to do some involuntary flexing of their own. Never too early to start the exercise. That unfortunate mouthful of cake wasn't going to disappear by itself.

Who wears jeans to a wedding? While everyone else was rocking tuxes and dark suits, Shane was embracing the American Dream with button-fly Levi's, weathered cowboy boots, and a sports jacket that stretched a little too tight over his annoyingly broad shoulders. Only after that snide thought had formed did it occur to her he had probably borrowed the jacket, likely from one of the other chefs.

Inexorably, her eyes inched up, up, up, taking in overlong, mink-brown hair that just begged to be raked. The melty brown eyes with a hazelnut corona ringing the iris. The jaw scruff that hadn't made acquaintance with a razor in a couple of days. The... Oh, she could go on and on.

So she did. Down, down, down, she traveled that granite-hard body before coming to rest on his large hands. Not that she needed visual verification. She distinctly remembered their size because she had awoken with one spread possessively across her stomach a week ago. She knew just how devastatingly erotic Shane's hand felt on her bare skin.

"Sure, I'm looking for a new dance partner," Shane said with that Irish musical lilt that did wondrous things to large segments of the American female population. Cara liked to think she was immunized against all that "faith and begorra" malarkey, but she reluctantly acknowledged Shane's accent was one of his most appealing features. Like the guy needed more help to sell the goods.

Shaking off her appreciation, she tried to draw on all the reasons she was mad at him. "What happened to your last one? Wear her out?" She looked to see where the cast-off Maisey had landed, but the poor girl was nowhere to be found. "Did you make her ill with all that jumping around?"

"Ah, I'm just too much for one woman," Shane said, exploding into that cheeky smile that had caught her attention the moment he'd stood up to offer her a seat in the bar at Paris, Las Vegas. A patchwork memory of the numerous drinking establishments they had crawled through flashed through her querulous mind. In every one, the guys had got there before the girls. And in every one, Shane Doyle had been first on his feet, motioning to his seat as soon as the lady mob arrived to meet up with the bachelor's posse for the tandem shenanigans.

A nice mama's boy, she had decided. Polite and mannered, the kind of guy she usually liked to date because they let her call the shots. Where to go, what to do, how to please her. A few tears might be shed when they parted, not by her, of course, but so far it had worked out swimmingly.

How had she messed up so spectacularly with Shane?

The band took a break and the music switched to DJ-determined wedding classics. First up, the oom-pah booms of the Chicken Dance, and Cara found herself just a tiny bit curious to see Shane's interpretation.

"We were talking about the cake," Jack said, defaulting to his one-track mind. Marriage to Lili or bust. In telepathic communication, both chefs' gazes slipped to the slice of maligned cake now insulting everyone by its mere presence on the table.

Shane scoffed. "Whoever made this rubbish should be shot for crimes against pastries."

That pulled a deep laugh out of Jack and a juvenile eye roll out of Cara. Ah, chef humor.

"So I'll expect something amazing for my wedding." He squeezed Lili's waist. "We both will. You up for it?"

A weird look passed over Shane's face, clearing his cheer. If Cara didn't know better, she would have thought he was annoyed. Even angry, which made no sense considering what an honor it was to have Jack choose the new guy for such an important commission.

"I thought you'd want to bring Marguerite in from Thyme," Shane said, his voice as tight as the set of his mouth. "She's your best pâtissière."

Thyme, Jack's New York outpost and Shane's stomping ground until two weeks ago when he transferred to Chicago, sported any number of culinary stars, and Marguerite was the brightest of them all. Cara was in full agreement with Shane. It wouldn't have surprised her in the least if Jack wanted to fly her in for the occasion.

Shane's mood change appeared to have passed unnoticed by Jack. "Yeah, she's great, but I want you to do it. You're a wizard with desserts and after chasing me around for months trying to get a job, I think you're ready for the big leagues."

Shane looked both pensive and oddly uncomfortable. There *was* something. "We could do angel food and pistachio cream, or maybe a rosemary-lemon to keep the Italian theme."

"I like how you think," Jack said, smiling broadly. "Keep it up and we'll talk next week."

Shane smiled back but it was as if the effort might result in the death of a puppy.

Lili hummed and flapped a hand at Gina's cake. "Oh, that's disappointing. For a moment there, I thought you were going to form a lynch mob to track down the criminal baker."

"Don't tempt me," Shane said with a dimple wink at Cara. Back to charming, sunny Shane. Flustered, she felt her hand move to the still-full champagne flute she had been avoiding since the toasts, but before her fingers made contact, he cocked his head. One of those, *Need a chaser of impaired judgment with that bubbly?* head tilts that decelerated her brain. Damn the man and his caramel-hued eyes, now narrowed and holding her captive.

"Back to the dancing," he said with a sly smile.

Cara had important things to say to Shane. Very important things. And avoiding him wasn't going to get it done. After years of unhealthy denial, she had vowed to meet her problems head-on, so she wasn't sure why she had let a whole week go by without pulling Shane aside and telling him how it was. How it will be. She'd put it down to how busy she was ensuring Gina's wedding wouldn't be a complete debacle. Declining to examine that closely was about the only thing preventing her from losing her ever-loving mind.

Before she went off on him, it might be easier to soften him up on the dance floor. Besides, there was something just so adorable about his enthusiasm. She uncrossed her legs and flexed a perfectly pedied foot clad in a Jimmy Choo peep-toe. Her feet looked stunning in fuchsia.

"Lili, would you do me the honor?" Shane's gaze brushed fire across Cara's skin as he reached for her sister. "That's if you don't mind, Jack."

Lili slid out of Jack's lap and Cara's heart slid into her stomach. "Oh, you wouldn't catch Jack dead on the dance floor," Lili said. "He's much too image conscious."

"I'm not afraid of looking foolish. You've heard me sing," Jack said blithely. "I draw the line at the Chicken Dance, though."

"It's ironic," Cara said, aiming for levity after being snubbed by Shane, because there was no doubt that's what had just happened here.

"Ironically stupid," Jack replied. "Just make sure I see daylight between you two."

Laughing, Shane led a willing Lili out onto the dance floor and jumped into flapping his arms with gusto. Lili fanned her hips with both hands, then moseyed into the fray.

"We're doing the right thing, aren't we?" Jack asked, his eyes glued to Lili, who was jerking her feet to the music like she'd just been Tased. "I don't want to upset her."

"You won't upset her, Jack," Cara said, her heart in a mad gallop as she struggled to recover her aplomb. It was easy to see why Shane would prefer to dance with Lili, who was never afraid to get into the spirit of things. Unlike stuck-up, no-fun Cara, who needed to drink her weight in vodka to go a little bit wild.

"You know how she feels about being the center of attention," Jack continued, his tone flat. "Sometimes I think she's serious about getting it over and done with at city hall. I just want her to be happy."

Cara worried her lip. Jack and Lili's relationship had been almost derailed by the merciless teasing Lili had suffered on the Twittersphere when they first got together. The online hordes, as capricious as twelve-year-old schoolgirls, had ragged on everything from her big Italian hair to her generous curves, and Jack's hotheaded propensity to punch anyone who insulted her had loomed large between them. Even now, with Jack in the bosom of semiobscurity, he guarded his privacy and Lili like a Doberman pinscher trained to kill at the first sign of trespass.

But there was still that side of him that loved to put on a show.

"Every girl wants to be the center of attention on their big day," Cara said casually, the irony that Jack was the attention-seeker here not lost on her. "And we're talking about the DeLucas. Relatives from both sides of the pond will be there, and they'll expect the usual pageantry."

Jack's lips curved up in a brazen grin, the one that still sold cookbooks and had once earned him millions. Cara knew how much he enjoyed the spectacle, but more than that, how he loved being part of the DeLuca clan. In-laws get to choose their family, to a certain extent, and Jack was eager to be a part of her big Italian one almost as much as he wanted to be Lili's husband.

Cara wouldn't be needing that dream wedding anytime soon—maybe never, if she bought into everyone's view of her. Career girl, destroyer of pastry chefs, a woman apart. But she was perfectly happy to let Lili borrow it—even if her sister didn't know she wanted it yet.

After all, managing was what Cara did best.

* * *

If Shane were to look up "pissed off" in *Roget's*, he had a feeling Cara DeLuca would be one of the synonyms.

He wished that didn't turn him on so much.

Every time he so much as dared a glance in her direction, he got dismissive ignoring or the brittle blond stink eye. Exactly how long could she stay mad at him?

She's a woman, Doyle. There's no expiration date on female fury.

The ballroom of this swanky hotel was filled with everyone in their Sunday best, apart from the horrific bridesmaids' garb, but Cara stood an elegant head and shoulders above the crowd in a classy black number that exposed one of those beautiful shoulders to the world. That same shoulder his lips had grazed when he'd wrapped his body around her a week ago and slept the sleep of the tired, drunk, and stupid.

Scout's honor, his lips were only resting on her silken skin. Lying beside her in that Vegas hotel room, he hadn't dared to kiss any part of her, beautifully curved shoulder or otherwise. Well, he was far too plastered to make a decent job of it, and there was no sense in ruining the moment, not when there would be plenty of time for that later. The morning after had a tendency to throw the brilliant decisions of the night before into sharp, rueful relief.

Instead of returning to Cara's table at the end of the Chicken Dance, he beelined for the bar. Not to order a drink, mind you. After a childhood spent with a constantly wasted father, he'd vowed not to fall into that cycle or become the stereotype of the Irish drunk. So much for his vow of moderation. One night in Nevada had kicked his principles to the cure, leaving in their wake a night of idiotic mistakes, a throbbing head, and the wrath of a beautiful woman.

He really should have kissed that shoulder.

At least then he might feel justified in his role as the fall guy, because the way Lemon Tart was carrying on, you'd swear it was all his fault. For the past week, she had known exactly where to find him—elbow-deep in pastry dough at the restaurant where they *both* worked—but not a whit of effort had been put forth by those killer gams. She'd been avoiding him since Vegas, click-clacking in to pick up something from her office and click-clacking right out again before he could catch her. And now she had the nerve to look down her nose and make him feel like rubbish? Hell, he had enjoyed wiping that pinched look off her face when he'd asked Lili to dance. Let her stew awhile.

Which would give Shane time to stew on Jack giving him the royal nod on his wedding cake. Shane was a great pastry chef—a stellar, award-winning pastry chef—and there was no doubt he could create something jaw-dropping with both hands tied to his feet, but he had still felt blindsided by Jack's request. This is what he wanted, wasn't it? To prove himself, to show the arrogant, Limey prick that he was worthy. A woman's fury might have no expiration date, but this job as pâtissier at Sarriette did. Two months max, then back to London to open his own pastry shop. More than enough time to satisfy his curiosity about the great Jack Kilroy. There was no room in the plan to take pleasure in Jack's compliment. There was no room for any pleasant thoughts where the man was concerned at all.

He needed to stop thinking so much. Stop being so maudlin, so melancholy. *So Irish.* Time to hit the head for a slash.

A strong hand on his shoulder arrested his progress.

"You're going to miss the best bit," Jack said, bowing to an all-female congregation now forming in the middle of the ballroom. Shane had attended and catered enough weddings to be well attuned to the signs, and today the ramp-up was as quick as he'd ever seen. Gentle nudges swiftly turned to less-than-subtle jabs as the ladies jockeyed for position.

"Now, girls, no need for violence," Cara said in a firm yet seductive cajole that sent a ripple to every nerve ending in his body. Silky with hints of bossy. Bet she used it in bed, or she would if she wasn't passed out in a drunken stupor. "But if you really hope to be next in line down the aisle at St. Jude's, remember your weapons. Nails, elbows, and, of course, heels."

She turned to her cousin Gina, or the munchkin bride as Jack called her, usually to her face. Gina clutched the purple and white posey bouquet, a remarkably classy floral arrangement considering the bride's proclivities toward the tacky. Shane's mind slipped back to that night and recalled sharing several laughs about Gina's "special requirements." Cara must have slipped the sophisticated bouquet past her during a drunken moment of weakness.

"Ready, bitches?" Gina called out, and twisted away from the madding crowd, whose nostrils flared and feet pawed the hardwood floor like the bulls behind the gate at Pamplona. The dark-haired throng of DeLuca women was broken by Jack's blond half sister, Jules. She'd wisely elected to hover on the edges with one eye on her six-month-old, Evan, now cradled in the arms of Cara's mother. But like all women in thrall to the marriage scent, she inclined her body to the crowd in readiness for the prize. Even cute-as-a-button Maisey with her purple-streaked hair was getting in on the act. Serious business, this.

An amused snort from Jack let it be known the fun was only beginning. Cara's aunt, the one with the bouffant that added a foot and change to her height, manhandled Cara from her role on the sidelines and placed her directly in the line of fire. Just as Gina's bouquet arced over her head and landed in a shocked Cara's hands.

"Oh, that's not good," Jack said, and not for the first time in the last couple of weeks, Shane wanted to work over that *GQ* magazine-cover face of his. Because he agreed, and Shane loathed being in agreement with Jack Kilroy on anything.

There was no way Cara could have known Shane's position about thirty feet kitty-corner from the main action, but somehow her ice-blue gaze found him like a heat-seeking missile, binding his chest in knots tighter than the hold she had on that bouquet.

No, not good at all.

The ladies groaned, a rather mean-spirited response to a supposedly fun end to the wedding festivities. Cara's expression changed from pissed to pondering as she turned the flowers over in her hand, her chilled gaze no longer on Shane. A gaze he now missed.

Gina placed her hands on her hips, all bridezilla spunk. "Probably wasted on you, Cara. Should I throw it again?"

The shadow that crossed Cara's face was impossible to miss, but it was immediately displaced by a slice of sun. Cara had a gorgeous smile, even when it was forced.

"Sure, cuz. Go for it. Though there's probably some bad luck associated with throwing it twice." She crushed the bouquet into Gina's hands and stalked off. Looked like a case of bad blood, bygones that were never gone. Cara's connection to her family had struck him as being a little crooked, not that Shane could claim bragging rights in that area. His own history was proof enough that families were fundamentally untrustworthy.

"Christ, these women. Weddings turn them into crazy people," Jack muttered, which was amusing considering how gung ho Jack was about joining the ranks of the smugly married.

"What's that about?" Shane asked. "Cara not big on marriage?"

"Cara's not big on relationships." Jack leaned against the bar and rubbed the weathered grain before meeting Shane's eyes, his expression flinty. "She's very career-focused," he added, as if that explained everything.

Shane kept his peace. Silence usually got better results.

"Don't get me wrong—I'm very fond of her," Jack continued. "But she's so tightly wound that I pity the guy who takes her on, even for a short-term thing." There was steel behind his words, sharp as a blade in that accent that made everything sound like an order. His eyes softened slightly, once he decided his message had made an impression on Shane.

Message received all right, but not in the least bit understood.

He found her in the foyer near a large potted plant, her back diagonally bisected by that classy dress, her shoulders shaking. Shit, she was crying.

Before he could touch her, she spun on her killer heels and the look she speared him with said she'd been expecting him. No tears, just frost turned to fire. Not crying, just pissed.

"You took your time, Paddy." She crossed her arms beneath her breasts, which plumped them up from B to double Ds, or that was his best guess.

"Are you all right?"

The morning after their night together, she'd been more embarrassed than annoyed. Too busy calling for a cab despite the never-ending train of taxis outside the hotel. Too busy looking for her shoes so she could put as much distance between them as possible. Now the anger shimmered off her in waves, leaving a mottled swatch of pink across the exposed skin of her chest. Two furious disks of color resided high on her cheeks.

"No, I'm not all right," she hissed. "I suppose you think it's funny."

He shook his head. "No, not at all. I'm as upset about this as you are."

That garnered him a growl, a response on the highly upset end of the spectrum. So she had him beat for vexed. "We have to fix it. It's bad enough Jack thinks I'm some sort of man-eater with my claws embedded in your hot Irish ass. If my family finds out about this, there'll be hell to pay."

Hot Irish ass? Huh, he kind of liked that. He opened his mouth to make a joke, then closed it because it didn't seem to be the wisest course of action. Besides, she was right. They did have to fix it. Put it behind them and return to normal or whatever the hell passed as normal in his lately complicated life. The animosity prickling the air around them sizzled, making a nice counterpoint to a distant, low-rumbled rendering of "I Am...I Said," one of Neil's schmaltziest numbers. Guilt that he had dismissed her so cavalierly ten minutes ago tightened his chest, because now he wanted nothing more than to lead her to the dance floor and hold her tight.

Jesus, Doyle. Get your head out of your hot Irish ass and focus.

Taking a tentative step forward, he placed his palms on her golden shoulders. Might have let his hands wander over a few inches of her soft, sleek skin. Just to stop her trembling. The angry rash on her chest was fading now along with the wild-eyed fury, but her eyes were still as big as headlights. He gathered her close, willing her stiff, slender frame to soften.

"Cara," he said. Quiet. Soothing. As if dialing the volume down might keep her from bolting like a wounded doe. "It's going to be all right."

She lifted her head and those sapphire blues knocked his heart out of his stomach and into his mouth.

"Yes, it is," she said, her chin strong and proud. "As soon as we get a divorce."

THE DISH

Where Authors Give You the Inside Scoop

♥ ♥ ♥ ♥ ♥ ♥ ♥ ♥ ♥ ♥ ♥ ♥ ♥ ♥ ♥ ♥

From the desk of Jaime Rush

Dear Reader,

Enemies to lovers is a concept I've always loved. Yes, it's a challenge, and maybe that's what I like most. It's a given that the couple is going to have instant chemistry—it is a romance, after all! But they're going to fight it harder because they have history and a good reason. Each person believes they're in the right.

That's how Kade Kavanaugh feels. Being a member of the Guard, my supernatural world's police force, he has had plenty of run-ins with Violet Castanega's family. They live in the Fringe, a wild and uncivilized community of Dragon shifters who think they are on the fringe of the law as well. And mostly they are, except when their illegal activities threaten to catch the attention of the Muds, the Mundane human police. Because Rule Number One is simple: Never reveal the existence of the Hidden community that has existed amid the glitter and glamour of Miami for over three hundred years. Mundanes would panic if they knew that Crescents—humans who hold the essence of Dragons, sorcerers (like Kade), and fallen angels—lived among them.

Violet is fiercely loyal to her Dragon clan, even if it does sometimes flout the law. But when one of her brothers is murdered by a Dragon bent on firing up the clan wars, she has no choice but to go to the Guard for help. There she encounters Kade, whom she attacked the last time he tried to arrest her brother.

My job as a writer is to throw these two unsuspecting people together in ways that will test their loyalties and their integrity. And definitely test their resolve to resist getting involved with not only a member of another class of Crescent, but a sworn enemy to boot. Juicy conflict, hot passion, and supernatural action—a combination that truly tested my hero and heroine. But their biggest lesson is never to judge someone by their name, their heritage, or their actions. I think that's a good lesson for all of us.

We all have magic in our imaginations. Mine has always contained murder, mayhem, and romance. Feel free to wander through the madness of my mind any time. A good place to start is my website www.jaimerush.com, or that of my romantic suspense alter-ego, www.tinawainscott.com.

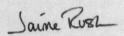

From the desk of Kristen Ashley

Dear Reader,

While writing MOTORCYCLE MAN I was in a very dark time of my life. An *extended* dark time, which is very rare. Indeed, it's only ever happened that once.

In fact, I wrote nearly an entirely different book for my hero, Tack. He had a different heroine. And it had a different plot. Completely. But it didn't work for me and it has never seen the light of day. I abandoned it totally (something I've never done), gave it time, and started anew.

I had thought it was rubbish. Of course, on going back and reading it later, I realize it wasn't. I actually think it's great. It just wasn't Tack. And the heroine was not right for him. But never fear, I like it enough; when I have time (whenever that is in this decade), I intend to rework it and release it, because that hero and heroine's story really should be told.

Nevertheless, when I finally found the dream woman who would belong to Kane "Tack" Allen in MOTOR-CYCLE MAN, I was still questioning my work because things in life weren't going so great.

You see, sometimes I battle my characters. Sometimes they urge me to take risks I feel I'm not ready to take. Sometimes they encourage me to glide along an edge that's a little scary even as it is thrilling. And when life is also scary, your confidence gets shaken in a way it's tough to bounce back from.

But Kane "Tack" Allen is an edgy, risky guy, so he was pretty adamant (as he can be) that he wanted me to just let go and ride it with him. Not only that, but lift up my hands and enjoy the hell out of that ride.

But as I was writing it, I still fought him. Particularly the scene in Tyra's office early on in the book, where they have a misunderstanding and Tack decides to make his feelings perfectly clear and in order to do that, he gets Tyra's attention in a way that's utterly unacceptable.

I fretted about this scene, but Tack refused to let me soften it. I even sent it to my girl, a girl who knows me and my writing inside and out. If I remember correctly, her response was that it was indeed shocking, but I should go with it.

Ride it out.

In releasing MOTORCYCLE MAN, I was very afraid that my life had negatively affected my writing and the risks Tack urged me to take would not be well received.

As you can imagine, I was absolutely *elated* when I found I'd done the right thing. When Tack and Tyra swiftly became one of my most popular couples. That Tack had rightly encouraged me to trust in myself, my instincts, my writing, and give myself to my characters to let them be precisely what they were, let them shine, not water them down, and last, give my readers the honesty. They could take it. Because it was genuine. It came from the soul.

It was real.

And because of all this, MOTORCYCLE MAN will always hold a firm place in my heart. Because that novel and Kane "Tack" Allen gave me the freedom I was searching for. The freedom to ride this wave. Ride it wild. Ride it free.

Lift up my hands and ride it being nothing but me.

Kristen Ashley

♥ ♥ ♥ ♥ ♥ ♥ ♥ ♥ ♥ ♥ ♥ ♥ ♥ ♥ ♥

From the desk of Christie Craig

Dear Reader,

Here are two things about love I took from my own life and used in TEXAS HOLD 'EM:

1. Love can make us stupid.

Sexy PI Austin Brook is a smooth-talking good ol' boy Texan. Where women are concerned, he wings it. Why not? He's got charm to spare. But one glance at Leah Reece and he's a stumbling, bumbling idiot. First he accidentally blows his horn as she's passing in front of his truck, causing her to toss up her arms and drop her groceries. Wanting to help, he snatches up a plastic bag containing a broken bottle of wine and manages to douse Leah with Cabernet from the waist up. And since he likes wine and wet T-shirt contests, it only makes her more appealing and him more nervous.

For myself? On a first date with a good ol' Texan, we were both jittery. I'd dressed up in a short skirt. The guy, thinking he should be a gentleman, pulled my chair out in the crowded restaurant. I had my bottom almost in the seat when he moved it out. *Way out.* *He* might've looked like a gentleman, but there was nothing ladylike about how I went down. All the way to the floor, legs sprawled out, skirt up to my yin-yang. Laughter filled the room. Snickering in spite of his apologetic look, he added, "Nice legs."

Later when he dropped me off at my apartment, I struggled to get the door of his sports car open. Forever the gentlemen—hey, that's Texans for you—he rushed to open my door, and then shut it. Standing close, he heard my moan, and completely misunderstood. He dipped in for a kiss.

I stopped him. "Can you open the car door?"

"Why?" he asked.

I moaned again. "Because my hand's still in the door."

With a bruised butt, and three busted fingernails, I eventually did let him score a kiss. It's amazing I married that man.

2. Love is scary.

Divorced, and a single mother, I wasn't looking for love when I met Mr. Craig. Life had taught me that love can hurt. And I'm not talking about a sore backside or fingernails. I'm talking about the heart.

Neither Austin nor Leah is open to love. Isn't that what makes it so perfect and yet still so dad-blasted frightening? We don't find love; love finds us. And like me, Leah's and Austin's pasts have left them leery.

At age six, Leah realized her daddy had another family, one he obviously loved better because they had his name and he called that home. Oh, when older, she still gave love a shot, got married, expected the happily-ever-after, and instead got a divorce and a credit card bill for all his phone sex. It's not that Leah doesn't believe in love; she just doesn't trust herself to know the real thing.

Austin, abandoned by his mother at age three, passed from one foster home to another, and learned caring about people gave them power to hurt you. His last and final (he swears) heartache happened when his fiancé dumped him after he got convicted of a murder he didn't commit.

As scary as love is, Leah and Austin give it another shot. Not to give away any spoilers, but I think it'll work out fine for them. I know it has for me. I'll soon be celebrating my thirtieth wedding anniversary. So here's to laughter, good books, and getting knocked on your butt by love.

Happy reading!

Christie Craig

♥ ♥ ♥ ♥ ♥ ♥ ♥ ♥ ♥ ♥ ♥ ♥ ♥ ♥ ♥ ♥

From the desk of Laura Drake

Dear Reader,

There's just something about the soft side of a hard man that I've never been able to resist—how about you?

Max Jameson looks like a modern-day Marlboro Man. He's a western cattleman, meaning he's stubborn, hard-working, and an eternal optimist. But given his current problems, there's not enough duct tape in all of Colorado to fix them.

To introduce you to the heroine of NOTHING

SWEETER, Aubrey Madison (aka Bree Tanner), I thought I'd share with you her list of life lessons:

1. Nothing is sweeter than freedom.
2. It is impossible to outrun your own conscience.
3. "When you're going through hell, keep going."
   —Winston Churchill
4. There are more kinds of family than blood kin.
5. A stuck-up socialite can make a pretty good friend when the chips are on the table.
6. Real men (and bulls) wear pink.
7. "To forgive is to set a prisoner free, and discover that the prisoner is you." —Louis B. Smede

I hope you'll enjoy NOTHING SWEETER. Keep your eyes open for a cameo of JB and Charla from *The Sweet Spot*, and watch for them all to turn up in *Sweet on You*, the last book in the series!

♥ ♥ ♥ ♥ ♥ ♥ ♥ ♥ ♥ ♥ ♥ ♥ ♥ ♥ ♥ ♥

From the desk of Rebecca Zanetti

Dear Reader,

I met my husband camping when we were about eight years old, and he taught me how to play Red Rover so he could hold my hand. He was a sweet, chubby, brown-eyed boy. We lost touch, and years later, I walked into a bar (yeah, a bar), and there he was. Except this time, he was six-foot-five, muscled, with dark hair, a tattoo, a leather jacket, and held a motorcycle helmet under one hand. To put it simply, I was intrigued. He's still the sweet guy but has a bit of an edge. Now we're married and have two kids, two dogs, and a crazy cat.

People change...and often we don't know them as well as we think we do. In fact, I've always been fascinated by the idea that we never truly know what's in the minds or even the pasts of the people around us. What if your best friend worked for the CIA years ago? Or the mild-mannered janitor at your child's elementary school is a retired Marine sniper who didn't like retirement and has found a good way to fill his life with joy? What if your baby sister was a criminal informant in college?

What if the calm and always-in-control man you married is one of the deadliest men alive?

And what if you're now being threatened by an outside source? What happens to that calm control now? That was the main premise for FORGOTTEN SINS. Josie Dean, a woman with a lonely past, married Shane Dean in a whirlwind of passion and energy. Then he disappeared two years ago. The story starts with him back in her life, with danger surrounding him, and with the edge he'd always partially hidden finally exposed.

Of course, Shane has amnesia, and in his discovery of finding himself, he reveals himself to the one woman he ever truly loved. He'd always held back, always treated her with kid gloves.

Now, not knowing his deadly training, there's no holding back. The primal, arousing man she'd believed existed has to take the forefront as he protects them from the danger stalking him from his past. Yeah, he'd always been fun and sexy...with hints of dominance in the bedroom. Now the hints disappear to unveil the true Shane Dean—the man Josie hoped she'd married.

I hope you truly enjoy Shane and Josie's story.

Best,

Rebecca Zanetti

RebeccaZanetti.com
Twitter, @RebeccaZanetti
Facebook.com/RebeccaZanetti.Author.FanPage

♥ ♥ ♥ ♥ ♥ ♥ ♥ ♥ ♥ ♥ ♥ ♥ ♥ ♥ ♥ ♥ ♥

From the desk of Kate Meader

Dear Reader,

FEEL THE HEAT is the first in my smokin' Hot in the Kitchen series, about an Italian restaurant–owning family and the sexy, sizzling chefs who love them. And don't we all want a hotter-than-Hades, caring, alpha chef like Jack Kilroy in our lives? A man who cooks, defends his lady, and knows how to treat her right both in the kitchen *and* in the bedroom is worth his weight in focaccia (and the British accent doesn't hurt). But sometimes we've got to work with what the gods have given us. So if you have a husband/boyfriend/sex slave who believes guy cooking = grilling, but outside of the summer months, you won't catch him dead in an apron, read on.

"But he just makes a mess" or "I'm a better cook," I

hear you whine. Who cares? The benefits to encouraging your man to cook are multifold.

1. Guys who cook know how to multitask. If he can watch a couple of bubbling pots, chop those herbs, and pour you a glass of wine, all while *you* put your feet up, it'll eventually translate to other areas. Childcare, taking out the trash, maybe even doing the dishes as he whips up that *coq au vin*.

   Guys who cook know how to get creative. You might ask your man: "Is this made with sour cream, babe?"

   Cue worry crease on guy's brow that looks so adorable. "No, I didn't have any so I used Greek yogurt instead. Does it taste okay?"

   Hold praise for a beat "That's so creative, babe, and less fattening."

   (Positive reinforcement is key during the early training phase.)

2. Guys who cook have a direct correlation to a woman's TBR list. He's brought you that glass of Pinot and he's back in the kitchen where he belongs. Now you can get down to the important stuff—making a dent in your stories about fictional boyfriends who probably cook better than your guy. (In the case of Jack Kilroy, Shane Doyle, and Tad DeLuca, the sexy heroes of the Hot in the Kitchen series, this conclusion is a given.)

3. Guys who cook will evolve into guys who shop for groceries. Nuff said.

4. Guys who cook make better lovers. Chefs have very skillful hands, often callused and scarred from years

of kitchen abuse. Those fast-moving, rough hands are going to take your sexytimes to the next level! As long as your guy is burning himself while he learns, it can only be beneficial to you further down the road.

So get your guy in an apron and let the good times roll. Remember, chefs do it better...

Happy cooking, eating, and reading!

Kate Meader

www.katemeader.com

About the Author

Kate Meader writes contemporary romance that serves up delicious food, to-die-for heroes, and heroines with a dash of sass. Originally from Ireland, she cut her romance reader teeth on Catherine Cookson and Jilly Cooper novels, with some Mills & Boons thrown in for variety. Give her tales about brooding mill owners, oversexed equestrians, and men who can rock an apron, and she's there. Her stories are set in her adopted home town of Chicago, a city made for food, romance, and laughter—and where she met her own sexy hero. For news, excerpts, and recipes, check out her website at http://www.katemeader.com.